The Afflicted Saga
Devotion
Tale of the Fallen: Book I

Katika Schneider

ISBN: 978-0-9974268-0-9

For Kiga
Thank you for sharing the path with me.
You showed me what it truly means to be devoted.
Rest well.

ACKNOWLEDGMENTS

Thank you to my beautiful beta readers for helping me shape Abaeloth into a tangible place. May I someday be able to help you the way you've helped me.

Thank you to my wonderful cover designer, Sarah Anderson, for her continued patience and amazing skill.

Thank you to Dominique at Priceless Proofreading for helping me apply the final polish.

Continuous thanks to my writing colleagues—especially Lacey, Amy, Chelo, Grace, and Ronnie—for their endless patience and bountiful knowledge.

And a special thank you to Blackshire Equestrian for helping me depict the perfect warhorse.

ONE

Mathias Sagewind was no stranger to the uncanny. Eternal life blessed as the avatar of the Mother Goddess did that to a man. Even after ages spent maintaining balance on the world of Abaeloth per Etha's will, it never got any easier to face complaints from the mortal world. Such duties came with his title, one which Etha had forced upon him, and he upheld them as diligently as he could stand.

The mists of his corner of the heavens failed their attempts to thwart an incoming intruder, and Mathias stitched his brows together in frustration. He treasured his quiet meditations away from civilization, and seldom enjoyed the hassles brought by interruptions. An overwhelming urgency and despair preceded the day's visitor, and the paladin's gut welled with gloom. He lacked the ability to disregard a noble cause.

Mathias surrendered to the inevitable confrontation, stood, and opened begrudging green eyes. Willing the haze that concealed him to part, he revealed himself to his audience. The man strode toward Mathias with a confident air, reminiscent of a glorious past life. He possessed the handsome facial build typical of the elves, but a foreign brawn challenged further speculation to his heritage. He towered over Mathias by at least a head, each of his arms larger than one of the human's own legs. Dark hair offset eyes pale with trouble.

"White Paladin," the man said, his voice every bit as powerful as the frame that housed it. "I've heard much in regards to your abilities."

Mathias churned over the foreign dialect with his hard-earned linguistic skills to form his reply. "Have you?" he asked. "May I inquire on how you came about such knowledge?"

"Death opens your eyes to quite a bit, as I'm sure you know." He appraised Mathias with eyes keen on judging opponents. "My name is Laes Teradhel, General of Elidae." He confirmed his origins as he bowed.

"I assume you mean late general, sir," Mathias replied coolly, nodding at the gesture, but more interested to hear that the ancestors of the violent banished elves of Drailged now populated Etha's blessed homeland. Sent there centuries ago, the bulk of Abaeloth contently assumed the elven refugees and the pirates who harbored them had perished to the demon sea, Havoc. Compelling evidence to the contrary now stood before Mathias. Despite his curiosity of this new information, Mathias loathed his next question. "What is it you want from me?"

"I came to beg for your aid."

Laes's voice waned, revealing the fragile spider webs of his forged heart. The request left Mathias unsurprised, but he took note of the fallen general's tender emotions. Intrigued or not, he raised an eyebrow to feign astonishment for Laes's behalf.

"To beg?" Mathias was unable to cloak the entirety of his disdain. Few people without selfish motives ever wanted to speak with him.

"If need be, yes." Laes strained to maintain his temper under Mathias's patronizing tone. His life had paid him with a sound political mind, and he knew what consequences awaited a hasty tongue.

A deep sigh drifted from Mathias. "I cannot help you if you are already dead," he said. "Forgive me, General, but you have to trust your troops in the hands of another."

"I already am!" Laes pled. "And my troops are the least of my concerns."

This piqued Mathias's interest just enough for him to keep

listening. "Then why are you here?"

"Please, sir." Laes dropped to a knee and bowed his head to conceal his vulnerability. "I cannot begin to worry about the troops, because I worry too much about their general."

Mathias watched Laes, humbled by the helplessness radiating from him. Most generals who came to Mathias sought only to implore him to bail their armies out of trouble, but not Laes. Something else drove this man to grovel before him with so little regard to pride.

"Continue," Mathias requested, his voice softened by this new development.

"Evil is marching on Elidae," Laes said, forlorn gaze fixed on the ground. "I know this because I know Elidae. I flourish when she flourishes. I hurt when she hurts. I fear when she fears." He shook his head with an uncertain reluctance. "Her new general is far from ready to handle the coming war, and for that, I am terrified."

"If your successor is so incapable, how did he gain his station?"

"*She*," Laes corrected promptly, "became general through blood."

Mathias frowned. He should have guessed as much. "This new general is quite close to you?"

"She is my daughter." Laes's words trembled with the confession.

Mathias's incredulous scowl declared his opinion on appointing such officials through any means besides skill and proven performance. He valued the bond of family more than most, but allowing children to gain station through privilege alone seldom yielded a positive outcome. Beyond that, Mathias knew of very few soldiers willing to follow a woman's guidance on the battlefield. It was no wonder Laes feared for his country. In all probability, this little girl lacked the skills and experience necessary to fulfill the tasks at hand.

Laes sneered at Mathias's assumptions. "She might be young, but do not doubt her. The flemans were born of survivors, and we haven't forgotten that. The men would follow Nessix to their

3

deaths if she asked them to. She trained for this position since the day she could hold a knife, and serves as a fine general against our common foes, but under the coming circumstances…" Laes closed his eyes and shook his head. "The men won't be able to follow her for long unless she has help. Elidae will be crushed under this threat, and my Nessix will be dead."

Mathias blew out a slow breath, balancing this equation carefully. Laes bled with his sincerity and the despondency which pried its way from Mathias's own heart threatened to thwart his more rational thoughts. Torn, as his vows forbid him to make any attempts to consciously alter fate, Mathias actively fought off the benevolence sprouting inside of him.

"How did you find me?" He hoped to uncover some flaw in Laes's ways to justify declining this inconvenient mission.

"I saw the threat to Elidae and prayed for help to rid my mind of these visions. They never left, and I saw my troops fall and my daughter's brutal fate. I saw the tortures that awaited Elidae. These thoughts overpowered me and I—" Laes choked and looked up at Mathias with a haunted expression. "A young woman in robes of silver and white came to me and asked me why I'd been crying. She told me how to find you and here I am now, begging for you to answer my prayers."

Mathias quietly internalized the grim fact that his personal preferences no longer held merit in this decision. "Did this woman have a name?"

"Not that she told me, but she had infinite patience. Just being near her eased my fear. I don't know how she found me, but she told me you would help. I've tried everything else."

"And what was this threat you told her about?" Mathias asked, stomach slowly flopping with the direction this conversation had taken.

"She forbid me to tell you." The answer crept cautiously forward, as if Laes feared frustrating the man he considered his nation's last hope. "She said you didn't need to trouble your mind over it yet, but assured me you've been through worse and would know what to do now."

Mathias shook his head and turned from Laes. Etha enjoyed

playing games with him, and he knew of no one else capable of erasing this man's fears. She'd given Laes her blessing and had appointed Mathias as her means of assistance. Only one option remained for Mathias, whether he liked it or not.

"Rest your soul at ease, General," Mathias sighed. "Come tomorrow, your daughter will have disposal to my services."

"May Inwan bless you!" Laes breathed. His eyes brightened with hope. "You will never know what this means to me."

With nothing else, Laes vanished, leaving Mathias to churn over this mysterious commitment alone.

* * * * *

"They're nothing but rumors," Brant Maliroch scoffed, brown eyes narrowed at Sulik Vakharan's stony expression. "You can't possibly think the hells just opened up to spew their garbage out." He turned to plead his case to the young woman in their company. "I'm telling you, Nes. This is ridiculous!"

"The scout saw it himself," Commander Vakharan countered peevishly, casting an uncertain glance toward his general. "It was a winged demon, just like in the murals. Why would he lie about it?"

"Can both of you let this drop?" Nessix groaned as she stared across the training field where her ranks plugged about their daily activities. She wanted to trust the integrity of her scout's report, but without witnessing the event firsthand, had trouble believing it. She heaved a sigh, looking from her cousin to her life-long bodyguard. "We will remain on guard until things straighten out."

"But, Nes—"

"That is my order, Commander Vakharan." A waif compared to the man in stature, it took only her station and the flash of her chilly blue eyes to demand no further debate. "Double the watch around the fortress and add an extra rotation of scouts. We'll worry about this after I have some sort of tangible proof."

"Of course, General," Sulik agreed curtly. He speared Brant with a perturbed glance. "I will address the ranks promptly."

Nessix and Brant watched Sulik leave, his rigid strides a clear

5

display of his agitation. The young general hated all of this. Common sense told her the exact same thing it told Brant, but a foreboding apprehension still tugged at her judgment. Historical fact stated that demons no longer existed. The Demon Wars she'd learned about in stuffy childhood lessons allegedly saw the beasts to their end ages ago. Nessix kept trying to convince herself that a return of such a threat made no sense, especially on the remote island she called home. All of this tangled her typically carefree mind in a web of frustration.

"Square something with me," Nessix said to Brant, still tracking Sulik's departure. "Is this the first time you've heard these reports?" Silence prompted her to turn and face her dear cousin with an unspoken and indignant demand.

"I didn't think there would be a need to tell you!"

A deep breath and quiet excuses sifted away her irritation with him. "What have you heard?"

Brant rubbed the back of his neck, darting his eyes away, but indulged Nes's question dutifully. "Creatures creeping around the forests, mysterious masses blocking out patches of stars at night." Concern snuck onto Nes's face in the form of anxious eyes and tightly tucked lips. "Any of this could easily come from hitting the keg too heavily, though, Nes."

Nessix chewed on Brant's confession, struggling to believe his attempt at reassurance, but a twist continued to tighten her stomach. "Find out which soldiers had these encounters. I'd like to meet with them. If there really is some sort of threat out there, I need to know about—"

A winded scout dashed up to them, interrupting Nes's thoughts. "What's wrong?" She prayed to her departed god against any further confirmation of such reports.

"A man is approaching, General," the scout panted.

Nessix shook her head, her mouth falling open as she tried to process why that demanded such urgency. "That's a problem?" A quick glance met Brant's eyes. Perhaps her men *had* gone insane.

The scout nodded and choked against the rasp in his throat. "When we asked his intentions, all he said was that he was the White Paladin, sent by General Laes to—"

"My father?"

The scout cleared his throat at the frigid inflection of her question. "Y-yes, General."

Nessix turned from both men, remembering a much more innocent version of herself stumbling upon her beloved father's body contorted on the war chamber's floor. She'd been the one to find him. Brant laid a hand on her forearm in silent comfort, but she ignored the gesture, too stunned to pull away from his touch.

"This man... he's not... normal." The scout sent a sheepish glance at Brant, wishing the commander wasn't there to witness the absurdity of his report. "If I didn't know any better, I'd say he doesn't even look fleman."

Nessix hefted a sigh and returned her attention to the present. "Brant, forget your previous order; I want you to investigate this. I'm going inside to get a drink."

"There is no need for this to be investigated, General," a cheerful voice hailed from nearby. "Or at least I'm assuming you are the general."

Nessix whirled around to find a man casually leaning against a tree, dressed in alabaster plate mail that appeared innocent of battle. The emblem of a kite shield laced in a ring of lilies decorated the breastplate, and the simple suit's glistening perfection contrasted sharply with the battered and darkened steel better suited to Nessix. The man's features were rough and exotic to her eyes, lacking the powerful elegance that even the men of Elidae showed. His pale hair and rich jade eyes, both foreign hues on this island, held the bulk of Nes's bewildered attention, followed closely by his fair complexion and smoothly rounded ears.

"Who are you?" Nessix demanded, laying her hand on the hilt of her sword. At her reaction, both Brant and the scout drew their blades, taking note of the massive weapon in the man's scabbard.

He gave a lax chuckle and batted a hand to dismiss their startled response. "I am Mathias Sagewind." He pushed against the tree to stand at full height, nearly a foot above Nessix, though well-met by her commander. "I am the White Paladin." He ignored the unconvinced glares his words received. "And your father did send me. I mean, you *are* Nessix Teradhel, aren't you?"

"That proves that you're bluffing," Nessix seethed. "My father's—"

"Dead," Mathias finished, nodding. "Yes, I know. I'm not enough of a fool to think I can force you to believe me, but I am a paladin and can communicate with spirits. Your father is the one who sent me here."

"Impossible!" Brant scoffed, initiating an advance on this boastful man.

"Brant, hold!" Nes's exasperated order stopped her cousin before he completed his first stride. "Go find Grandfather and see what he knows about this White Paladin. You," she said, striding up to Mathias to unbuckle the scabbard from his belt, "are coming with me."

"Nes, are you sure that's safe?" Brant whispered upon her return to his side. "I don't trust him."

Nessix didn't trust him either, but matters regarding her father concerned her alone. "You don't trust anyone when it comes to me," Nessix said, handing Brant the weapon she'd procured. "Besides, Logan will keep me safe. You know that."

Brant accepted the sword and stared at his cousin in search of comfort. "If those are your orders."

"They are."

Nessix forced a reassuring smile, more for her own sake than his. Too many concerns gnawed at her already, and she wanted to avoid adding Brant's to them. Reports of demons, the appearance of a paladin, a human on Elidae. Nothing made any sense, and Nessix desperately needed a way to maintain authority over the situation before she completely lost control.

Brant snagged this unwelcomed guest with a mute warning, daring him to offer any form of danger to Nessix. When Mathias's tempered gaze confirmed receipt of the admonition, Brant turned to seek his elder as instructed.

Nessix dismissed the scout, and strode toward where she last saw Logan, whistling sharply to summon her warhorse. She needed to plan the following conversation with care. This man's testament infuriated her, but reality had been skewed enough to leave her at least a little bit curious to the explanation of his brassy claims.

Facing such disconcerting times, the most obvious answer suggested Mathias's story held some degree of merit, and Nessix owed it to her kingdom to look into it.

Logic caustically laughed at her, demanding Nessix rethink such notions. Her father died and her god, Inwan, left shortly after. No more paladins existed, and she lacked the sense of mind to deal with some zealot's prattle. Logan bounded up to her, scattering her thoughts with the playful toss of his mane. Nessix took the massive horse's head in her hands before he noticed Mathias and gave him a wary inspection.

"That's quite the mount you have there." Mathias ceased his action of reaching forward to pat the horse's shoulder upon catching an intelligent eye.

"Yes, he is." Nes smiled at the great black animal in front of her. This horse, one of Elidae's revered fecklans gifted to nobility at birth, had walked with her every day of her life and she still marveled each time she saw him. Dwarfed easily by Logan's sheer size, her height barely matched the length of his forelegs. "And I consider him among the most valuable in my ranks."

Mathias quirked his lips and gave a skeptical nod. "Is that so?"

"It is," she said. "And you are in no position to question my words right now."

"Yet you question mine?"

"Of course I do," Nessix laughed. "You came to me, so I'm the one who gets to judge you, not the other way around."

"So you doubt my standing as a paladin?"

"I have no reason to believe you." Nessix released Logan's head to allow him a disapproving snort at Mathias. "I've never seen you before, never heard of you. Inwan, I've never even seen a human before. Certainly, if you are some great *White Paladin*"—her tone shrouded the title in disdain—"your works and righteous deeds must be grand enough to have preceded you to my humble island."

"I suppose you would think so," Mathias granted. "Maybe it'd clear things up if I told you I've been dead before and spent a good amount of time being blessed on the ethereal plane. I'm not your average human."

"That's impossible."

"I'm sure you've seen your share of miracles."

Nessix's bitter laugh alarmed Mathias. "Not in nine years. I don't have time for games right now. I don't know who you are or how you got here, but you can't come claiming miracles are going to help us."

"As long as the gods are around, there will always be miracles."

Nessix fixed Mathias with a cold glare, hating him for his faith. "There is no god," she spat. "He left this world. If you really think you are a man of the gods—"

"Goddess," Mathias corrected politely.

"If you think you are a man of the *gods*," Nessix repeated, stressing her words against his belligerence. "I ask you, paladin, what purpose do you have on this faithless island?"

Mathias sighed, hopes for a pleasant introduction dashed. "I told you. Your father sent me here to help you, but it seems you don't need me and it was a fool's quest to come at all."

"And that would make you the fool."

"Your father is the one who sent me," he opposed smoothly. "Perhaps that makes him the fool?"

"Son of a bitch!" Nessix lunged at Mathias, eyes alight with dangerous intent. She reached for her sword with her free hand, but her blade never left its scabbard.

Mathias countered the attack effortlessly, reaching forward to push her elbow up and wrench her shoulder. More angry than hurt, Nessix dropped to the ground and out of his grasp, rolling to the side to catch his legs in her own. He fell to the ground beside her. Not wasting a moment, Nessix sprang to her feet and crouched as she grasped a hold of one of his legs and rushed her weight toward his chest. Removing his limb's mobility, Nessix held Mathias in place as her fury bore down on him.

He groaned a strained laugh. "You really think attacking me is going to change that fact?"

Nessix drove her weight harder against him. "There is no such fact to be changed."

"You really ought to trust me, Nessix."

"You will address me as General!"

"I will address you as my equal," he corrected, irritated with this girl's behavior. "Consider it a favor."

A commotion clambered across the training fields, putting an instant halt to the current debate. Nessix's battle sense eased in her attempt to survey the cause. She freed Mathias from her hold as she straightened.

"We'll finish this later," Nessix promised, her attention already gone from their confrontation.

"I'll hold you to it." Mathias climbed to his feet to trot after Nessix as she hastened toward the uproar.

She focused her will against glancing at him. "You are unwelcome to follow me."

"You have faith enough to leave me unattended within your establishment?" Mathias asked. "That's strange, considering you don't seem to trust me at all."

Clenching her teeth so fiercely they ached, as not to give Mathias the pleasure of goading her further, Nessix continued toward her gathering troops. A small group hustled her way, burdened with a limp body, and she quickened her pace. Injuries from this field typically warranted banter from comrades and a couple days' worth of soreness. Whatever happened to this man not only immobilized him completely, but successfully worked his colleagues into a poorly maintained panic. The closer Nessix got to the approaching group, the clearer it became that the soldier suffered from something far more serious than a training mishap.

Mathias stopped quietly to observe how Nessix handled a crisis. With as much fire as she'd spent this far, a considerable part of her must have already burned out. The longer he watched, the more Laes's reason for concern became evident. Nessix held heaps of confidence, but the tell-tale fear in her eyes testified to her lack of experience.

The paladin's compliant halt almost caught Nes's attention, but she'd already wrapped her concerns around the injured man. Jagged lacerations shredded the side of his face and a fistful of hair had been ripped from his scalp. The smaller pieces of armor no longer protected his body, and a clean slice stretched across the chest of his leather breastplate. His limbs hung loose around him as shallow breaths barely offered proof that he still lived.

"What happened?" Nessix asked.

"He was attacked, General," came the immediate reply. "We don't know what hit him, but we heard a struggle and a call for help. We found him like this, perhaps with a bit more life."

Nessix grudgingly shoved the last piece into the puzzle. "Get him back to the fortress and to one of the surgeons." She turned to Logan and rested a hand on his shoulder, taking a moment for her mind to quit reeling. "The rest of you, gather as many troops as you can. Leave only those posted within the townships, and establish a curfew. If there's something attacking at will, I don't want to tempt it further until we can identify what's going on. Logan will see to it this man gets back faster than any of us could carry him."

An echo of compliance rose from the soldiers. The majority departed as the remaining few peeked at their wounded comrade, captured by morbid curiosity of the mysterious cause of his condition. No one spoke and Nes's discomfort balled in her throat. The group hoisted the man onto Logan, careful to drape him across the animal's broad back without aggravating his seeping wounds.

Nessix shot an unspoken challenge to Mathias. This soldier clearly held hands with death, and any paladin worth his mettle ought to go to the aid of someone in such a state. Mathias smirked in acceptance of her invitation, intent on proving himself to her.

"Might I assist?" He made sure to speak his offer loud enough for the group of soldiers to hear.

Nessix exaggerated a roll of her eyes, ignoring the confused expressions of her troops. Rightfully unnoticed until now, no one knew what to make of Mathias's bold declaration. Their general's calm expectation of the outburst offered them some relief.

"I was afraid you'd offer." She spoke with a delicate charm, eager to put this man to the test. "Do not give them hope if you cannot deliver. It's bad on morale."

Nessix's assumption that she knew that better than him amused Mathias, but his glee at proving this proud child wrong left the instant his resolve settled in. While Nessix tried to wrap her mind around the origin of the soldier's injuries, Mathias had made his appraisal of the man's condition and couldn't waste any more time. He'd seen these wounds before, and his heart pounded an oath of retribution for the defilement that had found this island. Etha should have told him.

"I do this for him." Mathias nodded in the soldier's direction. The humor in his voice sank beneath his cold and serious tone. "Not to gain your trust, and certainly not for my own glory." He stared Nessix down until his haunting eyes forced hers to dart away. Mathias drew a deep breath and bowed his head as he approached his patient.

Logan pinned his ears at Mathias's advance, flinging his head stiffly into the air. A reassuring hand from Nes stopped him from stepping away, though both the girl and her mount remained wary of whatever would happen next. The crowd was anxious to see what spectacle awaited them from this strange, bold visitor, but Nessix raised a hand to signal them back.

"If he wants to humiliate himself, by all means, give him his space. He thinks he can save this man," Nessix told them, continuing with her haughty show. "He calls himself the White Paladin."

A smattering of nervous chuckles left the unit, though Nes's dwelling concerns prevented her from joining them. Humored exclamations regarding the time of the named hero's glory rose from the few who recalled tales of him. Most found it entertainment enough to hear this man considered himself a holy knight. The paladins of Elidae, or at least those who avoided suicide after Inwan's abandonment, went mad following their god's departure. The taunts continued until concern shifted away from the purported human and back to the wounded soldier as Mathias reached him.

Mathias paid the jeers no mind. Humility would find his audience without verbal reprimand soon enough. For now, he concentrated only on his patient.

Etha, grant this man your mercy, he prayed, silent to the skeptical gathering.

Lifting his head to study the wounds more critically, Mathias murmured his prayer aloud. He spoke too softly for any of the surrounding ears to catch his words, and the crowd unconsciously pulled closer. Mathias remained focused on the soldier, raising a hand toward his subject. A white aura grew from his palm as he laid it on the man's arm, and a pale light enveloped the pair. As Mathias spoke louder, pallid sparks drifted from the haze around him. Every spectator felt the divine brilliance burning from Sir Mathias Sagewind, whether or not they wanted to admit it. Open wounds stitched together and color flowed into blanched cheeks. Mathias whispered a few last words before the soldier murmured a subdued groan. A gentle smile crossed Mathias's lips. He straightened and turned to face Nessix.

She stared at him mutely for several heartbeats, unable to comprehend what she just witnessed. Her hopes that she could write this off as a coincidence reeled toward a perilous reality, and she wanted nothing more than to blame this looming misfortune on someone else. Mathias served as the most convenient candidate.

"What did you do to him?" Nessix demanded.

Mathias ignored her question and precarious resolve. "Let him rest until nightfall. He'll live, but likely won't regain consciousness for a few hours." He politely disregarded the crowd's growing wonder for the sake of their insecure general.

"Answer me!" Nessix insisted, unaccustomed to such public defiance.

"You said I can do nothing, so that's clearly what I must have done."

Nessix glowered at his mockery, but snuck a glance at her recovered soldier. Dried blood still crusted his flesh from where wounds had poured. Flaws still marred the remaining pieces of his armor in testament to whatever put him so close to death. Hardly any of the padding remained salvageable from where it peeked from his breastplate, but he showed no further proof of his ordeal. He would live and provide Nessix with a full report once he woke. Genuinely thankful for this outcome, Nessix still refused to swallow Mathias's arrogance.

"Logan, take this soldier back to the fortress," she said. "The rest of you will gather the troops as I instructed."

Mathias crossed his arms as he contemplated his best course of action to address the danger Elidae faced, watching Logan hasten off and the troops dispatch with unwavering obedience.

Nessix studied her guest as his mind worked, unable to fit words to her steeping turmoil. Trust was never a virtue for Nes, and she found no reason to start such nonsense now. "I don't have time for games, paladin."

"Ah, so I have a title now," Mathias mused. A blink of his eyes exchanged his brooding for levity.

"How in Inwans's name did you do that?"

"I did nothing you could comprehend, at least not right now." He answered honestly, too indifferent to her reaction to bother watching for it. "I have come to you, as was requested of me, but it seems I might be wasting my time."

Nessix sneered at his attempt to take control. "If my father sent you, then you're not here by your own will and you're certainly not here on mine." She brushed off the chuckle Mathias offered in reply. "You would be disgracing him if you left, and I will not allow that."

Mathias couldn't decide if Nes's complexity intrigued or irritated him. "Your father did ask me to come, but mark my words, I am not here on his accord."

"Then what are your intentions?"

"I am here to prevent disaster from tearing apart this holy land."

"Holy?" Nessix scoffed.

Mathias nodded. "This is Etha's blessed homeland."

Nessix rolled her eyes at his ridiculous statement and exceedingly reverent tone, no longer viewing this conceited bastard as dangerous. "There is no threat that's ever risen that my people haven't handled on their own," she said. "And I don't plan to let that change."

The playful smile faded from Mathias's face, aging him from the brash youth who first introduced himself to the sagacious man time forged him to become. As he regarded the horizon in a bid for lenience, he pitied how little the flemans saw. Elidae boasted the most diverse topography in all of Abaeloth. Mountains towered from the carnivorous ocean that held the island captive from the world, safeguarding this lush valley from drowning. What remained of the morning sea mist rolled down the rocky faces. Deserts supported the minotaur past the forests to the west, and the ogres' swamplands mirrored in the east, buffered by rolling hills and gentle grasslands. The nation's water supply originated from the Great Spring, located central north, feeding four rivers which flowed to the caverns in the mountains, where a fifth ran back inland. Long ago, Etha created Elidae to serve as its own world; it was no wonder the flemans showed no interest in the rest of Abaeloth.

"You are young," Mathias said. A wistful patience turned his lips down and softened his eyes.

Unmoved by his demeanor, Nessix scowled. "And I have seen more in life than you'd ever understand," she swore, too caught up in her memories to consider any of his. "Besides, you're not that old, yourself." Grudgingly, she appraised Mathias's youthful face and capable limbs. Appearing not more than a few years into adulthood, no trace of mortal age decayed his strength.

Mathias stretched his arms out and weighed his physical condition. "I suppose you're right." He smiled at the clench of Nes's jaw. "I seem to be a pup as well."

"And," Nessix continued, fueled by his compliance to accept her scrutiny, "your confidence is obnoxious."

"I only need to know my own place." Mathias stowed his impression of Nes's pride to himself. He read her intentions clearly, and lifetimes of similar disbelief had taught him how to deal with it. "I'm content to let others decide the rest for themselves."

Nessix pinned him in her sights and approached. "What disaster are you here to prevent and how could helping us possibly be worth your while?"

"The rumors coming to you are true," Mathias said, his gravity halting Nessix as she stood to full height. "It seems they've become more aggressive, as your soldier can now attest to. Things will get worse from here, I assure you."

"They?" she piped.

"Demons, General. We're looking at a holy war."

16

His words severed the breath from Nes's lungs. She knew how to fend off ogres and minotaur, but not demons. Her mind lurched, trying to sort through how to handle this foreign prophet's confirmation of fears that shouldn't even exist, and she felt her composure slip. Desperate to protect herself from Mathias and his troubling assertion, Nessix forced out a short and unconvincing laugh.

"You expect me to believe that?"

Mathias caught her waver of self-doubt and softened his expression. "You already do. Just like you believe you'll need help to fight back against them. I am that help, Nessix, and if you'll let me see to it, I will not let you fall."

A tremor of confusion muddled her reservations as Nessix took in Mathias's reconstructed disposition. She peered at him curiously, wishing she knew more about him. Years of learning to read people judged this man, and Nes knew he likely kept his secrets well hidden. No amount of doubt shook what her gut whispered to her, though; always her guide, it told her Mathias truly intended to help.

"You are not a threat to me." Her words wielded a civil force.

"I never was," Mathias replied.

A warm voice bubbled in Mathias's head. *Her caution isn't a bad thing. If she's got sense enough to be wary, she may not be as much work as we thought.*

A gentle smile traced his lips, bewildering Nessix even more. *I guess we'll find out soon, Etha.*

"You know what I think of you," Nessix stated, drawing Mathias's attention away from his goddess's reflections.

"Yes, I do. I've given you much to consider for now, and I believe you said something about meeting with your elder. If you have nothing else for me, I'll let you on your way."

"I did not dismiss you," Nessix said.

Mathias smirked as the young woman waged between her want of him to leave and her desire to maintain authority. "And I'll forgive you for that," he said.

Nes's mouth fell open at his flagrant disregard, but no words of correction reached her tongue. Satisfied with his assessment of what he had to work with and that he'd found a way to silence her, Mathias gave Nessix a polite smile and turned down the road that led to the city of Sarlot. He'd find time to reclaim his sword later.

* * * * *

"I would like to meet this paladin," En mused.

The way the wrinkled corners of his mouth pleated in a diminutive smile flew warning flags in Nes's mind. Even before she found her grandfather tucked away in his study, word of the soldier's inexplicable recovery had infiltrated her fortress. Now facing En's enthusiasm, Nes's annoyance pressed her upper limits.

"I don't see why you would," she muttered, pointing her peevish gaze away from her grandfather. "He's no greater than Veed—a charlatan and dabbler at best."

En chuckled, his warmth persuading Nes's attention back to him. "I consider mending the flesh of the dying a bit more impressive than anything General Astaldt has ever managed. I would be honored to meet this paladin."

"Just because he claims to be some hero from one of your books doesn't make it true," Nessix said. "Miracles do not happen anymore and you know it. It was luck that let his spell work at all."

"And a poor twist of fate that's drawn monsters of horror stories to Elidae?" En asked. "Child, I know you're afraid, but whether or not you like it, we need help. I think if I had a discussion with this man, I could clear up quite a bit."

The hour spent arguing with her grandfather had drained Nessix, and though she feared for his sanity at the hands of Mathias, she was through with this debate. Her very own stubborn streak came from somewhere, and En had several decades' more experience to master it. No amount of bargaining would thwart En from subjecting himself to Mathias's drivel, but what troubled Nessix more was what it meant if Mathias's ominous predictions were accurate.

"If the reports given to me are false, it'd be a waste of time," she tried once more.

"Then let me entertain myself with it. I don't have much else on my schedule. Besides, what if the reports *are* true?"

Nessix frowned at the reminder of her own apprehensions. "Then we'll need a lot more than hasty actions and the goading of one man to see us through. If demons have existed this long and somehow reached our home, they're no less survivors than we are."

En nodded in consideration, pleased with the sound development of Nes's tactical mind. "Perhaps you should have paid a bit more attention to the histories, my dear. The White Paladin knows how to handle a couple of demons."

Pressing this subject promised to only frustrate Nessix more. "I need to have a chat with Veed," she said, "see if he has any similar news to share."

En nodded and began to tidy up the collection of papers on the table in front of him. "And what of my meeting?" His genial eyes remained directed on his task.

"You won't give up, will you?"

En's steady smile provided Nessix with the most unsatisfactory reply.

"Reports say he's been staying in Sarlot. I'll send Sulik to ask about him with orders to bring him to you." Gauging her grandfather's enthusiasm knotted Nes's stomach. "I trust you'll wait in a manner appropriate to your hard-earned status until he gets here?"

Added warmth to En's expression answered her. Standing and stretching her arms, Nessix walked over to the old man's side.

"Just between you and me, what do you think about all of this?" she asked quietly, pulling En's chair back and offering her arm to help him rise.

En sighed and stood beside his granddaughter. "Neither the reports nor Mathias should be taken lightly. Things have changed far too much since Inwan's departure."

Nessix lowered her head, nodding silently. She still grieved her god's flight from Elidae, and each reminder dug another finger into that wound.

"I suppose you're right," she answered tightly.

En smiled again and patted Nes's hand with a gentle affection she allowed few others to express toward her. "It isn't fair that you are troubled with all of this, child."

She returned the smile, though more distant. "It's in our blood to accept this fate, Grandfather. Nothing's entitled to be fair." Staying long enough to ensure En had nothing else to say, Nessix left the library with a heavy heart and climbed the stairs to her quarters.

TWO

Sulik, less than enthusiastic with his assignment, reached the nearby town of Sarlot not long after receiving his orders. Regardless of his personal preferences on the developing issues, Nessix had dismissed him before he'd had the chance to meet Mathias, and his curiosity sought answers about this strange new guest. Anything able to work Nessix up so thoroughly was usually well worth the while.

After sorting through excited accounts spun by the townsfolk, Sulik discovered that Mathias had taken up residence with the local smith. The so-called paladin had found quite the name with the civilians during his brief stay, and Sulik began to side with his general's caution over Mathias's validity. Hindered by the teary farewells from the smith's children, Sulik collected Mathias to escort him to the fortress. Sizing up his charge, the grizzled commander saw nothing outwardly impressive. After the human voiced a catty opinion about Nessix summoning him, Sulik liked him even less.

The men walked in silence for some time, Sulik uncertain what to say, and Mathias not entirely caring. Townsfolk crowded as near as they respectfully dared, watching the pair leave. Hushed speculations of Nes's intentions with Mathias filtered anxiously between friends, but neither of the two men allowed themselves to respond.

"The general doesn't seem to care for you," Sulik said, once they left the more populous main street.

"Yes, I got that impression," Mathias replied thoughtfully. "What about her advisor?"

"En is her grandfather, removed from his position as general due to the death of his mount. He is a cunning man and a master strategist, and was intrigued enough by the general's account of your confrontation to request a meeting with you." Sulik glanced at Mathias, who still wore a relaxed expression despite the wariness floating around him. "Do not make the mistake of assuming it was the general who wanted to speak with you."

Mathias wasn't nearly that foolish, but kept as much to himself. "Is her grandfather going to doubt me, as well?"

"En is rational." Sulik caught his tongue to avoid disgracing Nessix through any direct comparisons. "He won't rush to call you a fraud, but he'll expect proof before believing anything you have to say."

Mathias nodded. "I would be wary of anything else from such an experienced man." He pondered this a moment longer before allowing a glance at the sullen commander. "And what about you? Do you think I'm here to help?"

In truth, Sulik hadn't yet formed his opinion. "I don't believe you're in the position to be asking questions, Sir Sagewind." He raised a hand in response to the town guard's farewell gesture.

Mathias swallowed a frustrated sigh. Though he favored caution over blind faith, the extent to which Nessix and her men took it surpassed necessity. Regardless, he planned to work with what little these people offered, and prayed for a way to wake them up. With Etha willing, he'd be able to provide sufficient evidence of his intentions before the demons gained momentum.

"Then by all means, ask me your questions," Mathias said.

Sulik chewed over the request. "I was told you think you're a paladin."

"Then you were told wrong. I *am* a paladin."

"Very well." Sulik chuckled and shook his head. Nessix had warned him of Mathias's propensity for irritating mischief. "Paladin or not, how do you know about demons?"

Mathias caught his sharp intake of air in inflated cheeks and his initial enthusiasm hissed away through pursed lips. Two more attempts to deliver different takes on his explanation ventured to leave his mouth, but careful consideration censored the truth out of concern for credibility. Sulik deserved an answer to this question, and Mathias hoped his awkward response fit his expectations.

"I faced the demons a long time ago. I came to offer your people assistance as you prepare to do the same."

"I'd hoped for something a bit more in-depth."

"Then you should have asked for it."

Half a smile unveiled faint wrinkles at the corners of Sulik's brown eyes. "You enjoy avoiding my questions, don't you?"

"I answered exactly what you asked. I chose not to elaborate."

"Then will you tell me about these demons you fought?" Sulik asked, playing into Mathias's game.

"I can tell you they first made themselves known to us much like they have here. It's foolish of your general to ignore the reports given to her," Mathias said, emotions too distant and intentions too guarded for Sulik's comfort.

The commander fit his companion with a stern warning. "And you would be foolish to question General Nessix's judgment again."

"Besides her having *terrible* judgment, she's already decided I'm not a threat to her. I consider it fair that I view her the same." He wrote off the slack in Sulik's jaw. "You'll learn, Commander, there isn't much in this world that can bring irreparable harm to me."

Sulik no longer knew where to steer this discussion. Typically, Nessix exaggerated anything she deemed a problem, but her warnings about Mathias appeared more accurate than not. Sulik considered himself efficient at assessing character, but not even a sliver of doubt hid in Mathias's conviction. Frustrated, he pushed the matter, concerned for En's safety.

"Seeing is believing among my people, Sir Sagewind. The only ones who believe demons exist are those who have witnessed the attacks firsthand."

"The fact of the matter is that there *have* been men among

your ranks who have seen demons," Mathias said, "and your general witnessed me heal a soldier who encountered one today, yet she still doubts."

Sulik squinted in contemplation. "General Nessix is a stubborn one, I'll give you that." He tossed around a few ideas on the path to his next question. "Can you heal anyone?"

Mathias nodded, an amiable smile showing his contentment. "As long as their will lies with being healed. I cannot force well on anyone."

Sulik had hoped for such an answer, committed to unveil proof of these claims. Drawing his dagger, a grimace flawed his seasoned face as he slid the blade across his palm. Sulik held his bleeding hand toward Mathias and gave his order.

"Show me."

Mathias gave the wound only half a glance. "What I do is not meant for show, Commander."

Sulik flushed under Mathias's disregard and pulled his hand back to nurse grudgingly. "I am in pain," he pressed. "You will do nothing to help me?"

"You brought that on yourself out of stupidity." At the moment, Mathias considered Sulik worthy of the insult. "There is no reason for me to waste my efforts on such foolishness."

The commander's mouth snapped shut in his determination to avoid further prodding until the fortress gates greeted them in the distance. "I suggest you plan your arguments more carefully when addressing En," he advised tightly.

"If he's your wise elder, I expect more sense out of him."

Sulik stalked his way ahead and led them into Nessix's fortress. Mathias watched actively as they passed through massive halls large enough for horses to navigate, constructing a mental map of the labyrinth Nessix called her home. Whoever designed the building either lacked sanity for the haphazard layout, or possessed exceptional ingenuity by designing a structure able to thwart intruders.

The trip to En's study was short, though Mathias caught several interested glances from soldiers they passed. As the paladin still awaited his interrogation, Sulik barked prompt orders to impede such curiosity. Amusement tugged at Mathias; Sulik offered him no threat if he truly wanted to disobey. Breaking any silent musings, Sulik reached out to pull open a plain wooden door and nudged Mathias ahead before following inside.

Brant stood to the right of the door to serve as Nes's ears in her absence and to protect her grandfather from Mathias's nonsense. His cynical gaze swept over Mathias, sneering once again at his foreign face. The door shut and Mathias, bored with the commanders' scrutiny, surveyed the room.

Deceptively small racks of ancient scrolls and shelves of tomes Mathias hadn't seen in ages crowded the chamber. A large wooden table sat centrally with several of the room's volumes cluttering the top, illuminated by an ornate chandelier hanging a yard overhead. An old man sat in a chair directly opposite the door, aged past his days of glory. He stooped over one of the larger volumes, neglecting even the slightest acknowledgement to his company. His fine robes spoke of nobility, and Mathias knew beyond a doubt that Nessix lavishly pampered her grandfather.

Brant and Sulik took no further action after posting themselves guard on either side of the door. The paladin took his time to enjoy the comfort of books and smell of parchment. His eyes travelled to En, who still refused to look up from his studies. Half the volume still waited to be read and Mathias decided it best to speak first.

"Nice place." He meandered over to one of the shelves to better view En's collection. "Reminds me a bit of my own study."

En's eyes dragged away from the text at the sound of Mathias's voice, and instantly set to study the human with equal intensity. Mathias marveled at En's calm. This elder embodied everything Mathias expected of a proud race's leader.

"Careful with those. They're old enough to make you seem a boy, regardless of who you truly are. If it's history you enjoy, I'd be happy to have you accompany me one afternoon," En said, not at all unkind. "But I'm afraid there are much more pressing matters to pursue at this time. Please, take a seat."

Mathias nodded and did as he was told.

"I am sure you'll forgive my disbelief, but you must

understand the discord surrounding your arrival."

"I do," Mathias replied. "Which is why I agreed to meet with you to provide what I must."

A firm nod preceded En folding his book shut, and Mathias met the old man's wizened gaze with quiet resolution.

"What do you think of your past?" En asked.

"The past is important to me, but the present is what I aim to preserve."

"The present will not be touched without your compliance, Sir Sagewind," En said. "I assume you've come to terms with certain events of your youth?"

Thinking back on the matters En alluded to tied up Mathias's insides. "What do you want to know?" he asked, though with limited enthusiasm.

"Tell me how you gained your passage to the heavens."

Sucking his teeth, Mathias bowed his head to hide the brief surge of remorse that always accompanied rehashing this history. "The first time I fell was the defeat at Redthorn. I received word that Krystan, the woman I'd fallen for, had been captured by demons at our rear. There were no immediate threats apparent where I stood, so I left my men to rescue her." A ragged sigh shook Mathias's capable frame as he recalled the woman with bitter contempt. Ample time helped him move past the event, but her name still stung his lips the way shame stung his heart. "When I reached her, I learned she was a succubus."

En watched Mathias's inner struggle intently, accepting the account without interruption.

"I destroyed her," Mathias confirmed, to this day unclear how he felt about it, "once I discovered the truth, only to get word that the town I'd been entrusted with had been hit by three legions of the fallen." For now, Mathias considered it too bold to ensure such a mistake would never happen again. "I returned to my post with all the strength I could find, but by then, the demons had already breached the walls. I ordered both my troops and the civilians to fall back to Zeal.

"My duty had been to protect Redthorn. I promised my men no demon would get past me, and so they fled. Etha kept me fighting longer than my body wanted to, and everyone reached safety." He shook his head, lip twitching. "Hundreds of demons fell to me, but there were too many for me to hold, and I collapsed. I betrayed the trust of my men for the petty love of a cursed woman."

Silence enveloped the room for long heartbeats.

"That is the manner of my death," Mathias murmured at last.

"Your Etha found it in herself to test you so?" En asked, appalled by the goddess's ruthlessness. "After all you'd done for her!"

"True devotion expects no favors," Mathias said. "She was disappointed with me, but I held true to my word. The people escaped and the fortress was prepared for the demons' approach. For that, she gave me a peaceful rest." Flattered by how much En knew of him, Mathias ignored the dubious glares he felt piercing his back.

"Do you regret your mistakes from that day?" En asked.

Mathias took his time answering the question, not expecting En to understand the peace that time had granted him. "I wish things would have gone differently. In the end, it was Etha's will, and as such cannot be debated."

En thought this over and smiled. Leaning back into his chair, he reached out to tenderly pat the day's chosen literature. His gaze lingered on its worn binding. "This volume holds every detail of your life known to those besides yourself, up until my ancestors were forced from Drailged. If you are not who you say you are, then you've spent more time researching the old histories than I have."

Mathias curbed his amusement behind a smile. "A living artifact has come strolling into your home, of course you're going to doubt its authenticity." Part of him wanted to get his hands on that book to see what bogus tales of heroics En took as truth. "I have not faulted any of your people for that."

"You have not, and I hope it can stay that way. Your goddess is not known here," En explained carefully, hoping Mathias wouldn't take offense.

Mathias had feared as much. "Yet she was here long before

your ancestors were."

"That is indeed how it's written, but we've no way to confirm such legends."

"She watches you in place of her irreverent son," Mathias said. "Even if you doubt her, she hasn't left you."

"One must also keep in mind that in the absence of nourishment, the body grows intolerant. Times change. I'm sure you understand that."

Mathias almost laughed at the irony. "Of course I do. Etha wouldn't coddle the children of Abaeloth, anyway. She enjoys seeing independence in her creations."

En looked up at the commanders, his brows fixing in a straight line. "I believe the two of you are no longer needed here."

"But, sir! Nessix—"

"Oh, hush, Brant!" En snapped. "This man will not harm me."

"Nessix will have our heads if anything happens to you," Sulik persisted.

"Then I will send my wandering spirit to set her straight," En said. "Now, go."

Neither caring for the order, both commanders forced themselves out the door. Even removed from power, En maintained weighty influence over Nessix and demanded respect. If they followed this order, they risked infuriating Nes, but disobedience to her lineage threatened something much worse. The chamber door fell shut and after their footfalls disappeared, En continued.

"Is it true you can speak to your goddess?" He leaned forward, an intent wistfulness flooding his eyes.

The memories streaming from En's soul pained Mathias. To think an entire nation no longer felt the touch of the gods discouraged and frightened him. "Yes," he answered. "And you could, too, if you'd listen for her."

"I'm afraid the gods have remained silent to us for some time now." En's expression wiped clean of his prior longing. "But enough of my regrets. Nessix tells me demons have come to Elidae."

"They have."

"And you, White Paladin, are here to help us."

"I am."

En's focus shifted to the table. "She doesn't seem to care for you much," he murmured. "But in her defense, the poor girl has had much to deal with in her short life."

"She has logical reasons to distrust me. I'm sure she's only acting as she sees fit."

En smiled, his shoulders settling. "Then I suppose it's a good thing I am her respected elder. She will listen to me better than anyone else, and I have a request to make of you."

"I thought you might."

Despite the fact that everyone else had left, En lowered his voice. "In my many years of command and research of combat, I must admit that none of my people have the knowledge to battle demons."

Mathias offered no response. He already knew that.

"I am not daft, Sir Sagewind," En stated in the absence of a reply. "I know I cannot force you to do anything against your will, but neither am I a desperate man. If you deny us your aid, we will do as we always have."

"I will lead those who will follow me," Mathias assured. "In the end, my path would force me to stand against the demons, regardless of anything else. To deny assistance to those in need would be blasphemous to my nature. It would take years for me to teach all I know of demonic warfare, but I will do what I can."

"We are a race of warriors," En reminded Mathias. "We are well aware of the dangers that wait for us and will adapt around them."

Doubt crept from Mathias's gut, despite his efforts to suppress it. "I pray that's true." He sighed, wondering if the island nation boasted the manpower to make a difference. "I will show those willing to listen how to defend themselves, and I swear to cleanse this place myself if no one else—" Mathias had almost said "survives," but the hope beaming from his modest audience choked the word away. "Will follow me."

A moment of silence passed as En processed the information. "I have no fear of the men opposing your guidance, but you must be careful when dealing with Nes. She sees you as a threat, and I beg you forgive her for that."

"I've not held it against her yet," Mathias said.

En nodded in appreciation. "If you will grant me a moment to send someone to prepare quarters for you, we would be deeply honored for you to take up residence within the fortress."

Fighting back a smirk, Mathias speculated on Nes's reaction to the offer. No matter, En acted as though he had quite a handle on her. "As you see fit."

"I thank you, Sir Sagewind." En bowed his head reverently. "We are forever indebted to you for your service. I trust you won't disappoint us."

Mathias sighed, wishing history depicted him as less of an infallible hero. "Whether or not I fight for you, this war will charge a heavy price."

The elder's eyes hardened. "We do not have a choice in the matter. We are unafraid of death, as it is a part of life."

Mathias nodded. "It is."

"Unfortunately, with Inwan gone, too much is unknown for all to be without fear, though we continue to accept the dangers life puts on us," En said.

"I know a man such as you would." Mathias stood and bowed respectfully. "Give me the day to gather my belongings from Sarlot, and I will return to be at your disposal." With nothing more, he dismissed himself from the room, easily retracing his steps to leave the fortress.

* * * * *

Nessix detested her visits with Veed Astaldt. Formerly Laes's dearest friend, the late general's death pushed Veed to branch off from the Teradhel family and develop a territory of his own. Too inexperienced and stricken with grief at the time, Nessix allowed his grab for power, a move she now regretted. Veed raised his fortress on the northern border of his province in favor of keeping a close eye on Nessix and to allow visits with her to be quick and as frequent as his muse desired.

As the garrison rose mockingly to greet her, Nessix let Logan slow to a trot. The guards swore no loyalty to her, but Veed's fondness for the young woman prompted their polite respect. Nessix stopped Logan before the entryway to gather her resolve before dismounting. Dismissing Logan, she invited herself inside. After investigating Veed's usual haunts, Nessix found him on his private training field within the courtyards.

Nessix observed him in silence for some time, watching as concentration creased fine lines across his aging face. Veed bragged of some sort of magical abilities, but Nessix only ever caught brief glimmers of tricks and pageantry from him. His focus centered on his sword as he held it pointed ahead of him with both hands. After a pair of controlled breaths, he proceeded with a series of deliberate slashes before his left hand dropped its hold and he lowered the blade to his side. Pleased to witness Veed's shortcomings, Nessix laughed at his frustration.

"How's training going?" She crossed her arms defensively when he turned to face her.

"Quite nicely, actually." Veed gave her a charming smile and straightened to sheathe his blade. "To what do I owe your lovely company?"

She inclined her head toward the door. "I need to talk to you about war plans and the like."

Veed passed her and led the way inside. "I thought you wanted a break from our games until we finished off the hordes in the east."

Nessix narrowly contained her irritated sigh. "That's not what I'm talking about."

He chuckled and looked her over with eyes keen on more than these proposed war plans. "I love it when you snap at me."

"Shut up," she sneered, purposefully avoiding his patronizing gaze. "The reports I've heard are much more alarming than a few ogres. Certainly more dangerous than any threat from you."

"Oh?" Veed opened the door to his conference chamber. His dark eyes tracked Nessix as she strode past him to take her usual seat at the central table. "Please share," Veed prompted, closing the door behind them.

Nessix fixed Veed's back with a firm glare as he walked by to select a drink from his abundant wine rack. She dreaded his response to her pending claim.

"Demons."

Veed offered no reply as he finished his task and returned to the table. "Care to elaborate?" He slid a glass to Nessix and sat across from her, hands folded before him on the tabletop.

She took a lingering drink. Honestly, she didn't want to try to explain. "Apparently, some of my soldiers have been reporting demon sightings."

Half a smile traced Veed's lips as he contemplated Nes's disclosure. "Do you believe them?"

"I'm not sure," she answered slowly. Besides not wanting to admit as much to herself, Veed's likely response to such a bogus assertion remained unclear. "I haven't seen anything myself, but one of my men was attacked today. Those who were with him claimed a demon flew out of the sky and tore him apart."

Confessions of an attack seized Veed's interest too much for a humored response. "Did he live?"

"No." Lying to Veed came easily to Nessix, and she felt safest keeping Mathias a secret for now.

Veed sighed, and finished his serving of wine in one long drink. "I cannot doubt you," he told her. "My men have reported similar events."

"And you hadn't bothered to tell me?"

"You hadn't bothered to ask."

"Have you lost any men to them?" Nessix pressed, fretting over Veed's implications.

"Two have been reported missing, but that's not enough on its own to go crying about creatures of lore."

Veed's self-assurance typically concealed his doubts, but today, Nessix saw through that wall. "Then let's pretend it is demons," she fished. "If that was the case, how would you propose dealing with them?" Hopefully, his more seasoned mind had some idea.

The man shrugged, tucking his apprehensions in the crevices

where he hid things from the world. "I haven't thought it out yet; probably engage them if they came out in force and see where it took me."

The brightness left Nes's eyes and she frowned at the ominous suggestion. "I wish you'd have laughed at me over all of this," she murmured.

"It was either this or lie, Nes," Veed said. "And you know it just kills me to lie to you."

His snide remark rolled past her as her mind reeled with far more treacherous thoughts. Nessix had come here expecting Veed to call her mad or prove her wrong, but instead, he gave her this. No matter how much she resented Veed, her ingrained respect of him led her to trust him over serious matters, and this one trumped anything she'd faced before. Her brooding consumed her until Veed grew bored with her quiet loss of resolve, and cleared his throat.

Nessix blinked once, flushing under his gaze. "I came to you to report and see what your thoughts were, nothing else." Not wanting to give Veed the chance to prolong their visit, Nessix stood. "I think I need to head back to my troops."

Veed eyed the remaining wine that nerves kept Nessix from drinking and realized how frightened she was. He rose as well. "I'll keep in touch."

"I'll hold you to it," Nessix said through a dry throat. "I'm going to do some scouting for myself. Try to stay quiet about this until I get back to you. There's no need to cause concern over the tales of drunkards."

Veed nodded at her request. "Take care of yourself, Nes."

Outwardly, Nessix ignored the hint of concern in Veed's voice and answered him with the strongest smirk left in her. "Keep working on your magic, Veed." A bolder laugh slipped from her. "Inwan knows you need to!"

Veed allowed Nessix the last word since she needed the boost to her confidence. In truth, only a sliver of his valor looked forward to what these rumors suggested; the rest of him felt every bit as lost as Nessix seemed. He watched her leave, the slightest hints of delicacy her toned body showed intriguing him as she moved. If

Inwan still watched any part of Elidae, it would be Nessix. With that in mind, Veed prayed for her safety.

THREE

Nessix's anxiety eased as she rode farther from Veed's stronghold. Relieved from the immediate duties of her position, she took her time on the return home, soaking in the gentle breeze, the sweet fragrance of native foliage, and the chipper songs of lighthearted birds. Not long ago, her only responsibility consisted of exploring these fields with Brant, daydreaming of her future glory. Nessix expelled a bitter sigh. Those excited dreams now twisted into a reality she wasn't prepared for, and greater concerns than chasing happiness commanded her attention.

She needed this time to decontaminate her mind from Veed's influence over her and, more importantly, to prepare herself for En's post-Mathias excitement. The level of fascination her grandfather showed toward the paladin concerned her, and she refused to acknowledge En's speculations might be more accurate than her own. Even if nobody else in her kingdom shared her suspicions, Nessix vowed to keep an eye on Mathias. A truly seasoned veteran ought to avoid someone else's war, especially when he insisted wanting no recognition. Besides all of that, the last human on Elidae died hundreds of years ago, her father had been gone for ten, and her beloved god left soon after.

An ancient tree waved to her, tenderly offering the solace of its shade, and Nessix needed no further motivation. Many years had passed since she last shimmied her way into tree tops, but some things needed to be remembered. A faint smile toyed at the corners of her lips as she swung up to the first sturdy branch and leaned her back against the solid trunk. Her gaze travelled over the plains to watch the sunlight dance along the currents of the Bastin River. If she bothered to look farther, the Great Spring and its surrounding oasis broke up the grasslands closer to home. The warmth of the sun eased her mind, tempting her toward the comfort of dozing.

The stillness defied the fact that the hells sat poised for their chance to ravage the land. Nes's mind tugged at the fragments she remembered learning about demons as a child. History spoke of a Demon War, though most of the particulars escaped her recollection. The only significant details that stood out were from the murals hiding in the scattered caverns. She and Brant used to make up enthusiastic stories behind those scenes, and it never once occurred to her that those tales waited for their chance to come to life.

Demons were brutal creatures, according to those images, heedless of who they slaughtered and delighting in it. The accompanying text claimed they originated from mortal roots before twisting into corruption when the Divine Battle tore the lands apart. Nessix vaguely recalled hearing about several types of the creatures, though she had only seen the difference between those with wings and those without. Previously, the murals provided her with wild fantasies of glorious battles. Facing such peril now, Nessix desperately wanted to deny such horror lurked in her future. The longer she sat, the more dread choked out the peace she'd hoped to find.

"Beautiful day, isn't it?"

Nessix jumped at the words, grasping the branch for stability. She glared down at the man who started all of this. "Where did you come from?" She tried her best to maintain her dignity.

"If you'd care to join me on the ground, I'd be happy to explain myself." Mathias stepped aside to allow her passage down.

After brief consideration, Nessix cooperated with his invitation and swung back to the ground. "Alright, so why are you here?"

A mischievous smile dashed across Mathias's face. "I'm here because your father—"

"Oh, enough!"

"Enough of what?" He raised his hands in mock surrender. "I was answering your question."

"You know damn well what I meant."

Mathias needed Nessix to calm down and think rationally, and softened his approach. "Walk with me a bit," he requested, stepping around her to continue toward the river. "It would serve you well to talk to your grandfather about me, but for now, my knowledge of myself will have to suffice."

"I suppose it will." Nessix blamed her instinct to follow Mathias on her growing fear of being alone.

Her compliance surprised Mathias and stole his chance to plan his approach. En mentioned how Elidae no longer found divine guidance, and Mathias's stomach soured at that thought. "What do you know of the deities of Abaeloth?" he asked at last.

"I—" Nessix hesitated. She'd heard the names of gods before, but never paid attention to any of them besides Inwan. "I know enough for my purposes," she finished casually. "Why?"

"Whether you believe me or not, I am the White Paladin, of the Order of the White Circle, and I serve the Mother Goddess, Etha."

Nessix scoffed, prepared to repeat her opinion of powers foreign to her, but straightened her behavior under Mathias's chilly glare. Up until now, he'd kept his demeanor peaceful, but the silent warning that flashed in his eyes suggested she might want to stay in his good graces. He took insults to this goddess he believed in quite seriously.

"Alright," came Nes's grudging reply. "Keep going."

"Etha's most ancient temple is on this island."

An unchecked laugh burst from Nessix. "You mean the old cave temple? Yeah, it's here."

Mathias expected a similar response, and accepted her amusement with a firm nod. "I would like to see it."

"And I'll bet you're wanting me to take you there."

He grinned at how easily she caved to his unspoken suggestion. "I would be honored."

Nessix regarded his self-assured smirk, approving of him even less. How dare he come to her home and mock her so! Divine powers left Elidae when Inwan turned his back on the flemans. Nessix had poured her all into finding direction for her godless nation, and now Mathias wanted to shake that up? Her nose wrinkled at the foul taste these considerations fed her.

"Shouldn't your goddess be able to show you the way?"

The vehemence behind Nes's question assured Mathias of how much she disrespected the gods. "I asked her for guidance," he said, dreading how to fix such a deep and mortal flaw, "and she guided me to you. Something about building trust."

"Wait." Nessix waved her hand in a feigned dismissal. "Out of all of your goddess's greatness and goodness, she told you to come bother *me* with this nonsense?"

Mathias shrugged, indifferent to her accusation. "Etha does what she wants. I can only settle for the guidance she gives me."

Teeth clenched to prevent any unplanned outbursts, Nessix stopped and glared at his back. Mathias continued a few more steps before halting beneath Nes's scorn. He turned to face her, confusion exaggerated across his features.

"Is something wrong?" he asked.

"Yes," Nessix snapped. When a gentle shake of Mathias's head conveyed his proposed ignorance, she huffed, "You!"

A broad smile made his face much more irritating. "I assure you I'm in good health, though I'm touched you're concerned." Mathias flexed his lean arms and craned his neck to look himself over and ensure they passed inspection. Satisfied, he nodded at his assessment. "Yes, I believe I'm quite fine."

Nearly shaking at Mathias's casual provocation, Nessix flung her hands in the air. "I have more important things to do than cater to your whims!" She wanted nothing more than to storm off, but Mathias was testing her, and she steadfastly forbid him to get the better of her.

Mathias lowered his head, disappointed by how quickly Nessix gave up. "As you wish, my lady," he murmured. "Leave, if you must."

Nessix balked at the idea of swallowing his orders, but something about his words disturbed her more. She used a long blink to look away from him, and had difficulty meeting his eyes again. A tight frown creased her face and, while it silenced her tongue, it disheartened Mathias.

"Did I say something to offend you?" he asked, genuinely uncertain how he'd stifled her frustration so effortlessly.

Nessix mumbled her reply. "What did you call me?"

Her confusion triggered enough of Mathias's curiosity to pursue the matter. "I'd thought it safe to assume you'd accept such a title, given you're from the noble house."

Nessix had inherited her position with pride, but the duty of her birthright often left her wanting. Every day, she bound her chest and kept her dark hair tucked into neat war braids to prevent her body from posing as a liability. The dirt and grime of battlefields and training barred any attempts at primping. To serve as a strong and capable leader, she kept her body toned, foregoing the feminine softness expected of women. Nessix wore her title well and served her people diligently, but she only did so by hiding this vulnerable side of herself. She swallowed hard. Mathias would never understand.

"The days of lords and ladies died out with the last of the humans and elves. Such titles hold no meaning."

Mathias took note of the veiled trouble in her eyes. "Well, I'm a human, so we're not all dead yet," he assured, trying to steer their conversation back to their pleasant banter. "But if you'd prefer a different title, I'll do my best to oblige."

Nessix eased her haunted expression with a tired smile. "General is all you need to remember." Unconsciously, she continued walking toward the bluffs.

Relieved by her response, Mathias followed without hesitation. He let their trek progress in silence, but the lack of a distraction gnawed at Nessix until her need to busy her mind surpassed her desire to hear nothing more from Mathias.

"You know the cave temple's been abandoned forever, right?"

"Forever's an awfully long time," Mathias mused. "I'm sure

you're exaggerating, at least a little bit."

She blew out her exasperation with his wit and shook her head. "Maybe a bit," she admitted, "but nothing's there anymore. I don't know what you're expecting to find."

Considering Nessix's personal state of spiritual health, Mathias spared himself the headache of explaining the extent of his motives. "It may not mean much to you, but this is my goddess's most sacred temple, and I couldn't come all this way without seeing it." He looked ahead, spotting a crude entryway into the cliff face. "Once the war starts, I won't have this luxury, so I'm making it a priority now."

Nessix glanced at Mathias as he walked ahead, not caring for the tightness of his jaw or the stern concentration set in his brows. He'd just confirmed his certainty that a war with demons was inevitable. Dignity insisted she protect her self-doubt from this stranger, and Nessix hid behind a belligerent puff. Mathias accepted her unspoken opinion for its worth and knew better than to overlook her pride. An open challenge to any bouts of wit or strength promised to accomplish nothing at this point, no matter how badly he wanted to test her mettle. Pushing aside his whims, Mathias continued their walk in silence until they reached the rocky foothills of the cave's modest entrance.

"Well, here it is." Nessix waved her hand in the opening's direction.

Mathias walked two paces ahead before realizing Nessix had quit moving. He stopped and turned back to face her. "You're not coming? Aren't you the least bit curious what's in there?"

Nessix shook her head. "I already know what's in there and it's nothing interesting. Brant and I used to play—" She stopped abruptly. Even though she considered Mathias's faith erroneous, Etha meant no less to him than Inwan meant to her.

"No." A cunning smile crossed his face. "Go on. You and Brant what?"

She shook her head, willing Mathias to dismiss her slip. "Look, it was before I knew there was anyone who might actually think this place was sacred. All that's in there are a bunch of little rooms with cots, a big hall with some old murals, and a boring throne room. Like I said, nothing interesting."

Mathias's smile broadened. "Would you mind showing me to this boring throne room?"

His persistence wore on Nessix and a sudden wave of caution swept over her. She'd just led Mathias to one of the more secluded locations on Elidae, even out of Logan's current reach. "Why are you so eager to get me in there?" Her voice failed to hide her reservations.

Mathias would have laughed at her ridiculous assumption if he hadn't thought she was actually concerned. "Do you think I want to hurt you?" When Nessix stubbornly kept her mouth shut, Mathias sighed and rolled his eyes. "If I wanted you dead, I'd have knocked you out by the river and thrown you in, let your armor drown you."

She balked at his bluntness. "You think that makes me feel any better?"

Mathias shrugged. "I'd like to think it does," he said. "Now, are you going to help me find this throne room? The sooner I satisfy my curiosity, the sooner we can get back to discussing what to do about the demons."

He made a valid point, and though she still refused to admit it, Nessix needed to keep him happy in order to access what he knew about this new danger to her people. Curses jumbled beneath her breath as Nessix trudged into the cave, followed by a grinning paladin. Pairs of torches danced to life with blue flames as Mathias passed deeper into the temple. Nessix led the way around a turn that opened into a large room. They stopped as Mathias took in the sanctity of the moment and Nessix waited to see what other demands he wanted to make.

"Alright," Nessix said. "We're here. Now what?"

"Now, you wait."

Mathias stepped forward while Nessix's mind still formed its reply. She opened her mouth to dispute his order and a massive stone door from Inwan-knew-where slammed shut between them.

* * * * *

41

Mathias entered the room slowly, each footstep tainting the purity of the chamber. The room displayed a simple beauty, unmarred by manmade luxuries. Nes's promise seemed accurate. No mortal had worshiped here for some time, yet neither dust nor spider webs littered the marble floors or graceful cornices. Undoubtedly mundane to the average man, it clutched the breath in Mathias's lungs.

A single throne sat in the middle of the room. Three pairs of arching columns made of white marble, silver, and gold flanked either side of the seat. The room illuminated itself, though the expanse behind the throne faded quickly into darkness. A narrow hallway curved downward off the right-hand wall.

Nessix's angry curses forced their way through the thick stone door and Mathias subconsciously flinched each time her fists struck. His sympathy soon passed as the sacred moment overcame him. He'd seen thousands of temples devoted to the Mother Goddess, but the hands of men desperate to please her had built each of them. Etha constructed only one herself, in the image she most desired, and Mathias savored this blessed opportunity. He would be sure to spread word that Etha found the gaudy tapestries as hideous as he did.

"You've come to see me?" A playful voice wafted from the darkness behind the throne, chasing away his solemn considerations.

Mathias's face eased into bliss. "Of course, Mother," he answered. "I couldn't come to Elidae without paying regard to your holiest of temples."

Bubbling laughter chimed from the hallway to his right. "Your manners are stifling. I thought you considered ours a friendly relationship?"

"One more gesture will never hurt."

A gentle hand fell on Mathias's arm, turning him around. There stood a young woman, barely in her teens, though her eyes held boundless insight behind their tawny glitter. Amber hair fell straight and far down her back, gleaming with its own radiance. A brilliant grin paired itself with a nod of approval at the man who stood a solid six inches taller than her.

Nes's persistence faltered, but her fierce curses still filtered through.

"That girl is relentless," Etha murmured, a disturbing amount of awe trickling into her voice. "You've certainly done a fine job getting *her* worked up."

Mathias shot a glance at the doorway, still uncertain what to make of Nes's temperament. "She's stubborn. More so than most."

"She needs that spirit," Etha assured. "Life hasn't dealt her a very fair hand."

"And her father?" Mathias asked as Etha moved to settle on her throne. "How is he?"

"Oh, Laes." Etha sighed, wiggling about to make herself comfortable. "He's well enough. Nervous as any man who lost his god and maybe his daughter, but that's to be expected." She watched Mathias beam at her for some time before continuing. "I know you didn't come here just to see the temple, Mathias."

"I'm worried about these people," he answered, thankful Etha let him choose his words, rather than diving into his thoughts. "They know nothing about the gods and lack faith in anything they can't see. They aren't ready for a holy war."

"Forgive me for hiding the purpose of your visit," Etha said, regretting that she'd caused her disciple's grief. "I thought you wouldn't have come; your past encounters with demons left you scarred inside and I can't bear to think of you bleeding any more."

"Etha, there will never be a time when I won't have to face the fallen." A bitter laugh escaped Mathias. "It is the prophecy you wrote for me."

She reached out and caressed his cheek, gazing at him thoughtfully. "I'm amazed you're still so devoted to me. I don't mean to abuse you so."

Her touch refreshed his weary soul. "The past should have proven that I'll accept whatever trials you demand of me," Mathias said. "But in Elidae's current state, I don't think I'm enough to save these people on my own. Despite their recent blasphemy, I beg you to grant your blessing on those who seek you so holiness can return to your homeland."

"Is that all?" Etha asked. "I will grant that, but it's up to them to accept it. You know I cannot force my blessing on anyone."

"I know, my lady," he replied, delivering his gratitude through a relieved smile. "I just pray enough of them listen."

"They will believe once they see what I do through you. That can't possibly be *all* that's on your mind."

Mathias glanced away, concern overwhelming the mirth he'd found while goading Nessix. Reluctance kept his mouth shut longer than he'd intended, but Etha's patient gaze waited for him to continue.

"I cannot help but feel that there is something much bigger than the demons at work here," Mathias said at last. "I need to know how to stop it."

"You would have to figure out what it is, first." Etha raised a hand to mute his rebuttal. "Blood will be spilled in this war, yes, and there will be deep scars for Elidae, but even if I knew what was going on in the demons' vile minds, between the bindings of fate and free will, you know I could not lay it all out for you."

Mathias's heart plummeted. "You're telling me the demons are acting in a manner not even you can predict?"

Etha shook her head, gaze growing more distant beneath distracted brows. "There is a divine power at work here," she murmured. "We can rule out a few suspects from alignment alone, and I haven't noticed any suspicious conduct within my realm. This deceit concerns me greatly."

Mathias had little use for the younger generation of gods. He curled his lip at the thought of them hiding answers from Etha, and this betrayal would stay paramount in his mind until uncovered. Some force of the heavens threatened the outcome of this war, potentially the fate of Abaeloth as a whole. Beginning to wish he'd never asked, Mathias nodded slowly in acceptance of Etha's words.

Comforted that Mathias offered no debate on the issue, a firm resolve crossed Etha's face. "I will contact you if I suspect anyone on my end."

"If one of the children stands against you, should you allow me, I will punish them for this transgression," Mathias vowed.

A taut smile creased Etha's lips at his determination. All those years ago, she selected Mathias as her champion for his foolish grit and staunch loyalty, but she doubted his ability to face off against a god.

She concealed such apprehensions behind sweet words. "I would expect nothing less from you."

Mathias lowered his head reverently and speared the door with a critical glare. "Nessix is waiting for me, and it seems as though she has an unexpected guest."

Etha raised her pondering gaze and nodded. "Do as you see fit," she instructed. "And be good to the young general. She's confused enough with life as it is."

Mathias gave one final nod as he buried this conversation's trepidation in the depths Nessix was unlikely to find, then turned to wait for the door to slide open. He paused before subjecting himself to the girl's temper and made one last glimpse over his shoulder.

"Farewell, Mother," he murmured.

I know you will serve me well, my dear.

* * * * *

Blue fire seared into Nes's mind, burning her sanity as she sat pensively with her back against the stone wall. She grumbled her dissatisfactions and sent a loathing glance at the door once more. The pain in her fists had nearly subsided enough for her to try pounding again when a gentle scrape from the temple's entrance grabbed her attention. She peered down the hallway, but the torches didn't prove their worth enough to reveal the sound's source. Curiosity overwhelmed concern, and Nessix stood. The stone door slid open behind her and she acknowledged Mathias's presence with a raised hand of warning. He hesitated for her benefit alone.

Nessix drew her sword with care. Cautious steps moved her down the hall, leaving Mathias to contemplate his options. He wanted to save any grand displays of power for later, but without his sword, he had few options. Smiling contently, he followed Nessix and waited for his time to step in.

"What are you so afraid of?" he asked, defying Nes's efforts of stealth with his boisterous question.

"We are not alone!" Nessix hissed. She grabbed his arm when he began to stroll past her.

An abundance of smart replies popped to mind, but Mathias refrained from turning this into a joke. "We will be, soon enough." A firm hand pried Nes's grip from him and he continued ahead.

Cursing under her breath, Nessix followed. She strained her eyes to see further down the hall, only occasionally monitoring Mathias's steep confidence. A delicate laugh chimed behind them and Nessix froze in place. Mathias stopped at the halls' intersection and looked back to smirk at her. He gestured for her to continue. More reluctant than ever, Nessix tightened her grip on her sword and scrambled to catch up to him. The pace of a minotaur plodded, and ogres traveled with a lumbering gait. The footfalls in question sounded much like her own, but Nessix doubted any fleman with a lick of sense would think to spy on her.

Mathias released a labored sigh as Nes's tension overcame her. "As much as I would love to see how this turns out, I cannot allow such corruption in this temple. You are under Etha's orders to leave at once."

Slowly, Mathias turned in Nes's direction, the jovial expression wiped clear from his face. The tendons of his neck flexed to accentuate his clenched jaw, his eyes cold and serious beneath strict brows. He moved two steps closer to Nessix with calm deliberation, demanding all of her attention. Mathias raised his hand not more than six inches from the side of her face, a white light that spawned no illumination flashing against his palm. Faster than Nessix could comprehend, a bolt of light danced from Mathias's fingers, past her head, and above her shoulder. Nessix braced stiffly. Common sense frantically assured her that if Mathias had meant to hit her, he would have, but her mind staggered in its attempt to comprehend what just happened. She flinched, dropping her sword to cover her head as the beam exploded behind her and dimmed away with a gurgling croak.

"What was that?" Nessix breathed, not yet trusting her ability to control her limbs if she unlocked them.

"A cleansing," Mathias said, his amiable timbre returning. He picked up Nes's sword and placed it back in its sheath. Grasping her shoulders, he turned her around. "Look."

Still mending her nerves, Nessix peered at the lump the blast had hit. The stench of burned flesh flooded her nostrils and she sucked a great breath through her mouth. The figure came to an awkward rest, thrown against the wall where the halls joined. She stared at the smoldering body. Not much remained distinguishable of hair or flesh, but the extra appendages sprouting from its back gave the corpse a hulking mass. Nessix straightened abruptly, neither able nor wanting to retain her startled gasp.

"Love of the fled god!" she swore. "That was—" The word choked itself silent.

"A demon?" Mathias finished for her. "Yes, it was."

Nessix stared at the twisted figure, unable to move or even voice another protest. Color drained from her face and it took Mathias's soft touch on her arm to reawaken her senses.

"I've got to get back," she stammered. "Now."

Mathias accepted that as his cue to grab her hand. Pulling the startled girl to his chest, he chanted the words of teleportation. Nessix pushed against him, but found herself stuck as his other arm wrapped around her. The ground below them radiated with a soft pink hue and arcane characters danced in the haze around them. In a blaze of searing white flames, general and paladin disappeared.

FOUR

Logan loved it when Nessix roamed on her own and gave him the chance to kick up his heels like a foal. He trusted her to not find any trouble in such an open location. Temporarily relieved from duty, Logan galloped off as soon as Nessix slid from his bare back. He raced across the fields of his territory, shaking his mane as if pride no longer mattered.

Testing the air uncovered the usual pleasantries, but one scent caught his attention. Logan considered himself important enough to know most of the local equines, but he found one completely foreign to him. Ears pricked, he stood and listened for the other animal's approach, though no hoof beats drifted to him. Sharp breaths blew from flared nostrils and Logan walked in the direction of this mysterious horse, all senses on alert. Moments later, he discovered the cause of his concern grazing peacefully beside the Ceran River.

The other horse had a considerably more petite build, barely able to reach Logan's withers with his poll. Regardless, the massive feathered wings tucked neatly by his sides easily made up for this difference in size. Muscled to perfection, his golden coat glowed, interrupted by four uneven socks and a perfect blaze. His eyes, while sharp and enlightened, blissfully softened in the moment as he chomped up great mouthfuls of sweet riverside grass.

Logan watched the legendary beast nonchalantly dining and tossed his head at the informal provocation. He would not tolerate this intrusion, not in his territory and certainly not from a stranger! He trotted up to Ceraphlaks, snorting his authority. If this great golden gnat wanted to stay here, Logan demanded he prove his worth.

Ceraphlaks swung his head up to assess the situation, and met Logan with confusion. Mathias had warned him about a hostile reception, but never expected it from a horse. He studied Logan, realizing he'd seen too many battles to be an average equine. A feeling of kinship welled inside Ceraphlaks and he sounded a gentle nicker of salutation.

Logan halted abruptly at the greeting, appalled at the casual gesture. A chilled hardness fixed in Logan's eyes as he continued his approach. He swelled in collected pride, aiming to intimidate. Honoring his rider's judgment, Logan accepted Ceraphlaks as warmly as Nes took to Mathias.

Ceraphlaks hoped to avoid problems and set his interest to ignoring Logan. He dulled his gaze, lowered his head, and returned to his meal.

It seemed the pegasus wanted to avoid a confrontation, but that almost insulted Logan more. He rammed his forehead against Ceraphlaks's jaw to force him to cease his activities. Logan pinned his ears at his adversary, squealing his last warning.

No amount of ugly faces or valiant prancing daunted Ceraphlaks. Drawing his head as far from Logan as possible, he raised his forehand from the ground and unfurled his wings with a great gust.

Logan's mane stirred around him in the artificial breeze, but he mulishly stood fast. Ceraphlaks exhaled a playful nicker that Logan responded to with a belligerent squeal.

Determined to find a way to humiliate this rival, Logan charged ahead. Ceraphlaks had a close relationship with battle, but quickly took into account that Logan meant business. A ruffle of feathers lifted Ceraphlaks into the air, and he skimmed over Logan's head and landed behind him.

Logan knew his strength well and dwarfed his opponent by

size. Frustrated, he connected a kick with the base of Ceraphlaks's wing. The blow hurt, but a grunt and wringing of his tail pushed Ceraphlaks past the pain. This harassment had grown stale, and Ceraphlaks launched himself into the sky. He'd teach Logan how to tangle with a pegasus some other day.

Logan chased his afterthought to a hilltop, his whinny of good riddance echoing the pegasus's merriment.

The hill offered a flawless view of the land, and Logan stared across it until the sun suggested otherwise. Blinking away the brightness, he turned his attention to the grass Ceraphlaks had so kindly found for him. His muzzle plunged into the delicacy's sweetness as a second unfamiliar scent tickled his senses. Logan scanned the horizon and after long moments, caught activity in the south. The longer he stared, the greater the movement became until a small army speckled the plain. Pricked ears caught the sound of foreign war cries. Realization struck Logan hard as he spun and bolted to find Nessix.

* * * * *

Nessix lost all sense of time during their journey, and breathed her relief once her feet hit firm ground. She pulled her face away from where she'd tried to bury it in steel, knuckles white from how firmly she'd grasped the collar of Mathias's breastplate. Flushing, Nessix shoved herself away from Mathias, freed her hands, and flexed circulation back into her fingers. Mathias had safely deposited them to the only place of the fortress he knew, En's study. Once Nessix reestablished her nerve, she pushed through the door of her grandfather's sanctuary and into the maze of her fortress.

Mathias trailed after her. "Was that timely enough for you?"

"This is not a joking matter," Nessix scolded. En missing from his study compounded her preexisting fright; the only other place En spent his days was the war chamber, and that only happened from necessity. Thankful for the emptiness of her coiling stomach, Nessix glanced at Mathias. "Where are you going?"

"I'm following." He smiled at her attempt to push past her anxiety and bristle at his insubordination. "I don't know where else I'd go. Besides, considering I'm the only person here with any experience fighting demons, I might have something helpful to offer."

Afraid to admit he was right, Nessix briskly led the way to the war chamber. Guards greeted her in front of a closed door, a small chorus of muffled voices debating amongst each other behind it. Dutiful nods met Nessix's stern eyes and Mathias's tight smile as the door was pulled open. The room's quarrel ceased abruptly.

Prior to Nes's entry, En sat at the head of a heavy table, Sulik seated beside him, facing the door. Brant was on his feet, leaning forward with fists clenched. His chair lay tumbled backwards on the ground and his eyes sent pointed threats at Veed's sole commander, Renigan Falk. This man lounged in the seat between his own general and En, his attention fixed on digging grime from beneath his fingernails. Veed pushed his chair back to turn and smile at Nessix.

"My child, where have you been?" En breathed, eased to find her in Mathias's care.

Nessix hastened past shelves of maps and tactical pawns to her designated position opposite her grandfather. "Scouting got a bit sidetracked." She gave Brant a smile that prompted her cousin to turn from the table and breathe restraint into himself.

"And who is our company?" Veed's critical eyes combed over Mathias as he accompanied Nes inside.

"I decided to train myself a cleric," Nessix lied, before anyone else spoiled her secret. The less Veed knew about Mathias, the better. "Why in Inwan's name are you here, anyway?"

"A cleric!" Veed scoffed. He turned more completely and watched as Mathias moved to stand beside Nes's chair. "You really think someone like that can rival *my* abilities?"

"You only ever talk about what you can do," Nessix said. "I've never seen you heal anyone and would prefer to rely on my own sources."

Mathias examined Veed with a cold intensity. Too many secrets and undoubtedly foul intentions lurked within this man. His

51

arrogant eyes lacked honesty. For now, Mathias put his trust in Nessix's intuition. If she claimed him nothing more than a lost cleric, he'd play the part.

"So, Nes, why didn't you tell me about this new pet of yours earlier?" Veed pressed, slowly drawing his gaze from Mathias to the girl.

"He wasn't the topic of concern then, nor is he now," Nessix said. "Why are you here?"

An aloof smile crossed Veed's face as he slammed a sack filled with a bulky mass on the tabletop. "I've come with that proof you were asking about."

Veed hesitated for dramatic effect, allowing Nessix and her men the chance to exchange nervous glances. Mathias set his jaw and watched Veed closely. The dark general took his time loosening the stings that held the leather sack closed and carefully peeled it open. Inside the bag lay a petite humanoid head. Gray with death, it summed up Veed's take on war quite nicely. A small, scaled ridge rose from the bridge of an otherwise humanoid nose, disappearing into a mess of dark, matted hair. Haunting crimson eyes and predatory teeth remained trapped in a snarl.

En murmured a soft prayer under his breath as Sulik shifted uncomfortably beside him. Even Brant's temper quelled from shock, and Nessix went numb. Two of them showing up in the same day forced her into a most troublesome position.

Neither Renigan nor Veed expressed any discomposure, and Mathias hoped he hid his grimace before anyone saw it. The head belonged to an aranau, the demons left most physically and mentally blemished by the Divine Battle. They compensated for their smaller size with vicious natures. Grotesquely distorted, their hatred for mortals overcame them long ago and drove the subspecies to insanity. In battle, they served as violent and disposable berserkers, seldom controlled even by their own officers. Beginning this war against aranau concerned Mathias greatly, a fact he apparently displayed.

"Do you have something to share, cleric?" Veed asked.

Blinking away the morose premonitions that trickled into his mind, Mathias brought himself back to the present. "I—No, my lord," he said. "No, I do not."

"If you know something about this creature, now would be the opportune time to share it," Veed said. It amused him to see how tight-lipped the other side of the table became.

Staying on course with Nessix's deception, Mathias delivered a lie of his own. "There is an entire volume devoted to demons in Master En's study. I suggest you consult it sometime."

"I don't recall such a tome," En said before common sense caught him.

"There is," Mathias said curtly. "I found it myself."

Veed whistled. "Who are you to get away with such a tone?" He leaned closer to Mathias, though he made certain to speak loud enough for all to hear. "Good generals shouldn't bed their soldiers. It's bad for morale."

Mathias frowned at Veed's coarseness, more to protect Nes's pride than his own.

"And a smart general would realize there are more important matters to discuss right now," Brant said.

Bolstered by her cousin's voice, Nessix leaned back in her chair. She gestured to the head to avoid looking at it again. "You made no mention of this when we spoke this afternoon."

"If you wouldn't have been so anxious to leave, you might have been able to see it for yourself," Veed said. "It showed up at my gates not long after you and Logan left."

Nessix bit her lip to keep it from trembling. Her timing nearly left her up against a living version of what leered at her from the tabletop. The encounter she faced with Mathias had ended before she knew it began, and even that tattered her resolve. Nessix yearned to press Mathias for more information on what this meant, but blinked back the sting behind her eyelids and cleared her throat.

"How did you defeat it?" Nessix asked. Sincere hopes prayed against Veed using Mathias's method.

"Steel," Veed said. "And a lot of it. It kept fighting after being run through and losing an arm. It didn't fall until its head rolled."

Silence claimed the room while minds innocent of how demons fought toiled over Veed's report. The war had found them. Laes had given Nessix everything she needed to become a competent leader against Elidae's foes, but nothing had prepared her for a threat this severe. Her eyes fell on Mathias's back as she surrendered to the fact that Elidae's survival depended on him. Nessix dropped her face into her hands and ran her fingers through her hair.

"And we just killed one in the cave temple," she mumbled, keeping her eyes lowered.

"Oh?" Veed mused. "I've never heard of a cleric taking up arms. How'd you take yours?"

"A whole lot of might," Nessix said. She glanced up at En in haste, silently promising him a more complete report if he kept still for now.

"If they're so difficult to kill, a whole army will cut us to ribbons!" Brant said. "We don't have the manpower to back us up."

Still censoring Mathias's display in the temple, Nessix snuck a look at Veed. "Not on our own."

Veed smirked at her implication. "I'm touched, Nes, but do you really think your men would stand for any sort of treaty between us? I know mine would prefer to let you clean up this mess."

"I'll bet they would," Nes muttered. "And believe me when I say working with you is not something I want to do. I'll admit I don't think my force can handle this on our own, and I have no problem leading the enemy to your gates if you try to duck out of this war."

A smile crept across Veed's face. "I wouldn't put it past you."

Nessix rolled her eyes at him. "I've thought of much more pleasant ways to get rid of you."

Veed chuckled and turned his attention back to Mathias. "You've researched these beasts. How do you suggest we engage them?"

"I would suggest steel," Mathias said. "And a lot of it."

Veed scowled at Mathias's gall, unaccustomed to such obstinacy. Gritting his teeth, he blew out a sigh and glanced at Nessix. "If you're aiming for an alliance, you'd better be willing to share this man's insight."

Nessix wanted to laugh at Veed's slipped composure, but the

dreadful weight of their discussion suppressed that ability. "If anything relevant comes up in his studies, I'll let you know."

Veed's sharp smile returned. "That's my good girl."

The watch tower bells interrupted their discussion, drawing the whimsy from Veed's face and bringing Renigan to straighten at last. Color drained from Nes's cheeks as all eyes looked to her, the final set belonging to Mathias as he turned his back to Veed. The siege bells continued to pound and a muffled commotion brewed in the hallway. Mathias feigned a cough, prompting Nessix to blink away enough anxiety to resume function.

"Sulik, begin organizing the troops," she said through numb lips. "Order the archers and the fifth company under Veed's command for the extent of this battle. Brant, mobilize the cavalry."

The men constructed the necessary mental blocks and hastened from the chamber to execute her command. Nessix stood, leaning her weight on arms braced against the tabletop. Nerves and shame prevented her from looking at Mathias, but her words were for him.

"Tell me what to do," she begged softly.

Mathias still remembered his first tangle with demons, but Nessix's apprehension disheartened him. If she truly wanted to see the end of this war, she needed to toughen up.

So far, she's only seen the terrifying side of demons, Etha reminded him. *She's asking for your help. Count your blessings.*

I'm guessing by your tone that we're not facing anything insurmountable?

Little more than a raid. Several hundred, but no aranau, nothing with wings, and nobody that can manipulate divine energy. You should be fine.

Mathias breathed his thanks to his goddess. "First, you have to decide how badly you want to keep hiding me," he told Nessix. "I'll fight if you want me to. I'll clear the field for you myself if you don't mind revealing me this soon."

Her startled eyes snapped up to meet his. "You're telling me after what you did in the temple, you're not planning to fight?"

"I fully intend to fight when the time is right or when you order me to do so. Demons are cunning opponents. I doubt they'd field any more of what Veed faced without first knowing what they're up against. This should be nothing more than a scouting party."

Nessix slapped the table. "Do you hear those bells? That means there is a sizeable force—"

"And what they are after right now is information."

Nes's jutted chin and the glower she hid behind failed to influence Mathias's firm stance on the matter. "Then we should destroy them all," she said.

"We could," Mathias granted, "but if they recognize me, future battles will get much worse, and in a hurry. All it would take is one survivor to report that I'm here."

"And how long do you plan to hide from them?"

Nessix directed her heightening agitation at Mathias, but that meant some courage still lurked inside her. "I will not leave your men until this war is over," Mathias promised, "and I will take up arms at your call, but until you learn how to battle demons, your best bet is to avoid antagonizing them by brandishing me carelessly."

Every ounce of Nessix urged her to ignore his suggestion, but Inwan help her, there weren't very many other options. She had no idea what to make of demons, how to fight them, or what horrors they possessed. Mathias was the only person with a calm outlook right now, and if he had even a guess at what to do, her inexperience craved it. She cast a glance at her grandfather as he stared, tight-lipped, at the demon's head. She knew what advice he'd give her, and took it without even asking.

"So, what do I do?" she asked Mathias.

"Block what you can and keep them from reaching the fortress. Push them back until they get discouraged and leave. Demons might be crafty, but patience is not one of their virtues."

That sounded like a terrible plan. "But what happens when they attack?"

"Distract them with something rudimentary and aim a dagger for their eyes. The less skill you use, the better, and if you must reciprocate, try to kill it."

Nessix swallowed the last words, still unable to fathom how to successfully destroy a demon. "We aren't allies yet, Sagewind," she said tightly, "but I am going to trust you today."

Mathias nodded at her compliance. "You'd better hurry and don the rest of your armor if you want to deliver your orders," he said, noting Nes's limbs were currently exposed.

"There won't be time. I've ridden into combat in less." A new thought struck, chasing away the confidence Mathias built for her. "Logan's still gone."

Mathias had yet to appreciate the depth of Nes's relationship with her massive destrier, but abstained from questioning it now. "If you left him when we went to the temple, I can send Ceraphlaks to find him. I'm sure he's fine."

Nessix returned to her full height, nails digging into her palms. Logan never missed her battles, but without time to slap the rest of her armor on, she certainly couldn't set off to find him. Placing the fate of her army in her narrow faith of Mathias unnerved Nessix, but she had sense enough to know she needed his guidance to see this through.

Drawing a ragged breath, Nessix gave a curt nod and took inventory of the weapons on her belt. Before her tension resurfaced, she strode out the door, Mathias close behind. He watched this doubtful young woman attempt to prove her grit, and a small part of his heart ached for her. Not even adept veterans were fit to handle the horrors of a war with demons, and Nessix deserved the chance to mature without knowing of them. Regardless, she stood as her people's banner, and Mathias prayed she'd keep herself together enough to protect Elidae.

The pair emerged from the fortress to behold the Teradhel army falling in line. The demon regiment remained a churning blot in the distance, but the information Etha shared with Mathias proved sound. Given the modest size of the opposition, this fight should culminate to nothing more than a frenetic scuffle. Already mounted on horseback, both of Nes's commanders and Veed waited in earnest for her to arrive, though Commander Falk no longer stood by his general. Nessix maintained her rigid composure, but all three men had watched her grow up and her efforts did not fool them.

"Commander Maliroch," she said tersely. "I require the use of your mount to rally the troops."

Brant kept his concerns to himself and slid to the ground.

"We will not attack directly," Nessix told the men around her, attention preoccupied with adjusting a stirrup. She kept her eyes directed away from them.

"You can't be serious, Nessix!" Veed scoffed.

"Today, you are under my command, General Astaldt." Nessix swung up on Armina's back. "And you will carry out my orders. Keep your attacks basic and do not prompt more aggression from your units than is necessary."

Not wanting to hear any other snide remarks about orders she barely approved of herself, Nessix pushed Armina forward to address the rest of the army.

Standing eye to eye with Mathias, Brant glowered at him. "Did you put her up to this?"

"I gave her my advice," Mathias said. "She chose what action to take on her own."

Veed snorted and turned to watch where Nessix cantered before the lines, doing her best to inspire her army.

"For the sake of our people, I hope your guidance was sound," Sulik said.

Mathias didn't bother to reassure them, their dubious expressions conveying their thoughts with clarity. If they continued to doubt his expertise, he'd tend to their questions after this clash resolved.

Across the field, Nessix speared the sky with her sword, her rallying cry devoured by the distance between them. Veed crossed his arms and clamped his jaw, turning from the trio of men as the entirety of the army called back, "Then we raise our swords together!"

Mathias nodded his approval of the troops' vigor, his gaze lingering on the tension bracing Veed's shoulders. "What was that?" he asked Sulik.

The commander smiled. "If we must die alone, then we raise our swords together." A gentle smile tipped his brows. "It was her father's battle cry. She never grew out of it."

Dedication poured from the troops, restoring the smile to Nes's face as she breathed in the moment. If fate wrote victory for them today, she wanted to find it with no other army. She motioned for her officers to come forward and dismounted Armina. Mathias invited himself along, mindful to keep his distance from the others.

Jaw set resolutely to curb his animosity, Veed spun his fecklan, Solvig, to join the unit appointed to him. Brant and Sulik retained their opinions and once Brant accepted the reins from Nessix, the two commanders took their posts, leaving Nessix alone with Mathias. She stared at him as he studied the scene from beneath strict brows, debating whether or not she made the right decision.

The blare of a hollow horn ordered the demons to rush forward. Swords flashed free on both fronts, arrows resting in their nocks as enemy war cries flailed against fleman courage. Nessix turned to her troops to check the posts of her officers. Choking away the last of her uncertainty, she pointed her sword ahead.

A stout wall of soldiers braced for impact, weapons ready and wills firm. Determination masked their suspense so thoroughly Mathias almost missed it. He recognized their expressions, too bent on going down with a fight to worry about falling. The closer the demons neared, the more positive tension surged through the flemans until their heralds called them forward. The lines broke, and the army raced to engage their opponent.

Mathias's assurance of the enemy's objective encouraged Nessix to dart into the fray and away from his supervision to gather her own understanding of these foes. At first glance, they appeared no more extraordinary than the fleman warriors she fought alongside, comparable in stature and build. A second look proved physical comparisons were the limit of the two races' similarities. Insanity devoured all signs of benevolence in the demons, but their luminous eyes were otherwise sharp and clear with violent intent. Movement to her right cut Nes's observations short, and instinct raised her sword to intercept a blow aimed at her head. A startled yelp escaped her and her left hand reinforced her right on the hilt to ward off the strength of her assailant.

Distract them with something rudimentary and aim a dagger for their eyes.

Maintaining only basic attacks might work on a lesser enemy, but not this! The pounding of hooves reached Nes's ears, followed by a dull crunch, and the pressure left her blade.

"I thought we promised each other we wouldn't die!" Brant shook fragments of demon skull from the hilt of his sword.

"Very funny, Brant." Nessix's voice trembled past her shaken courage.

"I'm serious, Nes," Brant shouted over the chaos around them. "Be careful." He wheeled Armina back into combat before Nessix could reply.

Mind garbled with instructions, Nessix wondered why she was the only one not giving orders. A nearby tangle slammed against her left shoulder, the scuffle jarring her into the present. She looked down at the demon Brant killed, its fingers still twitching in death. Recalling Veed's spoken account, she refused to take any chances and quickly severed its head.

Mathias barely caught Nes's recovery, and the fight continued to challenge her. Frustration overpowered relief when her soldiers came to assist her. This care the army took of its officers facilitated the demons in sniffing out the leaders. A couple of nasty blows threatened Nessix, but she rebounded furiously, her lithe form slipping away from those too powerful for her to overthrow on her own. The more Nessix involved herself in the fight, the farther she drifted from the paladin's efforts to keep her in sight. Using the force of his limbs to fend off the surrounding demons, he prayed for the futile chance that none of them recognized his armor. Mathias aborted his efforts to stay near Nessix and turned his back to the bulk of the battle.

Commander Vakharan and the back lines received only a handful of demons, and any that made it that deep fell to the overwhelming odds without notice to the rest of the horde. Sulik kept his gaze forward, though Mathias couldn't tell if he watched for the next wave, followed Nes's progress, or glared enviously at the younger Commander Maliroch. The cavalry effectively pressed through the enemy, though Mathias lost his visual on Brant. He had seen the commander rescue Nessix before bolting off, and opted not to fear for the reckless youth.

Last, Mathias looked to Veed, no longer astride his mount.

The paladin curled his lip in distaste for the other man, the chill he received upon their meeting returning to the pit of his stomach. Veed proved himself a fine warrior; the demons barely seemed to see his approach before they fell to him. Previous conversations hinted that Veed dabbled with the divine arts, but that only explained so much. Mathias threw one last glance in Nes's direction then pushed his way toward the foul man.

Veed approached the battle on his own accord, gleefully striking down whatever traipsed within range, and his effectiveness in battle disturbed Mathias. Not even an hour ago, Veed claimed it difficult to best a single demon. Mathias considered the difference in aggression between these scouts and the aranau, but Veed's rampage still unsettled him. Whispering a prayer to Etha, Mathias drew his holy blade and drove it through the gut of the demon in Veed's sights.

"I thought we weren't supposed to kill the beasts?" Veed said.

"Just following my superior's lead." Demon blood steamed off the blessed steel. "What happened to Nessix's orders, anyway?"

"She doesn't know any better—"

"She gave you orders," Mathias insisted.

Veed spun around, fury in his eyes. "Do not interrupt me, boy!" Mathias kept a wary watch on the other man's sword. "Nes is a child and doesn't know any better. We can defeat them today."

Mathias studied Veed's imperious face. "Out of the two of us, who understands demonic warfare?"

A quiet laugh mingled with Veed's grunt as he blocked an axe blow. "I believe that's you." His eyes narrowed. "Though I doubt your studies loaned you such knowledge."

"So what if they haven't?" Mathias challenged, relieved to hear the demons signal their retreat.

Veed's silence cued Mathias to turn his efforts to ending the broken demons strewn on the ground. Etha frowned on him healing these abominations, and he suspected the flemans would feel the same. That would not keep him from giving them a merciful end. The surviving demons dragged themselves off, eager to share their reports with their kin.

Veed followed Mathias's clean up, his attention trained on the paladin. "Who are you to show such mercy?"

Mathias had assumed their discussion through and began to realize the reason behind Nes's aversion to Veed. "We were supposed to drive them off. What you insisted upon was mindless slaughter."

"Your point?"

"I have no taste for it, even against the fallen."

That answer sat poorly with Veed. "What is Nessix hiding from me?"

"Hiding, my lord?" Mathias asked, feigning respect a bit longer.

"Do not play dumb with me. Not even she is stupid enough to believe a cleric could keep his skills without a god's blessing."

A smirk crossed Mathias's face before he regained his composure. An eerie intelligence lurked behind the wild look in Veed's eyes and Mathias decided to play it safe. "Are you so sure?"

"I'm not here for your games. If you won't tell me, I'll force it from Nes, myself," he challenged. "You're turning your dear general into more of a liar with each breath you take."

"If that's how you see it." Mathias bowed his head mockingly, the action answered by a dark laugh.

"Tell me who you are," Veed ordered. "Unless, of course, you are ashamed of yourself."

Mathias ran out of patience. Etha would protect those under his care; for now, he had to tend to Veed. "I am a follower of the Mother Goddess, Etha," he answered. "And I am *not* ashamed of that."

The smile grew. "And how did you come to know of this Mother Goddess?"

"I learned of her through the teachings of my childhood caretakers," Mathias said.

"Your caretakers, eh? Did you have no parents of your own, boy?" Veed laughed. His keen gaze traced the kite shield and ring of lilies etched on Mathias's breastplate.

"My parents allowed me and my sister to be watched over where they could not." Self-consciousness crept over Mathias. Those eyes knew too much.

"Tell me, cleric, do you follow power?"

"I follow the source of power."

Veed shook his head and looked away, chuckling. "Would you like to experience mortal power?"

"Are you challenging me?" Mathias asked. He knew both his talents and limitations, and Veed did not intimidate him in the slightest.

"Leave Nessix," Veed commanded. "Certainly, I cannot offer you the same pleasant bed she can, but I can grant you much more meaningful gifts than she ever could."

Mathias hadn't planned on aligning with Veed to begin with, but after such vulgarity! "I assure you, my bed is as lonely as yours, sir. I know that mine is by choice, whereas yours…" He shrugged.

Veed's eyes darkened. "If it's power you're after, you're on the wrong side. All Nessix has is her charm. You're as good as dead in her hands."

"We'll see in time, old man," Mathias said.

Nessix limped toward the pair, interrupting their impasse. She pressed a hand against her left shoulder, but a wild grin concealed any further pain. "That was amazing!" she breathed. "The victory was on my land, Veed. That means you're bringing the provisions." Nessix laughed, but her smile faltered at Veed's snarl.

"They'll arrive at dusk," he snipped. Through, Veed stalked off to find Solvig.

"What'd you do to him?" Nessix asked, wincing as she lifted her hand from her wounded shoulder.

"Called him on his indecency," Mathias said. He looked down at the exhausted girl. "Let me take a look at that."

"Don't worry about it." She batted his hand away and resumed applying pressure.

"And your limp?" he asked.

Nes shrugged. "I must have twisted something. Really, I'm fine."

A roar of taunts escorted the demons from the battlefield and Mathias reflected on the impact of this victory. Fleman spirits escalated with good reason, but this meager scuffle played out inconsistent with normal demonic tactics. The flemans remained oblivious to the danger of their bolstered confidence. Mathias stilled his desire to correct them as swords raised to the sky with boisterous songs. He sighed and turned his attention to those laying wounded on the field.

"I didn't die, Brant," Nes declared triumphantly as her cousin neared. "Just like I promised."

"You still have more wounds than you should."

"Only because I was fighting on foot."

Just this once, Brant allowed Nes the last word. She rode too high on the rush of victory to give a fair argument, and he focused his attention more on Mathias's efforts, anyway. The paladin worked efficiently, feeling for pulses, lips moving in hushed verses. Occasionally, he splayed a hand across a warrior's chest before a ragged breath filled their lungs and they sat up in confusion. Brant watched silently and debated his options. He didn't like Mathias and didn't want him here, but seeing him restore their damaged army forced Brant's hand.

"I'm going to have the cavalry carry the wounded home," he told Nessix. "If that man really can fix them, he'll have an easier time of it there."

Nessix looked around at her recovering army. Soldiers recently sporting mortal wounds staggered to their feet as Mathias spread his miracles across the field. She nodded at Brant's assessment, and departed to inform Mathias of the plan.

"General?" he asked absently upon her arrival, his attention otherwise focused on his task.

"We're moving the wounded and dead back to the fortress," she said.

Mathias glanced up, uncertain if he'd heard right. "As you wish, General." He assisted two soldiers to their feet.

The human boasted very few injuries of his own and as Brant led his unit with their task, Mathias wasted no time in instructing those around him on how to most safely move their injured comrades. Eager troops followed Mathias's requests, recalling his previous work and reveling in his current wonders.

"Nes, you really ought to keep a better eye on him," Sulik said under his breath, moving up beside the girl.

She'd been contemplating the same thought. "Mind if I assign you to watch him for me?"

"You plan to try and imprison him?"

"I'm not sure we could," Nessix admitted. "I want you to keep the men safe from him. He's bringing a bit too much hope and I'd hate to see what happens when he can't keep up with this show."

"A sound decision."

"And keep him away from Veed," she added.

"I'm quite certain Sir Sagewind can take care of himself."

Nessix shook her head. "Veed's a clever bastard. I like to get my way as much as anyone, but Veed sees to it his will is done, regardless."

Sulik's smile slipped out. "Now, Nes, surely you don't believe Sir Sagewind's capable of these wonders he's been boasting."

"Of course not!" she huffed. "Just precautionary measures. Can I count on you for the job?"

"As always." Sulik's first encounter with Mathias left him far from impressed, but both his hand and pride were on the mend.

"Give Sir Sagewind his space!" Nessix said, taking a step toward the man as her troops unwillingly backed away from him. "Aid him now by helping your comrades home." Orders received, the soldiers dispersed.

"I'm not so bad now, am I, General?" Mathias asked quietly.

"You should have waited to start with your tricks." She looked at him through weary eyes. "You've just saddled yourself with a whole lot of responsibility."

He nodded. "My life's been full of it. I told you I came here to help you win this war and I'll accept whatever tasks come with it."

"I've appointed Commander Vakharan to act as your bodyguard."

Mathias marveled at Nes's authority. Barely a slip of a woman, he still considered her capable of controlling any man or woman on this island, save Veed, himself, and Etha. The warning Etha gave him, that Nessix had lived a difficult life, came to light, but Mathias pleasantly noted she refused to let her troubles defeat her.

"I doubt that's required, but I appreciate—"

"It is required because I've ordered it. Now, the two of you must return to the fortress to prepare an area for you to fix my men. I will remain on the field to aid those standing."

"Yes, General," Sulik answered with a prompt nod.

"And you." Nessix grabbed a hold of Mathias's arm as he moved to pass her. "If I were you, I'd see that my armor was shined and fit for ceremony. I expect many anticipate your presence at the festivities."

"I will do my best, General," Mathias replied. With nothing left to say, he followed Sulik back to the fortress.

FIVE

Mathias stood, stretching his arms as he left the side of the last soldier wounded in battle. Sulik remained with him through the extent of his work. Mathias hadn't needed the company and Sulik offered nothing helpful to the task at hand, but Mathias considered him a wonderful witness. In less than two hours, he'd shown Sulik hundreds of miracles. Hopefully, Nessix would take an account from her own commander to heart. Those lost on the field received Etha's blessing, and Mathias considered the evening's work through.

"Where are you going, Sir Sagewind?" Sulik asked as Mathias turned to leave.

"I'd planned on returning to my quarters."

Sulik smiled broadly. "You don't want to join the festivities? Veed's providing, and he very seldom leaves anything to be desired."

"The invitation is appreciated, but I prefer to spend my post-battle evenings in meditation."

Appointed as Mathias's chaperone, Sulik hoped to sway his mind as not to miss the anticipated feast. "And insult General Astaldt's gifts? Sir, even Nessix mentioned you deserve the honor, and I'm sure it would do much for the troops' morale."

Mathias mulled over Sulik's persistence. "Only for an

appearance." He needed time to ask Etha for insight on the next attack, but would take advantage of this chance to appease Nessix. Besides, his stomach reminded him that he hadn't eaten since leaving Sarlot, and the promise of food enticed him.

"You won't regret it," Sulik assured.

Sulik led Mathias from the confines of the fortress and out to a lush meadow illuminated by firelight, just outside the fortifications. Soldiers bustled about in the twilight, laughing over boisterous conversations. The crowd doubled what Mathias expected, and he spotted a substantial number carrying Veed's crest. Banners flew from elevated standards and music drifted across the gathering from an undisclosed location. Situated in the center of this commotion sat three remarkably long tables, arranged in an open triangle. Stewards ushered hundreds of smaller tables around the central fixture in preparation for the banquet. While Mathias kept his reservations about their degree of exuberance, it was hard not to smile.

Mathias scanned the area until he located Nessix. She and Brant stood by a wagon lined with kegs, filling their flasks. Everything about her radiated victory, and he saw no sign of the previous distress on her face. Relaxed brows softened her features, and a genuine smile lit her eyes. Seeing her so vivacious eased the paladin's heart.

A soldier approached Nessix and pulled her attention from Brant as he spoke and pointed toward Mathias. She looked in his direction, her expression falling as the soldier continued to speak. Mathias met her eyes, wondering what transpired to so easily sour her mood. Sulik touched his forearm to draw his thoughts away.

"Nessix wasn't joking when she said you were to be honored," Sulik shouted above the crowd's rumble.

"What do you mean?"

Sulik cast an uncertain glance at his general. "Traditionally, each general is seated at his own head of the table. Sir Sagewind, there are only two active generals present, but the tables are arranged for three."

Nes's response to his arrival made sense now and Mathias would honor her insecurity. "I cannot accept such a compliment.

I'm no greater than anyone else in these ranks."

"With all due respect, sir, if Nessix feels you deserve it, you must accept."

The commotion settled as everyone meandered closer to the tables. Of course, Veed and Renigan took their seats first, flanked by banners of ebony and purple. Nessix and Brant followed suit, her colors crimson and navy. Mathias's gaze drifted upward to find standards of silver and gold awaiting him.

"Sir," Sulik urged. "Take your seat."

Mathias moved to sit down, brooding over this development. These people adored Nessix, without a doubt, but ignored her suspicions in exchange for their own intrigue. Mathias felt confident about them investing faith in him, but his miracles swayed them faster than Nessix seemed able to cope with. Oblivious to the paladin's thoughts, Sulik sat beside him and the rest of the army filled in the remaining chairs. Attendants brought out carts of food to shuffle between the soldiers.

Veed waited for the clatter of dishes to cease before he stood again. "Gentlemen of war," he declared, reveling in the silence that pursued. "Women." He nodded to the nearest female soldier. "Tonight, we celebrate a victory over a foreign threat. Those who were blessed with not taking up arms today cannot understand what is coming. It is my firm belief that joining my army and that of the beautiful General Nessix will give us ample strength to thwart any plans these demons may have for us." Veed returned to his seat, nodding as a server set his plate before him. A handful of men, mostly his own, cheered his brief address.

Nessix rose next, gracefully accepting the small roar and fists pounding on tabletops that followed her movement. She speared Veed with a cocky glance. "It was my brave men, seated here and in the infirmary, who have seen this terror. General Astaldt, I believe *you* are the one who cannot understand!" Laughter from her ranks accompanied her remark. "None of us are allowed to look lightly on this threat. Sources have told me what is coming and we cannot let ourselves grow complacent. We've got some new methods of dealing with this danger and—" She disguised her reluctance with a deep breath. "I believe today's victory is owed largely to someone other than myself."

Saying nothing more and leaving the troops in an insecure silence, Nessix sank back into her seat. She studied her dish hard as the popping of fires and symphony of insects wriggled through the merry crowd. If Nessix wished to sulk, she reserved that right. Angry that Mathias allowed his cousin such humiliation, Brant skewered him with a steely glare.

"Sir, I believe they want you to speak," Sulik murmured, before the mood deteriorated further.

Everyone but Nessix stared at them, and Mathias easily guessed the same. Nes's pride forbid her to give Mathias an open tribute, but she respected the desires of the many. That spoke volumes in defense of the girl's character. Reluctantly, Mathias stood, scanning the eyes of his enthralled audience.

"I am sure all of you have heard your share of rumors regarding the past day." He spoke slowly, plotting his course with care. "However, I'm comfortable saying that I am the only one able to verify them. For those of you who I haven't had the pleasure of meeting, I am Sir Mathias Sagewind." The White Paladin part could wait for later. "It is true that I'm capable of the healing arts and that I have an extensive knowledge of demonic warfare. And," he added, almost as an afterthought, "granted your fair General Nessix allows me, I would be honored to pass such knowledge on to those of you seeking it with open hearts."

Bubbles of hushed excitement cascaded from the crowd. Nessix's head snapped up, her expression contorted between anger and confusion. She never granted him permission to attempt such intimate relations with her troops!

"Your comrades who fell to injury mere hours ago are now resting well," Mathias continued, "and the plan of attack, at least that instructed by General Nessix, was also partly my doing."

Nessix ground her teeth and latched a foot around the leg of her chair, infuriated by the threat to her command. Veed's sneer declared how little Mathias's hidden insults amused him. Neither of the generals concerned Mathias. They'd demanded a speech from him, and he told them what they needed to hear.

"My goal is to serve you until the demons are no longer a

threat, and let it be known that such a day will come."

He meant to say more, but the rest of his words drowned in the crowd's enthusiasm. Unwilling to fight them, Mathias sat. As he'd witnessed from Veed and Nessix, his plate was delivered and all eyes fell on him.

"They're waiting on you," Sulik whispered.

Mathias stared at the food, unable to identify the meal served to him. Respecting the custom, he grasped his utensils and cut into the meat portion. The first warm bite struck his tongue with a strong metallic taste, not incredibly to his liking. Each time his teeth closed around the slick texture and tough composition, a new burst of offensive flavor hit the back of his throat and burned his nasal passages. Mathias chewed slowly, indulging tradition. His eyes watered when he choked the first morsel down.

Veed flashed a smile. "Men, enjoy yourselves!" The troops obeyed without hesitation.

Mathias satisfied himself with eating bites of an unfamiliar yellow vegetable that subdued much of the meat's flavor.

"I'm unaccustomed to this taste," he murmured, as not to be overheard.

Sulik's brows furrowed as he swallowed a bite. "A man of your standing has never been honored at banquet before?"

"I must admit." Mathias coughed into his hand. "Not quite like this. What am I eating?"

"The main course? It's to restore your courage," Sulik said with an amused smile. "You're eating the heart of a minotaur."

* * * * *

Centuries had passed since the Order banished Shand Heltsa from Zeal. In the months prior to Shand's deportation, Etha had led Mathias to collect the first known god shard. Through the most deceitful means, Shand uncovered the artifact's worth. Born of the mangled bodies of Etha's children at the end of the Divine Battle, god shards contained the undying essence of those first deities. The priestesses believed a mortal host could become a god if bound to one of these relics, and Shand's attempt to test that theory resulted in her exile.

Desperate to keep the god shard in her sights, Shand had begged Mathias to find a pardon for her as he had in the past for equally blasphemous crimes. He chose to side with the Order.

Shand's desire for vengeance ran deep, but her mortal life had taught her the value of patience. Free from Zeal's petty laws and restrictions, Shand set out across Abaeloth, facing trials and torment to reach her prize. After her ascension, she flaunted her new station before the Order, delighting in how those same arrogant officials who first sent her away squirmed in the shadow of her might.

Keener than any of them gave her credit for, Shand bided her time, gaining influence over misled beings of simpler minds as she waited for the best time to strike. Brimming courage allowed Shand to confront the demons, and her persuasion gained them as loyal servants. Anything to take revenge on Mathias Sagewind.

Shand had waited decades with the demons, and successfully isolating Mathias from the rest of the Order finally allowed her to take action. She trusted the demons enough to ensure the paladin suffered before she swept control of Elidae away from Etha. After the Mother Goddess found humility, the Order would collapse at Shand's whim. She pressed her cheek in her palm, lounging in her gilded throne as she waited for her pawn to return with his report of the past battle.

She'd gone about clearing Elidae of competent threats carefully, and arranged to tear apart the Teradhel family to better exploit the land. Meeting the island's traitor helped her gain an unseen political foothold amongst the flemans. General Laes fell, leaving his child to govern the land, and when Veed separated from her lines, the scene grew even more entertaining. Abaeloth's divine council sentenced Nessix's watchdog of a god to repent for his liberal conduct with mortals outside his jurisdiction, and the naïve general practically gave up. The squabbles between Nessix and Veed amused Shand until the frightened child developed into an efficient warrior. Elidae's recovering strength concerned Shand, and so she put an end to her diversion and called her demons out to play.

A timid knock struck the door to her chamber. "Come in," she ordered.

The door crept open, revealing a fleman cloaked in black.

"Your report?" she prompted, leaning forward.

"Unless the description you gave me was invalid, Mathias Sagewind is here."

Shand's giddy laughter beat out her gasp of pleasure. "You are certain?"

"His armor, his blade, his physical features." The man shook his covered head. "That cocky personality. This man matches your words perfectly."

Shand nodded enthusiastically. "And has he made it into Teradhel's ranks yet?"

"He's following her, but she doesn't seem too inclined to accept him."

"Give it time." Shand's excitement cast her to her feet and she smoothed her silken robes as she paced about the room. "He'll weasel his way in soon enough, and once he starts truly caring for them…" She clasped her hands beneath her chin, violet eyes sparkling with her grin. "I expect you to help me find a way to weaken his divine connections," she said, mind scarcely able to stick with one thought.

Nervous laughter disclosed his concern. "My lady, I have no way to deal such damage to a man like that, not if he's truly as blessed as you say."

The delight flashed from Shand's eyes as she stalked up to her pawn. He cringed as she reached a hand into his hood to cradle his cheek. "Now, my dear, do not forget you will have my help." She patted him twice, withdrew the gesture, and wiped his sweat on the shoulder of his cloak.

"Of course, my lady," he breathed, lowering his head. "I will do my best to please you."

The smile returned. "I trust you will."

Facing the paladin exceeded the pawn's abilities of deceit, but he was even more afraid of what tortures awaited failure. He'd need a miracle to fulfill this task and doubted Shand's willingness to perform one on his behalf. Exotic eyes complimented by shoulder-length silver hair kept a careful watch over him. Worn from the past day, he bowed before his goddess.

"I will return with any further news," he promised, relieved by her nod.

Shand's eyes tracked the man's rigid departure, and she wondered idly if he realized the unfortunate fate awaiting him. Evading Mathias's suspicions only bought him until Shand was through dealing with the paladin, herself. Once her pawn's purpose was served, she'd dispose of him just the same. Luxuriating a sigh, the goddess sank back into the comfort of her throne and resumed her fantasy of Abaeloth without her champion.

* * * * *

Mathias wanted to avoid appearing impolite, but jumped at the chance to excuse himself from the table. He'd taken part in unusual customs in the past, but frowned upon the idea of eating a creature as sentient as his family and friends. Actions covered by an amused Sulik, Mathias vacated the bustle to search for a calmer place to speak with Etha. Awed gazes from adoring soldiers followed him until he'd wound deep into the confines of the fortress grounds to a secluded courtyard.

Haven't you learned to clean your plate by now? Etha teased as Mathias took a seat on a raised garden bed.

I suppose not. Do you have any information about who's backing the demons?

I'm afraid not, she said.

Mathias frowned. *How many of the demons escaped today?*

More than I'd like, but fewer than I'd expected. You can decide for yourself whether or not that's good.

Mathias retained his sigh. In his time, he'd grown to hate the act of killing. *Do you know how much they saw?*

I'm not sure, but I know their retreat began as soon as you drew your sword. Etha thought for a moment. *It was foolish of you to unveil yourself so soon.*

Mathias grimaced. He'd expected as much, and yet, he'd let Veed's actions provoke his indiscretion. *There's nothing I can do about it now.*

Etha fell silent and Mathias drew his brows together as boisterous singing infringed on his peace. The snort of a displeased equine indicated only one thing.

You should have kept a closer eye on her... Etha groaned.

Nessix spotted Mathias immediately when Logan rounded the corner and she grinned as the man cast a dejected look toward the heavens. Somehow, she steered her mount over to Mathias, the pleasure of her drink obliterating her previous reservations.

"Sagewind," she called. "What're you doin'?"

An honest answer would only confuse her right now, and Mathias wanted to limit his problems tonight. Besides, he needed to prove Etha's existence to Nessix when she was capable of full comprehension.

"I'm thinking," he answered at last.

"About what?" Nessix drew another drink from the flask held fast in her hand.

"Nothing worth troubling yourself over."

Nessix attempted to dismount Logan, but slipped, her descent narrowly intercepted by Mathias's steady arms. Logan eyed the human critically before deciding him harmless and trotting off to pass along the duty of tolerating Nes's drunken antics.

The girl shoved her half-empty flask toward Mathias, indifferent to Logan's departure. "I'll share'f you want me to."

Initially, Mathias doubted the sincerity of her offer, but one look into the deep vastness of Nes's eyes told him enough. "You would share your spirits with me?"

She nodded vaguely, mind stumbling along. "D'you not want any?" Mathias certainly seemed like a nice fellow when outside influences dictated her thoughts. "Oh!" she gasped, not allowing him the chance to answer. "You're waitin' 'til later, aren't you?"

Mathias nodded. "I think I've had my fill of the celebration for now. And you," he added before her mouth opened again, "should go get some sleep."

Nessix shook her head in firm disagreement and pressed her

free hand against her temple in a feeble attempt to slow the spinning. "The party's jus' begun. Wait!" she wailed in the closest thing to a commanding tone she could muster.

"I'm not going anywhere," Mathias assured her.

"You're not happy!"

He smiled patiently. "We were victorious today. Of course I'm happy."

"You can't fool me!" Nessix shouted in drunken defiance. "Are you friends with *them*?" She fumbled with her sword, fingers forgetting to unbuckle it.

"No, I am not." Mathias placed his hand over hers to ensure her blade stayed safely contained. "I'm just disheartened about the men we lost today."

Nessix smiled knowingly and ceased her attempts to jump to the offensive. "They fought by choice," she pointed out.

"Yes, but—" Mathias sighed, resigning his attempts to argue with her in her current state. "I suppose you're right."

"And we won!"

"Yes," he agreed again.

"So, they're dead with good reason. Let's go celebrate." Nessix grabbed his hand between hers to try dragging him along.

"You know…" Mathias pried her hands from him. "You did very well today."

She grinned and smacked him on the chest. "You didn't do too bad, yourself!" Satisfied, Nessix plunked down where Mathias previously sat and patted the spot next to her.

Mathias obeyed her unspoken suggestion and sat beside the young general. Nessix inclined her head toward the sky, the moon's cold light revealing the color of her flushed cheeks. Her mouth gaped open slightly and her mystified eyes soaked up the heavenly expanse. She stared up until her head felt too heavy for her neck, and then let it fall against Mathias's shoulder.

"You ever wonder what's up there?" she asked.

"I suppose I do," he replied, wondering where her warped mind wandered.

"Isn't your goddess s'posed to be up there somewhere?"

Mathias smirked. "In a way, yes she is."

76

"So part of her's down here?"

"Yes."

"How's she manage *that*?"

"We're all a part of her." Mathias enjoyed the feeling of Nessix's trust, no matter how distorted the cause. "Even the other gods are part of her."

"Like Inwan?"

"Yes, even your Inwan was part of her."

Nessix belted out a laugh. "What part're you?"

No one had ever asked Mathias that before and the depth of the drunken general's chatter fascinated him. "I like to think I'm a piece of her will."

"Sometimes," Nessix offered, "I feel like a piece of her hair."

"Oh?" Mathias asked, amused to hear Nes acknowledge Etha at all.

She took another drink. "Yeah."

"Why's that?" he asked, genuinely curious about her answer.

"'Cause." The response launched Nes deep into the realms of her own thoughts. "I'm always surrounded by a bunch of other hairs. And," she added quickly, "even though I *am* a very special hair, I think she sees me as just another hair." Her mind staggered behind hazy blue eyes. "Either a hair or a freckle."

It took a moment for Mathias to convince himself that Nessix had finished her explanation. Her logic amazed him, though this time, he was drawn by the proud girl's modesty. Could she really find it in herself to feel like nothing more than a commoner? Too bad it took so much ale to loosen her tongue.

"It's a good thought," he said at last.

Nessix nodded absently. "Yeah, I s'pose it is." The two remained sitting in silence for some time before Nessix blurted out, "Veed was talkin' 'bout you."

For the first time this evening, Mathias was truly compelled to listen to her. "What did he have to say?"

Nessix shrugged. "Somethin' 'bout you two crossin' swords. And I don't think he meant it in a friendly way, either." Nes sat back up and cocked her head in consideration. "Y'know, I didn't think you're the kind to betray me."

"I won't," Mathias said. "What made you even think that?"

"Well, Veed knows things. He knows things no one else knows." Nessix sighed dramatically and patted Mathias on his shoulder. "Just... don't kill me," she requested gently, as if she made the plea every day. "Or Brant. He's a good man."

Mathias returned the sigh. "I won't."

A cheerful, reassured grin seeped back to her face. "I don't think Veed likes you very much."

"Veed tolerates me from necessity alone."

Motioning for Mathias to move closer, then grabbing his arm to pull him there, Nessix whispered, "Can you be on my side?"

"I thought I was," Mathias whispered back. He tried to shift his weight to get comfortable, but her deceptively strong grip gave no intention of freeing him.

"You are?" she breathed.

"We fought the same enemies today, didn't we?"

Nessix squinted in deliberation, fussing at the effort of thinking. She definitely remembered Mathias ordering her *not* to kill the demons. He never tried to hurt her men, but he seemed to want to preserve their enemies' lives as well. She blinked a couple of times, her face blank until her decision solidified enough for her purposes.

"I think we did. Didn't we?"

"Yes," Mathias said with quiet authority.

"Oh," Nes sighed, finally letting go of Mathias's arm. He straightened instantly, gingerly stretching his cramped shoulder. "Okay. But I still don't get it."

"What don't you get?"

Nes shrugged and casually glanced away. "Veed's been my friend since I was born," she said. "Well, sorta." She shook her head, an almost sober solemnity crossing her face. "I don't think he'd turn traitor, either."

Memories of his conversation with Etha blew a chill across Mathias. "Who said there has to be a traitor?" Perhaps Nes's ramblings needed deeper consideration. The coincidence unnerved him.

"Well, Veed *clearly* wants to fight you, and he's not the type to go after someone without good reason."

It grew still as thoughts tumbled through both of their minds. Mathias doubted Veed ever found a reason for anything, save his own entertainment. The day's battle alone stood testament to his barbarism. Hostility dictated every action Veed made, and his eyes held too many shadows to prove trustworthy. Alongside these uncertainties lay Nes's impulsiveness and quick temper. The elves of Drailged were banished for their violence, and it seemed those tendencies still thrived. Mathias could only speculate on the flemans' potential in war.

Nes's thoughts lingered on Mathias. She knew enough to consider him a valuable asset. He healed her troops and showed her more tolerance than she deserved. Of course, in this moment, she also found him the most charming company on all of Abaeloth. She gave him a pat on the back.

"I'll keep you safe from him, okay?"

Considering the girl's current state of mind and what the alcohol promised for her tomorrow, the words gave Mathias very little comfort. "Thanks."

Nessix teetered on her perch, catching herself clumsily with her left arm. A wince accompanied the action and, up until now, her ceremonial cape had concealed the stained bandage which supported her wounded arm.

"Is your shoulder still bothering you?" Mathias asked.

"Only when I move it," she said. "The surgeon put somethin' on it and said it'd be better in a week."

"May I?" Mathias gestured to her arm.

At her nod, Mathias peeled back the dressing bound to her wound. He touched the glaze on her shoulder, and brought his fingers to his nose, recognizing the scent of medicinal herbs. It made sense in the days of a fled god that the flemans resorted to simple clerical techniques, but he knew what Nessix wore would not heal her in a week. Bruises covered the surrounding flesh, but the lesion showed no serious damage. Smiling, he closed his eyes to pray.

Etha, I know Nessix has done very little to impress you, but please help me make her understand. His careful hands traced over the stupefied girl's shoulder. *Lend me your grace so I may heal her and, though she'll most likely blame it on tonight's spirits, when she wakes to find herself free of pain, she's bound to make some connection.*

Tomorrow, she'll have much more to worry about than a blow to her shoulder, Etha answered.

It soothed Mathias to hear her reply. *I don't plan to ease her from her tonight's aftereffects.*

That's not what I mean, Etha warned. *The demons are regrouping to march out in the morning.*

The wound pulled together and Etha slipped out of Mathias's head before he offered a debate. They couldn't come again! Not this soon and not with the soldiers in their current state! Unsettled by the report and concerned about the magnitude of the impending attack, Mathias pulled his hands away.

"We'd better get going," he said tersely.

"Back to the celebration?" Nes asked with newfound enthusiasm. She moved her arm around and grinned at the lack of pain.

Mathias pushed the heel of his hand against his forehead and briefly grasped at his hair, distraught over the logistics of accurately treating thousands of hangovers. "Yes. They'll be wanting another victory speech, I'm sure." He stood, holding himself rigidly.

Unreceptive to Mathias's foreboding, Nes linked her arm in his to drag him back to the festivities. Two failed steps passed before Nessix realized Mathias remained immobile, and she turned to him, concerned.

"Answer one thing for me before we go," he said.

"Alright."

"Veed reigns over the south, right?"

"Yup!" she chirped, leaping forward only to be caught by him again. "Why?"

The demons had marched from the south today, yet Veed never reported any activity. "No reason." Mathias stowed the information away. "That's all I needed to know."

SIX

Distorted memories floated pleasantly through Nes's mind, urging her to stay asleep. Reminiscing on the three flasks she downed and those she'd forgotten tempted her just as powerfully. An irate voice intruded through the distant haze of reality, dashing her hopes of a peaceful and slow recovery from her impulses.

"General!" The shout pierced through her pounding head and Nessix pinched her eyes shut even tighter. "Duty calls!"

"Go 'way," she mumbled, neither knowing nor caring how accurately she conveyed the order.

"Your men are falling into formation. For the love of Etha, Nessix, get up!"

She didn't know where she'd ended up, much less how Mathias had found her. All she wanted to do was lay there and die. As consciousness crawled closer, her head whirling from last night's brutality, Nessix begged her fled god for Mathias to keep his opinions to himself. Grunting her defiance, she rolled away from the paladin's voice and slammed into a gloomy wall. No matter. At least it wouldn't yell at her.

"Did you hear me, General?" Mathias demanded. "We are under attack!"

Nessix heard him, alright. As much as she hated to miss the occasion, sleeping this off seemed much more enjoyable. Her men

81

knew their jobs well enough to handle one fight without her. Nessix threw an arm across her eyes and swallowed the sour taste in her mouth before it developed into retching.

Mathias snagged that limb in his firm grasp and he yanked her to her feet. "Nessix, they need you."

Nessix staggered, her legs protesting against the action. Her stomach twisted again, and she doubled over as much as Mathias's hold allowed. Effectively defeated, she leaned against his strength.

"No, you don't." He jerked her upright and drove her shoulders to the wall with his free hand.

Her eyes peered open, objecting to the dawn's light. Their best efforts at conveying curses to chase Mathias away failed. "Lemme alone," she grunted.

"And leave your troops without their general? I think not."

"Brant can handle them." She tried unsuccessfully to reach the ground again. "Tell 'im to take command."

"They won't follow Brant," Mathias said. "Not against demons. They need you for that."

But they just drove them off! Somewhere in the cobwebs of last night's memories, Nessix remembered Mathias promising more to come. Unable to fully process the danger ahead, she threw every ounce of her weight toward the ground. This attempt found success when Mathias let go and allowed gravity to punish her childish behavior.

"Damn it, Sagewind," she groaned. "Brant can handle them."

"So you'll abandon your army? Is that the kind of general your father raised?" Relief came in the form of Nes's savage, though short-lived, glare. "They're counting on you. It's not their fault you don't have enough control over yourself to be their leader."

"Oh, enough!" Nessix groped for her sword as she staggered to her feet, raising her weapon to point between Mathias's eyes. Nausea fought her temper brutally, and her arm sank to rest the sword's tip harmlessly against the paladin's breastplate.

"Do not insult me." She cringed as an influx of bile shook its finger at her. Morbid humor danced behind Mathias's stern eyes. "At least you can spare my father this shame."

"Good girl," Mathias commended at last, though without

enthusiasm. "Commander Maliroch is preparing your mount. We don't have time to waste."

Pushing herself from the wall, Nessix carefully found her balance and looked around. She'd passed out in one of the hallways, left alone either from kindness or respect for her station. Of course, Mathias lacked the sense to let her sleep. She stumbled her first step, seething at Mathias in case he planned to assist her.

"You're in no condition to fight," he scolded.

"If that's the case, why'd you bother to get me up?" Her tolerance for this zealot of a foreign goddess disappeared with last night's bliss.

"I never said you didn't have the responsibility. I just said you look a little rough."

Nessix growled at his tempered jest. "Where are they coming from?" She clenched her teeth against the tumult in her stomach, sweat beading on her eyelids and the nape of her neck.

"The east," Mathias answered.

"And the numbers?"

"About five times what we faced yesterday."

Either discipline or her numb mind held the appropriate alarm at bay. Nessix tried to focus on Mathias as he calmly led the way to the field. Her confidence rattled with each step, but she would try to borrow some of his. Shaking her head and regretting the drink that gave her so much pleasure, Nessix attempted to work out how Mathias knew so much.

This Etha very possibly fed Mathias all he knew; Inwan never hesitated to offer similar advice to Nessix and her father. However, her god had also assured her people that no other deities deserved their attention. Even after he silenced himself to Elidae, Nessix maintained complete trust in Inwan's word. Some random goddess giving half a damn about her home made no sense. The flemans belonged to Inwan and they didn't need Etha.

* * * * *

Nes's focus faltered as she rode Logan out to the front lines.

Her gaze swept to Mathias, who walked beside them, before casting over the troops. They all seemed well, if a bit disheartened at the speed of their opponents' recovery. Nessix wrestled her mind for logic, grasping at details from the previous night. Nearly her entire army had taken part in the festivities every bit as enthusiastically as she had. Brant—who had polished off at least two full flasks of his own—guided Armina forward without so much as a grimace. Suspicion boiled amidst the queasiness in Nes's belly.

"Sagewind." Nessix freed her foot from the stirrup to shove him in the shoulder. "What are you capable of?"

"There are many things a man can do, General."

Her mood was already foul enough. "You healed the men from yesterday's battle, did you do the same for last night's battering?"

Mathias flashed a smile that Nessix yearned to pummel from his face. "I can reverse the effects of poisons, yes," he answered. "But you were such pleasant company last night, I'd hoped it wouldn't wear off."

Clenching her teeth and keeping her groans to herself, Nes hunched forward in the saddle. Sifting through the few tangible aspects, she did recall talking to Mathias the previous night and they probably got along just fine, but Nes even enjoyed Veed's company after drinking so much. Scanning the expanse before them only exacerbated the misery of her physical condition. Thousands of demons stood against her troops. Nes's eyes shifted back to Mathias as they pulled up alongside her commanders. He remained silent beside her.

Brant greeted his cousin with little more than a twitched lip, annoyed to see Mathias with her. Nes's flushed cheeks and dull eyes made him even less pleased about the morning's events.

"What do you suppose the odds would be we'd all still be asleep if we'd have actually killed these things yesterday?" Brant asked.

Sulik rolled his eyes, tired of debating this matter with Brant, and focused his attention to the battlefield's activity. The younger commander made no attempt to hide his shoddy opinion of Mathias, and Sulik aimed to avoid getting stuck between the two of them.

Assuming Brant directed the question at her, Nessix answered with an incoherent mumble, not wanting to think harder than absolutely necessary. Mathias, on the other hand, knew Brant had directed the demand at him and gladly satisfied the challenge.

"You really think killing a couple hundred of them would have made today's force less intimidating?" Mathias folded his arms and refused to look in the commander's direction.

Brant bristled at Mathias's apathy. "I think showing them we were a force to be reckoned with would have made them think twice about coming back so soon."

"I can assure you that this is an insignificant fraction of their overall force," Mathias said. "If yesterday's game had concerned them at all, there'd be something much more frightening staring us down today."

Nessix bit her tongue, afraid of losing the narrow control over her stomach's reflexes if she joined this debate. Instead, she internalized every word Brant's feistiness pulled from Mathias. She almost fell to yesterday's raid, and Mathias just confirmed more lingered in the hells.

Only Sulik kept his full attention on the field, and the commander gasped. "They're charging!"

Adrenaline numbed enough of her pain to permit function and Nessix inadvertently looked to Mathias for guidance. Nobody else knew how to form an accurate strategy against demons, but her current audience and level of patience prevented her from asking him outright. The saddle squeaked beneath her fidgeting and she glanced once more in Mathias's direction. Her heart dropped at his clenched jaw.

"Commander Vakharan," Nessix said, desperately trying to form a sound tactic without Mathias's insight, "lead the lines with me and Commander Maliroch."

"What about him?" Brant jerked his head in Mathias's direction.

Nessix loosened her sword. "We need every able body we can find right now," she said, unable to declare what, exactly, she expected out of Mathias. "Now, go deliver my orders."

"Nes," Brant said, acutely aware of his cousin's scattered composure. "You haven't issued any."

"Give them whatever orders you'd planned on giving if I didn't show up," she said. When both of the commanders gave her blank looks, Nessix shrugged. "I trust both of you, and you had to have some idea. Now, go."

Unsure what to make of Nes's strange behavior, they tore themselves away to follow her instruction. Conditioned for leadership since birth, Nessix needed to prove she could handle whatever dangers came their way. Her wavering confidence threatened more than her own dignity, and Sulik and Brant hastened to protect the army from their general's uncertainty.

Once the commanders left, Nessix looked back down to Mathias. "What are we up against?" she asked quietly. If he saw her through one more battle...

Mathias narrowed his eyes, spanning his gaze across the force driving toward them. He saw nothing that openly displayed unusual power, but from this distance, it was difficult to determine what might be hiding in those mundane ranks. Mathias knew with certainty that a firm challenge awaited them, but cared more about bolstering Nessix's confidence right now.

"Most demons don't even merit a class among their peers. These are some of them. Consider this an army of foot soldiers," he said, unable to consider it a full truth. "Their biggest threat to you is their numbers. Don't be afraid to fight with your wits."

Nessix nodded slowly, her mind working plainly on her face. Somehow, she felt she needed a lot more than wit to see this through. In the distance, the strain of Veed's siege bells wafted through the air, and she frowned at the probability of him waking up to a comparable threat. Nessix almost regretted that he'd gone home last night, thinking of several ways she could have used his valor today.

"You cannot coddle me through this war, Sagewind," she told Mathias at last.

His expression softened. "I don't think there is a way to, General. If you can keep your head, you can beat demons. All I can give you is knowledge; you have to decide the rest for yourself."

With a deep breath and Mathias's reassurance, Nessix cued Logan to charge toward the rushing demon lines. Wishing he'd bothered to summon Ceraphlaks, Mathias stared dumbly after the pair before bolting to try to catch up on foot. He'd intended to fortify Nes's confidence by belittling the opposition, but his words fueled the fervent young general down a hazardous path. Mathias tried to assure himself of Nessix's ability to take care of herself, but he had little reason to believe it.

* * * * *

When the clash ended, Nessix still sat firmly in her saddle and Mathias finally allowed relaxation to find him. Once again, she'd evaded his sight for the majority of the battle, but appeared relatively unharmed. While her body showed little damage, her shoulders sagged and her mouth dipped in a bleak frown.

Nessix suspected they once again owed their victory to Mathias, but it took more than the holy man's presence and wisdom to cheer her. Many of her soldiers lay injured and dying, peppered with comparatively few demons. Nessix had no idea how strong foot soldiers from Mathias's homeland were, but this force far surpassed her expectations.

Dismounting Logan, she commanded her quaking legs to seek Mathias. He stood out like a beacon, the ivory radiance of his armor contrasting vividly with the dismal scene around him. She watched him play medic, gesturing for assistance from those of able body and amiable character, and considered leaving him to his work. Death came packaged with war, though, and Nessix accepted that readily enough to seek answers now.

"Sagewind," she growled. "I have a question for you."

He took his time responding, slow to turn his head toward her. "In a moment, General."

"Now!" Nessix demanded, painfully aware of the attention Mathias's defiance received.

"Not until the men are healed," Mathias said. "Don't let your selfishness cost them their lives."

87

"The men will be fine," she insisted, "provided this goddess of yours is as merciful as you say."

Centuries had lent Mathias the ability to withstand the most aggressive badgering, but he forbid such a skeptic to belittle his Etha. "What?" he spat, trusting Etha to stay with the wounded while he dealt with this child.

Up until now, Mathias had conducted himself gently with Nessix, and his harsh reaction gave her pause. Her authority stood no chance against his power, and her mangled nerves threatened to abandon her. Mathias had laughed before when explaining his age, but the wizened glower behind such ancient eyes challenged Nessix now.

"You have my attention, now what do you want?" Mathias demanded, moving in on her.

Nessix braced herself for whatever Mathias planned to deliver with his aggressive advance. "Those were not foot soldiers," she said. "The fleman casualties tell me that much."

"Perhaps you aren't at the level I'd assumed."

"No," she protested. "You lied to me. If you were half the man you say you are, you wouldn't want this bloodshed, not from honorable men."

Apparently, Nessix's finest attribute consisted of hoarding leverage for future use. Mathias would watch what advice he offered in the future. "Alright, so I lied."

"You sent us to slaughter!"

"I didn't think you'd charge ahead so blindly."

"It was not a blind charge. I knew everything I needed. By your words, we should have crushed them."

"I'm sorry," Mathias said, though with very little sympathy for Nessix. "It seems I've misjudged you."

"What about them?" Nessix waved her hand at the dying around her. "They'll never hear your apology."

"If I'd told you the truth, you wouldn't have believed me." Mathias readily noted Nes's stubborn silence. "And those who are not dead now will live, I will see to that if you'll let me."

Pinching her eyes shut, Nessix grimaced at the headache that overpowered the residue of her adrenaline. Her mind and body ached remarkably and her pride suffered nearly as much. A swell of doubt attempted to overtake her before she lifted her gaze back to Mathias's face. He claimed he came to help, but as of yet, he succeeded only in hindering her outlook and corrupting her men with feeble hopes of divine power. He'd found the nerve to lie to her—deliberately and with conviction—and she still couldn't convince herself to hand him over to Veed. Nessix shivered with misdirected rage, fists clenched so tightly her knuckles begged for mercy.

When Nessix lost the ability to continue the discussion, Mathias walked away, consulting Sulik briefly about something she couldn't hear. The ringing in her ears urged her to relax before she fainted. Nes's lack of experience screamed at her to trust Mathias. Her love of her father insisted as much. The way he performed, though, his readiness to act on his own accord, frightened and infuriated her. This White Paladin *did* know things, and Nessix needed to discover what they were before he ruined her.

SEVEN

The words never even reached Nes's ears, lost in the air somewhere between where she sat and where En perched across the table from her. She'd hoped to compare the day's events with textbook battles to help formulate future tactics, but failed to consider that her grandfather seldom left the study during his waking hours. Instead of something worthwhile, Nessix promptly received one of the old man's lectures. Her hair still frayed from her pinned braids and a thin spray of blood freckled her left cheek.

"Nessix!" En snipped. "Are you even listening to me?"

She blinked once and focused on him. "Yes, Grandfather, I am."

"Then you would have to agree with me," he said, well aware Nes had derived her reply from respect alone.

"I don't trust him," Nessix answered, relying on the generic response to flow with whatever he'd actually said. "And words alone won't change my mind."

En's face eased in the schooled patience Nessix grew up knowing. "My Nes, he's here to help us."

"He told me himself he was here because it's his goddess's cherished homeland." Nessix rolled her eyes at the notion. "Whether or not his master exists, he cares more about preserving her name than us."

En reached across the table to cup his hands over hers. "You're overreacting. If he didn't care about us, he wouldn't have saved our wounded."

"Veed says he can do the same," she said stubbornly.

"Would you really count on him to do so?"

Nessix shrugged. "Depends on the situation."

"Now look who's talking nonsense," En snorted. "You would be wise to keep Sir Sagewind in good terms."

"You can think what you want about him, but I know Father's dead and there's no way Sagewind could have spoken to him."

En's eyes softened, understanding her position at last. Laes was En's son – of course Mathias's claims unnerved him. Outside that single fact, Mathias had given him no other reason for doubt. En missed the days when Nes readily swallowed his advice. He appreciated her tactical mind and independence, but needed her to listen to him now.

"His valor will soon win the troops over," En tried once more.

"It already has, and that's why it's such a shame I have to order him away."

"Do you honestly expect him to listen? He is here to defeat the demons. The only way to get him off this quest is to kill—" En silenced himself quickly, unwilling to foster such thoughts.

"Oh, it's tempting, Grandfather," Nessix granted quietly, "but I wouldn't want you to turn on me if I did." Through with listening to the greatest man she knew so easily swayed by a foreigner, Nessix shoved herself from the table and left En alone with his books.

* * * * *

Brant stalked from the mess hall, unable to stomach the atmosphere. He understood why an exceptional soldier deserved acclaim from his peers, but the amount of excitement used in repeating the same stories and rumors disgusted him. Mathias commanded boundless charisma, and it launched him to an alarming esteem amidst Nes's troops. Brant tried to reassure himself that the men loved Nes, but their fascination with Mathias despite their general's reservations teetered toward a dangerous obsession.

Rounding the corner, Brant climbed the stairs, nearly colliding with Sulik. A tight frown slipped onto the older man's face as he glanced away from Brant.

"Is something wrong?" Brant asked, confused by his typically stoic friend's anxious tic.

Sulik was pleased to pass his concern to Brant. "You may want to talk to your cousin. She's in a mood that you're much better equipped to handle than I am."

Brant grimaced. He'd hoped to catch Nes in a pleasant frame of mind. "Any idea what's bothering her?"

Sulik sighed as the tension lifted from his shoulders. "I'd guess it's these past attacks. I can't really blame her, but I don't remember the last time I saw her take pressure so poorly."

"Last week, demons were a myth. This morning, we fought them for our lives. Of course it has her bothered," Brant said. "It has *me* bothered."

Sulik smiled at the younger man. "Both of you should talk to Sir Sagewind about this war. He may be able to ease your fears some."

Brown eyes narrowed. "It sounds like you're growing a bit smitten with him."

Neither of the two cousins had made any solid attempt to hide their animosity toward Mathias, but Brant's contentious accusation startled Sulik. "He is a valuable asset to our army, even you have to see that, and his guidance is what led us through that first battle to be strong enough to handle today."

"Nessix ordered you to spy on him, not cave at his words," Brant said. "She doesn't trust him half as much as she trusts Veed and is depending on you. Keep your loyalties in check, Sulik."

"Nessix is and will always remain my general," Sulik assured, "but I'm allowed to think she's ignoring something she shouldn't. The troops are calling Sir Sagewind our savior and—"

"Our savior?" Brant interjected. "That's a pretty hefty honor for someone who's not even one of us. What do you suppose fostering this sort of shit will do to morale when he falls?"

Sulik doubted that would happen, but kept as much to himself. "I pray we won't have to find out."

"Do you pray that to our god?" Brant asked, watching Sulik's response carefully.

"I pray that to whoever's listening."

No matter how badly Brant's support of Nessix urged him to continue berating Sulik for his commendations of Mathias, he had to accept the answer. Inwan had left Elidae without warning, taking all of his insight and support with him. The nation floundered to find itself again in the absence of divine guidance, and Nessix took a solid stance that Inwan would return in order to hold herself together. Brant hated the god for how he treated the flemans, but his love of Nessix restrained him from speaking his mind on the matter. If some other deity wanted to sweep in and rescue them, he almost welcomed it; just not from Mathias.

"Is there anything you want me to pass along to Nes when I see her?" Brant asked.

Sulik eyed the young man, knowing Nessix had already made up her mind about Mathias. "I really think it would do her some good to consult Sir Sagewind with an open mind." He raised a hand to postpone Brant's instant opinion. "He told me the demons are regrouping for another push from the west. He has some valuable insight that she should at least look into."

"And how, exactly, does he know all of this?" Brant asked.

"He never told me specifically, but I do know that his goddess tells him—"

"His goddess!" Brant snorted. "I've about had it with that!"

"Yes, Brant," Sulik replied curtly. "His goddess. It's no different than Nessix continuing to turn to Inwan, except there's still evidence of Etha. This man has brought us hope."

Brant's eyes flashed dark. "I will not remind you again. Keep your tongue in check."

Sulik met Brant's resentment with a refined calm. "Just because you are blood to Nessix does not make you a more experienced officer. One of these days, you'll understand how to value your resources, but until you do, I cannot help you."

Sulik gave Brant some time to formulate a response, but the youthful commander remained silent. Tucking his lips, Sulik delivered a brief nod of good will and left Brant in the stairwell.

* * * * *

Night fell across Elidae, shrouding the land in a deceitful comfort. Nessix shoved the day's accumulation of letters from the towns of her kingdom aside and settled at her desk. She folded her arms on the surface, lowering her chin to rest on them. Complaints came from Phyta, Grenbrough, and Sarlot regarding mysterious aggressors and distress to the sounds of battle so close to home. Midton and Dale both inquired as to why the noble guard occupied their towns. Even Veed had sent notification to confirm an attack on his territory. Nessix lacked the brain power to concentrate on these issues or any other right now.

Last night's drunkenness allowed only vague memories of her discussion with Mathias. He denied being a traitor then, even comforted her out of attacking him over it, and she'd believed him. Honestly, she *wanted* to trust him. Pride and intuition drove Nessix, and she considered those traits crucial to her survival. However, she'd learned much more than simple self-preservation from her father. It would be foolish to waste a resource like Mathias, but something about him sat poorly with her. Nessix knew how to handle a number of disasters, from ogre raids to famine, but trying to manage a single human and his enigmatic feats made her question her decisions all along. With an exasperated sigh, she raised her head and snatched up the nearest letter.

Lost in search of evasive answers, Nessix overlooked Brant's arrival and subsequent observation through her open door. Her attention shifted helplessly between scrolls, and she shook her head to scatter the unwelcome thoughts cluttering her mind. Hoping to avoid startling her, Brant gently rapped on the door frame to alert his cousin to his presence.

"I saw you standing there five letters ago." Nes waited to finish reading the complaint in her hand before she put it down to turn to him. "Is everything alright?"

Brant's smile relaxed his face and he invited himself the rest of the way inside Nes's modest chamber. "I came to talk."

"About what?" she asked.

"Sagewind."

Nes scoffed and turned back to her desk. "I've had about enough of him today."

"Well, I have news from Sulik."

She inclined her head toward him to let curiosity peek through her obstinacy. "So he's been doing his job?"

Brant shrugged and leaned a shoulder against the wall. "I suppose you could say that."

Nessix blinked and frowned, jerking her posture a bit more upright at her cousin's ominous remark.

"Oh, don't worry," Brant said at her reaction. "I'm quite certain he's still firmly grounded on our side."

"Let's hope so," she sighed. "What did he say?"

"Something about Sagewind predicting another attack. But come on, Nes." He snorted at her flit of concern. "I could tell you the demons will strike again. This is war."

Brant's logic offered Nessix some peace, and she pulled one of the letters from the pile. Weary, she dove back into the frantic script of town officials.

"Are those complaints?" Brant asked.

She nodded. "They've heard battling and want to know why the noble guard won't tell them what we're fighting. Others have found the remains of barbaric murders." Nessix quit speaking and stared at the plea from Phenton in her hand. "My people aren't well," she murmured, troubled eyes rising to Brant's in search of counsel.

"We could pitch the topic to our mighty paladin to see what he comes up with," he said. "He *is* the flemans' salvation, after all."

Nessix gasped. "Says who?"

"Says Sulik." Looking over to the stack of letters on Nes's desk, Brant wished he could offer her insight of his own. "So, what were you thinking about the townships?"

Nes's lack of experience in this regard prevented her from

finding an answer yet. "We could send out more of the guard, perhaps some ambush troops. Change the orders—What?" Her words trickled into silence at the shake of Brant's head and curled upper lip.

"You've already dispatched two whole companies for protection, Nes. If you send more, we'll lose too many troops for our own defense."

"Got any idea what Veed's doing?"

Brant coughed. "He's probably drafting the townsfolk. Don't look to his actions for guidance."

Nes expected as much. Whether or not she wanted to admit it, turning to Mathias over this issue beat imitating Veed's tactics. A gentle roar filtered up the stairwell, interrupting her comparison of the two men with an equally ill-favored dread. Nessix occupied a discreet, one-room chamber on the second floor of the fortress to allow easy access to whatever duty demanded of her, and she recognized the source of the commotion immediately. She tore her sword from its scabbard, letting the latter fall to the floor. Brant grabbed her arm as she sprang past him.

"Nes, I don't think it's an attack."

"It most certainly is," she hissed, dragging Brant two steps before he finally released her.

Mathias served a fine purpose in her ranks, providing Nessix guidance that neither her father nor Inwan had ever given her, but that was it. He had no claim to her country or her people, certainly no right to accept the title of their savior! All Nessix had left was her position, and this human was not allowed to threaten that. Pride stomped her insecurity into silence as she proceeded to bluster toward the stairs.

Despite his cousin's small stature, Brant often found himself jogging to keep up with her temper. No doubt, Mathias had found his way to the troops, resulting in the enthusiastic resonance seeping through the walls. Brant quietly envied how Mathias dazzled the men and raised their spirits, though he didn't share such thoughts.

More important than keeping Nes safe from the dangers of her own tongue, Brant feared the troops' reaction to her unmistakable view of Mathias. As much as either of them wanted to deny it, the men had appointed Mathias as their champion. They received him with more exuberance than they'd shown Nessix in quite some time. Brant refused to believe Nessix was jealous of Mathias, but her pressed lips and rigid stride stated her intent of shoving Mathias into the place she wanted him.

"Nes…" Brant laid a hand on her shoulder. "Think this through."

"Do not defend that man." Nessix stopped and spun on him. "Not to my face."

Brant balked at her sudden movement and bared teeth. "I'm not, but it might upset the troops to see hostility toward their hero."

"They're accepting it toward me. If you won't back me, go busy yourself someplace useful. I've lost Grandfather and apparently Sulik to this man and I won't have you contaminated, too." Ending the conversation, Nes dashed down the stairs, met by a hallway packed with excited bodies. Hoping Brant chose to follow her for moral support, Nessix dove through the crowd to instill order.

Once Nessix reached the main floor, the flow of positive energy directed her straight to Mathias. She made no attempt to hide her ire, pushing her way past starry eyed staff and soldiers. Brant trailed close after her, offering repentant smiles on his cousin's behalf. The troops cautiously folded in behind Nes's advance.

Just as she expected, a group of her men surrounded Mathias, warmly discussing something together. Dressed in simple breeches and a plain white tunic, Mathias's armor no longer offered to protect him from attacks. Muscles twitching in anticipation, Nessix rushed him before anyone tried to stop her.

Mathias's current explanation came to a startled stop as his audience debated whether or not to jump to his defense. In the same moment, the coolness of a sword's edge pressed against the paladin's throat. Recognizing steely eyes housed in a petite and dangerous body, he calmly held his ground.

"Do you have no concept of personal space?" His brows

furrowed in annoyance as he pushed an arm against Nessix.

"Oh, I do." She refused to let him move her. "And you've invaded mine."

The crowd trickled into silence at the unexpected interruption. Mathias glanced at the gathering then back at their fuming general.

"This isn't really a good time," he warned her quietly.

"Then when is?"

"These men love you," he tried again, delivering a reassuring smile to the uncertain eyes that watched them. "It would shatter them to see us fight."

Furious, Nessix shoved herself from Mathias and turned to the troops. "Go back to your dining!" she ordered. "Your training!"

None of them moved, staring at her with pleading gazes. The miracles they'd seen Mathias weave pacified them. His patient teachings of Etha comforted them in their bleak reality. Mathias was an outsider, yes, but they'd longed for this sort of hope for years. They needed Nessix to want Mathias.

"Nes, I think you'd better back down," Brant murmured. "Save Sagewind this ego trip."

She gnashed her teeth to keep from snapping at Brant. If it upset the men to see her assert herself, she would deal with Mathias in private. "Then you, sir"—she returned her attention to the paladin—"will join me in the war chamber."

Mathias shook his head. "General, I'm not through addressing their questions."

Her eyes sparked ferociously. "You most certainly are. My troops are capable of protecting themselves, and I'm more worried about those who cannot, the innocents and the townships." A spiteful air danced around her. "Unless, of course, you see some fault in protecting them? Reports are coming in." Nessix raised her voice for the troops to hear. "The people have seen and heard enough and are afraid. Are our efforts really better spent fawning over a foreigner or protecting our civilians?"

"Everyone here wants to protect them," Mathias assured her. "They are willing to give their lives to do so. Is it not enough for you to have your men strong in spirit before they go to face an enemy they don't understand?"

"What I want," Nessix said, enraged that Mathias so boldly placed words in her mouth, "is for my villagers to not be slaughtered by this threat that you only want to play with."

"Your men believe you're a strong leader, and I've seen you prove yourself with a sword, but I've yet to see wisdom from you, lady Nessix." Mathias ignored her flash of indignation and Brant's verbal attempt to enter the debate. "How do you plan to protect your people? By leaving no one to defend them after a reckless charge? Or maybe by putting troops in the villages and spreading your forces so thin we're left vulnerable?"

Unable and unwilling to directly seek Mathias's advice at the moment, Nessix blurted out the first thought that sprang to mind. "I will bring the people here, protect them in our stronghold."

"You will bring your people here. All of them." Mathias waited for the hasty plan to set into everyone's minds.

"All of them in my care." Nessix nodded once. "Do you have a better plan?" Hopefully, he did.

"I can tell you that your plan will give the enemy a single target."

"No," she demanded. "Veed wouldn't do anything like this. He'll give them plenty of targets to choose from."

"Veed won't do this because he's not stupid," Mathias said, brushing off Nessix's offended gasp and the shocked faces around him. "Harboring your country in these walls will make you more appealing. Quit lying to yourself."

"The people must be protected." Nes's eyes swept over the accumulation of troops around her. "Don't you agree with me?" she asked them.

A hesitant rumble of consent rose, offering cover for the hushed exchange to come. Mathias disagreed with Nes's decision wholeheartedly, but found solace in her genuine concern for those under her care.

"I will grant you that." Mathias kept his voice low. If Nessix wanted to mask their discussion, he'd honor her efforts to the best of his abilities. "But they will have no other choice but to die in your security."

Nes scoffed. "If you're our great savior, our *salvation* as they'll tell you," she said, nodding toward the troops, "you can keep us safe."

"Your plan is suicide." A hush stole over the hall as eyes refocused their attention back to the dispute. "Pull your people here and they will be protected within these walls. The demons will sit outside and watch, realizing they don't even need to attack. Days will go by and food will run short. The villagers will starve so the soldiers can live, and the demons will laugh as your force withers away."

Nessix was too proud to let Mathias publicly humiliate her, Brant too furious to form words. Soldiers gaped at Mathias in shock, swallowing everything he spouted for them.

"Then, when you are weakest, the demons will strike. You and your men will be wiped out in a matter of days, and the demons will sing of the great enemy who hid in a fortress and killed themselves."

"The people are scared," Nes insisted. "They've been attacked and heard our battles." She shook with rage and fear. "They don't know why the noble guard won't let them leave their cities."

Mathias didn't want to tell Nessix the truth she needed to hear, but had previously learned his lesson about lying to her. "If they have questions, answer them. Let your people know what this threat is and ask them to assist you, noble and peasant alike." He caught Nessix about to argue and hurried with his next statement. "If they know the demons are lurking, they'll be able to watch for them. You can only react to what you can see."

Nessix shook her head, aggravated but hopeful for answers. "They are not fighters."

"Your people are stronger than you give them credit for," Mathias said.

"None of them know how to fight!"

"Then teach them."

"The trained elite, the best warriors I've got, are falling to the demons. There isn't enough time to train them for this, let alone peasants."

Mathias tossed his hands in the air at her lack of faith. "Then hide in your fortress and give up."

Restoring her stubborn front, Nessix turned to her troops. Wide eyes stared uncomfortably. Mathias's words echoed in Nes's mind; her men loved her, so what kept them from standing up for her?

"We'll send out caravans to the townships," Nessix declared, gaining confidence at Brant's nod of approval. "The people come first, then bring any provisions they have."

The silence that responded to Nessix's order frightened her. She prepared a fierce reprimand before a handful of the troops tried to work their way from the crowd to move to action, only to be stopped by their comrades. Appalled by her army's lack of unity, Nessix spun accusingly on Mathias.

"Better to be sentenced to death by their own general than fight for their lives against the demons, right?" he asked her quietly. A wearied chuckle escaped him. "Since you're so set on your course, I'll buy you time from the demons. I'll do it alone, if I must. Your people are worth that much to me."

"With what you call fighting, you'll be torn apart." Nessix debated for a moment about how loudly to present the next before letting it ring through the halls. "I've yet to see you actually draw blood."

Mathias could never explain to Nessix what made him hate seeing the demons suffer. "Too much blood will be spilled in this war and I will not add to it needlessly, but if you want to bring your entire race to the verge of extinction, blood must be spilled. I will not let your people die out that way."

"We will *not* die."

"Not at first," Mathias said, regretting what the troops witnessed between them. "I will go make sure the roads are clear of danger. Someone must shield the backs of your people."

Nes's hand on his chest stopped Mathias's movement, and she turned to her men once more. "I gave you orders!" she barked. Uncertain gazes turned to Mathias. Eyes flashing with a vile potency never before directed at her own ranks, Nessix lashed out. "We do not have time to waste! Go!"

No one moved.

The defiance and betrayal pulled the breath from Nessix and

she barely kept from screaming. Brant grasped her arm, reinforcing the smallest pinch of sanity left in her before she sneered and jerked away from his support.

"You see this man as your salvation?" Her scathing tone won the shame of a few soldiers. "You honestly think he'll save us?"

"She's right," Mathias agreed, praying Nessix allowed his attempt to help her save face. "It's pointless to sacrifice yourselves for someone who won't even stand up to save himself." He looked at Nessix, accepting the wary eyes she held him with. "Keep to your honor and follow your general. Anything she orders will be no worse than the fate I'd lead you to." He stepped aside to divert attention back to Nessix.

Longing expressions and bated breath appealed to Nessix from the crowd. Just like the rest of them, she wanted Mathias to eradicate this plague, but not at the price it seemed destined to cost her.

"What happens if we lose you?" a timid voice rose from the back.

Nessix clenched her jaw, arms trembling in her struggle to maintain her composure.

"Within death, there's hope of future life," Mathias said, before Nes drew a breath to begin sputtering her agitation. "Take what hope I can give you and use it in my absence." He stared at Nes's pale face. "Step aside, General. I'll tend to your civilians."

Nessix shook her head fiercely. "Do what you think's best. As you don't want orders from me, you won't have any until the next sign of immediate danger." She turned to her troops. "Follow Sagewind, if you honestly think it will do you good."

The crowd parted in a hustle as Nessix spun to leave. Remnants of her pride trailed behind.

EIGHT

Two days and nights of ample rest brought Nessix to her senses. True to her word, more so to recover her dignity than prove a point, she stayed out of Mathias's interactions with her troops. They needed his expertise, and she craved it, but the only way to tolerate this split affection was to avoid subjecting herself to it altogether. Mathias worked diligently to repair the damages Nes's careless words had caused and, without her immediate misgivings, proceeded to educate the troops on demonic warfare.

Once calm enough, Nessix went to the training fields to observe the army's progress under Mathias's tutelage. She leaned against a wall, soaking in its warmth against her shoulders. If anybody noticed her, they made no indication of it, until a lively song from the watch tower announced the arrival of one of Veed's messengers.

Right as Nessix had found peace, she grumbled selfish objections and heaved her weight upright to attend to her uninvited visitor. No more thrilled with his task, the messenger shoved a pouch at her and turned his horse back toward home. Nessix briefly entertained the idea of discarding the message, but her more mature side prompted her to tend to whatever Veed wanted now rather than later. Removing the scroll, she broke its seal and glanced up to find Mathias politely dismissing himself from his prior obligations. He fit his face with a pleasant expression and made his way over to her. Unsure whether or not she welcomed his intrusion, Nessix skimmed over the message.

It mentioned only brief notes of demon movement, and Veed had kept his words much less provocative than normal. The bulk of the message concentrated on the one thing Nessix avoided dwelling on: Veed thought Mathias suspicious and invited Nessix to chat about the paladin's intentions. She'd grown up learning to trust Veed's insights and just as she'd started believing in Mathias's good will, Veed stirred up her doubts all over again. As Mathias reached her, Nessix rolled the message up and crammed it back into its pouch.

"Is that from Veed?" Mathias asked, mindful of the suspicion in Nes's eyes.

"Yes," she answered, whistling for Logan. "And I really don't want to deal with him right now."

"Then don't," Mathias suggested. He summoned his mount through his silent means.

Nes laughed. "I wish it was that easy." Turning from Mathias before her scrambled thoughts gave themselves away, Nessix stepped off to gather Logan's trappings.

"It is," Mathias called after her. Ceraphlaks landed beside him, as timely as ever. He vaulted onto the pegasus's back. "I'll go."

Nessix nearly dropped the satchel, but by the time she spun around, a flurry of wings had carried Mathias away. No amount of heated orders slowed them, and Nessix called out for Logan again. When Veed said he wanted to deal with Mathias, Nessix couldn't help but believe this was not what he'd had in mind.

* * * * *

Veed sat on the battlements, squinting against the sun as Ceraphlaks approached. Nes had told him the paladin rode a pegasus, and Veed doubted the girl would choose such a mode of transportation for herself. The animal landed on the rampart's stone surface, hooves clattering delicately, to reveal Mathias on his back.

"I sent for Nes," Veed stated plainly.

"Yes, you did." Mathias swung a leg over his mount's back and hopped to the ground. "But she said she didn't want to talk to you right now. I offered to drop by in her stead."

Veed raised his chin, contemplating how best to deal with Mathias. "Might I inquire why?"

"There couldn't *possibly* be any other reason you'd call for her except to discuss tactics," Mathias said, noting the other man's conceited smirk. "I assumed you wouldn't mind sharing with me, considering I've been serving as her tactician."

Veed circled Mathias slowly, weighing him through disdainful eyes. "I see you've still got some wit about you, boy."

"It's needed in such serious times." Mathias allowed Veed to pass behind him. "The men need someone who can cast light against the shadows. Their morale means everything."

Completing a full pass, Veed stopped in front of Mathias and sized him up. "If I'd wanted to busy my mind with such drivel, I'd have requested Sulik. He's easier to manipulate than Brant and ten times as pleasant."

Mathias rocked back on his heels with a speculative nod. He'd pass that along to his friend. "If that's how you see it. Manipulation is only a partial fix to control—I prefer loyalty."

"For the legendary White Paladin, you certainly are impertinent," Veed said. "You've already turned down my offer of service. I have no further use for you."

Mathias smiled slyly. "Much more power and I might explode, my lord, and that'd be a bit unbearable. So, for the good of keeping pieces of legend from showering down on your dear Elidae, I'll stand my ground on that matter."

"Then go back to Nessix. I've no more business with you."

"But you do," Mathias said, "as long as you have business with her."

"Go," Veed ordered, "and send Nes—"

"I'm here," Nessix barked irritably. She gasped for breath as she stalked up to the men.

Veed smirked at her physical distress. "Your haste is always a pleasure, love, but I wish you'd spared me the prelude."

"I didn't send him," Nessix muttered, placing her hands on top of her head to open her lungs. "The bastard came on his own."

"Mind ordering him off?" Veed guided her inside the fortress by two fingers behind her elbow.

"He wouldn't listen if I did." Nessix's imploring glance fluttered back at the paladin. Her embarrassment and concern over losing control aside, Mathias's presence comforted her against Veed's intentions, and she sincerely hoped he planned on staying. "Why are you so obsessed with him anyway?"

Veed waited until they'd left Mathias well behind before gripping Nes's arm to turn her to face him. "Can't you read?" he asked. "I don't trust him, especially getting close to you. Wouldn't you feel more comfortable with someone keeping a better eye on him?"

Nessix tore her arm from his touch. "I'm perfectly fine with the arrangements I've made regarding him. The letter you sent said you were more concerned about whether or not he was a traitor."

Veed grinned, continuing to direct her toward his quarters. "I had to get you over here somehow, didn't I?"

"So you lied."

Veed shrugged and opened the door to his elaborately maintained chambers. "Depends on what you consider honest." He ambled inside.

Nessix hesitated. Being in Veed's personal living space, with his eyes on her, always made Nessix feel indecent and small. "How do you figure that?" she asked, her voice stifled of its usual gusto.

"I told you I was concerned about whose side he was on, didn't I?"

"Yes, but I assumed you meant between our people and the demons."

"Maybe I did." He extended a hand toward a plush lounge to signal her to sit. "At the festivities, he ordered me to leave because of an attack."

She declined his offer. "Alright, but I don't—"

"Nessix, he was right. The next morning, I had demons marching on me. How do you suggest he knew that?"

Nessix rolled her eyes. "It was coincidence."

"Coincidence that our enemy split its forces to attack us both? Coincidence that he knew their timing?"

The quiet frenzy lurking behind Veed's features disturbed Nessix and she shuffled a step away from him. "This is war, Veed. Of course he predicted another attack."

"He knew it was coming," Veed insisted peevishly. "And he was giving orders to your troops, how does that sit with you?"

"It doesn't," she said, "but I'm honestly glad he did."

"You're glad he stepped in your position? He's working dark magic, Nes, darker than mine."

"Maybe so, but if he hadn't taken action when he did, we wouldn't have survived."

"And how did your commanders take it?"

"I'll worry about my officers," Nessix said. "I promise if I suspect any evil in him, you'll be the first to know."

"Liar."

"After Brant, then. If you're so afraid of him, let me keep him stored far away from you."

Internally, Veed frowned at how easily Nessix caught on to his intentions. Regardless of Mathias's nature, Veed's research implied whoever controlled the paladin controlled the war. Nessix seemed aware of this fact as well, and Mathias's actions suggested a sense of loyalty to her. The straight approach had failed, and now Veed had to come up with a more covert way to obtain divine protection.

Putting his motives behind him, Veed grinned at Nes's banter. "Come, Nes, have a seat and share some spirits with me." He pulled a chair back from the small table by the window.

"I'll pass, thanks. If you've nothing else to discuss with me, I'd best be leaving." Nessix turned to do just that.

"But we haven't even touched a conversation." Veed's smile fought between desire and charm as he sauntered toward her. "You can't tell me you really *want* to leave."

"My men must be trained and I have to get back to developing my strategies." She ceased proceeding toward the door when he blocked her escape. "Move."

"I told you, Nes, we've got more to talk about."

107

Nessix willed herself to keep calm. Veed only ever got worse when she was upset. "I'm serious, Veed," she warned. "Let me on my way."

"I think you'd best do as the lady asks."

Veed whirled around to find Mathias leaning against the wall just inside the doorway. Arms folded across his chest, he raised his hand from where it rested on his elbow.

"How did you get in here?" Veed demanded.

"By walking, my lord." Mathias entered the room uninvited and took the seat Nessix previously turned down. "Now, I suggest letting Nessix carry out her wishes."

"What did you hear?" she asked, voice betraying her attempt to mask her fear.

"Enough," Mathias said. "And I'll gladly discuss whatever's on your mind, if it is indeed still there, once we get back home."

Nessix straightened and crossed her arms as Mathias helped himself to a shallow glass of wine. Veed snatched the bottle from the table as soon as Mathias finished pouring. The two men stared each other down, Veed telegraphing his threats and Mathias calmly maintaining his walls. The instability in the air around them held Nessix immobile.

"What else did you need to ask General Nessix about?" Mathias asked at last, breaking the silence after he set his glass down. That, too, was promptly pulled from his reach.

"That is between her and me," Veed answered. "Order him off, Nessix."

Nessix never completely let her guard down when alone with Veed, and in this moment, she absolutely needed Mathias with her. "No."

"Be reasonable!" Veed persisted.

"I am. He's serving as my bodyguard and you cannot deny me protection."

"There's no reason to bring an escort to my home."

"And that would explain why you're forbidding her to leave?" Mathias kicked his feet up on the table. "I'd say imprisoning a general merits having someone step in."

Veed donned a menacing snarl and leaned over the opposite

end of the table. "You would be wise to keep yourself out of my affairs, Sir Sagewind."

"I will remind you again that business concerning General Nessix concerns me," Mathias said, disinterested in the other man's bid for control. "And if I recall correctly, I was the topic of discussion. I'd hate for the two of you to not get a complete story of what you're so afraid of. As wise a man as you think you are, I'd be more concerned over my own troops than anyone in Nessix's ranks. The general told you she's leaving, now let her go."

"Who do you think you are to be giving me orders, boy?" Veed sent a fleeting glance in Nes's direction. "Nes must be awful sweet on you to allow such confidence."

Coldness swept across Mathias as he slid his feet back on the floor. "You need to start investing your attention in matters that concern you, rather than those you will never obtain." Mathias considered Nessix more attractive than not, but Veed's apparent affection for her disturbed him.

The corner of Veed's lip twitched at Mathias's brass, but without yet understanding the extent of the paladin's capabilities, he tactfully backed down. "Fine then," he said. "I'm afraid of losing more men to the demons if I am left unassisted."

"Your men are nothing but objects to you," Mathias said. "I am serving under who I consider the most just. If you want your men trained by my hand, send them to Nessix and I will help them, but I will never command or serve under you." He looked back at Nes for a moment, eyes glistening with mischief. "Besides, Nessix told me you dabble with the divine arts, yourself. Why would a man as powerful as you need help from a boy like me?"

Nessix smothered a giggle in her throat, wondering if Mathias had been like this all along. She caught herself before admiration blossomed further and tucked such thoughts in the nooks of her mind she seldom exercised.

"What do you have against me, Sir Sagewind?" Veed asked, drawing Nessix's mind back to the drama.

"You're greedy and lustful, to say the least. And your heart is corrupt." Mathias shrugged. "I don't think Nessix has it in her to fall to your degree."

Veed sent a commanding glare at the girl. "The adults have some talking to do. You can leave now, Nessix."

At last, she released the smile Mathias had found in her. "And miss this? I'm staying, Veed."

Veed jabbed an accusing finger in Nes's direction. "Is that selfless? Using our concerns for her entertainment?"

"Concerns? No, I'm not concerned," Mathias said. "You're practically begging me for help, and I'm comfortable saying I don't need yours."

"You don't command anything," Veed reminded him. "If you did, you'd come crawling to me the same as Nes did."

"I can hardly imagine her crawling to you for anything."

Veed slapped a palm against the tabletop, livid from Mathias's offhanded jeers. Teeth bared, Veed dragged his glare away from his target until he successfully regained his composure. "What is it that Nessix is paying you to serve her?"

"If I told you a pleasurable bed, would you believe me?"

"Sagewind!" Nessix gasped, appalled by the notion.

"You do not humor me, boy," Veed said dryly, casting a curious eye at the flushed young woman.

"My cost need not be discussed," Mathias said. "Private treaty, between me and Nes."

"I'll double it," Veed promised.

Mathias laughed. A single room accommodated him just fine, and he'd never considered himself a glutton. "I cannot be bribed like that. I'm serving under Nessix, and as long as you remain in her good graces, I will protect your men when I can. If I were you, and I sing praises to the Mother Goddess I'm not, I'd be thankful just to know I was on friendly terms."

"Are you?" Veed asked.

"As long as you don't give me a reason otherwise. General," Mathias said, turning to Nessix and rising. "I suggest we start for home. We've both heard enough, don't you agree?"

Nessix smiled, delighting in Veed's shock. "For once, yes."

Mathias nodded and stalked past Veed to leave the room.

"You be careful with that man around," Veed warned Nes's back.

She laughed over her shoulder. "You be careful without him."

* * * * *

Nessix and Mathias rode away from Veed's fortress at a leisurely pace. She appreciated his levity when directed at someone else, and before she knew it, Nessix began enjoying Mathias's company. Thinking back on how easily he'd frustrated Veed delighted her, and more importantly, Mathias's unsolicited move to safeguard her gave Nessix a sense of security she hadn't felt in years. An unexpected trust passed between them, and it felt more right than wrong.

The more Nessix laughed at Mathias's antics, the more irate Logan became. Nessix needed to keep her eyes open and mind clear if she hoped to survive this war, not swoon over this human like those of weaker wills. Logan snorted his disapproval of this change of her affection, heaving greater breaths until Nessix caught his message and came back to her senses.

Afraid of her loss of discretion, Nessix dismissed Mathias and Ceraphlaks with the excuse of asking them to patrol the area from the sky. Mathias complied readily, pleased with Nes's more relaxed view of him, and left the general and her mount to traipse home on their own. The content smile and softness in her eyes stayed on Nes's face until Ceraphlaks flew from sight.

Logan's head bobbed with each great stride, an ear flicking a fly away. Nessix had spent the entire ride to Veed's reflecting on the dark general's thoughts of Mathias, embellishing his concerns with her own. Logan realized Nessix frequently overreacted to things she didn't understand, but Mathias clearly had dangerous potential. Going into this conference, Logan suspected a much different outcome than Nessix tittering over Mathias's foolishness. He telegraphed his opinions to his beloved rider, hoping to thwart her wandering mind.

"If you could have seen Veed's face, though!" Nes mused. She grasped the saddle's cantle as she leaned back. "I've quit getting those reactions out of him."

111

Logan grunted, skipping half a stride as he struck out a back leg. Nessix sat forward again.

"Now, Logan," she said, folding her arms midway up the crest of his neck. "All I'm saying is any enemy of Veed is a friend of mine."

The fecklan stopped abruptly, throwing his head—and Nessix—to the ground. He stared hard at her, pinning his ears and wrinkling his nostrils as she looked up at him from her back.

"I don't see what you're so worked up about." She reached up to tickle Logan's muzzle, pulled up a handful of grass, and held it for him. "Just because he gave me a laugh at Veed's expense doesn't mean I'm losing my head."

Logan nickered in contentment, accepting Nes's offer before nudging her to get up. She stayed still in the grass.

It never occurred to Nessix until then how dangerous Mathias actually was. She'd lost count of the reasons she hated Veed, but they needed each other to see their nation through this war. So far, Mathias only reinforced the distance between them, keeping the joint force weak. Beyond that, his charisma had weaseled its way to affect her judgment, something she previously thought impossible. Nessix speculated on Mathias's motives, and her bliss fluttered off. Catching Logan's head as he moved to nudge her again, she fondly stroked his noble face.

"I wish I knew what all this meant," she murmured. "Do you think—"

Daze gone in an instant, Logan jerked his head away from Nes's caress and stared off ahead. Nessix propped herself up on her elbows and followed his gaze, cursing at the sight of Ceraphlaks flying back toward them. She scrambled to her feet as Logan strutted a protective circle around her.

"The ride isn't that long," Mathias said once Ceraphlaks landed.

Nes's heart raced between the clash of intuition and willfulness. "Don't tell me you found something…"

"I wouldn't, if I thought we had time to play games on the matter, but there are demons currently marching away from one of your townships."

Nes's nerves coiled in her stomach, racing up her throat until their pressure hindered her ability to breathe. Her whimsy left as she thought of the tortures demons would inflict on civilians.

"They're marching *away* from the town?" she asked meekly.

"They are," Mathias said. "It was a smaller unit. They struck the outskirts, burned down a handful of farmhouses."

"Are the people…?" Her breaking heart intercepted the rest of her question.

"As far as I can tell, the city proper was not breached, but I doubt the demons left any they crossed alive."

Nessix turned her back to Mathias and placed her hands on Logan's shoulder, trying to siphon strength from him. She still hadn't issued an official statement to the public about the demons, choosing instead to let the people of her kingdom live in fear of a danger they knew nothing about. For the past week, Nessix denied the demons' existence to herself, deceitfully hoping for them to give up or disappear. Now, her fears and rejection of reality, her lack of action, had cost innocent people their lives. Whether or not the demons frightened her, Nessix had to step up.

She pulled in a ragged breath, missing her father and Inwan more than ever. "You're the only one of my forces capable of flight. Go keep an eye on where those demons are heading," she said to Mathias. "I want no one else to even see one of these beasts."

"Nessix—"

"Did you not just swear fealty to me in front of Veed?" she asked. "I gave you my orders, and you will obey them."

"Might I ask what you're planning to do?"

"I'm going to take the necessary measures to enhance the security of the townsfolk," Nessix said. "I don't want to see you again until those demons are out of my territory."

Mathias closed his eyes and prayed for patience. He wanted to shake sense into Nessix, remind her that she knew too little about demons to make these decisions completely on her own, but he refused to risk losing the sliver of trust she gave him.

"Of course, General," he replied curtly. Ceraphlaks took those words as his cue to depart.

Not even allowing herself the time to watch them leave, Nessix swung back into the saddle, and pushed Logan to a more vigorous pace. Even with whatever bridges she and Mathias had built, she scolded herself for not following her intuition from the previous week. The civilians needed more protection than what the simple units of noble guard provided. With or without the blessing of the only experienced man on the field, Nessix planned to bring them to safety.

* * * * *

Mathias's heart sank as he neared the fortress, baffled as to why Nessix continued to disregard his tactical advice. Hundreds of caravans fanned out from the stronghold, clouds of dust rising behind them as they set out to the surrounding towns. No matter how good Nes's intentions, the logistics of moving and housing an entire kingdom did not add up. Mathias wanted to believe Nessix had secured resources to make this work, but she seemed to not understand the mechanics of siege warfare, and the few days between her bold announcement and its execution suggested few preparations were made. Already tied to a prior engagement for the afternoon, Mathias repressed his opinion of her actions and aimed to pull a cheerful face.

The fact that the tent Mathias had requested still stood assured him that Nes's distracted mind kept her unaware of his prearranged class. Rows of eager soldiers anxiously awaited their lesson inside. Sulik stood at the entrance of the makeshift classroom when Ceraphlaks landed.

"Your report?" the commander asked, nervously glancing from the tent's crowded interior to the fortress gates.

"I found signs of mobilization in the east, but if they're moving in the interior, it's under the cover of the forests." Mathias rested a hand on Sulik's shoulder to keep him from running the report to Nessix. "She shouldn't expect me back quite yet. Don't trouble yourself with her temper until you have to."

Sulik twisted his mouth at Mathias's encouragement to delay

the message, but he trusted the paladin knew what he was doing. Curiosity overriding his motivation to please Nessix, Sulik followed Mathias into the pavilion. Each member of the mass shifted to allow them passage to where a modest desk and nondescript trunk waited at the back of the tent. Sulik took a seat in the corner behind Mathias, modestly boasting his connection to the man.

Mathias tried to open the session with a prayer to Etha, but a haughty outburst and several startled gasps disrupted the sacred formality.

"All of you, out!"

A grimace cut off Mathias's prayer and he requested Etha pardon the interruption. He peered his eyes open to find Nessix fuming at the tent's entrance, her cousin faithfully beside her with arms crossed and a presumptuous smirk across his face. Nessix stood with taut shoulders, fists clenched at her sides. The crowd fidgeted in apprehension, whispering questions of whose instructions to obey. Nervous eyes darted to Mathias and pointedly avoided Nes's. An eased expression settled Mathias's face as Nes's anger boiled, and he nodded to dismiss his students, satisfied by their desire to stay and learn.

With Mathias's gesture, the soldiers found their feet and filed out of the tent. Nes's nerves pinched as each man passed, her frown tucking lower with every murmured apology. Average troops made up the bulk of the group, but three captains and five lieutenants left with them as well. Her mind froze as Sulik strode by. The commander hesitated long enough to meet Nes's eyes until her scowl overpowered him and he ducked away without a word. Brant removed himself promptly to remind Sulik of his loyalties. Once everyone had moved out, Nessix turned her attention to Mathias. The tent flap fell shut.

"Weren't you supposed to be patrolling the skies?"

Mathias gestured for Nessix to take a seat and shrugged when she declined. "I already have, and Ceraphlaks is still scouting for us."

"And what did you find?"

"Nothing that merits immediate concern."

Nessix nodded, scoping out the simple interior of what usually served as a tactics tent. "You've led to me believe you're an honest man."

"I do my best to avoid telling lies," Mathias agreed.

"And I kept you safe from Veed today," Nessix said. "Was I right to do so?"

He debated correcting her. No part of Veed daunted Mathias on a physical level, and Nessix had no part in protecting him. He left those thoughts alone in exchange for directing this conversation to a more pleasant resolution. "If you want to defeat the demons, trusting me is the wisest thing you can do." He turned to retrieve the artifacts scattered about the room.

Mathias wouldn't get off that easily. Nessix rushed forward and snatched the pendant he reached for, unhindered by his frown. "What grounds do I have to believe you?"

"You've defeated the enemy twice under my guidance." Mathias held out his hand patiently.

"You cannot accept credit for that." Nes's eyes narrowed as Mathias plucked the bauble from her grasp. "You weren't the only one on the battlefield. You didn't even have wounds to show for it."

"And how many of your soldiers bear no scars from the battles, but bled just the same?" Mathias tucked the pendant into a pouch and continued his collection. "Whose doing mended the broken bones and maimed flesh?"

Nessix refused to stroke his ego by admitting the obvious truth. "For a man preaching humility, you're terribly proud."

Mathias shook his head, still not turning back to her. "I am stating facts, Nessix. You can't be conceited enough to think those I healed would have lived without Etha's blessing."

"Do you think Veed's just after your strength?" she persisted.

Mathias stopped and straightened, contemplating this sudden change of topic. "Veed *is* after my strength." If he placed his words with adequate care, he could possibly salvage the day's earlier progress. "He wants me to side with him and secure his power over others, including you. He's an indecent man who would just as soon hand you over to the demons as help you, should it prove to gain him more."

"And you think more of me than that?" Up until now, Nes hadn't bothered to question why Mathias insisted on following her.

"You care for those beneath you. Your desire to safeguard those who give their lives in your name comes before all else, I can tell as much from the actions you've taken. So yes, you are far greater than Veed."

"That's why you chose me over him, then," she concluded uncertainly.

"I chose to side with you, regardless," Mathias corrected, seeing Nessix with fresh eyes. The thoughtful woman standing with him now intrigued him much more than the temperamental girl who held her captive.

"Why?"

"Because you need help."

"So you're saying Veed's forces are more powerful than mine."

"No." Mathias drew the word out with tempered patience. "Your men fight for each other and for those they protect. Veed's work for greed and power, maybe even out of fear of him."

"But out of might," Nessix said, "they have me beat. Is that what you're avoiding?"

"Avoiding?"

"If you want me to admit it, I will. When it comes to brute force, Veed's got the upper hand. I know this. I *have* known this." Exasperated by her untimely bout of modesty, Nessix sank into a seat. "But there's something you need to tell me."

The humility gushing from Nessix grabbed hold of Mathias's attention. "What's that?" He sat across the aisle from her and rested his elbows on his knees.

Nessix faced him, constructing her defensive wall once again. "If what I've been led to believe is true, by not aligning yourself with Veed, you're weakening him. That indirectly strengthens the demon forces." She studied Mathias hard to ensure he followed. "Is that your plan?"

Mathias closed his eyes and smiled, hoping to ease her mind and coax this tolerant version of her to stay. "I can only grant finite power to any force. Victory will come to those with faith. Under

Veed's reign, his men are incapable of learning, and that will always keep him weaker than you."

She blinked and stared mutely at Mathias. Pretty words weren't enough for her and to think her men capable of overpowering Veed's was madness. Nessix had occasionally bested Veed in their war games, but only when she found a way to outwit him. She could not contend with Veed's strength, but his cunning edge had aged with his body.

Mathias caught Nes's disbelief and chuckled. "You witnessed the effect of true power in the temple, Nes. That is the power your men can learn, if you'll allow it, and that is what will defeat the demons."

Nes's teeth clenched and Mathias drew his shoulders back at her unexpected response to his reassurance. His soothing words had nearly whisked the image of her troops watching him in adoration from her mind before she caught herself.

"What have you done to them?" Nessix demanded. "Why are they so enamored by you?" A soft hand on her forearm halted her anxious spiral.

Mathias found patience in a slow blink and allowed Nessix to pull her arm from him once she had calmed. "They're looking to fill the void Inwan left. They're not too unlike you, in that regard."

"No," Nes corrected. "They think they *have* found their god. They're calling you their salvation." Nes's eyes scoured Mathias's serious face. "Do you know how dangerous that is?"

"I'm not a god and would never claim to be. Those I teach learn that lesson first. Perhaps you might—"

"You may not be a god, but they don't see that!" she pressed, discarding his invitation. "If you fall, this is all over. Whether I'm commanding them or not, if they see their savior defeated, there will be nothing left of us for the demons to challenge."

Mathias laughed. "Do you think I will suddenly fall?"

"You're no greater than anyone else out there. Mistakes still happen and war is still dangerous."

"Will you fall, Nessix?"

Straightening defensively, Nes's obstinance surged back to her. "As long as my men stand, I will stand beside them."

"Then we have a lot in common," Mathias said. It was a shame Nes found discontent so easily; she was much prettier without the scowl. "I will not fall until the day the spirit of your people breaks. Even then, I won't go down easily. Place your fearful eyes away from me and point them to your enemies."

Nessix bristled. "I am not afraid of this battle, do not forget that. If you think you see fear in me, it's because of you and nothing else. I forbid you to be my downfall."

"Should I have wanted your head, I'd have taken it with little trouble," Mathias said. "I will not be the death of you, but you must keep your pride in check if you want to see brighter days. Suck it up, General." He continued past her insulted gasp. "I am not after your men or your holdings."

Since the day Mathias first showed his cocky face, Nessix had kept a close eye on him, watching how he dealt with her people and the miracles he performed. The tactician inside her claimed it made sense to hold on to him, whether or not she wanted to admit his significance to her army and this war. At the same time, the tenacious girl in her stomped her feet and screamed that the paladin and the secrets he harbored threatened her. Unable to settle on which part to believe, Nessix stayed silent, tumbling Mathias's promise through her mind.

"You should help evacuate your citizens," Mathias suggested at the cessation of her debating.

"One more question."

Startled by Nes's compliance, Mathias weighed her volatile nature and cautiously asked, "What is it?"

"You don't like Veed, that's apparent enough." Leaning closer to Mathias, she gave him a critical once-over, eyes narrowed in consideration as they locked with his. "Yet, you took it upon yourself to warn him about the attack on his fortress. Why?"

A fine thread of trust existed between them, and Mathias clung to it desperately. "I have no love for Veed, but if he hadn't returned, his troops would have been crushed. I won't have their blood on my hands over my own pride." Mathias moved across the small room, feigning interest in a frayed edge of the tent after Nessix bit her lip and directed her gaze away. He hadn't meant to

119

push too hard. "It's a lesson you don't seem to fully understand yet."

Nes's ego doubled as her greatest fault, but she wouldn't give it up for any amount of salvation. Rationalizing Mathias's accusations by his lack of knowledge of flemans, Nessix let the comment pass her by. "That's all fine and well, but how did you know it would happen?"

"You said one more question." Mathias turned to face her. "Your time here is done, unless you wanted to join me for class?"

Nessix drew herself up with that pride Mathias had just warned her about. "That was the wrong one not to answer, Sagewind."

Mathias had already incriminated himself in Nes's mind, and didn't care if his honesty stung her. "I worship a present goddess, and she guides me when I need it." He walked to the tent's opening and pulled the flap aside. "You're welcome to consider that on your way out."

How bold! Advancing on him quickly, hand straying to the hilt of her sword, Nes stared into Mathias as deeply as he allowed. "You're no better than Veed, as far as I'm concerned," she hissed. "I'm going to apply myself somewhere useful and aid in the evacuation."

"As wise as ever, my lady," Mathias answered with the slightest nod of his head.

Nessix choked on her retort as the flap fell behind her. The back of her head burned from her racing pulse, and she rubbed it with one hand as she tried to calm down. Rhythmically working her jaw, she stalked from Mathias's location, purposefully avoiding the gazes cast in her direction. Brant's voice reached through the ringing in her ears, and an attempt to smile twitched her lips. He joined her on her trek back inside the fortress.

"I tried to ask Sulik what that was all about, but he disappeared in the crowd before I could catch him." Brant waited for Nes's response, relieved by her indifference. "I'd have gone after him, but thought you might need me more."

Nes nodded her appreciation and stretched her jaw. "Don't worry about it," she sighed. "I doubt he'd give you the same answers he'd give me, anyway."

Brant eyed Nessix cautiously, peering through her stubborn resolve. "What went on in there?"

"I'm not sure I could tell you if I tried." Brows drawing together, she toiled over the troubles Mathias had poured into her mind. "Have all the caravans been sent out?"

Brant's concerned eyes followed Nes's thoughts. "Enough to bring in the populations of Brenton, Dale, and Sheridan. Some citizens of Losson have found their way past the guards and come for safety. As soon as the first wave gets back, we'll evacuate them next."

"So we've already been exhausted?" The dreadful thought that Mathias was right nagged at Nessix.

"Yes."

"Make sure the first level of the dungeon is cleared out and made as suitable as possible for living quarters."

"May I ask what you'll be doing?"

"Talking to Grandfather," Nessix groaned. "Hopefully he can help me make more sense out of everything."

"Maybe I could help you sort out your thoughts before En has a chance to dictate them for you."

"My thoughts *are* sorted."

"Then what are we going to do about Sagewind?"

"What about him?"

"I don't know. The fact that he was just preaching to some of your finest soldiers, perhaps?"

"They weren't my finest."

"Quit rationalizing, Nes," Brant pled. "I thought you hated him."

"I do!"

"Then why are you defending him?"

"I'm not defending him," she said. "I just… have a lot to think about right now. We all do."

Brant shook his head, gently grasping Nes's arm to stop her and turn her toward him. "We grew up together, Nes. I'd trust my life to you before I would to Inwan himself. You know you can trust me."

"I do," she sighed. "But if I open my mouth now, I'm afraid I'll start spouting things I don't want to say and you don't want to hear. I won't let you get captured by Sagewind's witchcraft, and I need you sane enough to pull me out of it when the time comes. That's the kind of promise I need from you now."

"Would you listen to yourself," Brant snorted. "You don't really think you're falling for his garbage, do you?"

"The way I look at it, it's either his or Veed's."

She made a good point. Despite the fact that Brant had always deemed Veed a threat, Nes maintained a strange camaraderie with the dark general. Practically an uncle to them both, it had taken the events surrounding Laes's death for Veed to turn his back on Nessix, and as he forced more of Elidae under his control, Nes reduced from loving him to barely respecting him.

"I thought the two of you formed some sort of truce," Brant said at last, favoring Veed's predictable incivility over the unknown arrogance of Mathias. "Besides, he's even helped us recover from defeats he was responsible for in the past. He'll help us now."

"Didn't I give you orders?"

Brant flinched at Nes's reprimand, closing his mouth with purpose and setting his sights straight ahead of them. This war and that human brought out a side of his cousin Brant seldom saw and honestly resented.

"I'm sorry, Brant," Nessix said at his wounded response. "I have a lot on my mind right now."

It took a moment for the sting to subside, but he bent to her regret. "Alright, Nes. I'll keep my eyes on the evacuation. Go do what you need to; I'm here if you need me."

She smiled at last, and rested a hand on his arm. "If all my men were like you, I'd have no reason to be worried right now. I'll send for you before long. And tell Sulik I have a special assignment for him when you see him."

"You give him all the fun ones."

"Only if you consider dusty roads and irritated townsfolk fun."

The reminder of their current plight sapped the flippancy from Brant. "Isn't he supposed to be keeping an eye on Sagewind

122

for you?" He loathed the thought of taking over that job in Sulik's absence.

"I've seen enough of Sagewind's show and don't think he's much of a threat right now," Nes said. "Besides, Sulik's no good to me anymore, what with his opinion of the man. Please, let me count on you."

Brant smiled and tousled Nes's hair with a hand atop her head. "You always have and always will."

Nessix returned his smile with relieved eyes and departed to seek out En.

* * * * *

Dusk claimed the plains of Elidae, the chirping of nighttime creatures promising the demons remained tucked in their own realm. Such sentries failed to hold off deities.

"I am here, Shand," the pawn hissed, "as you ordered." He shot wary glances toward the shadows and buried his face in the folds of his cloak. Meeting his goddess exposed in the open hollowed his insides.

"I'm here." Shand's voice leapt from the shadows.

He spun to face her as she emerged from the night. "Couldn't we find someplace else to talk?"

"Immortality leaves me nothing to fear," she said. "If you're afraid to be seen with me, you should have posted guards."

"And who would you suggest I trust that to?"

"That's not my problem." Shand smiled, walking past him without so much as a glance, and leaned against a tree. "Trouble me with something I care about."

The pawn sighed and delved into his report. "I think the demons would do fine if Mathias wasn't here, but he's been throwing his power around, and I see that causing complications."

"Is that all you're worried about?" Shand scoffed. "You seem to forget that I watched the whelp develop those powers. He can be beaten."

"Then you're most welcome to the task. I don't see how a

mortal—"

Shand's hand struck forward and clasped around the pawn's neck, a scream he tried hard to muffle ripping from his throat as her flesh seared into his. Unable to catch adequate breath as his trachea burned, the pawn's knees gave out and he collapsed in the dirt. Shand threw him from her grasp and watched in arrogant pity as he writhed on the ground, clawing desperately at his throat.

"You know better than that," she spat. "I control the troops; you keep me informed on the mortals. Nothing more. Would you stop that?" She shoved him onto his back with a kick and his persistent sobs subsided into agonized whimpers. "Tell me how our opponents are faring. Tell me about that little Nessix."

"Nes—" he croaked, convulsing once more as the passage of air raked his throat. He tried to swallow, suspecting negative consequences if he failed to answer. "She's stronger than I expected." He pounded a fist into the ground in defiance to his pain.

"She's growing." Shand cocked her head as the pawn struggled. Wrinkling her nose at her servant's fragility, she flicked a hand in his direction and willed his damage undone. "Of course she's more formidable. It's a shame I went after you instead of her; she's quite fierce when she wants to be and has a much quicker wit."

"She's too innocent," he rasped, his skin slowly drawing back together.

Shand watched critically as the man wrung a hand around his tender flesh and hauled himself to his feet. "Then what about Mathias?"

"He hasn't shown much physical strength yet, but has been manipulating Nessix's troops."

"Oh?" Shand asked, interest piqued. "How does she appreciate that?"

"She doesn't. I'm sure if it was up to her, she'd hand him over to you without a second thought."

"He'd never come willingly. Centuries of mutual detestation would ensure that." Shand sighed, staring out at the distant lights of Nes's fortress. If Mathias fell here on Elidae, only High Priestess

Julianna would remain to protect the Order. "You must bring him to me."

"My lady?"

"Gain his trust and he'll follow you. Get him into the hells and I'll see to it he does not leave."

"With all due respect, I think he's cunning enough to know when he's being deceived. How else would he have survived this long?"

"He hasn't," she reminded him. "He's no different than the undead he loathes so much, only he's got Etha's blessing. He is weak; it took a mere woman to lead him to his death. I'm sure you can find something to entice him."

"The man reeks of humility. He cannot be bribed."

Shand's keen eyes narrowed in deliberation. When Mathias Sagewind first found his way to Zeal, his possessions consisted only of his clothing, the mount his sister rode, and barely enough coins to keep them all fed. His more recent heroics earned him tremendous wealth, but he turned it away in exchange for a sturdy suit of armor, smiths to tend to his weapons, a place to rest, and food to eat. Bribery and gifts had never appealed to Mathias, and the older he got, the less he wanted. Shand gasped, the answer plainly before her.

"No, you won't win him over by presenting him with wealth," she agreed, "but we can beat him if we can intercept his blessing."

The pawn snorted. "Lore says Etha physically bound herself to him with Affliction itself. I don't think he'd sit around and let someone rip a chunk of the god spear out of him, and you can sear all my flesh off before I'd ask Etha to turn away from him."

Shand laughed at his simple mind. "No, my pet," she cooed. "I intend to curse him."

The pawn stumbled over the concept. "I thought he was immune to those sorts of evils."

"He can halt them, yes, but only if he's aware they're present. His twit of a sister suffered from a curse that kept her from hearing Etha, and she's much more powerful than her brother."

"She is?" the pawn asked. He dreaded the thought of this sister coming to her brother's aid.

"For now, that's not important," Shand said, her mind working shrewdly to concoct the perfect means to ground her target. "We cannot curse him directly; he'd be able to counter it based on the caster's intent. But if we snuck a cursed object onto him, the effect would creep in slowly. He'd have no idea."

The pawn thought this sounded rather treacherous. "And how would we manage to get such an object on his person?"

"Must I do everything for you?" Shand snapped. "I'll provide you with the means of his decline, and you find someone to convince him to take it. The more hands it passes through, the less likely he is to feel malice from it."

"And what if he can tell it's cursed?"

"My dear, he'd blame the one who delivered it to him," Shand said. "Cover your tracks and you'll be fine. Your job is to do as you're told. Do not give me an excuse to replace you."

Respecting Shand's words as the warning she intended, the pawn bowed. "I will do my best."

"Of course you will."

Leaving him with no further guidance, Shand vanished into the dark. The pawn stood, pulse climbing as the nighttime creatures carried on with their eerie symphony. Before Shand, loyalty made sense. Now, shackled in servitude, all that mattered was appeasing the heinous goddess in hopes of surviving this war. She promised him reign over Elidae, but the deeper he wound down this path, the less he wanted that privilege. Failing to shut the dread from his mind, the pawn trudged toward home before anyone noticed him missing.

NINE

Days passed quietly as the caravans shuttled Nes's people to the fortress, unhindered by the demons. While the flemans rejoiced in their good fortune, each relieved face that stepped off the wagons and into perceived safety compounded Mathias's dread. Just as he'd first warned Nessix, the demons sat by and let the population draw itself together. Oblivious to this and overlooking the hints Mathias dropped, Nessix considered the operation an outstanding success, and Mathias prayed.

To distract himself and satisfy curious minds, Mathias continued offering his classes. When the daily questions about Etha and her miracles subsided, he trained the army to fight their new enemy. He spent the balance of his waking hours sharing tactics with En and Sulik. Brant never stayed past his opening statements, and Mathias withheld his insight completely the few times Veed stopped by. Nessix remained his wild card, her opinion of him drifting from each encounter and influenced by everyone and everything except for Mathias himself.

Despite her cultivating respect for him, Nessix avoided Mathias when possible. She acknowledged his talent as a fighter and gleaned the skills he offered her, but her inability to trust him confused her. Common sense and insecurity battled each other throughout the day, tearing at Nes's sanity. Her greatest concern on

127

the matter revolved not around her own well-being, but En. If Mathias managed to coax Sulik out of her control, she could always appoint another commander, but she only had one grandfather.

En's age furnished him the most experienced mind on all of Elidae, and though Mathias already influenced him, Nessix hoped her grandfather could offer something beneficial to help settle her troubled mind. She stared at the door of En's study, anticipating one of his lectures despite the advice she actually sought. Grimacing at the thought, she rapped a single knuckle against the door. Nothing happened, and Nes used that as her excuse to leave. She shuffled one step back before the sound of En's chair grating from the table filtered through the door. Plucking remnants of the nerves that tried to slip away from her, Nes waited.

She'd expected a warm welcome, so it startled her when her grandfather grunted at her presence and stepped aside to permit her entry. A tentative foot reached forward before she let the rest of her weight carry her into the room.

"Have your studies been going well?" she fished, scanning the titles of the day's reading selection.

"Well enough," En grumbled, sitting down again.

Nessix paused, chewing on the inside of her cheek before sinking into a chair. "What have you been studying?"

"Matters you wouldn't care about."

She tried a smile that faltered at the indifferent jut of his chin. "Grandfather, I'm always curious to know what you're up to."

"Well, you don't care about this!" he snapped irritably. "When, Nessix, will you grow up?"

Nessix started at his ferocity. "I don't—"

He interrupted her stammering with a hiss. "You're using him!"

Nessix rolled her eyes. Shame on her for not realizing what had worked him up sooner. "Not entirely. He's getting free room and board."

"That's not what I meant."

"Then enlighten me."

"All you care about is gaining his combat expertise. You don't—"

"That is the only thing applicable to war," Nessix said. "I don't need to be bothered with legends and potions."

En closed his eyes and shook his head. "You tried to play Veed this same way in the past, Nessix. It disgusts me that you would place our Sir Sagewind so low."

"Old man!" Nessix sprang to her feet in an attempt to gain authority. "If you have a problem with my actions, at least have the courage to tell me straight out."

"Look at what you've become," En murmured, a pitying scorn on his face. "You are a devious, disrespectful brat. Your father taught you to be better than this. If he thought you could handle a war on your own, he wouldn't have bothered to send Sir Sagewind to begin with."

"But Grandfather—" Nessix forced her argument to silence and dropped her head to scour the tabletop with her temperamental glare. It gutted her every time this debate went back to her father. "He trusted Veed, too, and look where that got us." She looked up at En through tired eyes. "I've been listening to Sagewind; I just don't take all he says to heart."

"Then the demons will defeat us."

"That's absurd. Sagewind knows a lot, I'll give him that, but he doesn't know everything."

"The people trust him," En stressed, "and they love you. Seeing your conflict with him will devastate them."

She snorted and cast her gaze to the ceiling. "They don't need me anymore. They have a new leader."

"Nessix, that's ridiculous."

"No," she insisted, leaning forward to emphasize her point. "It's true. You want to know why I've been so childish, it's because that man is tearing our kingdom out from under us. The troops are claiming him as our savior, and you're supporting it. Anyone who demands such a following is dangerous."

"Does that make you dangerous?"

"This is my kingdom. It used to be yours. I have no choice but to fight for it."

En remained silent for some time, trying to gauge the contents of Nes's mind. The family carried a stubborn streak, but this hang up with faith belonged exclusively to Nessix.

"Do you still believe Inwan is watching over us?" En asked at last.

"He *is* still watching us," Nessix said. "You cannot explain the ways of gods."

"Did you ever ask him about the heavens?"

"Of course." Childhood memories challenged Nes, happier days of watching her father train with Veed, Logan dozing nearby as Inwan answered her endless slew of questions. *Here's one for you,* she prayed bitterly. *Where are you?*

"And so you know Laes sees the decisions you're making. He's trying to help you, Nessix, and your pride won't let you accept that. Quit trying to shoulder this yourself. You're not as alone as you think."

Until now, Nessix hadn't comprehended the possibility that either her god or her father saw how she struggled. She flushed, her eyes falling at the thought of disappointing them. Only one person stood a chance at tapping into Inwan's reflections of her conduct. Nessix pushed herself from the table.

"Where are you going?"

She stopped and turned to En. "You wouldn't care." Nessix left the room before her grandfather asked any more questions.

* * * * *

It took very little investigation for Nessix to uncover Mathias's current location, and she trudged her way up to the battlements to meet with him. He stood half a pace from the wall, lines of concentration etched across his face, arms crossed as he watched the mountains in the north. Nessix announced her arrival with rigid footsteps and a forced sigh, but Mathias kept his attention directed on the horizon. He'd thought he and Nessix had shared a fairly enlightening experience earlier in the week, and the fact that very few snide remarks came from her in that time only bothered him now.

Nessix allotted Mathias ample time to address her, and his

refusal to do so only provoked her more. Scowling at his tender considerations of her kingdom, she stalked up to him and shoved him with all the might of her slight frame. She hadn't intended to push him over the ledge, but a piece of her almost hoped he'd lose his balance and tumble over.

Wincing at his ineptitude, Mathias caught himself and retreated a safe distance before giving Nessix his attention. "I take it you'd like to speak to me?"

Nes pressed her advance, shoulders drawn back and lips curled. "What else have you told him?"

His brows stitched together. "Told who?"

"Before you came here not only did I have an army, I had a family."

"I haven't taken anything that was truly yours," Mathias corrected. "And I've given you quite a bit more than what you started with."

"Like what?" Nessix spat.

"Knowledge and caution." Mathias stopped to think on those before deciding that Nessix had, in fact, improved from when he'd first met her. "Perhaps even a touch of discipline, if you look in the right places."

A nagging voice in the back of Nes's mind scolded her for admitting it took Mathias's arrival to give her self-control. "Those lessons are not worth the price of you leading the demons here."

"I didn't bring them. If anything, they brought me. Believe me, I've much more enjoyable pastimes than feuding with demons."

Nessix hissed and shook her head. "I've done my reading, and if you are who you say, you allowed them merciful retreats in the past. If you wouldn't have, they wouldn't be here now."

"Fate has a sense of humor."

"And I am left with people worshiping a legend and a grandfather who would just as soon watch me bleed dry as allow me to do my job." Nessix narrowed her eyes, melodramatic mind churning rapidly.

Her concern made sense to obscure parts of Mathias, but her method of expressing herself was obnoxious. "To be so jealous, perhaps you're not worthy to be your people's champion. This petty hate you have for me only weakens you in the public eye."

"But you"—Nessix shook an accusing finger at Mathias— "their proclaimed protector, lobby to keep the innocents in danger? The caravans are moving in and my scouts have reported increased activity surrounding the towns we've evacuated. If I'd trusted your advice, I could have lost two townships by now."

"You care about the land and the men, but fail to see the end, General." At this rate, Mathias doubted he could convince her of this before the demons forced it on her. "With our current strength, we may hold, but if you refuse to adapt and learn, to accept assistance when you know you need it, there won't be much left for you to protect when this is through."

"Did you learn that at Redthorn?"

Mathias blanched at Nessix's harshness and for a moment, he had no ready response. He stared into her aggressive eyes, realizing her self-proclaimed research taught her nothing of what actually happened that day. "I've learned a lot of things over many ages," he said, leaning against the wall's ledge. "I learned after that war that the heart of the people strives for much more than you'd want it to, and even officers can make stupid decisions."

"My men know how to fight."

"But your people don't."

"The people don't need to know how to fight. That's not their job."

"Your people are your strength, your will, your power. They are no different from you or anyone else in your ranks. The only things they lack are your blessing and training."

"They don't need training," Nessix insisted. "And they already have my blessing. That's why they have an army to protect them and I'm not drafting them like Veed."

"What would you do if they wanted to fight?" Mathias asked, mentioning the subject of his contemplation at last. "Would you deny them that spirit?"

"I would deny them suicide, yes. You met my father. You know he'd agree with me."

"Then perhaps he was a poor tactician and just as unfit to

lead. He was certainly not as arrogant."

Ridiculing Laes was Mathias's favorite way to infuriate Nessix. She responded predictably, slipping a dagger free as she advanced on him. Once in arm's reach, Mathias caught Nes's hand, trouncing her with little effort as he spun to slam her against the wall.

"And now that I have you here, you *will* listen," he growled. Past experience had proven gentle tactics failed on Nessix. "Your first lesson is to keep your emotions out of your fights. I should not have overpowered you just now."

Her expression remained placid through his criticism. "And your confidence makes you blind."

Mathias grinned. "You're really not as tough as you—"

Nessix invested all of her might in a swift uppercut that Mathias's objective of schooling her left him ill prepared for. The strike smarted and Mathias, cursing Nes's dirty fighting, freed her from his hold to assess for damage. Nothing broke, but the metallic taste of blood tickled across his tongue. Working his jaw back and forth, Mathias scoured Nessix with darkened eyes. She simply had no discipline!

Rather, she does, my child.

I wish I could see it. Mathias's thoughts scattered as Nessix threw herself at him again. Grabbing her wrists, Mathias twisted her arms over each other until she folded from his leverage and he shoved her away. *You're sure there's no way you can make dealing with her not... hurt?*

I could, Etha giggled. *But where's the fun in that?*

"How dare you handle me like that!" Nessix shrieked.

I'm getting too old for this... "Perhaps I wouldn't have had to if you'd behave yourself."

As much as Etha wanted to watch how this played out, more pressing matters needed Mathias's attention. *You should encourage her to save some of that energy,* she advised as her disciple fought to reclaim something akin to patience.

Are you suggesting she's going to need it someplace else?

"Is that it?" Nessix taunted, opening her arms before him. *Immediately.*

Hissing at his lack of focus and for letting himself get so

preoccupied with Nes's immaturity, Mathias snatched back his bearings. "No, it's not, and I'll be happy to finish this at a later time, but for now I insist you get yourself and Logan ready for battle." *What are we facing, Etha?*

Nessix laughed. "Reading minds again, Sagewind? That's convenient!"

Aranau, Etha confirmed bleakly. *Keep close to Nessix—she will be killed if you don't.*

"Nessix, I'm serious. Prepare your mount. Give me permission to draw the troops into formation and I'll see that it's done."

"Like I would give you that—"

Bells from the east watch tower sounded and Nes's features fell. The recklessness swept from her eyes as each toll reinforced her sense of duty. Horns echoed from the other towers, ordering the troops to the field. Instructions issued without her prior approval meant Nessix didn't have time to wait on Mathias's guidance.

"We will finish this later," she promised, her tone unconvincing.

"I look forward to see if you grow up by then."

You only grow from the hard times, Etha warned. *Be careful what you wish for, my dear.*

Banking on the hope that Mathias meant it when he claimed to care about Elidae, Nessix rushed down the stairs to dress for battle.

Urgent preparations rippled through the army, confirmation of the threat working its way to everyone. "Sarlot is under attack!"

* * * * *

Sulik reached the field before the other officers and made every effort to maintain order amidst the disorganized bustle. Nessix and Logan barreled through the gates, offering him welcome relief.

"Brant's at the stables," Sulik reported upon her arrival.

"Have you given any orders?" Nessix watched as members of the cavalry spurred their way onto the field. Captains turned their expectant eyes toward her.

"Only to gather the men to their companies," Sulik said. "Nes, I don't like the looks of this."

"Neither do I." She spotted Ceraphlaks landing on the battlements to gather Mathias. "How many are there?"

"We're not sure," Sulik said. "Scouts report the demons cycling through Sarlot's gates. It's a solid force."

"Spread the orders for the troops to fall in line."

"To what position?" Sulik asked.

Always one to push the initiative, Nessix hated her next order. "Defense." Not giving Sulik the chance to protest her unconventional decision, Nessix guided Logan to the top of a hill and looked toward her crumbling city.

Ceraphlaks and Mathias soared a low circle over the demon army that romped through the wall of smoke at the city gates. Their simple surveillance reaped a prompt and barbarous uproar from the enemy. The horde churned over itself, wretched hands snatching at the flemans' hope as Ceraphlaks turned back toward Nessix. Trepidation filled the void in her gut as she watched the enemy force swell to chase the pair away from the town's remains.

Sulik kept his attention on Nessix, fear tainting his clear eyes as he halted Brant and Armina's advance. "She's afraid, Brant."

Brant studied his cousin as she conveyed orders to a captain at Logan's side. "Whoever isn't deserves their death. Keep your mind out there, Sulik."

He nodded. "Same to you."

The men parted ways and Nes concluded her business with the captain as Brant neared. "Send the fastest horse we have southeast," she told him. "We have to stop the caravans."

Brant winced. He'd forgotten about them. "Armina is faster than Logan. Should I—"

"No," Nes said. "I need you on the field."

He nodded, but set his attention to watching Ceraphlaks bank their direction. "If the caravans are under attack?"

"They won't be."

Brant swallowed his apprehensions. "Of course not."

"Tell whoever you send to turn back if he's followed. I will not have him lead the enemy to our citizens."

Brant nodded again, giving Nessix the most sincere smile left inside him. It felt woefully lacking. "This is why we live, Nes," he said, trying to coax courage from her.

Indeed, the officer's creed dictated as much, but its author from generations ago had never encountered demons. Nessix finished the verse, the words out of place but much more applicable to her bleak outlook. "And that will kill us all."

Her forlorn demeanor threatened to erode Brant's resolve, so he settled for accepting his orders. "I'll get your message sent." When Nes tried a smile of her own, Brant turned Armina away and cantered toward his unit, a lump rising in his throat.

Nessix sat astride Logan, fretting over the odds of this battle ending with a positive outcome. Comfort arrived in the form of Ceraphlaks landing nearby and crossing his way to her. She waited in silent anticipation of Mathias's instructions.

One look at the girl's pinched lips and shallow breaths assured the paladin that Nessix was willing to listen. "Don't push forward. Have your men hold position here and rely on the archers to pick the demons off for as long as possible. We must not let them get into our lines while they have so many."

Nessix took in the size of the opposition once again. "My army's taken larger forces," she murmured.

"Remember what Veed told you about that first demon he brought to you?" Mathias waited for her hesitant nod. "This is an entire army of them."

A muffled whimper beat against Nes's throat. "Why aren't they charging?"

"They're waiting for you to go to them, aiming to manipulate you with fear."

Nes's most appealing thought was to run and lead this horror to Veed for him to dispose of, but she surveyed Sarlot's remains instead, thick columns of smoke spiraling up from behind the walls. Nes's heart ceased its pattern long enough for her to breathe. "Sarlot is gone, isn't she?"

"This is war, Nessix. Lives have been and will be lost. Any survivors have no doubt fled to the fortress for safety."

"You told me at the last battle that the demons we faced were foot soldiers," she said, recalling the magnitude of damage taken then. If the creatures waiting for them now possessed half the power Mathias claimed, worlds of trouble waited for her army. "You've lied to me before. You'll do it again."

Mathias stayed still for a moment. He'd never mastered the knack for lying, especially when confronted about it, but maintaining Nes's calm took priority. "That army *was* nothing but soldiers. These are far more vicious, but we can delay things before they grow impatient with us."

Nessix chewed on his advice for as long as she dared. Engaging this opponent at all sounded like a terrible idea, but they needed to be stopped. Silently, Nes guided Logan through the lines. Her officers looked up at her, unhinged by her grave demeanor. The General Nessix they loved hadn't made it to the field. No rallying motion called them to arms, fear snuffed the fire from her eyes, Logan didn't dance in anticipation. Those more seasoned and wise spun toward their troops to busy them with petty tasks, hoping to keep her fear from catching. Mathias watched as the general passed through the ranks, touched by the devotion her men showed and dreading the effect of her irresolute conduct.

Ceraphlaks trotted to catch up to Nessix's procession and Mathias prayed for Etha to give them their strength. He moved through the army, the knowledge behind his eyes imparting hope against the faltering of their charismatic leader. When Ceraphlaks stopped beside Logan at the front lines, Nessix didn't move, simply staring at her dying city. The demons roiled about in disorder, no obvious source of command in sight. Brant joined them moments later.

"Nes, the men need orders," he reminded her quietly. "This unrest will kill us before the demons have the chance if we don't do something."

Her gut suggested she tell Brant to split the cavalry and feign a flank attack, allowing her and Sulik the chance to divide the enemy force, but that seemed too simple. If Veed had struggled to defeat one of these, her men had little chance against an entire regiment. Nessix opened her mouth and an empty breath wheezed from her. The thought of condemning her soldiers to this savage fate turned her stomach, and she couldn't bear to order them to it.

"Signal the archers to open a volley and instruct the men to hold their lines," Mathias prompted as Nes's mind froze. He turned to her as Brant's perturbed eyes bore through him. "You must order your men, General. They are looking to you and no one else."

Mind treading through advice and terror, Nessix nodded slowly. "Tell the archers to prepare themselves. Open fire when everyone's set."

Sitting tall in the saddle, Brant carefully dissected his cousin's motives. On the exterior, Nessix appeared to find her calm, but the gnawing on the inside of her cheek and her thumb flicking the buckle of her scabbard betrayed what confidence she spun for her troops. Brant cast his wary eyes to Mathias.

"Are you sure those are your orders?" Brant asked.

Nessix wasn't particularly proud of Mathias's influence, but her options were limited at the moment. Acutely aware of Brant's implications against Mathias, she nodded again. "I am."

Reluctant to leave Nes alone with the paladin, but confident he meant her less harm than the demons did, Brant nodded. "I'll alert the captains," he told her as he gathered Armina to leave, "but my battalion will follow as soon as you move in." He waited for Nessix to respond, but received nothing more than her steady breathing. His own confidence wavering the longer he stayed there, Brant moved off, calling out his instructions.

"Sarlot is gone," Nessix murmured to Mathias. "I know it."

Perhaps Nessix remained more in tune with the spiritual world than Mathias gave her credit for. A new side of the girl revealed itself, her complexity intriguing him. She hid her fear behind a curtain of resolve, prepared to charge into what she saw as her death, not out of some prideful courage, but out of love for her people. And Mathias couldn't bring himself to confirm her suspicion.

"Let us focus on the here and now," he said. "We have to take care of these demons before we can worry about Sarlot."

"Do you really think we'll live through this?"

"We will." Mathias drew his sword and lowered it to his side. "Let your men find courage in you and they will not fail." The hilt of his enchanted blade spiraled and stretched into a long metal shaft.

Nessix missed seeing the magic unfold, and it took her a few moments to notice the spear clutched in Mathias's hand. If her men needed her courage to survive this encounter, she might as well surrender now. Swallowing her doubt, she looked down the line of archers, each of them ready, eyes trained on their chosen target. Whether or not they feared this battle, they were ready to carry out their jobs. Nessix had to step up and do hers. Locking eyes with Brant, she nodded to him. His arm fell and a shower of arrows pelted the demon army.

A few of the beasts dropped in the initial round, impaled in some vital location, though the number slain neglected to make a dent in their defiant standing. The last arrow landed and the flemans held their breath. With one throat, the demons bellowed a roar and charged toward their targets.

Mathias watched Nes's hands tangle in Logan's mane. "We will win this," he said. "Have your men continue the volley."

A few skirmishers ran ahead of the approaching force, and the nervous flush drained from Nes's face as she motioned for Brant to repeat the action. Arrows picked off the demons that skittered in front, but as each one fell, two more replaced it.

"Keep your head, General," Mathias soothed.

Nessix turned to him, her face lost in the currents rushing through her mind. "I can't do this," she murmured fiercely.

"You don't have a choice."

Mathias knew this battle would test Nessix, but he hadn't expected her to crumble so easily. Her hope and resolve disappeared, suffocated by her lack of faith in his reassurance. With Nessix frozen in place, Mathias took action. Sweeping the spear in a circle above his head, he struck it down by his side. Eight pillars of searing white flame erupted from the ground fifty yards ahead of the front lines, engulfing the unfortunate demons leading the charge.

"Steel yourself, Nessix!" Mathias barked. "Your men need their champion. You are more than capable!"

Nessix blinked at Mathias's command, wondering what he'd lived through to allot him such confidence. A touch of guilt floated by, a feeling she'd tend to later if it continued to weigh on her. Mathias had learned all he knew through his own trials and without expert guidance. Trepidation beat out her sympathy as the demons closed in. Her men sent anxious glances in her direction, terrified of her silence. Nessix had asked for Mathias's advice and he'd given it to her, expecting her to put it to use.

Nodding once, Nessix pushed Logan forward, and the fecklan threw his trust in her hands. Confusion flooded her ranks as captains bellowed their interpretations of Nes's movement, some holding their troops back while others encouraged support. The demons halted their advance, closing in on themselves to surround the advancing general.

Mathias leaned low on Ceraphlaks's back as the pegasus bolted after Logan. "For your people!" he cried. "For Sarlot, Nessix!"

Bolstered by Mathias's support, they reached the fray and Nessix moved to draw her sword. As suddenly as they came upon the threat, Logan jarred to a stop and Nes's fingers went numb. Neither of them moved in the horror around them.

The creatures they met wore blood as their war paint. A demon snarled up at her, close enough for Nessix to drive the toe of her boot into its face, blood seeping from below its eyes in streaks down its cheeks. Nessix's eyes swept across the extent of the brutality surrounding her.

Arms and legs of her people were wielded as flails, twirled through the air like gruesome banners, pale fingers still bent in their final actions. Heads adorned shields as standards and the demons hadn't discriminated on who they'd claimed, the face of a young man speared above the empty, cross-eyed gaze of an old woman. Innocents Nessix had pledged to protect floated in pieces through the enemy ranks. Entrails crossed over demon chests. All around Nessix lurked the only nightmare she'd ever have again.

Nes's stomach thrashed and she pulled her harrowed gaze

from the atrocity around her, compelled to grasp Logan's mane to keep her balance. An offending demon lunged forward and Logan twisted and reared, nearly dumping Nessix from his back in the process. The fiend scrambled away before Logan's hooves fell back down to crush it.

Another assault sprang at them and Logan danced, Nessix still struggling to regain command over her stunned mind. These beasts destroyed Sarlot and threatened the same destruction to the rest of her kingdom! Gnashing teeth surrounded her, claws raked at her breeches, and Nessix let out a startled scream as a spray of blood spattered across her side. The nearest demon's head tumbled to the ground, landing at Logan's hooves.

"Nessix, you must fight!" Mathias pled.

Ceraphlaks hopped into the air to avoid a demon preparing to unseat his rider. The pegasus's hooves returned to the ground and Mathias swept his blade across his assailant's gut. Blood steamed off the holy steel and Mathias grinned, a wicked expression Nessix never imagined him capable of. A rumble of confusion gushed through the enemy ranks as recognition dawned on them. For a moment, the tables turned, and the demons hesitated.

Gripping her sword, buying some strength from Mathias's courage, Nessix accepted her duty at last. When facing the usual minotaur and ogres, she fought easily from Logan's back, but these creatures were too short to allow her to land a hit. She cast her accumulation of fear aside and dismounted, sword held ready as she backed up against Logan's leg.

Mathias nodded in approval of Nes's renewed moxie, and joined her on foot. Ceraphlaks took to wing, catching the interest of a handful of snarling demons in the process. Clawed hands snatched at his legs in hopes of pulling him down. Beating a powerful gust, the pegasus drowned the field in a momentary haze of dust and dirt. When it cleared enough for visibility, he'd lofted far from their reach.

"I better not regret this," Nessix growled to Mathias. Her fear subsided enough for her to take action, but her peripheral vision caught an object soaring toward her head as she moved to engage. She raised her arm, hoping to deflect the attack and fingernails raked Nes's cheek as a detached arm linked around her own. A disgusted sob burst from Nessix, unchecked. The demon that brandished the severed limb tumbled onto its back as Mathias speared through its throat.

"This is why you're fighting!"

Nessix had seen mangled bodies before and knew how to tune gore out of her mind, but these were her people! Her innocents! A roar choked from Nessix and she rushed into the mass of demons. All the techniques her years on the field had taught her fled her mind, replaced by the very first suggestion Mathias gave her to aim a dagger for their eyes.

She swung her sword wildly at her first target, producing a dagger at the last second to wedge into the creature's throat. With their quarry finally in action, those demons closest to Nessix swarmed her, driving themselves between her and Mathias. Nessix fought to maintain contact with him until she noted his apparent lack of concern. Fear whispered to her as she parried blows, frantic to find a way out of this trouble. Mathias threw her a fleeting glance, and it made sense. If he showed honest concern about her, they'd tear her apart.

Nessix fought back. Jamming her heel against the nearest demon's knee, she swept her sword upwards beneath another's arm and pummeled its head with her blade's hilt. The uncertain song of the cavalry's horns demanding for the men to hold sifted through the field's chaos. Distracted, Nessix hissed as a blade kissed beneath her chin, too close to her throat for comfort. She staggered a two step retreat to recover before the weight of a body attached to her back. Her balance thrown, Nessix dug her elbow into another demon's shoulder to try and stay standing. Logan's cry neared and a few startled grunts left the throats of those his hooves landed on. Teeth dug into Nes's neck and she yelped against the pain.

Mathias caught sight of Nes struggling, and breathed a prayer as he muscled his way through the demons to reach her. He hated that Nessix insisted on learning her lessons the hard way. Holding back the urge to rally her, Mathias contented himself with ripping his spear through the demon latched onto her back. A gush of blood cascaded over Nes's shoulder, masking any injuries of her own as Mathias passed to resume his progress.

Shuddering at the warmth flowing over her, Nessix threw her shoulders back to deposit the demon's dead weight on the ground. She looked up at Mathias, who revered life so dearly, as he danced blithely through the enemy, his spear a seductive partner. The immediate threat had thinned out and he ceased the attack long enough to catch his breath and glare at those still standing. Nessix wiped at the blood on her right cheek as the sound of her army pressing into combat supported her. The demons bellowed out a cry and the entire army moved in.

TEN

Mathias set off to congratulate Nessix on her victory as the last of the aranau gamboled from the expended army. The soldiers promptly set to gather each other from the ground, and so Mathias put his immediate concern in assessing Nes's state of mind. Nobody walked away from their first encounter with aranau as the same person.

"I'm riding to Sarlot," Nessix told him as his steps neared. "To see what's left."

Mathias winced. "I'm afraid you'll be disappointed."

"Doesn't matter," she insisted. "I need to see this atrocity for myself." Not waiting for Mathias's common sense to talk her out of it, not wanting it to, Nessix mounted Logan.

The great horse's strides trod over bodies of enemies and allies alike. He crossed the field with a wary grace, nostrils quivering as the stench of fire and blood and burned flesh filled the air.

Sarlot's massive gates implored the pair away from the destruction beyond, the right leaning against its bottom hinge and the left only jagged planks. The watch tower hunched beside them, its old guard missing his arms from the elbows and legs from the knees, impaled on one of the broken poles that once supported his post. Logan balked at the sight, moving on only after Nessix choked her bile back down. Cautious hooves carried them into the

144

city's remains.

Blood paved the cobbled side streets and the bricks of the main road. There appeared no method to the slaughter, no form of collecting the bodies. Whatever buildings avoided arson stood in mournful shambles. Uncertain of what else to do, Nessix dismounted and wandered from Logan.

"Is anyone there?" she called, voice swallowed up by dread. "This is General Nessix. We've defeated the beasts who did this. It's safe to come out."

Silence cried back to her. No cats leapt through the wreckage, no birds darted through the thick air. The fires popped and smoldered their way to ashes. Screams of nothing audible filled Nes's ears, begging for help from the emptiness of what was so recently her most prosperous township. Her eyes flitted from the limbs and entrails strewn through what remained of the streets, careful to avoid any further desecration as she willed herself deeper into the broken town.

Mathias worried about Nes's frigid departure, afraid of the negative ramifications her seclusion might cause her. After finding Sulik to confirm safe transport for the wounded and dead, Mathias took Ceraphlaks into Sarlot. Whether or not Nessix wanted his sympathy, he knew she needed it.

The pair landed beside Logan, the massive horse's head lowered and eyes distant. Nessix stumbled through the empty streets, her strained voice piercing out for someone to answer her. An eerie chill saturated the barren town; doors broken through and thrown off their hinges, smoldering fires eating away at the rubble that remained of the smith's home and business. The demons had spared nothing.

Mathias's empathy for Nessix jammed in his chest as he watched her proud shoulders slump in defeat. She shouldn't have come. Her voice quit trying to reach any survivors as she slowly understood there weren't any. Whether or not Nessix considered herself an experienced warrior, nothing had prepared her for the demons' ravaging ways. A tremble rattled her and Mathias soaked in the magnitude of Nes's devotion. Motionless aside from heaving breaths, she stared at the debris of a school house. Mathias walked closer, allowing the sound of his steps to announce his approach.

Numb lips barely formed Nes's words. "I failed."

"You defeated the most vicious of the hordes today," Mathias said. "I would consider that a success."

"I lost my town!" she screamed, spinning around to face him. Tears glittered in the depths of her eyes, but she refused to let them fall. "The people I swore to protect with my own life—" Nessix waved her arm vaguely to her side, unable to speak further of her implications. "I *failed*."

Etha, don't let her break now. "You, your men, came out victorious," Mathias insisted. "If you feel defeated, take that passion and turn it into strength for tomorrow."

His words barely navigated through the dreadful pounding in Nes's head. Her passion to protect her people gave her strength, indeed. It was too late to use that strength to save them, but not too late to assert herself. Sucking in a deep breath, gagging on the smoke and death, Nessix stalked back to Logan and climbed into the saddle.

"What are you doing?" Mathias asked, falling short of patting the horse.

Logan wondered the same.

Nessix didn't answer, only clicking her tongue once to guide Logan back to the city gates. The fecklan lurched into motion, relieved to put this town behind him.

Dust floated from where the living troops trudged back to the fortress, carrying with them the wounded and what dead they could afford. Logan drifted toward them before Nessix brought him to a swift halt and jumped from his back.

Uncertain of Nes's intentions, Mathias trailed behind. As promised, Sulik had cleared the field; Etha had already greeted the only remaining flemans. Nessix strode through the carnage strewn around her, sword drawn and eyes frenetic. Her men comprised the majority of the dead, but she looked past that tragedy for now. Instead, she scanned the area for any surviving demons, kicking each body until she found one that managed to moan upon impact.

Mathias slowed his approach as Nes's eyes bore down on the mangled creature at her feet. It was a small female, origins indistinguishable through the wounds inflicted on her. Mathias thought to confront Nes, hoping to talk her out of the path she crashed down, but held back. She'd never witnessed this kind of bloodshed before, and needed to learn how to cope with it on her own terms. Justifying Nes's plans by her level of greenness didn't stop Mathias from flinching when she adjusted the grip on her sword.

The demon had crumbled, mortally wounded from a deep sever to her abdomen. Lip curled, Nessix pressed the tip of her sword into the gash, angling to push upward into the body cavity.

"Where was your mercy?" she spat, thrusting her shoulder forward to drive the sword deeper. "Where!"

The demon writhed as much as her wounds allowed, her attempt to cry intercepted by a sputtering cough. A trail of blood leaked from the corner of her mouth.

A maniacal smile flashed across Nes's face and engulfed her eyes at the demon's agony. "You won't answer me?" She nudged the sword again. "You've picked the wrong bitch to mess with." The force with which Nessix drew her sword from the wound sent a spray of blood back onto her greaves. "You've slain my men on this field." The blade fell cleanly across the demon's cheek. "Their deaths can be forgiven."

Mathias inched closer, hopes of Nessix conducting herself in a civil manner thoroughly dashed. He watched grimly as the tip of her sword flew to rest at the demon's throat.

"But to take the lives of the people! The commoners! The children!" Overcome by the surge of emotions at last, Nes's arm wobbled and she sank to her knees. "That cannot be forgiven." She slid the blade beneath the demon's chin, a tight smile following.

Vengeance, Mathias supported on many accounts, but not how Nessix intended to find it. "Nessix, that's enough. She was following orders."

"I can show you mercy," Nes cooed, ignoring Mathias's input as she fingered the demon's knife. "And I can show you all the pain in the world."

Disappointed with Nes's behavior, Mathias neared her side. The demon's eyes flicked toward him. Did she recognize him or simply want help?

Nessix stared down at the demon critically. "My people didn't want to die."

"Nes," Mathias said. "This won't bring any of them back."

Naïve confusion contorted Nes's face, her brows rippling and the corners of her mouth twitching in every direction. Overcome by the carnage, her stomach knotted. Nessix dropped her sword and collapsed forward, striking the ground as a single sob escaped her.

Mathias took a knee beside her. If she wanted comfort, he'd deliver it, but in this moment, he was obligated to save Nessix from this downward spiral. As coherence seeped back into her eyes, Mathias chanced his luck at trying to talk her out of her ruthless retaliation.

"Nes, perhaps—"

The sound of Mathias's voice sparked Nessix back into the present, and she flung herself at the demon. Her troops went into battle well aware of the risks, but the execution of the villagers wronged her entire kingdom. The fact that the demons' brutality managed to turn her stomach sealed their death sentence.

Mathias grasped Nes's wrists before she resumed her torture, and she fought with the remainder of her sapped energy to slip from his hands. A heel caught Mathias as Nessix squirmed, but his breastplate absorbed the impact. Pulling against him until her wrists stung, Nessix gave up, falling across the demon's chest. Mathias freed her carefully.

Nessix panted from the whirlwind in her head, and after her wits solidified, she sat up. "Do not stop me."

"Enough of this, Nes," Mathias begged. A fresh streak of blood flawed the girl's left cheek and for the first time, Mathias saw her feebleness. The braids securing her hair had fallen, a cut scabbed beneath her chin and another above her right eye. The blood on her side still glistened from when Mathias had beheaded that first assailant. "This will not bring anyone back," he repeated softly. "Let's go."

"These people took you in!" She reeled at Mathias, throwing her hands in front of her. "They were your friends! The men who died at this damned creature's hands looked to you as their salvation!" She shuddered, gaping at the carnage around her. "How can you sit there and accept this?"

Those words would have hurt a much younger version of Mathias. "There is no other choice," he said. "It happened. I can fix the damage done by sword and disease, but time cannot be undone."

Nessix sat quietly as her heart pounded, staring into those green eyes she struggled to trust. He was right, she knew, but that wouldn't bring anyone back, either. Pride, for the first time in a long time, meant nothing to Nessix.

"But revenge..." Her voice lost itself as she stuffed back a sob. She slammed her fist into the ground, releasing her frustrations with a strangled cry.

"Then avenge your people," Mathias said, shifting closer to the demon, "but don't turn into the beast. You're better than this." His eyes moved toward the dagger before meeting Nes's again.

She glared at him. He knew *nothing* about what her people meant to her. Moving faster than Mathias anticipated, Nessix's hands flew to the dagger and jammed it into her victim's throat. Half of a strained moan spilled from the demon and her eyes drifted into the glaze of death.

Mathias closed his eyes and looked away to keep from reacting to Nes's cruelty. "You are better," he repeated.

"I am loyal to my people," Nessix spat. "More than I ever will be to you or your pompous goddess. If I don't stop these beasts, who will?" She scowled as Mathias stood to look back at her fortress. "These actions will not pass in my kingdom."

Mathias wheeled on Nessix aggressively. "And if you can't control yourself, this violence will never leave it!" He neglected to correct his harshness. "Too many otherwise good heads of power have found corruption just like this, and I will not let you travel that path."

Nessix sat up, heart racing as her adrenaline siphoned away. Her breath came in quick gasps. Inside, she actively crumbled, and Mathias's assessment only helped scattered the pieces out of reach. She lunged at him, wishing she could throttle away his scorn.

He stopped her pathetic attack with ease, and as soon as his arms held her shoulders, Nessix collapsed against him. Mathias indulged her unspoken bid for comfort, remembering a time when he'd needed—but did not have—someone to do the same for him. The field continued to empty, taking the sounds of life with it, and Mathias let Nes go once her trembling subsided.

"Defending them isn't winning me over, you know." She kept her head tucked and sniffed back her grief.

"I am trying to save your spirit."

Nessix looked up at that, tears still prominent on the other side of her fragile temper. "I will not leave this field until every demon that hasn't crawled away is dead," she vowed, voice quivering with rage and regret. "How's *that* for spirit?"

"You may kill them all," Mathias said, as if he controlled their right to life, "but you will not resort to torture."

"What about what they did to my people? What kind of ruler am I to allow that? What kind of paladin are you, for that matter?"

Mathias couldn't decide whether or not to deem her acknowledgement of his station a milestone, but considering the intent of her words, he figured the title slipped. "You weren't ready for this." His eyes softened in his desire to find some way to fix this for her. "It isn't your fault."

Nessix straightened, nothing but her force of will keeping her from crying. None of his excuses or reassurance lifted the blame from her shoulders. She already made up her mind and this man's soft heart would not talk her out of her self-appointed duty.

"Get off my field," Nessix growled. "If you want to serve me, go conjure your miracles on whoever you can save."

Shocked by her abrasive tone and honestly a little hurt by it, Mathias averted his eyes. The vehemence in Nes's glare tried to assure him passion spurred her actions, but he feared for the girl's sanity. If Mathias stayed here right now, it would damage the fragile relationship he'd carved with her. Besides, the wounded needed him back home. Slowly, Mathias raised his head to look Nessix over once more, aching that there'd been no way to prepare her.

"As you wish, General," he murmured. Bowing his head, Mathias prayed for Etha to forgive Nessix and turned to walk back to the fortress.

Nessix tracked Mathias's path, frowning selfishly at his apparent sorrow. Her actions needed no justification. There was nothing wrong with them. The remaining demons had earned whatever tortures came next.

Absorbing the tragedy around her, Nessix pushed on to the next demon's body. It didn't move when she kicked it, but anything with even the slightest bit of sense had ample motivation to remain still. She raised her sword to strike, but stopped herself. Her blade had seen its fill of death for the day. She slammed it back into its scabbard.

Glancing around, Nessix spotted a great axe lying not far from one of the demon bodies. She needed both hands to lift the weapon and she hefted it into the air, letting gravity send it crashing through its former master. Dragging the axe along behind her, Nessix visited each demon she came across. The first few strikes landed awkwardly, severing the head at the jaw line or taking a piece of shoulder off as well, but after a dozen failures, the disturbing rhythm of systematic slaughter invaded her mind.

As each head rolled away, Nessix lost more of her strength, stomach tightening and arms burning. She strained her bleary gaze across the field as the setting sun mocked her efforts. With her last strike, the axe's handle fell from her hands and Nessix collapsed to the ground. Weak arms propped her up as her stomach wrenched again. She coughed up mouthfuls of the day's dining, gagging between heaves and fighting for decent breath, unable to stop until nothing but bile followed and her throat burned. A tear rested on the outside corner of each eye and she jumped when Logan gently reached his nose forward to nuzzle the back of her neck.

Nessix sat back, spitting up tainted saliva to purge the taste from her mouth. Death inevitably awaited those still living out here, and Nessix wobbled to her feet. Logan rested his head against her chest as she took him in her arms. A gentle rustle floated through the air, chased by a weak cough, and Nessix turned to locate the sound's origin. Commanding her stomach to lay still, she drew her sword. One more wouldn't kill her.

The mangled face looked up at her through a mask of blood

and dirt. A single hand reached out, the other missing at the end of a shattered forearm, and Nessix commended herself for not raising her blade.

"Blessed Inwan," she murmured, returning the weapon to her hip. Barely alive, her soldier dragged his way closer, indistinguishable words pleading to her. She rushed to him, Logan trotting close behind.

Nessix assisted the man to his knees and used the red half of her cape to wipe the blood from his face and eyes. "It's alright," she told him. "I'll get you home."

"I don't want to live."

Her hands ceased their work as she stared down at him, mouth agape. "The fortress isn't far off," she said. "Sagewind will fix you."

"But not the memories, General."

Nes's heart quickened and her stomach twisted again. "Battle makes us stronger."

A convulsion battered the man and he reached out his oozing stump, trying to grasp her shoulder. "Mercy, General!" he begged. "You ended the demons' pain… please…"

Laes never taught Nessix which morals to follow in a case like this. Killing had never bothered her before, but she'd never slain one of her own. Walking away now promised this man an agonizing death and her conscience would never allow that.

This broken man had no way to fight her, no way to keep her from stripping the armor from him and carrying him back home. His words, praising her for awarding the demons mercy echoed in her mind. These fiends earned gruesome deaths, but had she really handed them a favor she now kept from this soldier? His eyes fought to focus on hers and he made a failed attempt to stand.

Nessix blinked rapidly and cast a gaze to the axe that had helped her behead the demons before turning back to the man. She'd give nearly anything to trade places with him now. Her throat was parched, her knees weak. She still heard the gargles of death and afterthoughts of deranged laughter in the silence. This man deserved to put this behind him. Nessix drew her sword.

"Your name, soldier, so I can inform your next of kin," she

requested softly.

He managed a weak smile. "Dreyan Millis." His eyes pinched closed. "I'll tell Inwan of your mercy, should I find him, General."

Nessix stopped at the remark. She'd considered herself the last fleman who truly retained faith in Inwan. Gritting her teeth, Nessix batted away the urge to drag Dreyan back with her. She bowed her head and shifted her weight.

The tears Nessix had tried to hide surfaced and this time, she let them come. They fell as she pressed the edge of her sword against Dreyan's throat. Her other hand cradled the back of his head. "You can be healed," she tried once more.

"I'd rather be taken by your blade than a demon's. Mercy, General. Please."

Shoving her mind back to her core value, her dedication to her people, Nessix nodded. If anything else came from her mouth, she'd drop her sword and weep in the mud. Refilling her stomach with doubt and sorrow and rage, she nodded again.

"Thank you, General."

In one fluid motion, before her aching heart stopped her, Nessix pressed Dreyan's head against her sword as she drew the blade through his throat. His body slumped forward, shoulders falling against her legs. Nessix dropped her sword and supported him in uncertain arms. She eased his body to the ground.

Dry heaves shook her. She hacked until her throat rasped and tears cut their way through the blood and grime on her cheeks. Logan stood beside her, offering the comfort of his companionship. As the sun withdrew the last wisps of light, Nessix smeared the tears from her face with the heel of her palm and retrieved her sword.

Dreyan leaned into the earth, at ease after a life of service. Nes's heart no longer mourned his sacrifice, but it overflowed with remorse. Logan knelt down without prompting. Coughing once more, Nessix dragged the man's body in front of the saddle and mounted. Laying a protective hand on Dreyan's back, Nessix began the journey home.

ELEVEN

Men lined the halls. Words spoken in hushed tones peppered by moans of various stages of agony welcomed Nessix home. Every public space on the first floor served as a makeshift infirmary. Peering into the mess hall where the bulk of the mortally wounded lay, Nessix found Sulik dutifully tending to the soldiers. As much as she wanted to run to her chamber and wail over her own fears, Nessix stayed with her men. Several of them sported injuries mirroring Dreyan's, many far worse.

She trudged over to Sulik and touched the back of his arm. "Has Sagewind healed anyone yet?"

Her commander ran off anxiety and expectations alone and barely had the presence of mind to give her his attention. "Not yet. He instructed us to sort the men by severity, said a prayer and left." Sulik inched closer, speaking just above a whisper. "Nes, we won't have the manpower to fight if this happens again."

"Nonsense," Nessix insisted, though Sulik knew better than to believe her. "Do we have reports on the caravans?"

"They arrived safely." Sulik smiled weakly. "We're housing the citizens in the dungeon for now."

Nessix nodded, bereft eyes augmenting her gaunt appearance. "If there was room anywhere else..."

"I know," Sulik said, desperate to save Nessix from further

guilt. "There's little you can do here; maybe you should go get some sleep?"

Her aching body pined for rest, but flashes of carnage assaulted her mind each time she blinked and sullied the prospect of sleep. Caught between the two forces, Nessix took advantage of the opportunity to distance herself from this horror. "If anything needs my attention, let me know."

Sulik nodded. "Of course."

Almost drained of whatever courage allowed her to fake her calm, Nessix slipped away. She issued instructions to be left alone, toying with the thought of remaining undisturbed until she starved to death. Rounding the corner to ascend the stairs, an influx of dizziness battered her. The episode landed Nessix against the wall for support, and she wondered if Mathias's lessons could have prevented what happened today. The part of her that believed as much screamed at the other for her stupidity. At length, knowing how demons fought wouldn't make them any less terrible.

Cheers filtered from below her as Mathias undoubtedly returned to the crowd. With no desire to deal with any more of his lectures, Nessix bounded up the stairs to her room as fast as her swimming head allowed. She closed and bolted the door behind her, soaking in the familiar comfort of her quarters. Someone had tended to her desk during her absence, all of the scrolls tucked neatly to one side and her maps filed away. A tray of food sat where her documents once laid strewn on top of each other. Nes's empty stomach insisted she indulge, but after picking up the fork, everything inside her changed its mind.

Nessix dropped the utensil with a startling amount of loathing and began to remove her armor. Her body ached from the force of the battle and even the action of unbuckling the straps hurt. Limbs weakened from overuse protested the loss of support from her bindings, but Nessix was through wearing it today. She hung the pieces on their stand to be cleaned later then stood in front of her wash basin and mirror.

A stranger looked back at her, wearing a mask of blood and grime, her hair in a horrible state of disarray. She dipped a cloth into the water and pressed it against her face, letting its coolness soothe her muscles and erase the dirt of battle. Fibers caught the scabbing cut above her eye, opening the wound to allow a shimmer of blood to surface. Nessix squinted into the mirror. Her eyes had changed.

Usually her favorite feature, her weapon of charm, her eyes lacked familiarity. Where had her confidence gone? Her pride? Her fire? Promising tears betrayed her even further. Within their reflection, Nessix relived the past day's horrors. She shuddered at the thought of Dreyan facing this warped version of her in his last moments and angrily covered the mirror.

Nessix turned and strode to her armoire, eager to replace her dirtied blouse and breeches with something clean and ignorant of war. Pulling off her damaged shirt, she fished out a new one. A pair of pants accompanied her as she sat on the edge of her bed to pull off her boots. Halfway through the motions, a scroll case rolled across the mattress and bumped her back. After freeing her other foot, Nessix picked up the case and frowned at its seal.

"Arrogant bastard," she muttered, tearing the parchment free from its chamber.

The scroll requested she meet with Veed the following morning. She overlooked the snarky comment about such actions pending the stability of her physical condition. Nessix wanted to deny his request, but the last line proposed a bargain he assured she wouldn't want to pass up. The text failed to elaborate, sealing her curiosity. She cursed Veed again for knowing how to manipulate her so well. With one last gaze to the food on her desk, Nessix fell back on her bed, mind too numb to think and too haunted to sleep.

* * * * *

A rude pounding on her door jarred Nessix from the sleep that had found her. Groggy, she stretched the tightness from her muscles and rubbed the heaviness from her eyes before hauling herself upright. Her feet reached out to the floor uncertainly, waiting to be grabbed by one of the creatures childhood memories swore lived under the bed.

156

The knock sounded again, this time accompanied by a grating voice. "The day's already begun, Nes. You really ought to get out of bed."

Any shred of pleasure sleep had loaned her shriveled away at Veed's address. This was not at all how she'd hoped to start her day. At least he saved her a trip.

"I'm coming," Nessix grumbled back.

She shook the remaining dust of sleep away and stood. After a glance at the cold food on her desk, she picked up the bread and gnawed on its staleness. Her stomach demanded she devour it, craving even unappetizing nourishment, but her palate contradicted the appeal. Her throat wrestled the bite down.

"Would you hurry up? You're not the only point on my agenda today."

Nessix grasped the bread between her teeth as she folded the blankets back over her bed. Tearing off a second bite, she braced herself for the unpleasant encounter ahead. As soon as she slid the bolt from its locked position, Veed shoved the door open and pushed his way in.

"Your haste is appreciated." Glancing at the vile condition of Nes's armor and frayed hair, Veed smirked.

Nessix stalked farther into her chamber as Veed shut the door. "Not half as much as I appreciated your assistance yesterday."

Her attempt at distancing herself from him amused Veed. "I never received a call for help."

"You knew enough to assume I'd been hurt."

Veed grinned and drifted closer to her. His presence unsettled Nes's stomach even more, and she tossed the piece of bread back onto her desk, turning to keep a better eye on him. He snared Nes's attention by drawing three small leather pouches from his satchel.

Nessix bit down on the inside of her cheek, eager to know what those pouches hid, but equally reluctant to show Veed any amount of desperation. He waited on her patiently, and when she withheld her curiosity, Veed billowed an overdone sigh and spun her desk chair around to straddle the seat. He stared at Nessix so intently she shifted her gaze from him.

"You don't know what you've got, do you?" he asked.

Shaking her head, Nessix stitched her eyebrows together. "Charm? Seems to be all that's on your mind."

Veed laughed, idly wishing the circumstances allowed time to play with her. "He *is* the White Paladin, Nes."

She threw her head back with an aggravated groan. "You, too? This entire island's gone mad."

"Think, Nessix!" Veed demanded. "No matter how little you paid attention in your classes, you have to remember *something* about him."

"So, he's done some reading."

"He can bring men back from the brink of death."

"You claim you can do the same and there's no one spinning legends about you," Nessix pointed out with a mischievous grin. "Get to the point."

Veed sighed dramatically and exaggerated his action of loosening the strings on each of the pouches. "Nes, I dabble. That's as far as my talent goes."

Nessix craned her neck to try glimpsing inside the bags. "You seemed to be touting a lot more than that before this entire ordeal began."

Veed hesitated from reaching into the first of the bags, soaking in the pleasure of Nes's prying eyes. He had her firmly enough in his grasp to force her compliance. "If you're going to be like that, maybe we shouldn't be having this discussion."

She looked from the pouches to his calculating eyes. "I thought you had other matters to attend to? If this is so important, hurry it along."

Nodding, Veed busied himself with removing the pouches' contents. He produced an amethyst pendant first, half the size of Nes's fist and secured with a silver setting and elegant chain. Matching baubles in sapphire and crystalline hues came from the remaining bags. Each chain draped from a separate finger as Veed dangled them in front of her.

Nessix stared at the pendants and tried to shove the desire from her gaze. Her own kingdom's finances were in an ugly state, and Nessix deprived herself the luxury of wasting funds on such fine jewels. While Veed hoarded valuables for himself before addressing his people, Nes always tried to put her cities' interests before her own. Both generals knew these facts of the other quite well.

"Taunting me, Veed?" she asked.

"Never," he oozed, snatching the chains back. "Just trying to bargain with you."

She watched him place the amethyst's chain over his head. "I'm afraid I can't afford an equal trade for this, and the last thing I need is a debt hanging between us."

"You drive a tough bargain," Veed said. "Fine. What if I threw in enough coins to keep your people managed and your men paid?" He maintained the majority of his smirk as Nessix attempted twice to give him a response.

"I cannot put my men in your service," she said. "An alliance means nothing if—"

"Come now, Nessix!" Veed chuckled. "It's not your men or your land I'm after, at least not right now. I want you to pull your paladin into our deal."

"He's already at my side," Nessix said, "and he turned you down the last time you tried something like this. I thought you couldn't stand him, anyway."

Veed looked past her attempts to thwart his objective. "I'll keep your troops fed through the entirety of this war."

Money, jewelry, and food. The only thing left to want was victory. Mathias had assured her that he never planned to trust Veed, and Nes knew enough to consider him set in that regard. But beyond the joy of having a new, pretty trinket to flaunt about, she'd be able to support her troops and protect her kingdom properly. Mathias had to understand that! Nessix stared at the sapphire in Veed's grasp, keeping her hands busy tugging at the wrists of her blouse.

"The third one's for Sagewind, isn't it?" she mumbled.

"It's only fair, don't you think?" Veed narrowed his eyes and watched for her reaction. "Each general should be allowed the same luxuries."

A disappointed breath wheezed from Nessix. Veed certainly knew how to play his field. "What men do you propose he leads?"

"You said half your troops already follow him," Veed said. "I figured you could split your force."

"So generous an assumption."

"Tactics, love. You don't have to accept my offer, if you don't consider it fair."

Nessix could live without the necklace, but her troops and her people needed food and money to survive. "So, what is this? A test of my pride?"

"Your pride!" Veed snorted. "What about mine? You think it makes me feel more like a man to ask you for help?"

"You're asking for Sagewind, not me."

"Ah, but I can only get him through you."

So, Veed intended to use her as a buffer. Nes already felt insufficient with her place in this war. Veed possessed age and experience, and Mathias had the knowledge and skill. While the men won the battles, the role of diplomat fell on Nessix. No matter how degrading this was, she needed Veed's funding to keep her army functioning.

"I already told you I haven't been able to control what he does," she tried.

"For the sake of your people, you'd better find a way."

Nessix lowered her gaze, allowing only a fleeting glance at the other two pendants. "And if he won't comply?"

"Then I cannot pay you."

She puffed out a breath, figuring as much. Mathias hated Veed, and Nessix knew it would take a small miracle to get him to agree to work alongside him. Surely, her charitable Sir Sagewind considered helping the people more important than his own comfort.

"Why the silence, Nes? Don't tell me you're sweet on the fool?"

Nessix blinked at the accusation. "Even if I was, it would be none of your business." She took a moment under Veed's persistent air to sort her thoughts back in order. "As far as your terms go, I'll see what I can do."

He flashed a smile. "I thought you might."

Nessix glowered at Veed, resenting how he treated this as a

game, something else to hold over her to continue calling himself a man. "If that's all you've got to discuss, you can see your own way out."

Veed stood and meandered behind Nessix. She shuddered as a hand brushed the hair from the back of her neck, his fingers tracing vulnerable skin. "I thought you might want a drink after this," he murmured, unfastening the clasp of the sapphire to drape it around her neck. "Maybe loosen up a bit?"

Nessix stood rigidly as Veed secured the bauble and repelled from him as soon its weight fell against her collarbones. "I thought you needed your answer as soon as possible?"

Veed's grin faded. "I could always retract my offer."

"And I could just as easily keep my paladin to myself."

Veed tightened his lips in a dissatisfied frown and dropped the remaining pendant back in its pouch. "I don't like forcing things on you. Sir Sagewind seems to have a decent amount of affection for you, but if you're adamant I take the request to him myself, I will. Where's he at?" Veed turned on a heel and strode to the door.

"Veed, stop!" Nessix shot after him as he plowed into the hall, and flung the door shut behind her. "You wouldn't dare bring this up in public!"

"I don't see why it has you so bothered," he taunted over his shoulder. "You said he's already spread his influence."

Nes's desperate pleas chased Veed as he explored the fortress, three steps out of her reach.

* * * * *

"Sir Sagewind, where *are* you?"

A hushed, tense reprimand followed Veed's sarcastic call, cueing Mathias to leave the remaining patients to his students and rescue Nessix from the wretched man's intentions. He stepped out of the mess hall to greet his unwelcome opponent.

"No need to shout," Mathias said. "You could've asked anyone where I was and I'm sure they'd have told you."

Veed grinned and shoved past Nes's frantic efforts to stop

161

him. "That's funny. I asked Nes that exact question, and this is what I got."

Even as Veed spoke, Nessix darted in front of him, pressing one hand against his chest and waving the other in Mathias's direction to try to shoo him away. Now that Veed had located his mark, he stopped and let Nessix pretend such efforts could possibly make a difference. There were times when Nes's reactivity amused Mathias, but Veed's presence barred such thoughts. Clearly, she didn't want the two to interact, but the fastest way for Mathias to relieve her was to tend to whatever Veed wanted.

"Nessix was sleeping off yesterday's worries," Mathias said. "You can't fault her for not knowing."

Veed glanced at Nes's pleading eyes as her attention darted between the men. "Either way, she's got something to discuss with you and needed some motivation to get it out."

"Oh?"

Mathias walked closer to the pair and the arm Nes reached toward him fell to her side. Her mouth sagged and the huffs of her breath reinforced how badly she wanted to be someplace else. Mathias smiled his reassurance at her and looked to Veed.

"I take it you had nothing to do with such matters?" Mathias asked.

Aggressive shouts and the clatter of metal against stone interrupted the confrontation before Veed's wit had the chance to loan him a smart response. Losing his limited interest in what Veed had to say, Mathias turned his attention toward the sound. In seconds, a cluster of soldiers backed their direction, tension dictating their steps. The swish of thick velvet robes whispered from within the crowd, offset by an uncertain stumbling.

"Move aside, if you don't want trouble," a woman's absent voice cooed from the mass.

Grudgingly, the soldiers shifted away to reveal a young fleman woman tripping blankly alongside a sallow demon. His right arm draped across the woman's shoulders, his fingertips buried in the bloodied mass of her hair. He scanned the trio of officers ahead of him with hollow eye sockets. A grin of chiseled fangs pulled his skin tight across intricately scarred cheekbones.

Nessix's aggravation left in an instant. She threw her shoulders back and leaned closer to Veed. "Sagewind...?" Her voice quivered. "What did it do to her?"

The demon stopped his approach two paces from them, the collection of tiny bones and bejeweled trinkets secured to his belt chiming a vacant melody. His lips curled higher. The woman's head bobbed as she stumbled to a halt beside him. His sightless face studied the three of them in methodical turn and he drew a deep breath through flaring nostrils. Cocking his head, he pursed his lips smugly.

"How else do you expect me to talk to you, Nessix?" The demon's mouth whispered as the woman spoke his request.

Nes's cheeks chilled at the empty voice as she stared at the blood dripping from the heel of the demon's palm. Mathias rested a calm hand on his sword and cleared his throat. This was not the sort of situation he wanted to let Nessix sort out on her own.

"It's unusual for your kind to risk coming to the surface," Mathias growled.

"For the occasion of greeting our dear Mathias Sagewind, we made an exception."

Mathias frowned at the sound of his name hissed in demonic dialect.

"Sagewind, what's going on?" Nessix murmured.

"This demon's an oraku." Mathias kept his gaze focused on the fiend. "He's one of the few demons capable of independent magic and is using this woman to translate his message."

The demon hunched forward and drummed the air in front of Nes's face with palm-length, conical claws. "Though you seem like much more fun."

Mathias stepped deliberately in front of Nessix to block the demon's access, reinforcing her instinct to tuck herself behind Veed. With a direct threat now spoken, Mathias freed his sword and brandished it as a fair warning. "You must be smarter than to think I'll let you touch her."

"I wasn't asking your permission."

Veed reached for his sword, but only freed it halfway before Mathias motioned for him to stop. Displeasure rumbled in Veed's throat, but he slammed his weapon back in light of Mathias's educated lead. The paladin's lack of trust in Veed was beat out by his wariness of this magic-flinging demon, and he kept his back to the more mortal of his opponents. Etha's blessing ensured Mathias would survive anything this demon had planned, but these seldom-seen hell-dwellers and their gigantic overlords—the inoga—were notorious trouble makers.

"You've made your scene, now get to the point. What do you want with the flemans?"

Haunting laughter gargled from the demon, the eerie sound emphasized by his puppet's lost accompaniment. "The flemans? We don't want them at all. If they'd lay down like good dogs, we'd be willing to let them live, at least in the broad sense of the word."

Mathias frowned. "So you're after Elidae?"

"We will take Elidae when this is over, yes. But our objective is you."

That frown turned into a grimace. So much for his claims that he had nothing to do with the demons' presence. "Save your effort. The past has proven you can't take me."

"You're right. We can't. But you can be made to suffer."

Mathias's eyes darkened.

"And you *will* suffer."

Veed spat, having heard all he needed. "Is there any saving this woman?"

Still processing the oraku's message, Mathias shook his head. Veed needed no other motivation. He grabbed Nessix by the arm and flung her in front of him. The demon's mouth snapped shut around his words and broke into a toothy grin at Nes's startled shriek. Bony fingers fanned from his outstretched hand. Nessix didn't have the chance to catch herself, and Mathias sprang to whip her back by the shoulder. With his distraction a success, Veed stepped forward and severed the demon's free arm from its body. The creature wailed, his howl echoing off the walls. Seconds later, Veed silenced him by decapitation. Both the demon and the woman he'd preyed upon collapsed to the floor.

Mathias spared a glance at Nes as she crouched nearby, somehow in possession of one of his daggers. He sheathed his sword and spun on Veed. "What in Etha's name did you do that for?"

Veed tossed a smirk at Nes's wild eyes, blinked, and brought his attention back to Mathias. "Why are *you* objecting?"

"He was giving us information!"

"He told me everything I needed to know." Veed returned his sword and pulled out the last pouch. He strode past Mathias with no reservations and pressed the bag into Nes's open hand. "Don't let me be disappointed."

Her hand trembled beneath the weight of the pouch, and Veed sauntered down the hall, whistling to himself.

Mathias stared after Veed until the other man turned the corner, at which point he faced Nessix. Eyes wide and locked on the atrocity strewn in a heap before her, Nessix barely kept a grip on the bag in her hand. Her shock debilitated her, and Mathias stepped across her line of sight. Clearing his throat prompted Nes's startled gaze to flick up to his.

"Are you alright?" Mathias asked.

In truth, she wasn't, and until the unlikely time that demons seemed normal to her, she was confident it would stay that way. Regardless, Nessix nodded mutely.

Mathias sighed. "Can you tell me what Veed was talking about?"

Giving Nessix a problem brought her closer to the present. She frowned and pointed at the dismantled demon. "Is that thing actually dead?"

"Yes."

She nodded slowly, now able to turn her back to the creature. "Then come with me."

Mathias followed Nessix down the hall, abandoning the bodies against his better judgment. She led him to the war chamber, and after she poked her head inside to check it was empty, gestured Mathias in. Closing the door, she pushed against it twice to ensure it was soundly shut and kept her back to him.

"Veed's... developed an obsession with you."

This conversation launched in a most unsatisfactory direction. "What does he want?"

Nessix turned and stared hard at Mathias, squinting in an effort to gauge his possible reaction. Her shoulders drooped. "He thinks because of our work together I'm keeping important things from him. I know you don't like him. I've hated him for some time now, really, but he's not that bad if you try not to think about what he does."

"That doesn't answer my question."

Nessix pursed her lips. The concept of losing her men and influence terrified her, but she trusted Mathias to take care of whoever came under his power. "He proposed a three-pronged attack. He'd lead his troops and you and I—" Her sigh didn't buy her adequate time to feel clean saying this. "We'd split mine. He wants disposal of your services and your knowledge of the demons."

"I've already assured him I'll tell everyone what they need to know, when they need to know it. If he's on the field with me and will actually listen to my instructions, he'll learn. If not, I can't do anything for him."

Nessix twisted her mouth and shot a glance at the ground. "We need you to take a higher station," she blurted before pride stopped her.

A short laugh burst from Mathias, which he instantly regretted when a shamed flush flawed Nes's cheeks. "I share what I know and lead who needs guidance. Wearing a fancy title won't change that."

"I can't explain it," Nessix said, more to reassure herself than Mathias. "Veed says it's tactics. The damnedest ones I've ever heard, but I have to believe him."

Part of Mathias, while elated by Nes's relaxation of power, was dismayed. Her weary eyes and slumped posture plainly stated where she stood. "Maybe you should get some more rest before something else you don't want to say slips."

"Sagewind…" Her eyes met his, her soul reflected in them. "The people need food and the troops have to be paid."

Mathias shifted, uncertain how to best respond to her plea. If he doubted his aversion to Veed before, the manner which the vile man sought to abuse Nes's good will now solidified his opinion.

"I can't help my people much longer," Nessix murmured. "And I—" She paused, shoulders hunching closer. "I can't trust anyone else getting involved like this."

"He's offering you scraps in exchange for me operating outside of your power."

Nessix covered her mouth with curled fingers and looked away from Mathias. "Scraps are better than what I can afford."

"I was never yours to control."

Her head snapped up and she pinched her lower lip. "Sagewind, please—"

Mathias held up a hand to silence her desperation. He scolded himself for his prior assumption that Nes was nothing more than a spoiled child. "Pride won't fill the bellies of your people or compensate for the tolls of war. If you need funding and having me take station is the only way to secure it, I will accept."

Nessix released her reserved breath and her eyes drifted shut in relief. In this moment, duty let her look past the shame of recognizing Mathias as her equal. She hefted the pouch in her hand. "As long as you're in, I have something for you."

Mathias smiled. "Nessix, there's no need to bribe me."

She shook her head. "I might not, but Veed felt he did."

"I have patients to care for that are more important than any gift he might want to give me." Mathias moved to leave, but Nes's hand caught his.

Frantic to keep Mathias from turning down Veed's subtle gesture, Nessix fumbled with her free hand to pull the pendant out. "See? It's his idea of a peace offering."

Even as a poor apprentice, Mathias had never understood the appeal of such trinkets. Each facet met perfection and the stone shone with brilliant clarity, but it certainly didn't make him tremble with the awe Nes seemed to expect from him. This explained the sapphire draped around Nes's neck, and Mathias internalized a groan as he vaguely recalled Veed wearing a similar piece. Mathias frowned at the thought of gilding himself with such an absurd adornment.

"It's nice," he said.

Nes knew Mathias boasted of his humility, but his disinterest agitated her. "You have to accept it."

Mathias measured Nes's expectations against his own discretion before pulling his hand free from her grasp to take the chain. Patiently, he extended his other hand for the pouch.

"And wear it!" Nessix tossed the bag over her shoulder.

"I most certainly will not."

Her content eyes brimmed with dismay. "You must. It was Veed's offering and turning it down is a direct offense to his honor."

"Etha forbid I offend the man!" Mathias snorted.

Nes's eyes narrowed in the first whispers of anger. "I thought you had a better political mind than that."

"It's a heavy and useless decoration."

"Your petty distaste for nice things and your hatred of Veed are strong enough to put my people in danger?"

Nessix had caught Mathias in a delicate impasse, her sharp thoughts calculating in step with his. Somewhere in these past few weeks, Nessix had learned how to manipulate him, and that unnerved the paladin.

You are afraid of this little girl? Etha teased.

Mathias's frown set deeper across his face. *You're taking her side now?*

Come now, Mathias! It's just a necklace.

He grumbled his dissatisfaction. "Fine. I'll keep it on my person."

Nessix glowed, all anger and willfulness wiped free from her face. With a brilliant grin, she caught herself just short of embracing Mathias. Instead, she straightened with an approving nod as she continued to beam.

"I'll let you get back to your patients, then. We can discuss tactics after dinner."

Mathias heaved another, much more exhausted sigh. "As you wish, Nessix."

Grasping the massive sapphire hanging against her chest, Nessix allowed Mathias to usher her from the room. His eyes swept over the pendant in his hand and he grudgingly secured it to his belt.

TWELVE

Days passed and the army remained ignorant to Mathias's promotion. Broadcasting his new position would only dishearten Nessix, and he felt her decision lacked appropriate consideration to begin with. His job remained the same as before he slapped on a title, but the longer Nessix thought about the arrangement, the worse she felt.

Veed had cornered Nessix to make the pitch to Mathias and while the bulk of her agreed with the action, it left her chest hollow. Letting Mathias take charge unburdened her from responsibilities she considered unpleasant, but losing her troops to him was a substantial price. After pairing these notions with her vivid recollection of Sarlot's fate, Nessix detached herself from the public eye to sort out her personal apprehensions.

A courteous cough from the far end of the hall cued Nes to compose herself. She tried a smile, but the effort disappointed her.

"The latest round of caravans have returned," Brant said. "Word of Sarlot leaked out to the remaining townships and the guards have sent for permission to escort the people here."

"I'd prefer to move them quicker than they can march."

"It'll take at least two more cycles for the caravans to finish the evacuation. People in fear may travel faster on their own."

Brant raised a good point. The demons had permitted their

movement so far, but that left the flemans overdue for another attack. "Has Sagewind given us any more warnings?" Nessix followed as Brant continued walking.

He shrugged. "He's been in the dungeon, entertaining the townsfolk with stories and promising them things we can't give them." Brant glanced at Nessix. "There's something you haven't told me."

A flush swept across Nes's cheeks and she didn't bother denying her cousin's suspicions. "It's something you don't need to worry about."

Brant laughed. "I'm hurt, Nes. What's on your mind?"

Her guilt persisted past his cheerful tone. "Sagewind—" Nessix cut her words short, dreading the reaction she expected from Brant. "By Veed's orders," she clarified. It didn't matter how upset Brant got with Veed. "Sagewind now outranks you."

"Funny, Nes."

"No, it's not." Her heart raced with the confession. "Can we let it drop?"

Brant snorted. "Let it drop? We've never known a ruler—not a good one—outside of your lineage. This affects the entire kingdom. What could Veed have possibly bribed you with to do something so stupid?"

A reluctant hand pawed the pendant from its hiding place beneath her shirt and Nessix let it fall against her breast. "Food for those we're housing and money to pay those in our employ," she added. "You know I couldn't pass that up."

Brant glanced at Nessix as she continued to plod along, chin nestled against her collarbones and eyes fixed on the floor. "I'll support you in anything, you know that, but that doesn't mean I have to like it."

"You think I do?" she mumbled. A friendly smile concealed Nes's inner dread as they rounded the last corner to face the bulk of her kingdom. "Care to boost some morale with me?"

Brant heaved a sigh and nodded.

Well within the assembly, Mathias stood deep in conversation with a handful of rescued villagers and Nes was soon occupied with similar concerns. Brant turned his eyes to the soldiers who moved stiffly through the crowded expanse, and left to discuss current affairs with those he felt needed it most.

A pair of refugees inched up to Nessix, both her seniors, but reluctant to speak. Scuffling feet and fidgeting hands gained her attention. Oblivious to the size of her curious audience, Nessix snuck an envious glance at Mathias as he patiently tended to the anxious civilians. Consolation came so easily to him.

"Is something on your mind?" she asked, the greatest extent of her amiability charming its way through.

A third man stepped up beside his timid friends, and bowed his head in respect. "If you have a moment, General."

Nes smiled. "My time's not spent better anywhere else."

She braced herself for any number of concerns. With her own frightful view of demons, she couldn't imagine how terrifying they seemed to those not trained in manners of defense. The dreadful beasts destroyed Sarlot, Elidae's oldest township. Urgent evacuations drove fretting women and wailing children from their homes to take shelter in a dungeon. Nessix understood if they were afraid and could not fault them for it.

"We want to help." Spoken softly, the words almost drowned in the dungeon's racket.

"We're well equipped," Nessix said. "There's not much we need from you, save try and find some sort of peace."

The first shook his head, rebellious eyes begging. "The land belongs to us, too, General."

Nessix rubbed the back of her neck. Under normal circumstances, she'd allow herself a good chuckle and move on, but their sincerity kept her in place. "We're all strong in our own ways. You keep the kingdom running with your trades and let the army protect it with its strength."

"We're strong enough to plow the fields." This came from well within the crowd.

"And forge your weapons and armor!"

The sudden shouts caught Mathias's attention and he turned to observe Nes's reaction.

"I never called you weak," she said, "but I doubt any of you have ever killed a man or had one of your own take his last breath

171

while looking to you for help." Her modest audience shifted restlessly. "You have strength, but it's different from a soldier's. Now please, go back to your families and comfort them. You are safe in these walls."

"What happened in Sarlot will happen again. We want to stop it!"

"The general gave her orders," the nearest soldier grumbled in passing.

It hurt Nessix to dash the hopes of these men. Every fleman alive shared the blood of fighters, but peaceful times had softened the civilians. Beyond lacking the weapons and armor to fit them with, Nessix refused to endanger those she so desperately sought to protect. Her troops accepted the risk of brutal death in battle, but her civilians hadn't. Sarlot's devastation taught her that much.

As Nessix floundered, Mathias dismissed himself from his engagement to offer his insight. "It may not be a bad idea to train the peasants for war," he suggested quietly.

Nessix sucked in a deep breath and turned her stiff attention to him. "They would be cut to ribbons," she murmured through clenched teeth. "We don't have enough time to train the military, much less the peasants. Do not encourage them, Sagewind."

He could have listened, but figured this an opportune moment to abuse his new title and override her order. "We can train the soldiers, and those responsible for the townships can pass along their knowledge."

"They've never even wielded swords!"

"That's why we'll *teach* them."

"We've already seen the basics don't work on demons."

"The more people who know how to fight, the better."

Several nearby soldiers pegged Mathias with chilly looks, but the townsfolk beamed at their savior's support. Nessix scowled at Mathias's attempt to take charge over this precarious situation. Regardless of the rank Mathias held, the people belonged to her. Determined to keep the atmosphere as calm as possible, she snagged his forearm in a firm grasp.

"Excuse us," Nessix said, with what she hoped passed for an apologetic smile. She dragged Mathias to the stairwell and shoved him free. "It's hard enough to be responsible for the lives of my troops. How am I supposed to keep thousands of townsfolk safe on the field?"

Mathias meandered to the landing and rolled over his options. "If you don't feel qualified or able to watch over them, let me do it. They can be my force, and you can keep your soldiers."

"Haven't you taken enough loyalties from me?"

"This has nothing to do with loyalty," Mathias corrected. "This is for your people. Would you rather they hide in their storehouses to get burned alive or cut down as they fled?"

Nessix grumbled out her evaporating patience. "That's why they're *here*, to stay away from danger. The walls of this fortress will not be broken. Even if we did go under siege, there are deeper levels to hide in than the dungeon."

"I'm aware of that."

"They're in the safest place on the entire island, and you have no business arguing with me about it."

Mathias chuckled and shook his head at Nes's simplicity. "These people must be trained for war, if not to satisfy their desires, then to fill the growing gaps in your ranks. I can save a lot of the wounded, but we'll still lose soldiers to battle."

Nessix crossed her arms and glowered at the wall. "You don't need to remind me."

"So, we need the manpower."

"Veed's generosity will only stretch so far. Where will the funds to employ them come from?"

"I'll manage their compensation," Mathias said. "All you need to worry about is providing the rations and shelter they've already been promised."

Nessix shook her head, eyes setting more stubbornly beneath rigid brows. "These people have no idea about the hardships of war."

"You owe it to them to let them learn. The demons outnumber us in ways you cannot begin to imagine. Innocents have already died and they will continue to do so. Give them the knowledge so they can fight back."

He made a point Nessix understood, but the commoners had

simply become too soft. "We don't have the armor to protect them or the weapons to train them with." Perhaps she could thwart Mathias's goal with practicality.

"We most certainly do."

She looked up at him, put off by his plotting grin. "Mind telling me where?"

"In the catacombs beneath your fortress."

"We will not resort to robbing the graves of my ancestors!"

Mathias rolled his eyes. "Of course we won't. Now, come with me." He didn't wait for Nes's rebuttal as he set course down the stairs.

"Those are sacred halls!" Nessix scolded as Mathias continued his departure without her. "I will not allow you to desecrate my ancestors' resting place!"

"If you're so worried about my behavior, stop me," Mathias called back.

His silhouette shrank away as he descended, leaving Nessix too flustered to reply. How dare he so casually explore such a sacred place on his own! A thickening lump beneath her ribcage reminded Nes why she never ventured into the catacombs, but she was compelled to stop Mathias.

Growling at her foolishness, Nessix popped her way down the stairs to catch up to Mathias as he marched deeper into the ancient darkness. He smiled at her compliance until it became obvious she no longer followed him. Puzzled, Mathias turned back to face her.

"Is something wrong?"

Nessix hardly kept a visual on Mathias through the dimness, so sufficed for staring toward the sound of his voice. "I haven't been down here since I was a child."

Mathias thanked Etha for the poor lighting that hid his smirk at Nes's apprehension. Shrugging off her reluctance, Mathias resumed walking. Nessix stood fast, bringing him to stop once more. Was she afraid of the dark? As ridiculous as that seemed, Mathias ran his hand along the wall and located the nearest torch. His brows furrowed when the first sweep of his hand did nothing, but the second deposited a dancing flame and he removed the torch from the wall.

"Are you coming or not?" Mathias hadn't expected to see so much fear in Nes's eyes as the fire threw light against her elegant cheekbones.

A balmy hand pressed against the wall to steady her. "If I ask you something, will you promise not to laugh?"

This new dimension of Nessix delighted Mathias. "What is it?"

"When you came here…" She stopped and shook her head in frustration. "It's not important." Taking a deep breath, Nessix willed herself to the paladin's side and pretended none of this bothered her. Instinctively, she held her hand at her hip, ready to grab the sword she'd left in her room.

Mathias rolled his lips between his teeth to fend off his smile. "What? Are you scared?" Her innocent determination was quite endearing.

Nessix allowed her sullen eyes to convey whatever Mathias chose to make of them.

"I see." Saving her embarrassment by not digging deeper, Mathias proceeded down the corridor, taking the comfort of the torchlight with him.

The amusement in his expression exposed Nes's competitive side. Let him think her afraid; she'd come too far to run now. With her only light source actively moving away, Nessix hurried along to trail at Mathias's heels.

"Who gave you clearance to come down here in the first place?" she asked, hoping to reclaim authority over them both.

"No one. I came on my own."

"Did you find what you were looking for?"

"I found those I came to talk to."

Nessix's heels dug into the ground and she grabbed Mathias's bicep to make him do the same. The sudden stop nearly jarred the torch from his grasp. "We don't need to be down here." Nes's nails burrowed through his shirt and into his muscle as she attempted to drag him back.

Mathias wrinkled his nose at the pierce of her grip, but she held him fast. "Yes, we do." He drove his weight ahead and hauled her along.

Nessix struggled against his persistence, lowering her center of gravity to slow him. "No!"

"Now you're being obnoxious," Mathias muttered. "What has you so scared?"

"I told you it's not important!"

"If you won't come on your own, I *will* carry you."

Regressing back to the time when it only took a pout to get her way, Nessix shook her head. Memories leapt to life of heavy stone doors slamming shut and Brant's mischievous laughter taunting her terrified screams from the other side. She swallowed hard, wondering what had inspired her to ever forgive her cousin.

"Will you…" Gritting her teeth, Nessix sputtered a breath and looked away. "Great Inwan, Sagewind, make them stay asleep!"

Mathias's laughter pelted Nes's frazzled resolve. Things made sense now, but he tactfully avoided telling Nessix that to accomplish his goal, she had to face her fears. "Come on," he repeated.

Nessix shook her head stubbornly. "Not until you promise."

The words danced on Mathias's tongue to gain her compliance, but he'd already told her enough lies. "I promise nothing down here will touch you or bring you harm." That sounded more than reasonable to him.

Nessix trusted Mathias on the battlefield. She trusted him with her men. Her silly fear of ghosts? She barely even trusted that to Brant. Admitting as much to Mathias was out of the question, but she believed if anyone on Elidae could protect her from the apparitions of the long dead, it was Mathias. With a dubious nod, Nessix stepped forward. Mathias smiled at her resignation, though his brows met each other when he realized how closely she crept behind him. He never imagined something so trivial would terrify her so much.

They descended two levels, deeper into the catacombs than most people knew about. Nessix fixated on maintaining a steady breath, and Mathias bottled his amusement to her reaction. The hallway opened abruptly to a large chamber. Mathias allowed Nes to stop and gather her bearings as he entered and fed torches on either side of the entryway.

Intricate sarcophagi lined the walls, held four high by massive granite lofting. Ages of dust carpeted the stone floor and attempted to fill in the detail engraved in the abundant tombs. Directly across from where they stood, darkness loomed from a hall one hundred paces away. Between the two passageways, centered alone, rested three sarcophagi etched in silver, gold, and an unidentified metal that glittered red in the torchlight. The silence pounded against Nes's head, and she nearly choked on the musty air.

"You're not going to…" The absurdity of Nes's question snuffed her voice.

"Going to what?" Mathias held out his free hand to coax her closer. "This is the first hall of warriors. You'll—"

"I know what it is!" Nes snapped.

One of her favorite tales was of General Gathlin Teradhel, the second of Elidae's born guardians, and how he led the flemans to exterminate the savage creatures now believed extinct on the island. His commanders now flanked him in death. The rest of the room housed his elite guard, and the volume of bodies surrounding her quickly jolted Nes from daydreams of the past.

"I know where we are," she repeated. "That doesn't mean I want to be here."

"You're being ridiculous." Mathias grasped her wrist when she failed to take his hand.

She grudgingly surrendered to his influence and let him pull her forward. "They're all staying closed?"

Mathias twisted his mouth in brief consideration before answering. "All will stay closed." He hoped everything in this room heard him. "I promise."

Nodding, Nessix managed a bold step ahead before her eyes flew open and she took three more back. "And no one's already out?"

"Everyone's bodies are where they've been resting all these years." Mathias held out his hand again, smiling as Nessix gingerly took it and stepped up beside him.

He led Nessix forward, half the distance to the three central sarcophagi. Her confidence rebounded with each step and Mathias pried her fingers from his to hand her the torch.

"Nothing scary, see?"

I'm amazed by her lack of words, Etha said.

Mathias smiled and wandered from Nes to study some of the tombs along the wall. *She'll have plenty to say soon enough, don't worry.*

Nes's throat constricted when Mathias stepped away. "What are you looking for?" She drifted closer to him, the torch quivering in her hand.

"I'll tell you when I find it," he said absently. "Try to calm down. I think once you see how peaceful it is, you'll quit being so afraid."

"Who says I'm af—"

Nes's startled gasp cut off her retort as Mathias disappeared in a flash of light. Eyes darting around, she caught a glimpse of him passing into the hallway that led upstairs. Nessix dashed after him, abruptly halted when the doors fell shut in front of her. Her heart pummeled her ribcage and launched up her throat. She clasped the door handle with a sweaty palm and flung her weight against it.

"Sagewind!" she screamed, chest heaving. "This isn't funny!"

Cheeks tingling from hyperventilation, Nessix waited frantically for Mathias to answer, even with mocking laughter. Seconds passed in silence and Nessix spun to slam her back against the doors in an attempt to limit her vulnerability. Her gaze swept the chamber, watching each sarcophagus carefully. Forcing her dry throat to choke a swallow, Nessix pushed herself from the doors and crept to the column of coffins on her right. She deliberated each step and hesitated an arm's reach from the great stone cases. Clamping her jaw and annoyed by the dampness glazing her skin, she took one last step and faced them.

Nessix couldn't speculate on Mathias's reason for leaving, but she realized it wasn't nearly as scary as she remembered. Her gaze turned to the central fixtures and the final elements of fear thrashed about wildly before she extinguished them from respect of the moment. Pleased with her personal victory, Nessix took a deep breath and moved forward.

Only a few inches of stone separated her from her ancestors. Each sarcophagus bore its soldier's family crest centrally, embellished by elaborate trimmings. Timid fingers reached out to trace the crest—the profile of a noble horse's head—on the middle case. She grew up honoring that image, almost identical to the one she bore, herself.

Fear crammed where it belonged, it humbled Nessix to be surrounded by such greatness, even if they were dead. A smile tugged at her lips as she hummed an old bard's song and felt herself easing into history.

"General Gathlin led one-thousand men against a ten-fold army of gilum." The words trickled from her throat almost too softly to carry the tune. "Determined to cleanse our blessed land from the wrongdoings of their spite."

Merriment snuck up on her with the song of her childhood hero. To think, the proud General Nessix singing such legends to this audience! With a grin, the next verse rang out like it would from a rowdy tavern. No one was there to hear her, so she gladly let herself look foolish.

"His brilliant tactics could ne'er be stopped and the troops had nothing to fear! For General Gathlin had a pure soul—" Nessix straightened abruptly, all glee snatched from her. Someone was watching her. "Sagewind?" she piped, too unnerved to move.

"It's such a wonderful tale, please don't stop on account of me."

Wide eyed and pale, Nessix lost her ability to speak. The voice came from nowhere in particular and held wisdom that embraced the hollowness of the chamber. Her song continued its jaunty melody without her, the words rebounding off the walls. The torch fell from Nes's grasp as she rushed back to the doors, desperately running her hands across the seams.

"Sagewind!" she screamed. "You promised!"

The song filled the room, lifted by hundreds of voices as Nessix's hands fell helplessly to her sides. Mathias had held true to his word, she realized; the bodies had stayed in their graves. That meant, however, this strange company wasn't even tangible. Nessix inched close enough to grab the torch and threw her back against the closed doors.

Soldiers seeped from the far wall, dressed in armor they'd undoubtedly worn for centuries. The room seemed to shrink as more specters appeared, each individual vividly real. A handful

179

sported fatal wounds, one even cradled his head in his arms, singing along with the rest. The apparitions glimmered an eerie blue, their faces holding youth to defy empty, ancient eyes. Fearing magic almost as much as she feared the long-dead, Nes caved to a pathetic whimper.

"Be calm, daughter of war," the voice boomed. With it, the soldiers ceased their singing.

Nessix scoured her field of vision wildly, unable to decide which member the command came from. "Then go away."

The laugh that answered her ineffectual order melded power and kindness. In the racing heartbeats that followed, General Gathlin appeared, sitting on the foot of his sarcophagus.

Nes's objections grew to a full-fledged scream and many of the spirits flinched at her shrill tone. Their pain went unnoticed as Nes's eyes locked on the ancient hero. "Sagewind, you promised!" she shrieked. "*Promised!*"

"Be calm," Gathlin repeated, rising to feet that hovered a hand from the ground.

"Then go back in there." Nessix jerked her head at his sarcophagus.

"I cannot choose to go back. You summoned me."

"If I summoned you, then how do I get rid of you?" she challenged. "Inwan, I'm the general! I *order* you back!"

"I've held the same title."

"How dare you—"

Gathlin stomped three steps closer and promptly ended Nes's debate. "We are aware of your people and their plight," he said. "And to protect our home, we must speak truths you need to hear."

Dreading another sermon, especially from her current instructor, Nessix reminded herself that Gathlin wasn't even alive. "I did my reading, Sagewind!" she shouted. "Just like Grandfather ordered. You're supposed to hate the undead!"

Gathlin observed her calmly. "The paladin will let us stay. He owes us this right."

"Well, he's going to owe me a whole lot more once I get out of here," she snapped.

Mathias didn't hold exclusive rights to disregarding Nes's

temper. "If we could return to this world and fight, we would. We suffer as our people suffer and would join you in your next battle if you'd allow it."

"Whatever," Nessix muttered. "Unless you can wield a sword, you're of no help to me."

Gathlin nodded once, accepting her vague approval. "We may be unable to wield our swords, but our people can."

His eyes condensed into deep sapphires and Nessix stood transfixed by the intelligence within them. Slowly, she took a step forward. Gathlin lowered his head in reassurance and swept a hand toward the dark opening on the far wall. Curiosity tugged at Nes, anxious to know the room's connection to this eerie conversation, but acutely aware of the phantom army standing in her way. Gathlin had made no attempts to harm her, and if the legends of his greatness were true, she thought it likely to stay that way. That said nothing, however, about the members of his ranks.

"I'm not moving until they're gone." She swung the torch in the direction of the spectral warriors.

Gathlin nodded and the others faded as quickly as they'd appeared. Nessix hadn't expected him to agree so readily, and shook with a new reluctance. If a single nod dismissed them, how easily could they return? Distant ties of blood insisted Nessix trust Gathlin, but his apparent power suggested she play it safe and humor him.

"What do you want from me?" Nessix asked at last.

He drifted the last few inches to the ground, his boots hitting the floor in silence. "We want nothing from you but victory. Invest more trust in Sir Sagewind."

"Trust him?" she snorted. "Trusting him is what got me down here in the first place. Am I supposed to prove it further by hiring peasants I can't afford to pay and following you deeper into this hellhole?"

"Do you know nothing of our heritage?" Gathlin asked, tactically divulging his sorrow.

A growl seeped from Nessix at the insult. "I listened to my father well. Everything I know, I learned from him. Do *not* place the blame on me and Inwan help you, you'd better not blame him."

The threat blew right past Gathlin. "Did he not teach you that we are all survivors?"

A strained chuckle left Nessix. "A lot's changed since you've been—" The proper title stuck to her tongue. "In power."

"I see."

Nessix delivered a firm nod. Her people needed her protection right now, not have her gallivanting through musty crypts with a ghost. She understood that the civilians Gathlin knew were full of vigor, but the ones she looked after sent cries for help over bandits and minotaur raids.

"That warrior blood remains in each of us," Gathlin continued, as if knowing exactly where Nes's internal debate led her. "Some may have been tamed, but it's in every vein on the island. Now, come with me." Turning from her, Gathlin glided toward the other room.

This sounded too much like Mathias's banter for Nes's comfort. The connection struck her quite a blow and she held fast. Was Mathias capable of creating this entire illusion?

"It was not a request, child," Gathlin scolded.

Nessix hadn't been on the receiving end of orders in years, and stared at the specter's back in shock. Eighteen generations spanned her and Gathlin. That calculation tried to conquer her calm until a more disturbing thought came to mind. Burying the dead was a modern custom. Gathlin was the third general, so where were the first two? Her eyes flicked to the darkness of the room before her.

"Nessix!" Gathlin barked.

Gulping down her misgivings, Nessix crept deeper into the chamber. She hesitated as she passed between sarcophagi and looked behind her to ensure nothing followed. Three more strides brought her beside the spirit of her ancestor. Gathlin continued as soon as Nessix caught up, and they moved the rest of the way across the chamber together.

Nessix stood before the darkness of the second room and glanced to the spirit for further instruction. He lowered his head and extended his arm into the expanse. Cursing everything Mathias stood for, Nessix took a deep breath and stepped forward.

The torch took its time illuminating the chamber and Nessix, having feared the worst, dropped her jaw. Deceptive with its small entryway, this room dwarfed the previous one. A great table sat in the center with an intricate map of Elidae etched on the surface. Bunks fit for the living lined the walls clear to the ceiling. Between each set stood weapon racks, stocked and yearning for use. Ample space and weaponry for thousands of men filled the room and Nessix could only gape in awe.

"Shields are stored beneath the bunks of the west wall," Gathlin told her. "Armor is below those on the north and east. It's nothing as fancy as yours, but all have been tested and stayed true."

Nes's anxious eyes soaked in the scene, even as her mind tugged at disbelief. "How long has this been down here?"

"The great war room." Gathlin's smile spoke of nostalgia. "In my time, every soldier had the chance to be involved in battle plans. General Litarious was afraid of a traitor in his ranks and put the practice to a halt. Your White Paladin was the first living man to come here for counsel in fourteen generations."

Nessix wandered farther into the chamber and pressed her hand into a mattress. Even at its age, it supported against her. Forces much more complex than time alone preserved this room. Perhaps a similar blessing imbued the objects within it. The slightest smile fluttered across Nes's lips.

"I understand General Litarious's decision to separate the troops from politics, but why was this buried with the dead?"

"The tunnels of the dead were once the halls of the living," Gathlin said. "But it gets to the point where all that's remembered of the dead are stories and songs. Portraits, if he's lucky."

This belonged to the dead, Gathlin had just told her that. "Are you suggesting we desecrate your resting place to accommodate people who don't even know how to hold a sword?"

"It's not desecration," he assured. "Those who once rested in these beds and carried these goods of war miss the rush of battle; they're more than happy to pass along what they can."

"What is that supposed to mean?"

"I've given you all I was meant to, and look forward to seeing you win the coming battle. Trust your paladin for the answers you cannot find on your own."

As Nessix watched, Gathlin's features melted into one another, his broad form the only remnant of this encounter. "But there's still so much to ask!"

"Tell those questions to your children so they can ask me when it is their time for a visit." Gathlin's sorrowful voice slipped in and out of existence. "Do not let us be forgotten again."

"General!" Nessix gasped, rushing toward his fading form.

She needed more time! Desperate, Nessix resumed singing the ballad of Gathlin, driving her voice hoarse from her effort. What spell protected this chamber? What did he know of Inwan in this lonely time? Of Laes? The spectral chorus harmonized with her, though none returned to sight. The sea of voices soared with a new hope against her frantic strains. Gathlin disappeared and Nessix ran two paces into the crypt chamber, holding the torch high in search of any trace of him.

"Did you learn—"

Nessix screamed and spun around, nearly smacking Mathias in the face with her torch. He flinched and glowered at her reactivity.

"What was I supposed to learn?" she groused, turning from him to shield her embarrassment.

Mathias shrugged and eased the torch from her hand. "I don't know. I only caught the end of it. He asked me to send you alone. Fleman business, I presume?"

She nodded mutely, realization dawning on her at his knowing smile. Mathias had fully anticipated this outcome.

"Anyway, it looks like you found what I wanted to show you." He walked ahead into the old war chamber.

Nessix followed, unusually pensive. "We have orders to put them to use."

Mathias grinned, glad the spirits of flemans past had convinced Nes to take the right action. "Shall we begin preparing the quarters for a peasant militia?"

Reality struck Nessix, ripping her from her mystification. "There's no time to train them."

"You said we had orders from the divine plane to put this to use?"

Nessix nodded, her eyes narrowed.

"Then the divine plane will provide us with what we need. I told you before, I'll train them myself if I must."

"You can't!" Nessix insisted. Her heart tore between Gathlin's wishes and her stubborn inclinations.

"I can do whatever I want. You and Veed made me a general, remember?"

"If all your time is spent in the classroom and training fields, how do you expect to fight for us?"

"I've been on every battlefield, and so have my students."

Nessix moved closer and glared at him. "You've been filling our minds with garbage and sorcery and I will not let you take over my kingdom."

Used to Nes's temperamental show and expecting nothing from it, Mathias patiently stood his ground. "I won't take your kingdom from you. I have no right to it."

Nessix never planned to admit it, but Mathias was right. She'd sworn an oath to protect those beneath her, but no one ever taught her where the lines between shielding and repression began.

"Your people look to you," Mathias said as acceptance settled across Nes's face. "They follow you, even my students. They are loyal to their heritage and that honor will always bind them to you. Be strong for them and they'll return the favor."

Nessix lowered her head. Putting up this front of courage and determination was exhausting, and she no longer wanted to argue with Mathias. She couldn't bring herself to apologize for her previous wrongdoings, but she was capable of changing her current course. "I will extend the offer to the civilians."

Mathias nodded. "You are ever wise, General."

He gestured to the room's exit and Nessix scooted her way out, throwing a final glance at Gathlin's tomb. If that had actually been him, the divine plane did still act on Elidae. Nessix took comfort in that backing, and suddenly, her perspective looked much more appealing.

THIRTEEN

The wealth of weapons and armor harbored in the catacombs surprised even En. Part of Mathias expected Nessix to go back on her intentions until she took it upon herself to address the anxious citizens. She admitted the strength that still flowed in her people and graciously accepted those who volunteered to take up service under Mathias's instruction. Once anxious wives and mothers quit fretting over the safety of their inspired loved ones, recruitment flowed smoothly. Pleased with the outcome, Mathias shouldered his end of the bargain and began his preparations in earnest.

It took the remainder of the day and a portion of the following morning to issue equipment to the new recruits. The rooms beneath the fortress, so recently occupied by the lonely dead, were cleaned to provide lodging for this budding branch of the army. Veteran soldiers assisting Mathias voiced their concerns over the integrity of the ancient armaments, but Mathias hushed their doubts for the benefit of the enthusiastic volunteers.

Training progressed slowly, but Mathias ensured everyone who wanted to fight received proper instruction. Nes's declaration of the people having grown soft through the years proved correct, and it took staunch persuasion to motivate these men to practice combat against each other. The armor fit mostly like hand-me-downs, but held through sparring matches. Days passed by, and the peasant militia began to integrate their sessions with the main force.

Mathias's only disappointment came from Etha's silence. It was unusual for her to make it even a couple hours without checking in on him, so the days of not hearing from her struck him as odd. Eager to assume it was due to her investigation of the divine realm, Mathias did his best to keep his prying mind from distracting her from such an imperative task. He busied himself supervising three captains with the peasants' drills, occasionally shifting his focus to where Nessix and Brant practiced mounted attacks. Cannons pounded in the distance, and Mathias stood. The cousins halted their games and turned to look south. Nessix dismissed Brant to the fortress and maintained her surveillance a bit longer.

"It's coming from Veed," Brant answered Mathias's concerned brows.

"Does he make a habit of random fire?"

"He can certainly afford it." Brant watched Logan turn and canter toward them. "But I doubt he'd waste the time to load the shots."

Mathias nodded. "I suppose we should move to defend—"

Bells tolled from Nes's towers, interrupting Mathias's thoughts.

"Demon army, from the east!"

The training field gushed with madness as peasants scurried in frightened confusion. Seasoned troops wove through the disorder to fall in line. Logan's stride lengthened as he brought Nessix back to assess the situation. Brant dashed off to the cavalry unit, leaving Mathias to locate Sulik on his own.

"We'll have to move quickly," Nessix said to Mathias. Grooms rushed from Logan's stall with his armor and Nessix leapt to the ground to assist. "It'll be a difficult fight with the sun in our eyes."

Mathias shook his head and furrowed his brows. "The sun doesn't set in the east."

Nes's face paled. "No, they're coming from the northwest." At Mathias's grimace, Nessix doubled her efforts of dressing Logan. "Have we sent word to Veed?"

There wasn't time for them to fret over the dark general's

predicament. "The cannon fire suggests he's having his own trouble. I want all but my first four companies to return under your command."

"Are you mad?"

"My force has come a long way these past few days. All I need are a few hundred men to act as guidance. If you have any cavalry to spare, I'd probably put them to good use."

Nessix's practiced fingers danced across the straps and buckles of Logan's defenses. "Sagewind, they've hardly learned to attack, how are they supposed to defend themselves?"

"I'll pray they figure it out," Mathias said. "Now, gather your men and head west. I have faith you can handle anything we've encountered so far." He wouldn't bring up the dangers that existed if she found any of the winged alar.

"And if I can't?"

"If you must lead a retreat, run east and we'll clean things up together. Whatever you do, do not return home."

Nessix accepted Mathias's instruction silently and turned to her nearest assistant. "Go tell En to gather those not fighting and barricade themselves as deep in the catacombs as possible." After the man hustled off, she turned to Mathias. "How far along have your clerics come?"

"I'll send a dozen with you." Mathias glowed to hear Nessix indirectly place value in them, though he prayed she wouldn't need their skills.

Nessix nodded as the cavalry poured from the stables. She swung astride Logan, barking out orders to the captains, and rode toward Brant.

* * * * *

"They don't seem to be slowing, sir."

Veed's dark eyes focused on the advancing mass. "We have enough traps before they can storm our keep," he reminded the captain.

As Veed spoke, pitch boiled in great cauldrons below the

second story windows. His men reluctantly followed the orders given to them, not at all caring for the idea of demons marching up to the gates. Built to complement Nes's fortress, Veed's stronghold served as a weapon of its own. Of course, once it revealed its secrets, defense of both buildings would be compromised, but Veed preferred his odds of thinning out the demon army through the halls over facing their oppressive numbers in the open.

Renigan approached his general's side. "Have you sent for reinforcements?" He loosened his sword. "Perhaps Nessix can aid us?"

They lofted about distantly, but Veed heard Nes's siege bells over his own urgent preparations. "I think she has her hands full," he murmured. "Pray we all survive."

* * * * *

Although he hated doing so, Ceraphlaks removed himself from the field to survey all three fronts, trusting Mathias to a sturdy, mortal warhorse. Mathias took care to distribute the trained soldiers under his command through the less experienced portion of his ranks, and at least one of his clerical students remained in each company. The demons in the east rushed in fast and forced Mathias's advance to an abrupt halt. With his chance to rally the men stolen, Mathias defaulted to what he knew best. *Etha, they're in your hands. Let us find victory today.*

"Brace yourselves!" Mathias's voice rasped against its force. Uncertain what response to expect from either side of the field, he spurred his mount forward, the hilt of his blade stretching into the shaft of a spear. In the last moment before impact, he wheeled the horse to a stop and swept his weapon across three demons. Two fell, the third scrambled to retreat.

Seconds later, Mathias realized he'd made the charge alone. He trained his focus on the weapons crashing toward him and groaned at the prospect of holding the army off on his own. Sulik's hoarse orders beat into the flemans' hearts, echoed back by the seasoned warriors. Digging the butt of his spear into an offending demon's eye, Mathias found relief as reinforcements swept around him.

His horse ran out of room to move within the mass, and if Mathias forced it to hold its ground, he risked crushing his allies when the demons inevitably took it down. He pounded his heel into the animal's side and pulled sharply on one rein. The horse spun wildly and plowed a landing for Mathias to dismount. As Mathias's feet hit the ground, the horse bolted away from the peril. Odds momentarily stacked against him, Mathias willed his weapon to its conventional form. A fevered chorus rang out behind him, jarring Mathias from lifetimes of battle sense as he turned to face the call.

His forces dove into the demon mass with a reckless intensity, wielding their weapons with instinctive effort. Their modest preparations had barely instilled basic hack and slash methods, but fluid attacks streamed from the peasants now, cutting down their opponents with ease.

Demons fell at a steady rate, but Mathias saw no end to them. His force encompassed nearly a dozen townships worth of makeshift soldiers, and that gave him enough men to rotate units for recovery purposes. Passing command to Sulik, Mathias withdrew from combat to assess the damages.

Most of the veterans remained in the thick of the action, but an unsettling pattern emerged among the peasants who retreated to the security of the back lines. Those still clutching their weapons fought to resume the battle, regardless of the severity of their wounds. If the same man's sword had been lost or spear broken, he huddled against the horror, begging to return to his family.

They aren't fighting with their own skill. Mathias hailed the nearest cleric. "Take a task force to the fortress and bring back all of the spare weapons from the catacombs you can carry. Go quickly!"

The cleric accepted the order without question and Mathias passed through the rows of the wounded. His prayers brought renewed strength to each patient, but with every fighter Mathias healed, he felt his strength drain rapidly. In wartime, his healing often came with a creeping exhaustion due to sheer volume, but now, his head swam and vision blurred with each imparted blessing. By the time Mathias had seen to the current cases, his legs ached and his heart strained from his efforts.

Ladling a mouthful of water, Mathias turned to look at the battle while he tried to recover from this unforeseen impairment. The rotations flowed smoothly and Sulik handled himself with the grace Mathias expected of a seasoned commander. Multiple demons fell for each fleman casualty, and the push gained momentum. Impatiently waiting to recoup his power, Mathias faced west.

Etha, guide Nessix with brilliance. Protect her where I can't.

His brows inched toward each other as he spotted smoke against the fading sunlight. Mathias had put Nessix in danger by letting her head off alone, and fire with demons seldom meant anything good. Grumbling at his current limitations, Mathias closed his eyes to seek out Nes's spirit, trying to feel if she needed help. His efforts hit a solid force of rejection, and he wondered if Nessix fought his mental intrusion consciously. Considering her current relationship with the spiritual realm, he thought it unlikely. Mathias made a second attempt, answered by a numbing wave of dizziness. He must have been too tired.

Mathias cast a final glimpse at the columns of smoke and prayed Nessix chose to set camp. Gloomy, he dragged himself back onto the field.

"I know it's a lot to ask, but I need you to heal what you can of the next group," Mathias told Sulik as he blinded a demon with a slash of his blade.

Sulik appraised Mathias's haggard condition. "You're pale, sir. I've been managing things nicely, if you need to rest."

A grim smile pressed across Mathias's face. "I'll be fine."

Mathias pushed on. Etha chose quite an inconvenient time to take her leave, but even without her active support, Mathias knew how to fight. As he hefted his sword to the ready, the demons called a retreat.

Trapped in a wild bloodlust, the bulk of the fleman force gave chase before the veterans screamed for a halt. At that, the inexperienced members regrouped, flinging taunts and curses against the demons' backs. A mile closer to the mountains, the fiends ceased their retreat and lit small fires.

"Looks like they're giving us rest," Sulik mused, stretching out his shoulders. "Unless you'd rather press an attack?"

Mathias stared ahead silently for long moments. Dead demons scattered the field. Yes, the flemans prospered today, but a haunting number of the beasts still lurked in the nearby mountains.

"No," Mathias said. "We've got to tend to our wounded. We'll try again in the morning."

"You're not afraid of them calling reinforcements?"

"There's a possibility for anything." Mathias sheathed his blade. "But my experience says it's unlikely. The demon armies might fight for one cause, but don't usually work well together. Go see to our patients, I've got some of my own work to do."

Sulik noted the atypical exhaustion that streaked across Mathias's forehead and flushed his cheeks. He saw the extinguished embers in his eyes and the absence of any sort of confidence in his smile. The commander longed to press the matter, but trusted Mathias to bring up anything pertinent to the battle's outcome in good time. Uncomfortable, Sulik nodded and departed to carry out his duty.

* * * * *

The closest items to bedding carried by anyone in Nes's force consisted of cloaks and capes, if anything at all. Unprepared to treat this battle as a campaign, she refrained from sending a unit the five miles back to the fortress for items as frivolous as camp supplies. Complaints indirectly filtered their way to her, but the army accepted the orders to her face. They'd roughed worse conditions and needed to obey their general now as much as ever. Nessix instructed campfires spread, but the unit to remain compacted, and insisted they catch their rest fully clad in their armor.

"Not your most popular tactic," Brant murmured.

Logan shifted his weight, rudely bumping the commander with his hip. Brant shuffled a step to maintain his balance and glowered at the horse.

Nes's heart hammered with worries of everything that could go wrong, but she stood behind her plan. "Unless the demons beat us to the draw, this will go smoothly. It has to."

"But what if they do? You still haven't told anyone what's on your mind."

"I want to try to peel them apart and attack from three sides instead of one. We have the Leilan River to the west and the mountains to our north. Sagewind is somewhere in the east, which leaves the enemy only one way to push."

Brant scoffed at Nes's impulse. "You want to shove troops into the middle of that? They'll devour us!"

Nessix twisted her mouth with the uncertainty she refused to elaborate on. Gathlin had promised her some sort of support, but she had no idea what to expect, or when. Worse yet, her men—Brant included—already opposed her current actions. Rattling on about ghosts would most definitely push them over the edge.

"I'm going to send your cavalry unit east. The demons will launch a pursuit, assuming an easy target. I'll split the remainder of the army and while their attention's diverted, one wing will close in from the south and the other will circle around to drive them against the mountains and block their rear."

Brant nodded slowly and refrained from pressing for the secret Nes clearly held from him. "You think it'll work?"

"It has to," Nessix repeated. "It's the only plan I've got. Hopefully, we'll catch them off-guard. Distribute my orders and wait for my cue to move."

"Of course." Brant sighed and left to convey their projected movement.

Doubting her own plan, Nessix salvaged all of the faith left in her to hold course. If only Inwan would answer her! She needed to hear this wasn't a terrible movement and she wanted to ask how Gathlin intended to assist her. At one point in her life, spirituality had carried a strong meaning to her, and now that she needed it most, Nessix closed her eyes and breathed her tension out in a prayer for guidance.

* * * * *

"Douse the campfires!"

The order hastened through Nes's camp. She nodded once to Brant, trusting command of the cavalry solely to him. With specific instructions on how she wanted him to lure the demons and a vague mention of anticipating unusual assistance, Brant rode through his battalion to light the dozen torches scattered through them.

Nerves pinched thin as the demons' front buzzed with activity. Unable to hold the tension any longer, Brant bellowed to his men and the unit scattered, riding swiftly to the east. The rest of Nes's army held its breath, dreading to draw attention to themselves until an angry growl sounded from across the field.

A blue haze flickered around galloping hooves, tumbling among powerful legs. Silhouettes interspersed amidst the mortal cavalry, illuminated fleman soldiers matching the horses' strides. Hollow battle cries poured out of spectral mouths, and the horses protested their riders for permission to flee.

Nes's baffling premonition came back to Brant, and when he recognized the specters' crests, he pushed his alarm aside. "We're among allies, stay the course!"

Brant snuck a glance over his shoulder, wondering how Nes and her lack of magical know-how pulled this off. These men were real enough. Fires from Mathias's camp speckled the horizon, and Brant dropped his torch, signaling the riders—and this new army—to slow down. The entire branch of demons mobilized. Brant threw his hope into the hands of faith that tangible reserves still waited for his unit.

Nessix cursed the fact that the demons moved out of her plans, but neither had she expected the phantoms to actually appear. Logan carried her briskly between captains, sending a dozen units ahead to join those already in position. Not wanting to divide the army more than necessary, Nessix dispatched a regiment due north in case the demons were as deceitful as her. Unable to take the waiting any longer, she signaled a charge.

As predicted, the demons seemed unsuspecting of an attack from behind, though the disorder caused by her ancestors likely assisted with that. Nes's force swept through the demons like a storm through brittle leaves. Encouraged by their initial success, the flemans tore into the demon troops as gleefully as the beasts had obliterated Sarlot. It took several minutes for the enemy army to regain itself to counter and by then, hundreds writhed on the ground.

The units lying in wait in the east pressed in after the demons focused back on the west. Brant rallied his meager cavalry unit and they dashed into the fray.

Peeking out from its slumber, the sun gave enough light to permit sight, threatening to chase the spirits of Nes's forebears away. With time working against them, the phantoms whisked through the demon lines. Spectral limbs and weapons could not inflict physical wounds, but stirring such terror through the fiends gave their living comrades all the support they needed. Cheering a jubilant cry, excited to see the action of battle once more, the phantoms rushed into frantic claws and weapons swung out of desperation. Demons had never before panicked quite like this.

* * * * *

As dawn broke, the clamor of battle drifted to the forces in the east. Mathias grasped only part of the night's worth of ineffective sleep. More unanswered prayers flowed to Etha, and both his body and mind ached from his earlier expenditures. Nes's progress raised a noisy stir within Mathias's camp, urging him to rejoin activity in the muggy dawn. Viewing as much of the battle as his modest hilltop vantage point allowed, Mathias beamed at Nes's bold move. Her extravagant tussle pulled at the loyalty of the peasants, however, and before long, several voiced requests to go to her aid.

"General Nessix has everything under control," Sulik reassured them as Mathias tried to stitch a practical plan from his preoccupied mind.

"Then why is she coming to us?"

"The river won't allow her to move anywhere else."

"What if the demons catch them?"

195

Sulik bit back a sigh of frustration and cast a longing glance at Mathias. "The cavalry would have brought word to us if that happened. Besides, I think I hear the melody of victory songs. No more concerns about the west."

Mathias nodded. "It seems she's cleaned things up nicely."

Interrupting the chance for more questions, a barrage of arrows rained down onto the camp. Screams from unprepared peasants filled the air as veterans ordered shields to be raised.

"Move in pairs!" Mathias shouted, grabbing Sulik to throw him to safety. "One shield aimed to the sky, the other ahead!"

The flemans clustered into formation, their wall of shields holding while the demons contently pelted arrows against them. Men fell with each wave, shaking the remaining troops' confidence.

Sulik braced his arm against the impact on his raised shield. "We're falling faster than we did yesterday."

"They'll run out of shots soon," Mathias assured. "This is the only way to guarantee they use them all."

As Mathias promised, the assault continued for only a few more minutes. The roar of thousands of snarling demons replaced the attack and echoed back from the mountains. Lowering their defenses to assess the change of events, the men beheld a beautiful sight. Logan, with Nessix astride, tore across the field. Sword pointed ahead, she led nearly three hundred members of the cavalry and two fleman armies toward the enemy.

Who'd have thought the girl would have to come to your rescue?

The immediate circumstances hindered Mathias's ability to express his relief. *Not now, Etha.*

Before Mathias could evaluate anything else, Sulik dropped his shield and commanded a charge. Disorder erupted from the demon forces, not knowing which front to attack. The peasants, much closer to the enemy than Nessix was, clashed against the front lines with renewed enthusiasm, completely unaware of the spectral army that pushed centrally within the demonic forces. The creatures scattered from the untouchable opponents, devoured by the living flemans surrounding them. With their job through and the sun finally rising, the apparitions dissipated, but far too late to save the demons.

A call for retreat beckoned the enemy away, and Nessix only allowed enough of a chase to ensure their departure before returning to Mathias's weary force. As she and Logan passed, the men fell to their knees, spewing oaths of gratitude and loyalty. Her concerned gaze turned to Mathias. Sheathing her sword, Nessix dismounted and approached the careworn paladin.

"I didn't expect to be the first of us to win. Were the peasants having trouble?"

Mathias shook his head, aware of the inadequacy of his smile. "The peasants were fine. I just—" He took a breath to buy a moment to slap an excuse together. "I was busy all night treating injuries and it seems to have worn me."

Nessix believed his excuse no more than he did. "The wounded from my force are on their way back home. Your students healed most of them; I'm pleased with their progress."

Mathias's expression eased this time. "And I'm amazed by your own tactics. To think you'd rely on the dead!"

That coaxed a smirk from her. "I told you I'd learned a bit. Any word on how Veed held up?"

"Ceraphlaks has been watching the field. I trust I'd have known if we needed to rush south."

Nessix nodded thoughtfully and looked across the recuperating army. She caught Sulik send longing glances in Mathias's direction, recognizing the crestfallen confusion in his eyes. The commander had obviously picked up on Mathias's unusual behavior, and Nessix hoped the march home would give her a private moment to discuss it with him. Seeing Mathias so distracted soured Nes's stomach, and she slapped him on the shoulder to try to cheer him.

"If Veed doesn't need us, we should head back," Nessix said.

"I suppose so."

Your thoughts are a mess, Etha told him gently.

Yes, my lady. Mathias wanted to ask her about the past night's troubles, but his shame kept him from finding the words. Etha always corrected him when he tried to hide things from her, and he hoped she didn't hear his doubts now.

FOURTEEN

"You swore to me we would wipe that field!" the pawn hissed.

Shand glared at the man from the other side of his chamber's mirror. "You led me to underestimate that girl, and Veed's forces outperformed the expectations you gave me, as well."

"Of course they fought back!"

Shand spun from her pawn to reconstruct her composure.

"At least your curse seems to have neutralized the paladin. Wasn't that what you wanted?"

Shand's form stepped away from the mirror to pace in agitation through the marbling of the window, her features distorted by the puzzle of glass. "That is the closest thing to criticism I ever want to hear from you. All I have given you can be taken away in less than a breath. Do not forget that."

"Never, my lady."

"And the next time I ask you about the field conditions, you'd better tell me who I need to watch. That Nessix summoned an army of phantoms, drove confusion into two fronts and picked us apart. Why didn't I know she was capable of that?"

The pawn laughed at the ridiculous claim. "Nessix can't summon anything."

Shand's head snapped forward and she stepped out of the window into the room. A chill swept through the pawn, scattering his boldness. "Then perhaps you can explain to me how it happened?"

He balked at her request, unable to create even the most basic explanation. "Nessix doesn't have those abilities and Veed loves himself too much to help her while he's still in distress."

As the pawn tried to slink away, Shand strolled up to him and laced her fingers into the folds of his cloak to jerk him closer. "Which means, my dear servant, Mathias is still strong enough."

He squirmed in her clutches, glancing at her calm eyes and tight frown through his cringing. "Perhaps the need to protect his army gave him the strength to push past it? I did everything you told me to," he insisted. "If something went wrong, it wasn't a mortal error."

Shand released her pawn slowly and scalded him with critical eyes. The thought that she had failed never crossed her mind. After all, she was a goddess. The impact of such implied inadequacy soaked Shand through with rage, and she flung the mirror to the floor. She'd reached perfection! How could one pesky man and a witty little girl best her? The shards of broken mirror sparked and danced with the flames of her fury. The pawn shuffled two steps backwards.

"Never again!" Shand spat. "He cannot have this control over me!"

Shand whisked away to her plane, leaving the pawn to breathe in his relief of surviving another encounter with the goddess. Once he trusted the integrity of his legs, he stalked to the burning glass and smothered the flames of one sliver with his boot. He'd followed Shand's instructions flawlessly; the curse carried itself out as well as she'd designed it to. Hating the ways of women, he sighed and kicked the pile of tiny mirrors, sending them dancing into a corner.

* * * * *

In typical fashion, En requested a meeting as soon as he received word of the officers' return to the fortress. The four progressed quietly, each reflecting on their personal takes of the battle's outcome. Nessix and Brant led the way, and halfway down the hall to the war chamber, Brant snapped under the weight of his prying mind.

"Nes, how did you—" He snuffed his question as the sound of footsteps reminded him how closely Mathias and Sulik followed.

Nessix glanced at him, too busy toiling over Mathias's peculiar demeanor to catch any of her cousin's unspoken cues. "How'd I what?"

Brant loosened his jaw and ducked closer to Nes's ear. "I mean, *what* happened back there?"

That put a smile on Nes's face and lit her eyes with mischief. "Oh, come on, Brant," she teased, purposefully raising her voice to allow it to travel. "Certainly, you don't believe in ghosts."

Brant squared his shoulders, imagining the snide chuckles shared by the two men behind him. These past few weeks, he'd worked diligently to get Nessix to laugh again, but he hadn't expected her to find it at his expense. She poked him with a smug smirk and sly eyes that he batted away under the guise of solemnity. Brant reached forward and yanked the war chamber's door open.

En gestured them in with quick sweeps of his hands. "Losses?" he asked as soon as his guests sorted to their seats.

"Minimal," Nes replied promptly. "Especially considering the numbers we were up against."

"We allowed as few as possible to escape," Brant added. "Figured it'd help in the future."

Mathias frowned at this. "Did they call a retreat?"

"Not a formal one," Nessix said. "We did what we had to and you're damn lucky we did."

"Our front would have likely had significant casualties had Nessix not arrived when she did," Sulik agreed.

En turned to Mathias. "You needed Nessix's aid?"

"The offer stood both ways, sir," Mathias answered shortly. "I was fighting with a green force."

"You said they were ready!" Brant insisted.

"They were."

"Then what happened?"

"Brant!" Nessix hissed, bringing her cousin to a bitter silence with her pointed glare. "It's in the past. We won." Her eyes wandered from her relatives to the human seated across from her. He still displayed his regal confidence, but she unearthed a vein of guilt. "Perhaps you ought to see to the wounded?"

"My students can handle what's left," Mathias said.

"I don't believe her words were a suggestion," Brant snapped.

Nessix pressed her lips in a tight line and glanced away at Brant's harshness. Matters regarding the flow of this campaign needed to be discussed without Mathias's influence or interjection. Looking around the table, even Sulik's dropped shoulders and shifting eyes suggested he shared concerns about Mathias's recent performance.

"And I am not hers to command," Mathias clarified. He knew he was the cause of the tension trapped in this room. "If you must discuss my actions, I'd rather hear about it now than later."

En turned his wizened gaze to Nessix. "Sound fair?"

Nes's lips puffed out in a brief pout. She'd grown fond of Mathias and no longer enjoyed trying to humiliate him, but her personal sentiments could not validate his underwhelming performance. Nessix averted her eyes from him.

"Sagewind has proven valuable, but I can't help but think we've overestimated him." She held up a hand in a silent bid for patience from the rush of replies thrown across the table. "I'm not saying we'd be any better off without him, but I think if we let this obsession with him continue, it won't be long before morale's destroyed."

"Everyone has bad days," Sulik said.

"Bad days on the field mean death for more than just yourself," Brant countered.

"Are you saying you've never made a mistake out there, Commander?" Sulik challenged.

"I've never held as much power as your Sir—"

"Even Nessix has called poor tactics, needlessly costing lives."

"Enough!" En sprang to his feet, shaking on legs that debated the wisdom of his hasty action. Flushing, both commanders jumped to support him, but he swatted them away.

201

"I've learned from my mistakes," Nes said, recalling the slew of tactical defeats in her past.

"May I not learn from mine?" Mathias asked, aiming his question to Nessix alone.

"We trusted you under the assumption that you already knew what you were doing. You remind me all the time that this isn't one of your first campaigns."

Mathias closed his eyes and concentrated on his breathing. Without Etha to answer him, he had no satisfactory justification for the errors he'd made. Trying to explain how his steadfast goddess had overlooked him through this last battle promised to cripple Nes's opinion of Etha even more. On his own, Mathias saw no way out of this, and so he said nothing.

En looked between the commanders and settled back into his chair. "Nessix has made her stand. Can either of you confirm?"

Brant rolled his eyes with a dry laugh. "You know I agree with her. You would, too, if you saw how often he spares the demons."

En nodded once, accepting the answer before the brash commander continued to vent his personal grudges. Three pairs of anxious eyes waited on Sulik, but Mathias's shamed gaze remained fixed on the center of the table. Sulik vowed long ago to maintain loyalty to the Teradhel family, but he couldn't find it in himself to betray Mathias.

"I cannot speak for his intentions," Sulik said, "but perhaps he could explain himself?"

No one debated the request, though Brant made his heaved sigh no secret effort.

"If he can explain why he's gone so easy on the demons, I'm willing to listen." Nes looked to Mathias, begging him to have a good reason. "Please do not disappoint us."

Unlike the initial judgement Nes used for protection, this single botched encounter threatened to hinder all of the actions necessary to defeat the demons. If Mathias failed to convince them to maintain trust in him, he anticipated the flemans charging to a rapid defeat.

"I've drawn more than my share of blood in my time, and have lost the love of doing so." Mathias looked away from the repulsed glares his words received. "I've been around far too long to seek violence, and I know there will be no escaping it once the demons bring out their true wickedness."

Brant pounded his fist against the table. "Fuck, Sarlot wasn't wicked enough for you?"

Nessix blanched at her cousin's outburst, but nodded in agreement. "Elidae has never lost a township, not in war."

Mathias's voice lowered. "I won't try to tell you that it wasn't devastating, but the demons still have much more to show."

"Then from a tactical point, sir, wouldn't it be better to defeat them as they come?" Sulik asked.

Nessix shook her head. "We'd be better off to lead a proper campaign against them and finish this off."

"How many men are in your army?" Mathias asked. "Eight, maybe ten thousand? Veed's got, what? Five thousand more than you? Even with your entire forces combined, the demons have enough to wipe you out on the road. It's best to draw them out where we can still control some of the variables."

"Is that a threat?" Nessix murmured.

"Never, General. It is a fact."

"War is a deadly game. If the demons aren't killed, then we will be." Nessix stood up slowly. "I believe we've sorted enough onto the table for now. If a general won't lead his army to do its job, what good is he?"

"I think you know that answer, Nessix," Mathias said.

She lowered her eyes, hearing the implications that slipped past the others. If Mathias resigned his station, Nessix wouldn't have much of an army left, let alone Veed's backing. A gentle rap at the door announced a young messenger's delivery of Veed's recent victory. Brant shoved back his chair and dismissed himself, through with politics, and once Nessix's shame waned, she followed.

* * * * *

Disheartened after the recent meeting, Mathias returned to the mess hall to resume pouring his increasingly finite energy into those who needed it most. Nes's behavior suggested she wanted to protect him from prosecution, but her initial assessment of him looked more accurate than ever. Mathias wasted a moment trying to reach Etha for answers and was met with disappointment. Catching himself before his doubt caved in around him, Mathias sighed and entered the makeshift infirmary.

Regardless of his damaged self-worth, these people needed healing, and the chunk of Affliction his heart beat around provided the necessary divinity to get Mathias started. Desperate to save face and avoid indirectly damaging Etha's reputation, Mathias dismissed his students. As he walked through the cots of the ailing, he found the simple wounds tended to and the more severe cases stabilized. The full reach of Etha's power eluded the clerics in training, but it reassured Mathias to see their growing capabilities.

Most of the patients rested soundly enough to miss Mathias's current instability, but those still conscious lit up with instant relief when he set to work. Well aware of the ramifications of his dour conduct, Mathias put on a comforting smile and trudged through his best efforts.

As with the past battle, each blessing Mathias imparted dripped more lead into his arms and sand in his eyes. Etha's influence continued to pass through him, but the channel that allowed her grace to flow with Mathias's will pinched off to a debilitating trickle. By the time he'd tended to a dozen men, Mathias regretted sending the students away. Rows of wounded troops remained, and he could only sit among them and pray for his own recovery.

"Should I send for Sulik?" Brant asked, noshing a bite from an apple as he walked into the room.

"Commander Maliroch," Mathias said. He sat upright and eyed the fruit, stomach rumbling. "I thought I'd removed all of able body."

Brant grinned. "This fortress's been my home longer than it's been Nes's. I go where I please."

Mathias stood and feigned wellness. "I'm afraid your presence may upset the patients. You tend to share your cousin's love for drama."

Brant's smile faded. "You've won over many, but remember you're being watched."

"Always, Commander."

The disgust in Brant's eyes suggested he'd been doing that for quite some time. Bearing a substantial influence over Nessix and too little respect for Mathias, Brant's reconnaissance sapped the paladin's sense of security.

"I thought you'd be inclined to accept my offer of finding help, but may as well be off."

"Are you mocking me?" Mathias asked dryly.

"Never." There was no honest conviction in the answer.

"If you've got other things to do, Commander, please don't let me keep you from them."

Brant nodded. "Very well. Finish patching up the army. I'll leave you be."

The commander tossed his apple core onto an empty waste cart as he turned and left. Mathias had no way to know how much Brant had seen, and he considered that dangerous. He closed his eyes once more, trying to relax enough to regain his confidence and subdue his lurking headache. For the first time in a long while, pride told Mathias to prove his worth.

* * * * *

It took Mathias far longer than usual to bless all of those in need. The eventual success of his remedies proved Etha's prevailing presence, which left Mathias wondering why such simple tasks wore him so. He took the most secluded staircase to his quarters, and quickly tucked himself into the room before he gained anyone's attention.

Almost delirious with exhaustion, Mathias loosened his sword belt and batted through the sparse articles in his armoire. Plucking the first shirt he found from its hanger, he turned, startled to meet stern amber eyes in his mirror. Etha offered him no words. Her look alone assured Mathias she'd heard his earlier doubts, and he bowed his head in submission.

"I haven't been this weak since I was mortal," he murmured. "I searched for you, Etha, for the entire battle. I needed you!"

"I was there, as I am now and always."

He refused to look back at the mirror, trembling under the pressure of her eyes. "If I'm doing wrong, please correct me."

"You've done nothing to wrong me. Perhaps you've wronged the flemans with your soft heart, but there's yet to be any serious repercussions from that." Etha studied Mathias, from his concerned brows arched carefully over ancient eyes to the shirt now threatening to fall from his wavering grasp. "My dear, you're doing all you can."

Mathias shook his head and resumed changing his clothes. "If you were watching, then you know I can barely pull scratches together now. The flemans need more than that to survive this war."

A gentle trickle of amusement flowed from Etha. "You're not giving yourself enough credit. You've done much more than that."

Mathias distracted himself with scraping grime from his belt buckle with a thumb nail. "Have I lost your faith in me?" His heart dashed at the blunt question.

"Your accusations are not becoming, Mathias!" Etha gasped, abhorred by the senselessness of her disciple's doubt.

He looked up at her, comforted by the reprimand. "I didn't mean to accuse. I just want to understand."

Etha's face softened, her concern almost overwhelming him. "Your failing powers are not my doing. Dark magic is in use here."

Mathias nodded briefly. His mind flicked to Veed, the only fleman he knew capable of divine power, but that still didn't add up. "No one on Elidae is capable of magic powerful enough to thwart you."

Etha cocked her head and twisted her lips. "With the protection of one of the lesser gods, any magic user could be shielded." Her eyes deepened in consideration. "That could also be why any curse placed on you went undetected. Just as my divine power blesses you, it can just as easily cripple you. The new children are crafty. You know as well as I do that the demons haven't risen so boldly on their own."

"So you're confirming one of the children is involved? Selfish or not, they can't possibly be foolish enough to defy you."

Etha silently reflected on Mathias's words, having assumed the same. She only trusted two of the new gods, and hoped their influence over their peers could shine light on this mystery. "I'd wanted to avoid involving them, but I'll ask Azerick and Drao if they suspect anything."

Mathias nodded, trusting the greater gods of both good and evil to help reestablish balance. "The children must learn their place."

"They know their place," Etha corrected, shaking her head. "That's why they're challenging it. I have a dreadful feeling this is about something more than power."

"None of them have a reason to follow some petty vengeance. Greed's the only motive I can see."

"Ah, yes." Etha sighed. "And I can assure you that mortals are delicately involved in those matters."

"Mortals controlling a god?"

Etha longed to approach Mathias, but not without understanding the curse he carried, and contented herself with keeping the layer of glass between them. "You think too simply, my dear. I believe it began the other way around. The lesser of the new children are selfish, and you know how desperate man can be. The tables of control can be turned much more easily than you or I care to admit."

"I've already been told I'm the target here," Mathias said, "but besides En, nobody knew who I was."

Etha's forehead scrunched in thought. "It's a deeply layered plan, to be sure. Gods protecting mortals, protecting demons."

"If there's a more elaborate plan, the fallen know nothing of it. They're bent on their chance to torture me and claim Elidae. They think they have this won."

Etha hated it when Mathias tried to find redemptive qualities in those so removed from her grace. "Not even the demons are vain enough to charge in, assuming victory."

"I've seen into their hearts. They're no more than toys in this foul game." Mathias kept his regret in check, channeling it into determination. "I agree that someone else is influencing them, and I will find this villain."

The goddess's ancient eyes softened at Mathias's fortitude. "If I cannot find them, how will you?" she asked gently.

"If they've chosen to come for me, then I'll let them come. I will not fall." Resolve alone kept Mathias's words brave amidst the apprehension dancing in his heart from the damage already dealt to him.

When Etha first resurrected Mathias, she had no idea what to expect from him or the depth their bond would reach. She'd always admired his confidence, but it doubled as her greatest burden. "You put too much pressure on yourself," she said. "You need your rest, my love. Trust me to find the help you need."

Mathias glanced away at the thought of a challenge he and Etha couldn't face together. "I suppose you're right, Etha." He pressed a hand to his temple and gazed at the welcoming comfort of his bed. "I'll get my rest. Thank you, as always, for your assistance. "

The pendant around his neck glittered back at Mathias from the uninhabited corners of the mirror. Etha gave him a gentle smile and was gone.

FIFTEEN

Two quiet months elapsed, raising fleman strength and spirit, but that said nothing of Shand's impatience. She held the demons back to give Mathias's curse time to fester and Nes's forces the chance to grow overconfident. Not even allowing raid parties out to stir up mischief, Shand's boredom pushed her to the brink of insanity. Torturing the few demons foolish enough to complain barely entertained her anymore as she reached the limit of her restraint. Ready to see how badly she could make Mathias squirm, Shand called on her sniveling pawn. She curled her lip at his arrival, offended by his proud carriage as he hid his expression in the depths of his hood.

A prompt bow spared him her retaliation. "Mathias is growing weaker, as you planned."

The immediate insight tilted Shand toward a more pleasant demeanor. "And what of those he's training as apprentices?"

"Don't worry about them," the pawn scoffed. "It took him ages to master his power. Others like him won't pop up overnight."

"Foolish mortal..." Shand murmured. "Do not speak to me like I'm ignorant. I watched that bastard serve his Mother for years. If neither of them have figured out how to fix him, they'll appoint others to work in his stead. They won't let innocents suffer."

The pawn frowned at the mention of Etha. "Has his goddess

caught on?"

"Enough that she's been asking about loyalties. Stupid wench is too trusting."

He watched an arrogant smile stretch across Shand's face. "With all due respect, if you left Etha on bad terms, wouldn't she have you under close watch?"

"Nonsense," Shand snapped. "She's more concerned over the neutral gods, worrying that they caught some sort of imbalance and are seeking its recovery."

"But don't you have the most bad blood with Mathias?"

Shand snorted. "Outside of Etha and the buffoons Azerick and Drao, we all despise him. He's Etha's pet and could easily outrank any of us because of it. None of us are *allowed* to touch him."

"We're still left with the problem of his influence over Elidae."

Shand twisted her mouth thoughtfully. "Then it's time to start distracting him. Is there anything on this island he seems terribly fond of?"

The pawn shrugged. "As far as I can tell, all he cares about is pushing the demons back and protecting the people. He seems set on his mission with little room for anything else."

His mission? The rumor floating around the divine realm said Mathias had been sent to Elidae to protect Nessix first and defeat the demons second. Shand's brows furrowed. "Is there any chance the girl would ever join us?"

The pawn laughed until he realized Shand had been serious. "No. Loyalty's been bred into her lineage for too long. She'd never support actions that would harm her people."

Shand sucked on her tongue and nodded slowly. "Then I suppose we have to force her involvement."

He stared at her mutely. He'd agreed to help Shand destroy Mathias, even if it meant sacrificing a large portion of the flemans, but threatening Nes had never been part of the plan. The thought of losing the noble bloodline unsettled the pawn, nearly as much as having the girl's death on his hands. Shand had a reputation of discarding the things she used, and he knew if she pulled Nessix in, the young general would die.

"What's your plan for her?" he murmured, honestly not wanting the answer.

Shand stared at him keenly and he lowered his head to look away. Even as a mortal she'd ignored her emotions, and could only speculate on where her servant's mind wandered. "Besides the fact that she's proven to be quite a destructive force, I think hurting her will be the fastest way to hurt Mathias."

The pawn tried not to encourage the flicker of hope that sprouted from Shand's mention of merely maiming Nessix. "But all she is to him is a mission. There's a good chance he doesn't care about her any deeper than that."

Shand's eyes lit with cunning. "It doesn't take much for Mathias to grow fond of someone. Even if you're right, even if he doesn't care, making him fail his divine quest would suit me just as well."

"And will she die?"

"At some point, I'm sure." Shand shrugged. "Whatever happens to her in the days to come will be up to the demons."

He winced, mind concocting the cruel ways those beasts could dismantle Nessix. A clenched jaw and forced breath shoved his feelings aside in favor of self-preservation. He looked up at his goddess with ramshackle resolve. "When will they begin the attack?"

Shand rose and turned to leave, delighting in her servant's blatant discomfort. "I'll leave the details to you. You're obviously deceitful enough to not disappoint me."

"Thank you, my lady," he murmured, bowing more stiffly this time. "Permit my dismissal and I'll begin planning."

A small tilt of Shand's head rid the pawn from her sight.

* * * * *

The morning started later than usual, but earlier than Nessix had hoped. Nothing in particular woke her, but muted percussion and muffled hums refused to let sleep return. She sat up and slipped out of bed to dress in tan breeches and a white blouse

211

before opening her door to step into the hall.

Curious, Nessix followed the noise to where it twisted up the stairwell. Her descent uncovered buoyant melodies and the sort of cheers that accompanied drinking songs. The commotion bubbled from the dungeon, boldly proclaiming the peasants' happiness. A grin blossomed across Nes's face and she trotted beneath the fortress proper, greeted by a swell of adoring faces.

Music flitted about the animated scene, and Nes met respectful bows with humble nods. Makeshift soldiers mingled through the crowd, and she even recognized a few seasoned veterans among the masses. Her gut mused that Mathias was behind this ruckus, but her mingling about the chipper convention didn't uncover him. Even absent, his charisma glowed through those preaching of his miracles and the occasional cluster of blushing maidens giggling at talk of his physique. Nessix shook her head at both modes of foolishness, but her mood stayed light and enhanced by her discovery of a pocket of dancers, spinning and skipping in step with the music.

Pairs floated past her. The girls, not too far in age from herself, flounced by, their skirts twirling playfully around their dainty frames. Nessix unconsciously tugged at the hem of her shirt. If she'd been born without station, she'd look just like these vibrant maidens. Instead, her preferred attire echoed a man's, with minor alterations to accommodate the obvious conformational differences. Dresses were silly garments that would only hinder her in battle. Smiles bounced across full cheeks and hair danced freely about delicate shoulders. Smooth arms curved with elegant softness. They glowed with a brilliant femininity that Nessix staunchly disallowed herself.

The strength and functionality of her body comforted Nessix, but a desolate part of her subconscious cried of her insufficiency. Her lean legs were chiseled and accentuated by the snug fit of her breeches. Her face shared a certain delicacy, but her gaunt features paled in comparison to the rosy complexions around her. The only true aspect that allowed Nessix to feel like a girl was the length she kept her hair, and even that stayed tamed in tight war braids.

Nessix smirked and shook her head at such petty notions.

Even if she wanted to trade her sword for a skirt, she was in a terrible place to try to settle down. It wouldn't make a difference if she looked the part of a voluptuous peasant maiden or not. A small frown flawed her brow, but Brant's wide grin as he spun up to her wiped it away. With a chivalrous bow, he offered his hand to her.

A giggle passed through Nes's defenses as she shook her head and took a step back. Brant exaggerated a pout, but nimbly traced a kiss on his partner's hand before passing her along to the next dancer.

Nessix laughed as Brant hunched over, hands on his knees to catch his breath. "What brought on all of this?" she asked.

The instant fall of Brant's expression confirmed her suspicions. "Sagewind did some scouting last night. Rooted out a pocket of demons."

"That's hardly a cause for such nonsense."

Brant held up a finger and glanced away. "No, it's not, but he allegedly took a group of the people—common folk, Nes!—out to fight them."

She shook her head in disbelief and threw her shoulders back. "What in Inwan's name was he— Did anyone get hurt?"

"No."

Nessix should have assumed Mathias had some way to ensure their safety. Even so, his promotion was getting to his head. Watching the excitement buzzing around her contented Nessix, though. She trusted Mathias to help protect these citizens, and the power he gave them illuminated the gloom of the dungeon. Not even Brant seemed entirely opposed.

Unable to come up with a legitimate complaint, Nessix blew out her breath and resumed an amiable expression. "I never knew you danced."

Brant grinned back. "Of course you didn't; you're not girl enough to pay attention."

The words stung, but not enough to harm her. "What's that say about you?" A playful jab to his shoulder and tilt of Nes's head drew Brant with her into the crowd. Nessix could spare the morning for her people.

* * * * *

For the following week, attacks from the demons came, varying only by time of day or direction from which they hit. Each battle ended with the flemans victorious and every time, more of the army began to consider the war won. This progress pleased Mathias, but his past experience with demons assured this was building to a larger, much more sinister objective.

Sorting out these speculations compounded Mathias's resentment with his spiritual disconnect. He removed the pendant Veed had convinced Nes to force on him, tossed it onto his desk, and peeled off his armor following the latest successful battle. Sounds of the evening's celebrations lofted from the halls and lower levels. Still half-dressed in his armor, Mathias shoved the maps on his desk aside and took a seat, resting his head in his hands. The pendant slipped behind the desk and fell to the floor.

Mathias had grown tired of hearing the flemans call the demons stupid. He'd seen before what dangers came from belittling these fiends, but through the continuous victories, everyone laughed off his warnings. His mind tangled with worries, most of them out of his control, but reining in this dangerous enthusiasm was something Mathias felt certain he could influence.

Situating himself well enough to prove presentable before a lady, Mathias followed the back halls to Nes's chamber. Her door stood open per her typical policy, and she spent her post-battle evening responsibly scouring tomes about demons at her desk, aggressively gnawing on her cuticles. Maps and open scrolls sprawled around her, even on the floor. She answered his soft knock with an absent order to enter.

Mathias proceeded cautiously and shut the door behind himself, approving of her chamber's modest décor.

Brows furrowed in concentration, Nessix kept one ear on Mathias's movement until she completed penning her current thought and looked up irritably. "You want something?"

"All I want is to clear Elidae of the demons, which is looking unobtainable at the moment."

Nessix pressed out an arrogant huff as she leaned back in her chair to stretch out the past hours of sedentary work. "For a man who boasts such wisdom, that's a foolish conclusion. Haven't you seen our progress?"

"Ah, yes." Mathias took two steps closer. "The steady trudge forward, great victories day in and day out." He wanted to slap that smug smile off her face. "Something's not right."

"That steady trudge begs otherwise."

"Does it?" Mathias almost laughed at her ridiculous assumption. "The demons are baiting us; I'd bet my life on it."

Nessix dragged her attention back to her maps and sighed. "You worry too much."

"I'm telling you, there's more going on here than we're able to see. Open your eyes and look for it."

The warning tucked itself away in Nes's mind. "You're talking like we haven't had any difficulties. We have. We're just learning how to fight them better."

The peak of Mathias's lip twitched. He couldn't stop Nes from trying to endanger herself, but ignoring his cautions threatened the troops and her people. "When was the last time a scout returned unsuccessful in the last week?"

Nessix ignored him.

Gritting his teeth, Mathias stalked to her desk and pulled the map from beneath her pen. "When have we not been able to outguess the enemy?"

Eyes flashing dangerous threats at Mathias's boldness, Nessix stared into the wooden surface of her desk. "Never," she said tightly. "And that is why you don't need to be concerned. We've outsmarted them."

Mathias shifted the map away from the hand Nessix sent to retrieve it. "Our enemy has far more wit than you give them credit for."

Nessix laughed. "The demons are nothing but stupid beasts."

The brief encounter Mathias had shared with Laes suggested he'd have never raised his sole offspring to be so daft. "Think of them that way."

"I will."

"And continue to think of them that way."

215

Nessix snatched her map away from him and slapped it back on her desk. "Don't you have to go teach someone how to cure a cold?"

He glowered at her, not due to her disrespect, but from her ignorance. "I suppose I do," he rumbled. "But in all my wisdom, the one thing I pray to never become is a prophet."

Mathias stalked away from her with nothing more and slammed the door shut behind him. His last words chilled Nessix and she stopped her reading to stare at the wall in front of her. What if he was right? The demons had offered little challenge since Sarlot. Nothing kept them from trying the same to any of Veed's towns or, worse yet, her own fortress.

"You're thinking too far into this," she grumbled. Shaking her head to shoo away the doubts Mathias planted there, Nessix returned to her work.

SIXTEEN

Following Mathias's frigid counsel, four more battles ended in the flemans' favor. Confidence warmed the hearts of Nessix and her men, and their pushes grew stronger with each encounter. They bore minimal losses and Etha's sweet voice resumed its frequent chatter in Mathias's head. He credited his ability to tolerate Nes's growing abandon in combat on this reunion, and quit dreading the sound of the watch tower bells.

Despite the victories, one thought rode in the back of Nes's mind each time she looked over a fresh challenge. Mathias had warned her not to push back when the demons shoved, told her it was foolish to pursue their attacks with her own. Her hasty judgment aside, Nessix valued the lives of her troops too much to ignore him, but with each victory, her confidence swelled. Whether her men grew more skilled or the demons lost part of their tenacity, it didn't matter to Nessix. All she cared about was riding this momentum until the demons learned their place. With those thoughts in mind, Nessix gladly led the enthusiastic masses onto the field to savor the conquest awaiting them.

The morning revealed a larger opposing force than the army expected, but the flemans still outnumbered the demons two to one. Brant mirrored his cousin as they surveyed the field, watching her closely for the motion to engage. Nessix turned in the saddle to look over the men behind her. The cautious approach of past battles had dampened their collective spirit, and Nessix felt they were overdue for a traditional fight. Her fingers tingled in anticipation.

"Open rush, boy," she murmured to Logan. "Nothing fancy; let's go have some fun."

He snorted his approval and tested himself against Nes's hold. Waiting for her nod to Brant, Logan leapt forward.

The lessons learned from the past weeks' tactics assured every warrior they had nothing to fear. Common sense lectured Nessix, sternly reminding her of Mathias's suspicions, but ambition drove her harder. Logan's massive strides quickly overtook the soldiers and the two forces soon met.

The energy emanating from the fleman warriors stifled their opponents' approach. Logan reared, crushing a demon's head upon landing. Nessix shot an optimistic glance over her shoulder and prayed Brant's side of the field held as strong as her own. She waited for Logan to settle and dismounted to proceed on foot. Drawing her sword with a wild grin, she jabbed the blade into an oncoming foe's throat, quick to jerk it free before the dead weight pulled it from her hand. She raised her arm back for a second strike when the demon horns of retreat bellowed across the plain.

Nearby captains turned to Nessix for instruction. Equally confused, Nessix stared in shock as her enemies scattered and ran for the mountains. Her adrenaline overload advised her to charge, but self-preservation chimed that the demons quite possibly anticipated a chase. Nes's brows furrowed. That last thought hadn't been her own. It hadn't even sounded like her own voice! Ignoring the unusual plea, Nessix swung herself astride Logan.

"Are we going to let them run?" she cried to her army. "That's not like us at all! Men, charge!"

Her herald sounded the flemans' song of pursuit, met by cheers from the troops.

A hard press caught them up to the demons and as the fiends tired, the flemans surrounded them again. Nessix returned to the ground, her sword still drawn from her previous engagement. Smooth progress led Nessix to the sounding of a second horn's bleat, this one unfamiliar to her.

A swell of chaos opened and engulfed the army. Time held its breath for an instant before rushing to catch up again, spinning the following moments into utter confusion. The first taste of reality pinched Nessix with the thin slice of a blade as it connected with her cheek. Her eyes darted to assess the evolving situation. Demon reinforcements poured from the nearby mountains, and Nessix realized her current numbers had no chance at holding off so many. She should have known better.

All around her, men were torn down, horses crashed to the ground. In the sudden surge, Nessix forgot herself and spun to locate Brant. The flood of demon bodies swallowed everything around her. Logan's scream pierced through the cries and haunting laughter. A hand grasped the back of her gorget and Nessix wheeled to jab her elbow into the chin of the foe behind her. Necessity forced her to abort her search for Brant, and Nessix dove through the bodies to reach her herald.

"Signal a retreat!" she pled.

The field froze at the terrifying song. Demons chortled as Nes's soldiers struggled to comprehend the seldom-heard command. Logan bounded over bodies to reach Nessix and she scrambled into the saddle.

The horns cried out their warning and while many of the flemans scratched together enough nerve through their shock to resume function, the demons pressed back against them. Cursing the determination of her men as they engaged once more, Nessix grudgingly employed her last resort.

"Logan, run."

The desperation in Nes's voice forced Logan to forego any concept of bravery. If the flemans stayed any longer, they would be obliterated. Launching onto his hind legs in hopes of catching his allies' eyes, Logan took a giant leap away from the field. With their flight, the herald turned his horse to follow, continuing to urge the men away until his lips grew numb.

Fleeing reminded Nessix of how far she was from being the leader her people needed. Shameful or not, the scene she made drew the army's attention, and they followed her lead to pull away from the demons' clutches. The rumble of the field and rush of blood in Nes's ears muffled every other sound. Her courage drained from her with every stride, chilling the fire that usually fueled her so well.

That foreign voice tore through her mind again, affirming she chose the right course. Her father had taught her to look out for her men and to never abuse their spirit. Against these odds, retreat was her only option if she hoped to save her army.

Once Nessix believed they'd adequately distanced themselves from danger, she pulled Logan to a stop and looked back at the field. The nearest enemy lines snatched at the stragglers, and Nes choked on the realization that most of them would never reach safety. The wounded no one found, those who sank too far in the masses, they were sealed to a torturous fate. Memories of Sarlot assaulted Nessix as she debated whether or not to order the archers to spare their brothers such an end.

A small roar erupted on the field as twenty riders darted from where they'd grasped sanctuary in a grove of trees, instantly surrounded by the enemy. With the welfare of these knights on the line, Nessix sent a quick look to Brant. He shook his head, eyes harboring stern disapproval of her telegraphed thoughts. The demons' attention lurched from the slim pickings of the wounded to the more exciting hunt of vibrant men. Horses were spurred hard, but a solid wall of bodies intercepted their flight. The knights fought fiercely to fend off the enemy and Nessix held her breath. She'd seen enough.

"Assign change of command to Commander Maliroch," she told the herald. "My order to retreat trumps anything he comes up with."

The herald conveyed the order as Nessix grit her teeth and focused on her mission. She only needed to gain the demons' attention for a moment to carve a path for those horses. Logan barreled back into the opposition and Nessix braced herself as he trampled six lines deep.

A spear aimed for Logan's eye sent him onto his hind legs. Distracted by trying to rally the soldiers around her, Nessix lost her balance. With only one hand free, she swung her leg over Logan's back to avoid an uncontrolled tumble. Her feet connected with one of the demons Logan had trampled and she stumbled on a rolled ankle.

"Fight, men!" she shouted. "Logan, clear the way for their mounts!"

Pain never fazed Nessix, but fear did. As the demons caved in on her troops, the unsettling need for Mathias's help surpassed instinct. That, and a powerful blow to her back that doubled Nessix over to gasp for air. She tried to twist around to engage, but the number of demons grounded her. Their attention left her troops once they recognized her, and Nessix prayed Brant had led the army home. She raised her sword for a strike that never fell.

A kick to the knee knocked Nes's legs out from under her, but a hand on the back of her gorget whipped her up before she collided with the ground. As Nessix attempted to regain her bearings, a shadow passed above and a booted foot crashed down on her exposed neck. A sickening crack reverberated throughout her being, and the demons allowed Nessix to crumble to the ground. In an instant, her mind detached from the terror around her. Only minutely aware of a snap in her leg, Nessix stared ahead, unable to move, as the demons followed through with their retreat at last.

* * * * *

Speaking with Etha over the past few days had revitalized Mathias. He allowed his doubts of Nes's skills to slip his mind, finally accepting the fact that she knew the terrain of Elidae far better than he did. Besides, her willingness to listen and her flourishing performance record suggested she'd be fine, and the easy progress bolstered the army's spirit. A raucous commotion beckoned Mathias over to his window. Fully expecting another jubilant procession from a victorious army, Mathias instead beheld desperate soldiers bolting for the fortress. Panic chased the army back to their perceived safety, and Mathias rushed out his door.

Shouting orders to cover the army's retreat along the way,

Mathias reached the main floor and burst into the mess hall, interrupting the casual dining of peasants and soldiers. "Forgive my intrusion, but we're reestablishing the infirmary." Mothers gathered their children and hastened away; those soldiers present hustled over for instructions. "Find Commander Vakharan and tell him to meet me here."

Seeing the men off, Mathias ran out the fortress doors and scanned the rushing mass. He spotted Brant, the commander slowing every dozen strides to scan the horizon and round up those who fell behind. Mathias hailed him over, surprised by his compliance.

"What happened?"

Brant met Mathias with worried eyes. "Nes ordered a retreat," he said, looking back once more. Concern overtook his predisposed notions of Mathias. "Some men got stranded, she passed command to me and rode back to help them."

A swell of regret hit Mathias. Stupid impulses always flooded Nes's mind when faced with emergencies, but she proved willing to give up both power and her own safety for the sake of her soldiers. It took a dedicated general to do that.

"So she's still out there?" Mathias strained his gaze to where the troops dragged themselves in from.

"My hope is that she's currently running from that," Brant said. "Her herald said she wanted to serve as a distraction so the men could run. I'm hoping she chose to go against her nature and avoided engaging."

"She's a clever girl. She'll figure this out." Even as Mathias assured them both, he couldn't shake his misgivings.

"I shouldn't have left her," Brant murmured.

"No," Mathias said. "If it was bad enough for her to call a retreat, you did the right thing." The faint jeer of the demons' horns echoed from the distance. "They're pulling back."

Brant shook his head and looked at the last of the wounded as they pulled each other closer to safety. "I'm going to find her."

"I need you here, Commander," Mathias said. "We need to organize the hospital again. We weren't ready for this." He'd wait to criticize Nes's hastiness after he found her alive and well.

222

"What if she needs—"

"I will tend to Nes's wounds if she has any. Right now, I need you to obtain some sense of order. Find the most critical and send them into the mess hall."

Brant frowned, clenching his teeth to contain his angry retort. A deep breath and heavy heartbeat later, he accepted that his duty to the people trumped his pride. Mathias knew how to handle this upheaval better than anyone else.

"I do not take orders from you, Sagewind." Brant dismounted. "I'm doing this for Nes."

"Thank you, Commander."

Content with Brant's compliance, Mathias hurried back inside to survey the damage that had already leaked in. Bloodied soldiers lined the halls. Women who refused to return to the dungeons wept at the sight of such suffering. If not for the grave emergency, Mathias would have taken the time to usher the peasants away, but right now he had more immediate concerns. Entering the mess hall, he found Sulik bustling through the tables, searching for the injuries he knew how to deal with. Mathias approached him with a calm smile.

"Sir, what happened?" Sulik breathed.

"Let's not worry about that right now," Mathias said. "These men and women need us."

Mathias passed through the ranks that had filed in, touching people on occasion, whispering prayers under his breath to buy them more time. With a resolute nod, Sulik hustled to his side.

"Have the students tend to the wounded. I have someplace to go."

"But, sir…" Sulik fretted over the responsibility saddled to him. "I don't think I can do it."

"Of course you can. Your actions may save them from finding paradise today. Now go and do. I must see to those who couldn't make it this far."

Sulik nodded, trusting Mathias's faith in him. "I'll tell Nes—" Sulik's words clipped short as he drew himself up and wheeled about to look over those assisting each other into the fortress. If she'd made it back, Nessix would personally drag them through by spirit alone. Features frozen, Sulik whipped back around to meet Mathias's eyes. "Yes, sir. Go quickly!"

Clapping Sulik on the shoulder, Mathias hurried from the fortress. Nessix quite possibly had limited time. Mathias whistled for Ceraphlaks, quickly met with the pegasus's snort. Ceraphlaks had kept an eye on the battle and knew exactly what concerned his rider now. Flying hard, they met Logan bolting toward the fortress. The fecklan reared and screamed for Ceraphlaks's attention, spinning to lead the way back to where Nessix had fallen. Traveling by air brought Mathias to a small group of soldiers well before Logan reached them. As Ceraphlaks landed, Mathias prayed these men guarded something more than a corpse. A sickening grasp clawed at his throat. *Etha, please...*

"No," one of the soldiers demanded. "I promise, I did some studying about this kind of thing and she'll be fine as long as we don't—"

"You don't know what you're doing!" A second soldier blocked the first with a firm arm.

"Maybe we could—" the third never got to finish his thought.

"Move aside." Mathias's barked words scattered the men abruptly. Fear clenched at him as he assessed Nes's wounds. One leg twisted unnaturally from her hip and again beneath her knee and a dent twice the size of his fist blemished the plate on her back. Her eyes remained open and blank, her mouth gaping for sporadic breaths. "Do not touch her. None of you have trained enough for this."

In truth, Mathias wondered if his own drifting powers could handle the injuries Nessix suffered from. Even with Etha back in his mind, this was the first opportunity to test how much he'd recovered. Pinching his eyes shut for a quick prayer, Mathias held his hands over Nes's back.

Warmth flowed from Mathias's core as Etha's grace patched up the minor scrapes, filling Mathias with a euphoric intoxication. Swallowing his doubt, he unbuckled the straps of Nes's armor to remove the back plate. He traced his fingers up her spine. *Etha, please keep her safe.*

Logan wheezed upon his arrival and shoved his way past the

concerned soldiers to stand opposite Mathias. Lowering his head, he planted his nose in Nes's open hand. Mathias allowed the fecklan's efforts as he continued to gauge Nes's injuries. His fingers reached the base of her neck and confirmed his worst fears.

If Mathias failed to heal her, he knew Nessix would prefer death over any other alternative. Careful not to dislocate the severed column further, he cupped his hands over the back of Nes's broken neck. *Etha, if you would be so gracious as to grant me your power even once more, I need it now more than ever. Please, allow Nessix the chance to live. Let her rebound from this to continue her ways and have faith in me that she will find faith in you. Etha, I need her*—His prayer wavered at the thought that slipped from him. *Her men need her.*

Nessix trembled beneath Mathias's hands, gently at first, then with increasing ferocity. Logan tossed his head with a startled snort and eyed Mathias critically. A broken whimper staggered from Nes's throat, cleaved by a sharp gasp. Tension built in her small frame and her eyes pinched shut. Two more breaths cycled before her body fell limp. Mathias lifted his hands and looked up to meet the bewildered gazes around him.

Thank you, Mother.

"She'll be fine." Mathias picked up the armor he'd removed from Nessix and handed it to whoever accepted it first. "I'll carry her back on Ceraphlaks. The rest of you should return home, as well."

Not waiting for any affirmatives or debate, Mathias supported Nessix in his arms and mounted with Ceraphlaks's assistance. They travelled home attentively, as not to jar Nessix any worse, and arrived at the quieter back entrance near Nes's quarters. Mathias climbed the single flight of stairs, lips tight to the prying questions that chased him to her room. Fumbling with the door handle, Mathias used his shoulder to push his way inside and positioned Nessix carefully on her bed.

Mathias pulled a chair over to the bedside, ladling a small bowl of water from the wash basin. Staring down at Nessix, he frowned and adjusted the pillows so she lay more evenly. Satisfied, Mathias washed the residue of the field from her face and neck. A cough sounded from the door.

"Nes know you've gotten so friendly with her?" Veed asked, inviting himself in.

"Nes isn't aware of anything right now," Mathias said. "The battle's barely through and I only just got her home. What are you doing here?"

Veed craned his neck to wait on the rise and fall of Nes's chest. "Rumors travel fast. I heard she ordered a retreat and I came to see if she needed me."

Mathias straightened and dropped the washcloth back into the water. "If she hadn't done so, her entire army would be bedridden or dead. Sometimes more honor is found in cowardice than foolish pride. It makes a man stronger."

A lazy smile sketched across Veed's face. "Apparently, it makes a woman fall." He sauntered over to the bed and looked down at Nessix. "I trust she'll live?"

"Yes," Mathias answered curtly, swallowing Veed's previous cruelty, "but I'm quite sure she'd prefer you to leave."

"She'd understand my concern." Veed chuckled and brushed his fingers across Nes's cheek. Tension crackled between the two men, Mathias's jealousy tangible. How *very* unlike him. Veed turned his head and withdrew his hand. "You healed her, I'm guessing?"

"Who else would have?" Mathias wanted so badly to swat Veed's hand from Nes's pillow. "The talents you dabble with would have done nothing for her."

"Do you consider her more valuable than the others?" Veed asked, well aware of Mathias's displeasure. He leaned forward and slid his hand against Nes's palm. "Because last time she and I discussed your tricks, she told me you'd been losing your touch."

The barbs in Veed's statement struck Mathias, but no blood flowed from the wounds. "Nessix is the most valuable body on the field," he confirmed. "Etha had been silent for quite some time, but I don't expect you to understand that."

Veed lowered his eyes. "You sure she's ever been there?" Slowly, he lifted Nes's fingers closer to his lips.

The bowl fell from Mathias's lap and shattered on the floor as he jumped to his feet to grasp Veed's wrist. "Leave my patient be."

"No harm's ever come to her while I've been on watch. Seems

to beat your record."

Mathias met Veed's malicious eyes with steadfast anger. "You will remove yourself."

Veed had stumbled across the line Mathias refused him to cross. "Very well," he sighed, storing this information away and gently laying Nes's hand on her chest. "I'll be back to check on her."

"You are not needed for her recovery," Mathias assured. "Keep your concerns on the field, General."

Veed scathed Mathias with his glare. "Have you relinquished our camaraderie?"

"I tolerate you for the same reason Nessix does."

In the time it took Mathias to draw his next breath, Veed produced a dagger and laid it against the paladin's chest. "Or perhaps my offering wasn't good enough for you?"

Nessix had warned Mathias about Veed's propensity to find insult so easily, and in all honesty, he couldn't recall where the gaudy bauble went. "Must have lost it in battle." He shrugged. "I'd never disrespect authority."

"Of course you wouldn't."

"Is she going to—" Brant's frantic words cut off the moment he saw Veed aggressively positioned in front of Mathias.

Veed chuckled and tapped Mathias's chest with the blade. Already distraught, Brant would be after trouble, and this could be finished later. "No need to worry, Maliroch. I was on my way out." Bowing his head in a mockery of respect, Veed turned and left.

Brant had seen Mathias perform on the battlefield and at the mercy of Nes's tongue, but he'd never seen such a dangerous air about him. The commander considered asking what happened, but thought better of it. Instead, he hustled past Mathias, and grasped Nes's hand, kneeling beside the bed. Brant had been prepared for Nes to bear injuries, but his eyes dampened at her paleness and degree of battery. He should have stayed with her.

"I thought you said she'd be fine." Brant held his breath between each of Nes's own as he tried to work heat back into her cold fingers.

Mathias swallowed the tension that fogged his mind, Brant's

devotion to his cousin easing his troubles. "She will be, but she barely made it. She's best in your hands for now. I'll send for a maid to change her into whatever will be most comfortable. There are more patients to supervise Sulik with. I'll be back before dark."

Brant lifted his head, gazing at Nes's still face. The brat even griped in her sleep; he couldn't recall a time she'd been so still. He set his jaw firmly, unable to deny how much he owed Mathias.

"What do I do for her?"

A gentle smile crossed Mathias's face. "Stay with her. Clean her up a bit. If you find any wounds I missed, bandage them until I return. She's no longer in danger from what happened to her on the field, but there are other factors that determine whether someone lives or dies."

Brant nodded, carefully laying Nes's hand back down. He unpinned her braids and picked at the mats of blood in her hair. Pleased at his patient's safety, Mathias snuck out of the room to check on Sulik's progress.

* * * * *

Mathias brooded over what had made him stay with Nessix for so long. While he fussed over her, more than a few of the critical cases waiting in the mess hall had succumbed to their injuries. Without Nessix, the war would be over, and her well-being needed to come first. But if she knew others died while Mathias's jealous mind tried to come up with ways to torture Veed, she'd hate herself and Mathias both. To keep from dwelling on the limitations of human motives, Mathias concentrated his efforts on praying for mercy and divine intervention.

"Sir." Sulik's quiet voice startled Mathias from his stupor. "I found enough of the healthy willing to give up their bunks for those in need."

"Very good," Mathias said. "We can clear the main halls, then."

"And Nes?"

Mathias smiled. "Provided Brant will let you in, you can check

228

on her yourself. She's unconscious, but resting well."

"Will there be any lasting damage?"

"Only to her pride." Mathias briefly wondered if that would make Nessix any more reasonable. "I've got to catch some rest, myself. I expended more than I meant to today. I'm sure you did, too."

Sulik nodded as the day's efforts rushed up on him at the mention of sleep. "I'll make arrangements for the wounded, sir. You've done much more than I have."

Staving off weariness long enough to peek in on Nessix once more, Mathias found Brant still at her side. Bloodshot eyes stared at a soldier beside him. Having not intended to interrupt anything, Mathias prepared to leave until the commander's attention flicked toward him.

"We'll give what we received," Brant grumbled. "That's all."

Mathias entered as the soldier bowed and left the room. "Is everything alright?"

"With Nes?" Brant's gaze returned to his cousin, the same troubled expression wreaking havoc on his face. "She hasn't moved."

Mathias nodded. "She likely won't for a few days; her injuries were greater than my touch alone could heal." He reached forward and gauged her pulse. "But my question was in regard to that soldier."

"An army's marching on Veed," Brant said. "The men well enough to return to battle wanted to know if we'd aid him."

"Did he send up a flare?"

"No."

"If he does, the men will assist," Mathias said, "and it would be best for you to lead them."

Brant didn't particularly care for the declaration, considering it more than generous that he tolerated Mathias at all. "I'm just a lowly commander." Brant stifled a yawn. "If you feel we need to take action on Veed's behalf, you are welcome to cover the actions yourself, General."

"If I outrank you, then my words were an order. You know how your men fight better than I do, and should anything change in Nes's condition while I was gone, what would you do for her?"

Brant cursed Mathias's willingness to use Nes's fragility as leverage. "Then let us pray no flares are sent."

Mathias sighed, but accepted that as compliance. "Make sure you get some rest. The demons are bound to take advantage of their new position."

Closing his eyes, both from weariness and the urge to rid his sight of Mathias, Brant nodded.

"And remember, you have me and Sulik at your disposal."

Brant never accepted the offer verbally and Mathias took that as his cue to leave the room. The flare would come and pull Brant back onto the field, and Mathias would get his chance to check on Nessix in due time.

* * * * *

Nessix lay in her bed, carefully tucked in and the covers smooth. A chair sat beside her, Mathias's sword and the bulk of his armor resting in a pile nearby. Her eyes traveled the room, trying to recollect any wisps of a memory to explain what happened, and it took a moment for the battle to return to her. Blinking in reality, Nessix spotted Mathias leaning against the windowsill.

"If you came to lecture me, I don't want to hear it," she said quietly.

Mathias stared across the field in silence. Nessix pushed herself up with her hands, atrophied arms shaking beneath the effort before a jolt of pain shot up her spine and leveled her again.

"And if you're waiting for me to tell you I learned my lesson, you'll be disappointed."

Mathias dropped his hand from the sill. "I'm not here to lecture you, only think."

Her eyes returned to his belongings. "About moving in?"

"No," Mathias said gravely, turning to face her. A flood of relief hit him as he met her clear eyes. "I was thinking about how the butcher forgot to bring a sharp enough axe."

Nessix pointed her chin away from him. "I didn't ask for your help."

"You didn't have to," Mathias said. "I did what had to be done. I—" The words that fought to form remained lodged in the back of his throat. Nessix had neither the need nor the desire for him to share his thoughts. "Forget it. You survived."

Nes's glower subsided, replaced with a keen curiosity and a hint of egotism. "No. Tell me."

"Don't worry about it. What matters now is that we've learned how strong the demons have become."

"Nonsense." Gritting her teeth, Nessix tried once again to raise herself to a seated position, coaxing Mathias away from the window and closer to her bed. "We'll still win this."

"Please, stay down," Mathias urged. "I'll bring you your notes and maps, but you're in no condition to move about."

Nessix didn't care for his assumptions, but pain scolded her persistence. She sufficed for leaning against the headboard to wait for the agonizing pulses to ebb so she could try again. "Give me a minute. I'll be fine."

"If you strain yourself now, you could put yourself out for another week." Mathias tucked his relief away as Nessix settled back against the pillows.

"How long until I can take the field again?"

"Two days until you're mobile, assuming you actually rest. Even then, you'll have to get back in condition."

A tiny smile tugged at the corners of her mouth. "You're not looking so good, yourself."

"Taking charge of your force was tough," Mathias confessed. His eyes drifted to the window again. "Your army's impressive and this war is brutal. I hope you take to heart how much I admire your ability to keep up with it."

Nes's lips broadened in contentment. His praise pleased her immensely, but not quite enough to overlook her bedridden condition. "How long have I been out?"

"Eight days."

Reflex ignored her previous failed attempts and Nes's instinct to sit up resulted in another frustrated cry. "Impossible!"

Patiently, Mathias returned to her and helped ease her back

down. She initially resisted his efforts, but a firm look persuaded Nessix into compliance. Her eyes strayed to the chair and armor again.

"Eight days," she murmured. "And you stayed here with me?"

Mathias's slack jaw preceded a verbal answer. "I couldn't leave you to anyone else; none of my students could have handled your condition."

Nes's gaze lofted to the ceiling. Over a week had passed since she'd seen her army, and her heart ached to know how they'd fared without her. "What about the demons?"

"Brant's been waiting to give you a report." Mathias knew both Nessix and her cousin would appreciate sharing the victories. "I'll find him for you."

"Wait."

Mathias paused on his way to the door.

"What was bothering you just now?"

Mathias turned slowly and moved two steps back into the room. "I was worried about you not making it for a while," he admitted. "Foolish of me, huh?"

"Was I really that bad?" Her voice shrank with the question.

Nessix proved her competence on the field time and time again, but Mathias had no idea what she'd have thought of her own injuries. Apparently, her recollection of the event was fuzzy, and Mathias figured that best.

"I don't know," he lied.

The flimsy tone of his words left Nessix feeling tiny and vulnerable. Pride gone in this private moment, she called on one more favor. "Help me stand."

Mathias glanced away from her, incapable of meeting her frightful determination. "Your wounds were grievous and you shouldn't move yet. I understand your resentment for your condition, but please let me bring you what you need."

Nessix shook her head as firmly as her firing nerves allowed. "You were concerned about the field," she insisted. "I need to see my men."

No amount of reassurance would convince Nessix everything was fine, and Mathias knew that. He didn't want an argument any more than he wanted to see her disappointment and purposefully avoided looking at her. "Your commanders are managing well." A stab of weariness forced Mathias to lean an arm on Nes's bedpost. "If you'll dismiss me, I'll find Brant for you. Now please rest."

Nessix reached out and grabbed Mathias's free wrist, oblivious to the tension that flickered through him. "You're hurting."

"I'm doing no such thing." He wriggled his hand free. "I'm just tired; I've been up for the past two days."

"Were there others worse off than me?"

"Only the dead."

Nes wanted to hear that only slightly less than Mathias wanted to say it. Uncomfortable at once, she pulled her hand back to her chest. "Go find Brant," she ordered quietly. "Tell the troops I'm well."

"They'll be glad," Mathias said. "The entire fortress has been anxious, thanks to you."

A gentle laugh surprised them both. "They shouldn't have been. I'm stubborn, remember?"

"We both are," Mathias agreed, though his smile couldn't quite surface.

"Get yourself some rest." Nes's smile broadened just a touch, and she gave him a wink. "I promise I won't let anything happen on my watch."

Caving to her words and his weary mind at last, Mathias returned her smile. "If you insist, General."

Mathias turned, ushering himself out of her chamber. Nessix yawned and pulled the blankets around her shoulders. Her eyes drifted closed. Unobserved, a sinister face poked through the open window, grinning at the girl's serene form, and took wing.

* * * * *

If injuries hadn't killed Nessix, boredom would. Interacting with her army secondhand irritated her, and she scorned her body for not holding up to her efforts of answering the watch tower bells. Mathias had appointed Sulik to impede Nes's activity, the commander reciting threats about how she shouldn't push herself, and her generally sour mood crept back. The war persisted despite Nes's condition and while reports attested to her army's valor, she fussed over how much better they'd be with her marching with them. The army returned, raising their jubilations through her open window, and Nessix sighed out her frustration.

Throwing the blankets off herself with a busy grumble, Nessix gingerly drew her knees up and grit her teeth in anticipation of pain. Feeling nothing but the tight protest of neglected muscles, she eased her toes to the floor and tested her weight on numb legs. Tingling prefaced the rush of fatigue in her calves, and her knees ached when she asked them to bend. Biting her lip, Nessix pulled herself the rest of the way from her bed, resting her hands on the mattress for temporary support. She straightened after not falling over the span of three breaths and took her time dressing. Once she deemed herself presentable, Nessix wobbled toward the door.

She aimed to keep to the back stairwells and passageways on her way out of the fortress, hoping to leave the building before debility subdued her. Her head swam by the time she reached the main level and she wondered if leaving her chamber had been a wise decision. Stepping into the daylight reawakened her senses. A faint breeze tickled her face and the sun brushed her skin in the delicious way no number of blankets could imitate. Nessix tilted her face toward the warmth and basked on the side steps until she remembered why she came out in the first place. Her gaze lingered on the tent where Mathias conducted his classes.

By now, Nes's legs protested her activity and her lungs worked quickly, but determination sustained her to the pavilion. She quietly slipped inside and plunked down on a stool in the back of the class, grateful to rest her feeble body. Mathias muttered under his breath in a foreign language, his back to his audience as he rummaged through a trunk.

"It seems someone in the heavens is playing a game with me," Mathias grumbled, giving up on his search. "You'll have to take my word for—" He paused when he turned around and saw Nessix. "What it's worth. Review what we've gone over for a moment," he said, waiting to see everyone turn to his requested task before making his way to Nessix.

She watched him approach, eyes openly curious. "You didn't have to stop on my behalf," she whispered, wrinkling her nose as her voice gained the attention of those nearest to her.

Mathias grasped her shoulders and moved her to face him squarely. "I wanted to look you over, since you're out and about earlier than you ought to be." Regardless of what Mathias wanted, at least Nessix was in good spirits.

More of the students turned their eyes to the pair, opting to ignore Mathias's directions. Nessix fidgeted under their attention.

"I'm fine," she insisted sheepishly, batting his hands away. "A little dizzy, but nothing I can't shrug off."

"To be expected, considering how hard you're pushing yourself," he said. The diffidence in Nes's gaze prompted Mathias to turn and look over the gawking students. "You're all on break for the next hour."

Despite some apparent disappointment, the class filed past Nessix to give the generals their privacy.

"In all honesty, I'm surprised you didn't start running around earlier," Mathias said as the last student left.

Nessix smirked, but refused to look up at him. "You told me I shouldn't and I really don't know much about how to get better. I held out as long as I could stand."

"Well," Mathias said, completing his evaluation. "I can't say I approve of your activity, but I'm sure the men appreciate seeing you for themselves."

"Was I really that bad?"

"I don't think anyone else would have survived."

Nessix tried to laugh, but it lodged in her chest. "I don't think I was meant to."

A small frown pressed Mathias's mouth. "I'll remember that next time, if you'd like."

"Why'd you do it?"

"Do what?"

"Was it to prove yourself?" she asked. "I mean, with you here, there's really no need for me." Nessix picked at her cuticles, afraid of what Mathias's eyes might tell her.

This timid side of Nessix dropped an uncomfortable weight in Mathias's stomach. "You are the banner of hope for your people. They *do* need you."

Nessix shook her head. "But I..." Even though everyone was gone, her voice shrank to a whisper. "I was *dead*. I felt it."

"Even the next realm can't take you if the faith protecting you is strong enough," Mathias said, whether or not Nessix wanted to believe him. "The gods knew you weren't meant to leave this world yet."

"Would I have lived if you weren't here?"

He ruminated on the thought. "Perhaps. The pleas of your people were strong and their voices were heard."

She laughed, an empty tremolo. "I thought you told me you were done with the lies."

Mathias adjusted his weight, unable to gauge Nes's intentions. "You were the one staring at the gates of death, and you still doubt the gods?" He watched her consider his words. "You are as intriguing as ever."

Nessix hung her head as she tried to decipher if Mathias meant that as an insult. Resistant to change and still madly devoted to Inwan, she didn't necessarily doubt Mathias or Etha. She was simply afraid to accept them and move on from the past she cherished. She shrank with her doubt.

Mathias softened his approach. "It's alright, Nes. You're well again and that's what matters."

Attempting to put order to her jumbled thoughts taxed Nes's brain and made her long to go back to bed. "Do you think the demons expected my recovery?"

"They left you with fatal wounds. They must have thought you fell."

Nessix sighed, grasping the pole beside her to aid her standing. Reflex told her to wave Mathias's hand away, but no one had to know she needed his help. "The reports I've been given tell me you sent a unit to the north. If you'll give me permission, I'd like to ride out to them."

Mathias nodded. "Sulik's there now. Brant should be sending a unit shortly to give the soldiers a chance to rest."

"You've controlled them well, I'll give you that."

Nes's simple compliment filled Mathias's belly with a giddy warmth and modesty swept over him. "There were no epic battles for bards to write songs about. It was more paperwork than anything."

Nessix grinned and gave Mathias a pat on his forearm. "Has my song been composed yet?"

"I believe they were waiting to see if it would be the song of a martyr or a champion."

A tide of guilt washed over Nessix and she lowered her head again. "Would you ride out with me?" Her gaze dropped further. "I'd hate for them to think I'm the only champion to sing of."

Uncertain at first if Nessix intended those words as gratitude, Mathias was moved by her request. "I'd be honored to."

SEVENTEEN

The strength of the northern lines satisfied Mathias. Nes's presence bolstered the army's enthusiasm, which renewed her own light. With contentment working back through the Teradhel army, evening settled over Elidae.

Although Mathias lived for others, he anxiously retired to his quarters, escaping the fuss and bustle of the lively fortress. Since the attacks had eased enough to allow plentiful rest, his strength mended daily. From his window, Mathias watched the sun slink away. Ceraphlaks would watch over the land, and so Mathias reveled in the anticipation of a full night's sleep.

"It is in your will I trust, Mother," he prayed, as usual for his evening routine. "May I fulfill your desires through the pending trials."

Laughter trickled from beneath the door and condensed behind him. "This is a trial, is it?"

He wished he could smile. "Aren't all things I do in your name?"

"We've already discussed your recent limitations, my dear," Etha murmured. "But I've noticed vast improvements since then."

Still not turning to face her, Mathias hung his head. "I'm thankful for what you've given me, but it's still barely enough to do what I need to for these people."

Etha opted to ignore Mathias's sour mood and pranced impish steps in front of him. A wide grin parted her face. "You *did* have enough, no?"

Her efforts warmed Mathias's soul. "Yes," he admitted, "but I'm curious if it's your doing or dumb luck."

Brooding, Etha scavenged a brighter thought, one that had scratched at her over the past several days. "There's something else I'd rather talk about."

Mathias smirked, allowing Etha's gaiety to affect him. "I should smite myself for blasphemy. Whatever insight you have, I'd be grateful to hear it."

Eyes twinkling, Etha pushed Mathias back a step with a finger to his chest. "I know what's in your heart!"

"Fear?" he asked with a bitter laugh.

Etha's expression dulled for a moment, disappointed by his ignorance or denial, and lowered herself to playing dirty. Before Mathias's weary mind registered the changes, he gazed into clear sapphire eyes. Etha's features sharpened toward maturity and dark locks tumbled about her shoulders. The grin previously lighting her face melted into a cocky smile.

Seeing Nes's hair down captivated Mathias, and he ached to run his hands through the raven tresses. A spear of laughter reminded him at once of Etha's playful nature, prompting Mathias to scramble away from the goddess. What had come over him?

"It's not what you think!" Mathias insisted, clawing at his fleeing composure. One blink and Etha returned to her preferred appearance of a mischievous girl.

"It isn't?" She threw him a sidelong glance.

"My faith and devotion is to you and you alone. I have no room for anything else."

"You spent eight days doting over a single patient. You made room for *something*."

"Nes's death would have meant the defeat of her people," Mathias insisted. "I couldn't sit idly and let her die. It was too difficult a task to chance to anyone else." He planned on sticking to that explanation, too.

"Even if you could have trusted her to a student, would you

239

have?"

Mathias shoved down a modest flush. "Of course," he said, doubting the claim under Etha's pressure. "There were too many suffering and so few able to help. I would have gone where I was needed."

The goddess shook her head, the grin persisting and still suspiciously similar to Nes's. "Don't think I wasn't watching."

"Watching, but not answering."

"I let her live, didn't I?"

Ashamed, Mathias lowered his eyes. "Yes, by your grace alone did she live. I am grateful."

"I know you are."

After a couple breaths, Mathias snuck a glance at Etha to catch her glittering eyes and a brow arched in elegant jest. His cheeks burned beneath Etha's glee. "Grah! Why are you doing this to me?"

Etha burst into laughter, flustering him even more. "What are you ashamed of? She's not an ugly girl."

Mathias rolled his eyes and stared at the ceiling. "Besides the distant past, there's nothing I regret." He seldom grew impatient with his goddess, but the feeling crept on him now.

Catching the desperation of his thoughts, Etha cleared her throat and attempted maturity. "Why won't you admit it, at least to me?" Good intentions failed to keep the glint from her eyes. "You're afraid of her, aren't you?"

"Afraid of that brat?" Mathias scoffed. A patient stare demanded his elaboration. "She's cocky and stubborn."

"Nothing at all like you at that age, huh?"

His mouth wrapped around excuses he didn't have.

"Go on, my dear."

"So what if I was like that once!" He wondered where Etha hid all of these cheap shots. "I wasn't my nation's sole guardian."

"She didn't *choose* her position, you know."

"There were *good* leaders when I was a boy, ones who stayed true to their faith and oaths. Ones who earned their station through merit and not blood."

"She honors her oaths and has stayed remarkably true to the

only faith she knows."

"Her faith is based on false traditions and a failed god."

"Perhaps that's why you feel so close to her?" Etha suggested. "To protect her?"

Mathias had taken his fill of this goading. "What good is it to lead a child who won't listen to reason or acknowledge holy power when it's right in front of her?"

"I am ashamed, Mathias Sagewind," Etha scolded. "After Nessix came to you today, you think she assumes she's alive for any reason not directly tied to you?" She offered him the chance to reply, but her harshness had silenced him. "She may be spoiled and stubborn, but she isn't as foolish as she comes across."

"I'm sure she's already come up with excuses," Mathias muttered.

"Is that what's bothering you?" she asked. "The thought that she may not need you?" Etha searched his face and found nothing but the very stubbornness he claimed to detest. "Are you *wanting* her to come up with excuses?"

"It'd be easier on her people if she'd accept a miracle for what it is and not need constant proof."

"And it would be easier on you to accept your feelings," Etha said. "Things would straighten themselves out if you did."

"I don't know what you're implying," Mathias said, anxious for this teasing to lose its novelty.

"I can see into your heart, dear, and you know exactly what I'm implying." If Mathias wanted to be difficult, Etha would gladly accept the challenge. "Unless, of course, your motivations are as indecent as Veed's."

"Veed is a repulsive man," Mathias sneered.

"But maybe you're jealous of his connection with Nes? He's known her much longer, certainly he must mean more to her on some level?"

"That's ridiculous. She hates him."

"But also respects him."

As the thought set in, it became increasingly valid. Something in her past made Nes resentfully appreciate Veed. Mathias had heard her refer to him as an uncle before, but saw no apparent blood between them. Once Etha got this mischief out of her system, Mathias would ask Sulik about the two generals' history with each other. His mind wandered to the exchanges he'd shared with Veed and he doubted he really wanted to know the truth.

"If she knew how he talked about her..." Mathias startled himself with the emotion he only vaguely realized lurked inside of him. "There is no love in his words, only selfish desire."

"And you pride yourself on being unlike him," Etha clarified.

"What does that have to do with anything?" Defense turned to frustration. Mathias welcomed Etha's games, but this neared torment.

"He has no love for her?"

Mathias gave in. "Even if I did have feelings for her, they'd only complicate matters and distract me from my duty."

"I suppose it would." Etha sighed and slumped her shoulders in disappointment. She'd hoped for this to play out differently.

"Since when have you cared about the passions of men, anyway?"

"Not men," Etha corrected. "*Man*. Is it wrong for a mother to keep an eye on the affairs of her dearest son?"

Heat returned to Mathias's cheeks under Etha's grin. "Do all mothers meddle in their children's affairs?"

Etha gasped, raising a hand to her chest as she shook her head. "*This* is meddling? If you'd prefer, I could stop by her chamber for a chat about what goes on in that head of yours. *That*, my dear, would be meddling."

Mathias cringed at her enthusiasm. "You wouldn't." He scanned those deep eyes he knew meant trust, though he found it difficult to scrape enough of it together right now. "Would you?" he asked meekly.

A delicate shoulder rose in a shrug. "You'll never tell her, and politics don't give her a great selection of suitors."

Heaving a sigh, Mathias sagged on his bed. A whole new war prowled after him, this one far more dreadful than most. It had been ages since he'd dealt with lost breath and fluttering hearts, and the physical war on Elidae wouldn't allow him time to assess both threats. "You don't fight fair."

"I don't have to."

"Was this the only reason for your visit, or is there something I actually need to know about?"

Etha's grin faded, replaced by a more serious expression. "The demons are moving again."

Mathias stared at her, dumbfounded. "Couldn't we have opened with this?"

"We could have, but where would be the fun in that?" Instantly catching on that nothing at all seemed fun to him, Etha composed herself into the serious mother Mathias always wanted. "I've told Ceraphlaks to avoid the western forests. It would be no good if they saw him."

"Do you have an idea on how many?" Mathias was already at his desk.

"They're rivaling an even match for your forces, but you know the way demons fight. More are bound to follow."

Mathias nodded, eyes sweeping across the maps and fingers tapping the edge of his desk. "Anything else?"

"Not unless you're concerned about the scuffles they've started elsewhere on Elidae. They've taken quite an interest in the minotaur lately. You're welcome to help them in the next lull, if you so please, but for now your duty is with the flemans."

"Of course," Mathias said. "If you've got nothing else, I'd best get word to Sulik."

Etha crinkled her forehead. "Sulik? What'll he do about it?"

Mathias looked away. "Tell Nessix."

The corners of Etha's mouth tugged, but she hid her smile in her eyes. "Because you wouldn't dare confront her yourself."

Concentrating on the danger awaiting the kingdom, Mathias maintained his composure past his blushing. "My lady, I have plans to start laying out. Sending Sulik with the message is efficient."

Etha rolled her eyes. "I suppose I'll be off. Do give Nessix my regards."

"Of course, Mother," he muttered. "If anything else suspicious shows up, please bring it to my attention."

I've influenced Sulik to find you. He should be by shortly.

Mathias turned in his chair to find Etha already gone. Heaving a sigh, wondering how to write off the more awkward of the evening's topics, Mathias diverted his attention back to his maps.

* * * * *

"He wanted proof that Nessix is as well as the reports say," Renigan insisted, attempting once more to shove past Brant. "You are trying my patience."

"And you have overstayed what little welcome you had," Brant seethed. "If Nessix wanted Veed to celebrate her recovery, she'd have gone to him herself."

"You would send me back to my general with nothing?" Renigan asked.

"If that's all you gathered, then yes. If you're trying to threaten me, know it's not working."

Renigan opened his mouth to retaliate, but his eyes locked on something more interesting. He leaned against the wall and crossed his arms. "Good evening, Sulik," he greeted as the third commander bustled over.

"Oh, Brant, thank Etha I found you!" Sulik ignored Renigan completely. "Sir Sagewind reported movement in the west. Their expected charge is tomorrow afternoon. He asked me to alert Nessix and have her begin working on plans, but I'm overbooked tending to the—"

Brant held up a hand to curtail Sulik's excuses. "Do what you have to. I'll let Nes know about the demons."

Sulik nodded his appreciation then turned his eyes to their company. "I trust you can see yourself out, Falk."

Brant's chuckle stole Renigan's smile. "You heard him. We've got more important things to tend to."

Renigan blustered off in a tiff and Brant turned to find Nes. He resented the fact that Sulik, no doubt under Mathias's guidance, saw fit to use him as a simple messenger, but he wasn't keen on the idea of gambling with the people's lives. Resolving to restore his standing in this nonexistent bout for power, Brant searched for a happy medium between asserting his position and saving the day.

So caught up in plans to protect his pride, Brant nearly collided with Nessix as she descended the stairs with an armful of books. She smiled at him and continued on her way.

"Hey, Nes, you have a minute?"

"Maybe two. What's up?" She resumed skipping down the stairs and Brant followed.

"I think we're due for another attack."

"I thought Sagewind said we just had one," Nessix said thoughtfully, leading the way to her chamber. She shoved her books into Brant's arms to open the door, and gestured to her desk. "Have the patterns changed?"

"I think they've stayed the same for too long." Brant deposited the haul where Nes had directed. "Just try to keep plans in the back of your mind and your senses sharp."

Nessix furrowed her brows, but refrained from asking what had him so concerned. Regardless of his answer, she trusted Brant. He'd never led her astray in the past. "I will," she said. Cursing the dull ache in her neck, Nessix winced and gingerly stretched it out. "I'm still not feeling quite as spry as I ought to."

Brant smiled. "Get your rest. I'll see to it your kingdom's safe tonight."

She laughed shortly. "You expect me to trust that face?"

Brant winked. "You can never be sure, can you?" How he'd missed having her well!

"I've got some reading before bed, but I'll get on those battle plans first thing in the morning. Maybe we can lead an attack on them for a change."

He nodded in approval. "I'd love to see how those brutes handled it. If they're smart, they'd tuck their tails and run."

"Let's hope so," Nes answered with a yawn. "Good night, Brant."

"You too, Nes."

As Nessix cracked open the first old tome, Brant excused himself, content with her ease.

EIGHTEEN

Even in sleep, Nes's mind worked rapidly, winding her deeper into the world that mirrored her imagination and taunting her with the life her position barred from her. Music beckoned Nessix to the great hall, chipper melodies accented by trills of laughter. She turned the corner, and met the enchantment of lively dancers twirling about in their skirts, hand-in-hand with dashing young men. Each member floated by without a care, coaxing Nes's lips to part in contentment. The circle of dancers spun past until she met Brant's bright eyes. His hand caught the tips of her fingers, and she allowed him to lead her in to the dance.

In all honesty, Nessix felt foolish. Besides not knowing how to dance, her frazzled war braids and worn breeches contrasted against the blushing elegance around her. Her psyche refused to let her make excuses and proved Brant a fine teacher for such a silly form of expression. In less than one pass through the crowd, the steps started to come to Nessix. By the second, her hair tickled her cheeks and shoulders in luscious waves and the swish of a skirt caressed her legs.

Feeling so helplessly feminine elated Nessix as much now as pressing into battle did on any other day. The thought of war scolded her to shape up, but when she tried to escape the soiree, Brant drew her back in. Worry creased the space between her brows, but the jovial faces around her begged her to leave responsibility behind, at least for tonight. Needing a respite, trusting the towers to alert her if any danger lurked in the waking world, Nessix surrendered at last.

Just as she figured everything out, reveling in the joys of being a girl, Mathias entered the hall, dressed in the handsome attire of a nobleman. Nessix flushed, uncertain of what came over her, and attempted to avoid acknowledging him until magnetic curiosity forced her to look up. In that moment, the softness in his eyes and the charm in his smile stifled her breath. Brant raised his free hand to motion Mathias over. Modesty choked Nessix, and she suddenly felt the skirt made her vulnerable and indecent.

"Brant..." she begged. "Don't make me do this."

He answered her with a devious smile and inclined his head toward the far side of the circle where Mathias waited. Nessix shook her head, pleading with Brant to stop as she squirmed her hand in his grasp, but the methodical steps of the dance pushed her ever closer. Flustered and insecure, Nessix could hardly breathe as they neared Mathias and he held out his hand to take this dainty version of the haughty general from her cousin.

"Show her around!" Brant laughed, twirling Nessix once more before casting her free from his hold.

In that breath of freedom, Nessix had the chance to run from the encounter, but her pounding heart numbed her senses. Instead of trying to escape, she timidly stretched her arm toward the human who captivated her so much. She *wanted* to dance with him, for him to teach her. True to his chivalrous nature, Mathias swept his arm grandly and bowed. He strode forward to take her hand.

Mere inches from touching him, an overwhelming dread twisted Nes's gut. Her joints locked against movement and held her fast, impeding her attempts to withdraw. Time withered to a crawl as Mathias's fingers reached for her, and the absolute need to keep him from touching her flooded Nes's unresponsive body with panic. Mathias's skin brushed against hers and a concussive force scattered lights across her field of vision. The sounds of happiness drowned in an empty ringing.

For several heartbeats, Nessix heard only her own gasping.

She dug the heels of her palms against her eye sockets to try to flush out the flashes of light. Her senses crept back to her, and she peered down an unfamiliar, dimly lit corridor. As she stood there and fumbled over what happened, the haunting sound of siege bells reached her ears. Someone clad in armor marched several paces in front of her, barely visible, and waved toward himself before dashing off down the hall.

Completely disregarding her previous experience with dream folk, Nessix chased after this stranger, cursing the confines of the dress she wore.

"To the field!" she ordered, gaining on this figure despite the handicap of her unfamiliar garment. "Our brothers are—"

A startled yelp squeaked from Nessix and she fought momentum as the man spun around and leapt back at her, easily wrestling her to the ground. Nessix ordered him off, but only managed a scream before a cold hand clapped over her mouth. One arm held down by her assailant's free hand, the other by his knee, Nessix kicked fiercely in the skirt's masses of fabric. Screams smothered, she looked into luminous green eyes.

Reality crashed around her, launching Nessix from the realms of sleep. A demon straddled her waist, crushing her diaphragm and hissing condemnations at her struggles. With her arms pinned and her legs tangled in her sheets, Nessix bit down on the demon's palm and choked out the loudest scream her lungs allowed.

Cursing in his foreign tongue, the demon shot a glance over his shoulder then lowered his mouth over hers. Nessix twisted her body beneath his, tried to scream again, but her efforts were suppressed by an intolerable burning that flowed down her throat and into her lungs and stomach.

In a flash, the demon propelled himself off of her and vacated the room through the open window. Too shaken for anything else, Nessix recoiled against her headboard, wringing one hand around her neck and wiping the demon's blood from her lips with the other.

* * * * *

Fleet footsteps clamored down the hall, chased by frantic exclamations that tugged Mathias's concentration from his prayers. Etha made no objection to his concern and answered his question before he'd even asked it.

They're running to Nessix.

In the moments it took Mathias to grab his enchanted blade and race down the hall, the handful of soldiers that first alerted him had beaten the door to Nes's chamber open. With only the troops' urgency and Etha's brief information to go off of, Mathias assumed the worst.

"Step aside," he demanded, quick strides carrying him to Nes's room. "All of you."

The anxious crowd parted readily, content to let Mathias handle whatever caused Nes's palpable terror. He passed by the men and rounded the partition separating her bed from the rest of the room. Nessix kneeled on her bed, her back pressed against the headboard as she clutched a sheet around body with one hand. Blood smeared across her chin and half of her mouth, stains of the same dappling her blankets and a trail to the window. Eyes helplessly beautiful, it took half a dozen heaves of her chest for Nessix to recognize Mathias and succumb to the quivering of her lower lip.

Mathias lowered his sword. "She'll be fine," he called to the soldiers in the hall. "I ask you spare your general her modesty and return to your posts."

The troops trusted Mathias's assessment and obeyed his instruction, leaving Nessix in his capable hands.

Tears flooded silently down Nes's ashen cheeks. As her hands trembled and shoulders slumped forward, Mathias hurried over to her. At any other time, Nessix scrambling into his arms would have startled them both, but as Mathias perched on the edge of her bed, he made her feel safe, and she needed him.

Nessix shook in his arms, able to bite back her tears in the security of his embrace. Mathias held her close, her heart pounding against his bare chest, and his eyes stung at her anguish. She pressed close to him, his strength building a sturdy rampart around her that vowed to never let another demon touch her again. His hand unintentionally clasped the hair at her shoulder blades.

"Mathias, what happened?" Nes murmured.

The sound of his given name on her voice left him dazed, but her question struck him harder. "I was hoping you could tell me."

She pushed herself away from him, eyes flitting across the room. None of her thoughts made any sense. "Dreams aren't supposed to hurt."

Mathias clasped her hands between his. "Nes, I don't think it was a dream."

She shook her head and pinched her lips together in an effort to dam her tears. "It was a dream," she said. "It *had* to be."

Mathias drew her hands closer and pried them apart to grasp one of her wrists. His thumbs brushed across bruised skin and he glanced up to see her staring down at the blemish. "Dreams do not hurt," Mathias agreed, "but something *did* hurt you. You're safe with me. You can tell me what happened."

Their turbulent past aside, Nessix knew she could confide in Mathias and he'd keep her shame a secret. "It *was* a dream," she insisted, lips quivering as she frowned. "There was dancing, and Brant was there, and—" She stopped the recollection before she admitted dreaming about him. "We were attacked, and there was this man, and…" Her voice faltered as she tried to distinguish the tangible parts of the truth. "A demon grabbed me, too strong to fight."

Mathias stood, letting Nessix's frantic hand clutch his as he inched over to her wash basin and soaked a cloth. When he returned to her side, Nessix let go of him as he dabbed at the blood on her face. "Clearly, you did fight it," he said.

Her face contorted in her next wave of denial, but as she saw the demon's blood staining the cloth in Mathias's hand, it became harder for her to argue against reality. "I couldn't fight him," she said. "He pinned me down and I couldn't get free."

Mathias frowned, his unsettled stomach prompting him to pause his actions. "Then what happened?"

"He…" Nes looked away from Mathias, lashes fluttering rapidly. "He kissed me."

A filthy rage engulfed Mathias, and he barely contained the

urge to slam his fist into the nearest nonliving object. He clenched his teeth and swallowed the emotion before it blew out of his control. "What else did he do to you?"

The distress from Mathias's assumptions tugged a thread of regret from Nessix, and she shook her head. "Nothing," she said. "But it burned."

Mathias's relief that Nessix had been spared one of the demons' more appalling forms of torture lasted just long enough for a new concern to surface. "It burned?"

She nodded. "Everything in me—my tongue and throat, stomach and lungs. I-I can still feel it in my veins." Her lips tucked downward again and she sniffed back her next swell of dismay. "What does this mean?"

Any sympathy Mathias had ever tried to show the demons drowned out in his fury of them targeting Nessix in this manner. He veiled his anger in the hope of keeping her calm and lifted his sword from the bed to will it into a much more practical knife. "It means," he said, coaxing the fingers of her left hand to uncoil. "That I have to hurt you. Just a pinch."

Confusion compounded her fear until Mathias swept his dagger across the tip of her index finger. Nessix gasped at the sting, recoiling the cut to her mouth as she looked up at Mathias. Still too frightened to react to his audacity, Nessix followed his gaze down to the blade. As she'd seen countless times before, the blood simmered off the enchanted steel in a wisp of steam. Experience taught her demon blood behaved in that manner, only this time, the blood was hers.

Nessix whimpered helplessly, her face wrenching in a terrified frown as tears poured past their boundaries. Her mind raced with the possibilities—a prolonged death, corruption forcing her to turn on her people, or worse yet, becoming a demon outright. She saw herself clinging to her honest past as her future fell into darkness, and she realized how badly she wanted to stay alive. As Nessix crumbled before him, Mathias's heart splintered.

He held her head in her hands, trying unsuccessfully to force her to face him. "It'll be okay." He ducked his head to try catching her eyes. "It's a curse, nothing more, and it's something I can help you purge. You'll be okay."

His words burrowed through the ringing in Nes's ears, and she sniffled before looking up at him. "A curse to what?"

"I don't know," Mathias admitted. "But the demon who put it on you was sloppy and got caught. We can stop this before it has the chance to develop into something serious."

She nodded, the tears ebbing. "Please fix me."

His expression softened. "I'll get the ingredients to—"

When Mathias tried to move from where he cupped her jaw, Nes's petite, shaking hands grasped his forearms. Mouth stuck in mid-statement, the tiniest fleck of a much more intoxicating emotion than anger or fear muddled Mathias's thoughts.

"I don't want to be alone," Nessix murmured.

Mathias stared at her desolate eyes as she sought to hide them beneath bashful lashes. He felt her insecurity through the repeated clenching of her jaw, the desperation of her calloused hands, the urgency of her words. Nessix didn't want to be alone and, quite frankly, he didn't want to leave her. Drawn to her vulnerability, Mathias rested his forehead against hers.

Nessix kept her eyes lowered and her tear-induced congestion forced her mouth agape to breathe. From the moment they met, Nessix had masqueraded as a self-reliant woman, strong enough to fight her own battles, but right now she teetered on the cusp of a dependency Mathias ached for. He tilted his chin and parted his lips.

Mathias, Etha warned gently. *She's tainted.*

He pinched his eyes shut, internalizing a tormented sigh. His mortal desires urged him to forego the reminder and prove his devotion to Nessix, but his wizened side overwhelmed such longing. If he truly wanted to protect Nessix, he had to keep himself honest. A rude throat cleared from behind him, and they both jolted.

"Is this something I should know about?" Brant's tired eyes expressed how little he wanted to play right now.

Mathias blinked away the last fancies of his wandering mind and stood. Nessix briefly caught his hand, but he deftly wriggled it away under Brant's suspicious glare. "She was attacked. Quite shaken, but she'll be alright. I'm going to prepare an herbal remedy to help ward against any lingering effects, if you'd be so kind as to keep her company."

Brant's frown deepened when he saw Nes's forlorn gaze track Mathias. "And who was it that attacked her?" he asked as Mathias passed him.

Mathias met Brant's eyes. "A demon," he said. "I'm sure she can fill you in better than I can. Now, you can keep on with this pissing contest and we can wait and see what happens to her overnight, or you can comfort her and let me prepare my remedy. I know what I'd prefer, but the choice is yours."

Brant sneered at Mathias's words, but one look at his distraught cousin begged him to obey, just this once. "You—" By the time Brant turned to deliver his statement, Mathias had slipped out of the room. Hostility melting in concern, Brant approached Nessix, offering his embrace.

* * * * *

Between the tea Mathias had prepared and Brant's guard, Nessix snatched enough sleep to wake refreshed. Drowning the night's events in the second dose of the elixir, she was more determined than ever to chart out an attack. Her door stood cracked open, enticing Mathias to peek in on her.

"Are you feeling better this morning?" He paused in the doorway until Nessix motioned for him to enter.

"Much." The reply was genuine, though absent enough to prove her mind engaged elsewhere. "You're looking a bit rough."

Mathias smirked. "Call me concerned is all. Do you have plans to give me?"

"I've been working on some, yes." Nessix laid down her pen. "But I'm not too sure how much you'll like them."

"We don't have time to worry about my preferences." Mathias studied Nessix hard, curious about what bounced through her mind. "I'm ready to hear what you've got."

Nessix leaned back in her chair. "I'm sick of the demons

shoving us where they want. I know you said it's dangerous for us to stray from the fortress, but it's time for us to raise our weapons the way we were meant to."

Mathias squinted. "I'm not sure I follow. If we press an attack now, that'll leave us completely open to the east."

Nessix shook her head, ignorant to the information Etha had provided Mathias last night. "I never said there weren't risks."

"Are you *wanting* to fail?" Mathias pressed a hand to his forehead and turned from Nessix to redirect his frustration. "Did you even listen to Sulik's report?"

"Sulik?" Nessix asked. "I haven't spoken to him in two days. Brant dropped a hint that it's been quiet and I—"

Sliding his hand to cover his scowl, Mathias spun around to interrupt her. "Did Brant elaborate on his reasoning?"

Mathias's agitation quickened Nes's heart. "Sagewind, what's wrong?"

"The demons—a lot of them—are positioned in the west and moving to strike today."

Nessix looked back at the plans that would no longer be effective. "Why didn't you come to me yourself?"

He opened his mouth, ready to tell her that Etha's sense of humor almost kept their current conversation from happening, but stopped. "I was busy with other matters and asked Sulik to deliver the news."

"Well, he never showed," she said. "I thought you had him booked in the infirmary." Casting a glance at Mathias, Nessix sighed. One of them needed to keep their head right now. "Don't worry about it. We've handled worse before."

A distant pop sounded and Nes's head snapped up. The bells rang from the watch towers. East tolled twice, west tolled once. Echoing each other in this pattern, the alarm called every man and woman in the Teradhel fortress to attention. Color faded from Nes's face and she looked over to Mathias, eyes wide.

"What—"

"Veed sent up his flares," she murmured. "He's in distress."

NINETEEN

Madness animated the masses as weary soldiers scrambled to the field. Nessix ordered Mathias away as she prepared herself and Logan to rescue Veed. He never pled for aid, and that immediately raised her concerns about the pending conditions. Mathias brooded over a much more disturbing thought. For the first time, Etha had given him inaccurate information. Yes, an attack came, but not from the anticipated direction. At least it pummeled someone other than Nes.

By the time Mathias reached the field, Nessix actively rallied the unit she'd take to reinforce Veed. Urgency prevented her from enjoying her rival's distress and her goal was to distract the demons long enough for Veed to muscle his way free. Brant and Sulik, neither particularly pleased with where Nessix had left them, waited with the rest of the army, prepared to send supplements to Nes's task force if needed.

She schooled her resolve firmly, channeling her focus on the task at hand. Personal preferences aside, Elidae could not afford to lose Veed. Nes's unit rode hard and fast, and as Veed's domain loomed over the rise, her distress brimmed to the top. Flaming arrows pierced the sky from the southern side of his borders. Hopefully, the horses would last that long.

Raising her arm, Nessix signaled for the unit to stop. "I want the third line to follow me," she called. "Everyone else, circle west. I'm banking on them assuming I'm out of commission."

"Will our numbers hold?" one of the horsemen asked.

Nes wondered the same. "Keep the flares ready in case we need backup." It was little reassurance, but she wouldn't lie to them.

Logan's ears caught a rapid scurrying from his left. He skittered nervously to turn around, but Nes pulled him back to continue facing her troops. Securing the bit against the roof of his mouth, Logan pulled his head downward to demand his rider's attention. For now, Veed needed to save himself. Gaining the freedom to do so, Logan spun, giving Nessix full sight of a secondary force rushing their way.

Grossly outnumbered, Nes's voice trembled. "Call for supplementation and steel yourselves! We'll let them strike first."

* * * * *

Brant sulked over Nessix riding off alone. Telling himself that the men would keep her safe did not soothe his desire to personally secure her welfare.

"Think she brought enough with her?" Sulik asked quietly. He hoped to discuss matters with Mathias, but the paladin had reserved himself for prayer.

"No," Brant said. "Otherwise she wouldn't have told us to watch the sky. I should be with her."

Sulik sighed, straining his eyes to where Nessix disappeared over the horizon. "You can't protect her from everything. Trust there are others who love her as much as you do."

A frown creased Brant's lips. "Perhaps you've forgotten the orders Laes gave you, but I haven't. Nes is able, but she'll always need protection. That's dictated by her station and ordered by her character."

"I honor Laes's words as much now as ever, but I've also accepted that you and I can't do it alone. Keeping up with Nes has always been a challenge."

"And I thrive off them." The reply came curtly and Brant pushed Armina to a swift departure, raising a fist to command the men to hold.

Sulik watched the pair climb a hill. Ideally, the young commander would have at least tried to hide his concern. The troops settled into small units, anxiously mingling amongst each other. No one strayed far from their posts, and with Brant on watch, Sulik set off to locate Mathias. He found the paladin absorbed in thought, unresponsive to the turbulence around him. Sulik almost left, but then Mathias turned to face him, the brooding wiped from his eyes.

"Is everything alright?" Mathias asked.

"Brant's pretty agitated, but I can't blame him." Sulik shifted his weight and asked the question on everyone's mind. "Will Nessix be alright?"

Nes's last battle provided a chilly reminder of her mortality, and while Etha couldn't explain the inconsistency of the demons' attacks, Mathias felt certain Nessix would return on her own feet. "She's learned a lot. I doubt she'll make the same mistake twice."

For the first time since the initial ride from Sarlot, Mathias disappointed Sulik. "A mistake? Would it have suited you better if she'd left the back lines to the demons' discretion? She did what had to be done."

"She made the right choice, but chose the wrong actions. I doubt she'll ever tell anyone what happened, but she lived and learned from it."

"Will she need our reinforcements?"

Mathias bounced the thought between tactics and experience. "If she's just supplementing Veed's force, she should be fine with what she has." He debated the next for a moment before speaking. "I want you and Brant to carry on with your assignment, but leave a strong unit behind for me. There's a mass approaching from the west I'd like to intercept."

"On your own?" Sulik asked. "If Nes will be alright, I could go—"

"You've never been one to argue before, Sulik," Mathias chuckled. "I'll be fine. Brant can't watch two fronts and the fortress

257

on his own."

Sulik had grown accustomed to believing Mathias's words and trusted his experience. A breath short of accepting the directions, a flash of movement caught Sulik's eye as Armina streaked back toward the troops. Tension buzzed through the men on standby as they sped back into order.

"Have you ever led an independent attack?" Mathias asked grimly.

"I've elaborated on orders."

"And I'm assuming Brant's had little more practice than you." Mathias's calm wavered from Sulik's fretting. "The two of you will lead what you don't give me toward whatever startled Brant. I'm more than capable of handling the remaining threats."

Arguing would only waste time, and Sulik nodded. "Please don't let pride get in your way. Nearly losing Nes was too hard."

Mathias nodded. "All will be well."

Fleeting nerves the only thing urging his hesitation, Sulik rushed to convey the order to Brant.

* * * * *

The air brimmed with cries of men falling to their ends as handfuls of those with no business on the field bolted from it. Veed scowled toward the north, wondering what held Nessix up. He knew her too well to think she'd allow this devastation; if nothing else, her need to protect her kin came before any lesson she might try to teach him. Exuding a fierce roar as he turned to fend off a trio of demons, Veed muscled his way back to his fortress. Chaos spread around him, but his forces would hold. He didn't pride himself on the might of his army modestly.

Veed's retreat garnered attention from both sides of the field. His men covered him the best they could from demons seeking to impede his progress, and he reached the security of his stronghold's interior, battered but breathing. Captains waited in the halls with wary, expectant gazes. Veed shook his head and moved past them. Cursing Nessix and her casual approach, he rushed to his balcony and looked north to see blots of men hastening in every direction but his.

"What game are you playing, love?" The distance between them prevented Veed from telling who led what front, but the flash of Ceraphlaks to the west suggested Mathias's actions.

"Sir." Renigan stopped on the top stair. "Burrington has been breached. She's in the process of falling."

"Is that so?" Veed narrowed his eyes at a previously missed tangle on the field. "Encourage a hasty clean up and see if we can afford to send assistance."

"We've only just begun to gain ground. I don't think we can save her."

A flurry of red and blue danced from atop a great, black horse and Veed barely identified Nessix turning in the saddle. She raised her sword in a valiant attempt to encourage her men, and Veed studied the demonic masses surrounding her meager assembly. The first of the flaming arrows left Nes's unit.

"It may be her only chance," Veed murmured.

* * * * *

Mathias hadn't expected to intercept the enemy so cleanly, but the demons' keenness on storming Nes's fortress blinded them to the thought of hindrance. Progress through the lines moved more rapidly than Mathias had prepared for. Suppressing the urge to order a simple defense, he relied on stamina to shove, rather than slaughter. The opposition was strong, and the demons easily outnumbered the flemans. Sounds of battle resounded across the field; cries of forced might and the occasional choke of pain mixed with a more relieving sound.

A great sigh, hushed in its sounding and flowing through every fleman under Mathias's command, flooded the expanse. Sensitive to the toxicity of hope, the demons' ferocity wavered. The most resilient of the fiends continued to strike, but the more sensible secured a retreat.

"A steady push!" Mathias urged those nearest him. "Keep

them moving back and we'll have accomplished our goal."

Mathias left the troops to clear the field and sent a dozen students out to tend to the wounded. Murmuring his prayers, he braced against his task of ending those demons that remained. Mathias's conscience nagged at him about the slivers of goodness hidden somewhere in these creatures, and at that point, he turned his eyes away from the suffering. Watching the southern sky revealed Veed's flares had stopped. If the demons had won that encounter, they'd have begun a charge for Nes's fortress. Content that their rushed plans followed through, even relieved at Veed's apparent well-being, Mathias tucked a prayer of gratitude where it belonged. With any luck at all, he'd get the troops back to the fortress in time for supper.

As suddenly as fear swept over the hordes, a great cackle of supremacy shot back at the flemans' taunts. Startled, Mathias abandoned his reflections to return to active command. A strong push enveloped the first few lines and Ceraphlaks lowered his flight to distract the assailants.

"Remove the wounded," Mathias instructed the nearest of his students, "and return to the field as fast as you can."

Mathias didn't waste the breath to inquire about what happened as his blade swung in a searing arc to scatter his opponents away. His efforts were immediately effective, but short lived, as the demons regrouped just out of his reach. Anguished cries bellowed from the soldiers, telling Mathias something much more dear than the upper hand had been overcome.

Etha, I can protect myself. Watch over the others.

"Flares!"

Shock rippled through the ranks while the demons grinned. Mathias turned to look for the call's origin. The beacons shot up too far east to be Veed, and Mathias finally lost his patience with the conniving once-men standing against him. He spared a thought to Ceraphlaks, asking the pegasus to scout out what sort of danger Nessix had found.

"If they want to play games, we'll meet them on their terms!" Mathias shouted. "Your general's counting on us to help her!"

Taking their commanding officer's words to heart, a tenacious heave beat against the demons. Unsure of Sulik and Brant's position, Mathias counted on himself alone to make it to Nes. Grimacing at the inevitable, he readied himself for violence.

* * * * *

Years of service had programmed both commanders to follow Nessix, but never each other. Long before any backup showed, Brant initiated a fierce attack. When Sulik arrived with reinforcements, he concentrated first on harnessing Brant's temper. The two men quarreled against each other's tenacity more savagely than against the enemy's strength. Sulik scolded Brant for his recklessness, while Brant insisted they had to dominate the field immediately. As the officers sorted through their differences, the remaining force pressed ahead to defend their grounds and bickering commanders.

"The men want to fight!" Brant insisted. "Quit wasting time."

"This is the sort of thing that almost took Nes from us," Sulik snapped.

"No, she was securing those who fell behind. She's not the beast Veed is."

The hasty reply confirmed Sulik's suspicions. Brant was afraid. Not for himself, or the troops, or likely even Nes's safety, but of the demons themselves. They'd come a mere breath from taking the general's life and ending the noble line. What limited itself to terror when the war began now overpowered Brant's sense. Known for his calm as much as Nes was known for hers, Brant's desire for vengeance and a brisk end to this threat had driven him to the cusp of insanity.

"Sir Sagewind is marching west," Sulik said, hoping to tear Brant from his web of fear. "There's a front moving there as well."

"And why aren't you with him?"

"He said he could handle command on his own. Right now, we need each other more than he needs us."

Brant sneered at Sulik's implications, the words insulting him in the midst of his frenzied conclusions. "I suppose he appointed you over me?"

"No," Sulik sighed. "We're supposed to be working together."

Sulik respected Brant, despite his propensity for questionable behavior, but didn't doubt Mathias's suggestion had been more to protect Brant than anything else. No one expected the cousins to part ways willingly, but Sulik thought Brant reasonable enough to accept it. Arguing with the young man never worked any better than telling Nessix Inwan would never return. Sulik left to distribute orders after Brant accepted his silence as permission to ride off.

Cursing under his breath, Brant called the cavalry to action. Armina's sturdy body pushed through friendly and enemy forces alike, sorting the two armies where Brant wanted them. He met the first strike this time around and as he retaliated, the grind of battle comforted him. Consistent battering prevented noticeable progress for several minutes, but the point at which Brant gained the advantage struck too quickly to not raise his concern. He pulled Armina back and scanned the field for answers.

The unit Brant shared with Sulik showed no trouble, and the number of their opponents routinely trickled off. What was he missing? Turning Armina to survey the other fronts, Brant stared dumbfounded at the pleas for help shot from the east. With Nes's recent brush fresh in his mind, Brant's need to save her trumped all other obligations.

"Men, clean up! Our general needs us!"

Those immediately around him cut into the enemy with renewed determination. Brant anxiously followed his decree as it rode a wave of enthusiasm to Sulik. Right now, Sulik outranked him by experience. The wiser of the two commanders could not stop Brant from rushing to Nes, but he very possibly could hold the troops. As the report sank in, Sulik spun to face Brant and decisively swept his sword in Nes's direction. Brant's tension prevented a sigh of relief, but he wouldn't make Sulik signal twice.

Brant turned Armina and searched for his herald, finding his body crumpled amidst the other aspects of battle. Grimacing at the boy's unfortunate fate, Brant dismounted quickly to snatch up the horn and raised it to his lips to deliver orders to a third of the cavalry. With a final glance at the field now commanded by Sulik, Brant led the charge to save Nessix.

* * * * *

The fortress sat quietly as the majority of the troops either marched into battle or stood poised to assist. Most of the civilians harbored in the dungeon had locked themselves away in the safety of layers of stone. The men and women willing to take up arms waited for their calls to duty a level above the rest. A mere half hour after En saw Nessix and Logan out the gates, a messenger came by his study to inform him that Mathias had left his guard position, and Brant and Sulik had marched away. En dismissed the messenger, trusting the joint experience of the four officers to flow through this operation.

Another twenty minutes passed, and a second knock sounded. Irritated, En swung the door open, rather than inviting his guest inside. "Can't an old man have his privacy?" he gruffed. "What do you want?"

"General Nessix has sent flares," the soldier said quickly. "Reinforcements are in transit."

Immediately, En brushed the cobwebs off the parts of his brain he'd once kept so shiny and clean. "Has Veed fallen?"

"His beacons stopped and Nessix's rose shortly after, further north."

"What's the status of Sir Sagewind and our commanders?"

"It's unclear, sir."

Burying Laes had devastated En and he couldn't bear the thought of putting Nessix in the ground, too. Age had degraded his body from the typical fleman might, and his gentle hobbies only enhanced his debility. Either way, En was old, and if he died protecting his family line, he'd go without regret. Aiming a prayer to the heavens for the refugees' safety, En's rickety legs carried him through the door.

"Do we have enough soldiers to defend the fortress?"

The soldier glanced about, uncertain of his jurisdiction over

En. "Yes, sir."

En nodded. "Have them stand ready. I'm going to help Nessix."

The watch towers tolled for assistance, saving the soldier from his awkward position. Troops jumped to mobilize in the halls, running to their posts as fearful gasps accompanied the civilians to the lower levels.

"Demons, from the east!"

An entire kingdom of people would die if the demons breached the walls. En's heart ached for his granddaughter, but his place had to be safeguarding the civilians. Moving with a haste long forgotten by his worn frame, En hurried down the hall to his quarters and dressed in as much armor as his shrinking limbs would accept. Caring for the restriction much less than he remembered, he hustled from his chamber to reach the battlements. As the bells pounded and adrenaline urged him along, En slid back into the role he'd long since passed on to younger generations.

"Archers, aim for the outside ranks!"

Relieved by the receipt of official orders, the troops leapt to action. The pattern of fire compacted the demons, squeezing the force together to prevent them from surrounding the fortress. Nodding enthusiastically, En personally shoved bows into even inexperienced hands. Exhilarated by the nostalgic rush, En passed command to a senior officer and panted his way down to see if the cannons would still pound with their former glory.

* * * * *

Nessix ducked beneath a blow she caught in her periphery and sank a return strike into the demon's underarm. *Where in Inwan's name is my backup?*

The flow of battle had separated her from Logan, and neither he nor Brant were around to pick her up if she fell. That in mind, Nes flung herself at the opposition, fighting dirty enough to put Veed to shame. The fate of this fraction of her army depended on her performance.

One demon fell, having not seen Nessix approach from behind. She engaged a second, inflicting two slashes and a poorly connected jab before it jarred her with an uppercut. Nessix spit out the pain and repeated her attack, this time reaching vital organs. Suppressing the urge to spitefully return any favors the demon had planned for her, Nessix finessed her way across the field. Forget dreams and fantasies and festivities—*this* was dancing!

The fear of being overwhelmed dissipated as Nessix cut her way deeper into the enemy. Progression resonated beautifully between the ring of steel and mocking battle hymns rising from the men around her. She still hoped for reinforcements, but her urgency tapered off. With spirits high, it took Nessix several minutes to recognize her watch tower bells, muffled by distance and the clamor of battle.

That fortress was all she had left of her father. It harbored her entire kingdom. The unfamiliar pound of cannons echoed back at her. She frenzied against the fray, whispering assurance to herself that someone still stood for the fortress's defense.

The bells persisted, suggesting more than a few stray units threatened her home. What had begun as a fevered despair became an insulted pride. The demons made quite a bold assumption to think she'd stand by and let her kingdom fall to them! Her mouth fell open to shout her determination to the troops, but they'd already answered the same call. Nessix saved her breath for combat.

* * * * *

The back lines of Nes's unit trickled into Brant's view, motivating him to ask one more surge from his wearied mare. Hollow pounds of heavy weaponry called over the field, and his men pulled their heaving mounts to a hasty stop. Shock condensed through Brant's bravado and he turned to gawk with the others. The fortress bells hammered, rivaling Nes's flares. As the scene soaked in, the troops waited on their commander's instructions.

He needed to reach Nessix. Curling his lips between his teeth,

Brant turned Armina toward the flares and pinched his eyes shut against the thunder of cannon fire. There wasn't time for him to think, not if he hoped to help anyone. Armina's muscles shook in anticipation of her next cue. Tears stung the back of Brant's eyes. Muttering a futile prayer, Brant's head blatantly disobeyed his heart's most fervent demands.

Armina bolted away from where Nessix struggled and Brant frantically tried to calm his nerves with justifications. He'd reach the fortress much faster than he'd reach Nes. A larger force protected Nessix than their stronghold. She'd expect this from him. Decision made, Brant rode hard.

As long as Armina pressed on, Brant was only concerned with completing this mission as quickly as possible so he could return for Nessix. The horses behind him squealed, soon followed by startled curses from their riders. Brant loathed the thought of slowing, but the action was thrust on him when Armina slid to a stop with a startled grunt.

Flourishing massive wings twenty feet ahead of the pair, an alar dropped from the sky to intercept the rescue. Unarmed, his wingspan dwarfed those foes the flemans had grown accustomed to fighting. Brant didn't dare look back at his allies. Concern for Nessix and the fortress slipped away as Brant's mind set a course for survival. Not bothering to draw his sword, Brant pushed Armina into the demon.

The charge caught the demon off-guard, as he'd expected them to try to flee. Bounding into their foe, the mare's knees pummeled into bare flesh and pushed the demon off balance. Midway through Brant drawing his sword, Armina stumbled, nearly falling from beneath him. A leathery wing shoved her upright and a boney protrusion caught Brant above the ear, dazing him for a heartbeat.

"Where were you going, maggot?" the demon growled. His other wing swept beneath Armina's barrel, cradling the frightened warhorse in place.

Hearing the demon speak his language prevented Brant from relaxing into his landing back in the saddle. The demon's arms were close enough to wrap around his neck, but his calm demeanor persisted, almost noble. One hand grasped Armina's cheek strap, the other not readily visible.

Panic wouldn't do a single thing to benefit him, and Brant surrendered himself to fate. "You're underestimating our general if you think she'll just let the fortress fall."

"If your general wants another taste of the hells, arrangements can be made."

The threat catalyzed Brant's bid for freedom. Dropping a stirrup, he drove his heel forward and connected with all of his might into the demon's face. The demon released his hold on the bridle to cover his broken nose, and Brant pulled Armina sharply to the left to bolt away. They completed two strides before arms wrapped around Brant's waist and the mare ran out from under him. The next moment, when he could not draw his breath, Brant looked straight into the bloodied face of his attacker. A garbled phrase scorned him and the demon flung him unceremoniously to the ground. Using skills learned in the stables, Brant tried to right himself before impact. His armor broke the fall, but a snap in his shoulder told him his fall had broken something else. The demon turned and stalked toward him. Brant fumbled with his sword.

* * * * *

Mathias couldn't remember when he'd last dirtied his hands the way he encouraged the troops to now. Once the sight of Nes's flares penetrated the ranks, they acted on their own accord. Complicating matters worse for the demons, when the fortress announced her need, Mathias openly urged the men to tear through whatever they saw fit until the demons attempted their retreat.

"Let them run," Mathias shouted. "We don't have time for a chase. A dozen clerics will ride with half the cavalry to your general," he ordered. "The rest of us are returning to the fortress."

The orders ripped through the lines and in mere moments, hundreds of horses dashed past the paladin. Approving of their haste, Mathias turned from his men and ran back toward the fortress. With Ceraphlaks tending to more important matters, he'd resort to teleportation if he fell behind. Seeing the swarms of demons assaulting their home lit a fire behind the army. With Etha's will, they reached the gates, leaning on the side of winded, but still far from burned out.

"Go through the east gates!" Mathias panted as the doors opened to accept them. Locating the nearest captain, he completed the last important decision he hoped to make for the day. "Take your company and protect the civilians."

Pushing through hectic men rushing to the walls and frightened mothers searching for their children, the army managed its way to the far side of the fortress.

"Take down the barricades," Mathias barked. "Men, hold your ground; let them try to enter. We'll catch them at the bottleneck."

The steady volley of arrows prevented the demons from reaching the building proper, but arrows were a limited resource. Timid hands deconstructed the barrier standing between the demons and civilians. Leaving the ground troops in good faith, Mathias leapt up the stairs to answer the shouts from the battlements. Those accustomed to combat didn't acknowledge his presence, nocking spent enemy arrows to replenish their supply. The volunteer forces skittered about frantically under the threat of alar. Mathias cursed under his breath and snatched up a bow to take a position in line.

"Whose orders are you under?" he asked the archer beside him.

"Master En's taken command," came the quick reply.

A smile eased Mathias's face and he lowered the bow. "Continue your fire!"

Pulling away from the line of attack, Mathias climbed to the top level of the wall, stepping onto the ledge. The demons were after him and he accepted that. Alabaster armor gleaming against the sunlight, Mathias's blade flashed blue in the sun as he brandished it at his side, drawing thousands of eyes to him. The distraction served the archers beautifully.

What are you doing, my dear?

They've hurt too many. Mathias's usual affability was gone. *If I can get them to come after me, we'll have more time.*

"Sir Sagewind!"

Mathias kept his gaze schooled on the field. "A fine attack, master En. I'm sorry you had to take command."

"There's nothing like a good fight." Stress painted the old man's voice.

"I've got this now, if you need a reprieve."

"I've already gone through the trouble of donning my armor."

Mathias nodded respectfully. "What's their course of action?"

"We were firing until the demons changed course, help arrived, or we ran out of ammunition. There weren't enough left for a proper counter."

A harsh cry surged from the primary wall, prompting everyone to take cover. Shields flew up as enemy fire scattered across the defense. Peeking out at the enemy mass, Mathias consulted his tactical mind. The gates stood open, inviting the demons to enter the fortress, but none made a move for them. Locked against their wit, Mathias wielded patience against their intentions. Comfortable that the demons weren't yet ready to act, Mathias trained his eyes to the south. Nes's flares had ceased.

Is she alright?

She's rescuing Brant as we speak.

Mathias frowned thinking about the cousins. He wasted valuable trust in Brant by offering him control over the backup forces, and had seen enough of Nessix's fighting techniques. The two of them were together, struggling against a version of the enemy they'd never encountered before. Ideally, Mathias would hasten to find them and coach Nes through the new set of challenges, and in his perfect world, the demons attacking the fortress would pursue him in such endeavors. In the end, the demons frequently worked outside of Mathias's plans, and Etha had confirmed that Nessix was fine. Mathias's place was on the wall, maintaining the focus of both involved parties.

"The bulk of the army's waiting by the east gates," Mathias told En. "Nessix and Brant are somewhere in the south. Go—"

His instructions snapped from completion when a single alar landed on the wall and barreled his way. En staggered back at the demon's advance, his hands feeling behind him in search of stability. Mathias stepped in front of the old man and raised his sword level in front of him. Alar were blessed with superior strength, but they'd been known to reason.

"If you're not here to discuss tactics, I have no use for you." Mathias's tongue seamlessly wrapped around the demonic dialect.

The demon grinned and stopped at the tip of the sword, leaning forward to test Mathias's dedication. "A fine one for demands, Mathias," he answered in fluent fleman.

Mathias narrowed his eyes at the demon's cultural assimilation. "Speak what you know or leave." His arm maintained its firm position.

"I've flown the skies today. I know how the field lies."

"Then you're aware of your people's standing. I suggest an honorable retreat to your comrades."

You're in their sights!

Before Mathias processed Etha's omen, the demon flashed his teeth. "You know with certainty that we haven't grabbed up your pretty little sweetheart?"

"Foul bastard!" En spat, shoving past Mathias's security.

My child!

Etha's shriek pierced Mathias's mind, echoed by a gurgling choke from En. Answering with a fevered bellow, Mathias thrust his blade into the demon's chest. The weight of its carcass snatched the sword from his hand. En had already fallen and Mathias dropped to the ground with him. A roar gushed from the field and captains shouted for the archers to fire freely. It made sense now—the alar had served solely as a distraction. The demons wanted to see Mathias fall before moving in.

Tearing his sword free from its victim, Mathias scrambled to En's body, crouching low as not to impede the flow of combat. An arrow intended to ground him was lodged in En's neck. Grasping the old man's shoulders, Mathias rolled him onto his back and met the empty gaze of Elidae's last wise general. Mathias laid his hand on En's throat to search for the soul that had already soared from its withered shell. Heart falling, Mathias pinched the shaft of the arrow between his fingers, disgusted that such a pathetic attempt on him had killed a man so noble. Mathias curled his lip and pulled the arrow free. A small vial with a piercing tip replaced the usual arrowhead, drained clean of its contents.

Etha…

A girl scampered up to him, ducking behind the wall's cover. "You've got other things to worry about." She shoved a cloak in his arms, gesturing for him to hurry and disguise himself. "He will find his bliss today."

Mathias met Etha's eyes steadily and accepted the garment. The demons would not take one more life today.

"Sage—" A grief-stricken cry flew from Nes's lips as she ran to En's body. "No!"

Mathias had witnessed death and the devastation that went with it often, but a rope of sorrow noosed his heart. "Nessix, I—"

"It's just like…" She stopped, brows twitching in troubled confusion. Lost, Nessix shook her head, thoughts gyrating too wildly to catch.

"He was hit with a poisoned arrow," Mathias said, pulling his mind away from the battle long enough to attempt consolation. "He went quickly."

Nessix's eyes masked themselves from the man beside her, his words not reaching her. Besides herself, her bloodline had ended. En had died a glorious death, taken in battle the way every warrior hoped to go. She had gone in search of Mathias to try and coax him to repair her broken cousin, but now Nessix could only form three words.

"This ends now."

TWENTY

Exhaustion grounded Brant worse than any injuries had, and Mathias only uncovered two wounds he deemed worthy of divine assistance. He took it upon himself to manually reset Brant's dislocated shoulder without permission, and the commander declined offers to mend his flesh. Prescribing rest as the best treatment, Mathias left to assist his students. Nessix assumed the responsibility of burial plans on her own.

En's age had prepared the flemans for his inevitable death, and his defeat did not damage their resolve nearly as much as the demons had hoped. Brooding over this thought and Shand's opinion of it as he waited in the forest, the pawn savored another long drink to preemptively dull the pain to come.

"What's on your mind?" Shand asked with no other formalities. Curling her lip, she took note of the two empty bottles on the ground and the third clutched in the pawn's hand.

"You asked me to come. I showed up."

Shand glided over to him and gently coaxed the bottle from his grasp. "You are my eyes on the field." Placing a finger at the spirits' fill line, she traced a trail down to the bottom, the liquid draining with it. "I'm counting on you for insight."

The effect of Shand's magic slowly intoxicated him.

"The demon you chose missed his shot." He shrugged

indifferently. "If you'da used the alar instead, *like I told you*, I coulda been spared my sincerity at the old man's funeral."

Shand's ire bubbled inside and she forced herself to hold her actions. She was a goddess! A revered deity! Her plans should not keep failing. Eyes regulated by an inebriated mind plucked at her self-doubt.

"This whole battle was a waste a time an' resources," the pawn slurred, inhibitions trailing away without him. "Nothing was laid out right, and it was stupid to have the hordes retreat."

Shand's eyebrows rose sharply, shocked by the pawn's boldness. "Are you doubting my tactics?"

"I'm doubtin' the capability of your officers. Sagewind shoulda fallen. That was our plan and it's not what happened."

"Etha wouldn't allow poison to kill him," Shand assured. "Claim him until he could be summoned again, perhaps, but he'd still live."

"That woulda given us time to throw Nes's fortress. She may not be willin' to serve, but she coulda easily been captured. Stupid girl, she'da lost everything." The pawn looked around for another bottle and, finding none, slumped against a tree.

"What do you mean?" Shand asked, interest piqued by his rambling.

"No one's left in any of her towns," he said. "Ogres or minotaur, maybe some rebels of ours in 'em, but she's got every villager hoarded away in her dungeon for safekeeping." He laughed impulsively. "To think some people hoard people!"

Shand didn't see the humor in that last outburst. "Why haven't I been informed of this until now?"

"You never asked."

"Such insubordination will not be tolerated!" the goddess hissed, reaching her hand out for a disciplinary measure.

Snarling in his drunken state, the pawn grabbed Shand's wrist, currently unable to calculate the immediate repercussions for his action. He'd served this witch as loyally as he could stomach, and his state of mind prevented him from accepting such force from her. Shand allowed him to catch her, eyes calmly meeting his. Her gaze commanded him, a threat taunting him somewhere in those depths.

"How smart is this?" Shand murmured. "I don't have to hurt you every time we talk."

He hardly believed that. "You promised this'd be over by now. You promised I'd have somethin' to show for it."

"And when it's over, you will."

"Who're you lyin' to, Shand?" He ignored her gasp at such an informal address. "You've promised Elidae to both me and the demons now. They won't follow a mortal and I won't be able to fend them off on my own." One bottle earlier, he'd have been groveling at this point.

"Then keep me happy," Shand said tersely. "Lose my favor and you lose your only hope."

"No," he explained, annoyed. "You've already lied to me."

"Your interests have changed since we first met."

The pawn pulled her closer. "If there's one thing that hasn't changed about me in twenty years, it's my interests. You've got what you want, it's time to pay your dues."

Shand jerked her arm back with a force that sprawled the pawn to the dirt. "You are right. I have Mathias on the opposing field. What purpose are you even serving anymore?"

"I'm your eyes, *mistress*," he mocked, hauling himself back to his feet.

"I could easily find someone else to do the job."

"Who?" he snorted. "Who else d'you think can walk among those noxious nobles without suspicion? You need me, Shand."

She clenched her teeth, wondering why she allowed her peon to give the ultimatums. "My pet," she cooed. "Where would you be without me? Lurking alone in some ghost shell of pride, wondering all the what ifs and never finding any glory. I do need you, but you need me more. If not for me, your treacherous mind would have killed you years ago."

He rolled his shoulders upright, ruminating her words through pools of alcohol. "Information's all you want?"

"Information and loyalty."

A curt nod. "Sagewind's powers're restorin'. Don't know how, but your curse is failin'. Could be Etha—"

"No," Shand interrupted. "Etha cannot play with the fate of mortals without someone else wielding her will; it was a rule she made and is incapable of breaking. If I haven't managed to hurt Mathias yet, I guess we'll have to try harder."

Even drunk, the pawn saw Shand's intentions and he wondered if the goddess had paid mind to his previous concerns and demands on the situation. Resigning to the fact that this was beyond his control, the pawn bowed his head. He'd hoped to avoid senseless casualties, but in the end, he had no choice.

"I'll meet your commanders in the mornin'," he grumbled. "After tonight wears off, I'll talk tactics with 'em."

"Of course you will," Shand said. "I would expect nothing less."

* * * * *

"Why are you avoiding her?"

Mathias turned from Etha, carefully folding his shirt and laying it on his night stand. "What would I say?"

"You could offer your condolences, try to cheer her up." Etha's eyes bore through his back. "At least show her you care."

"What makes you so determined to get me involved with her?" Mathias asked, turning to face Etha at last. "I know her type. My place is out of her way."

Etha shrugged and kicked her legs playfully from her perch on the side of Mathias's bed. "I thought it would be a kind gesture to show your concern. She seemed shaken at the funeral."

Mathias nodded once in agreement, not denying Nes's emotions. Only Nessix remained of the nation's revered lineage, and Mathias knew her to be of great enough political mind to know the demands that faced her now. He did not envy her those burdens. Having left the funeral behind him after his prayers had set his heart at ease, Mathias's thoughts returned to the recent battle.

"I thought the alar would have shown themselves much sooner."

Etha twisted her mouth at his avoidance. "They'd been patrolling, but kept their attacks aimed toward the less civilized races. They seem to have their shock tactic completely thought out."

"Was their sole purpose of showing themselves to distract me?" Mathias asked, still trying to fathom why the demons wasted their effort on an attempt to poison him. "Or were they after something else?"

"I can't vouch for them all, but the one from the wall was sent for you. That arrow had a foreign poison from their side of the world. I doubt it would have killed you, but it would have taken you down long enough for them to snatch you up."

Mathias paused in his preparations to think this over. "I don't understand their motives. They could have targeted me from anywhere. Why did they lure me to Elidae?"

"Abaeloth only has one holy land," Etha said. "This is where life began."

"So it's a quest for vengeance?"

"If they were doing this for themselves, they'd be fighting much dirtier."

Mathias grumbled his dissatisfaction. "The last time I asked for your insight on their movements, they changed course on us. Is it safe for me to ask again?"

"They've retreated." Etha closed her eyes and concentrated on the lay of the land. "I can't tell what they're planning, but they haven't moved yet. There aren't enough surfaced right now to form a decent army. I'll notify you when that changes."

"Thank you, my lady." Mathias looked down at her and smiled. "My strength has been returning daily, so at least we have that to count on."

"I'm pleased."

Mathias suppressed a yawn. He didn't want to make his goddess feel unwelcome, but needed rest. "I suppose you could answer one more question for me," he said, preparing to pull back the covers.

Etha stood to accommodate his actions. "I'll answer what I'm able."

Mathias concentrated on fluffing his pillow to avoid looking at her. "*Is* Nes alright?"

Etha tucked her grin into her mischievous mind. "It would mean much more to her if you asked her yourself."

"You know I don't ask idle tasks. The important issues have been covered. Now all I need is a clear conscience before I turn in."

The smile returned. "You're an adult. You can solve problems by yourself."

"But—" Etha had vanished before Mathias's argument gained steam.

Muttering to himself about issues of maturity and warfare, Mathias climbed into bed. With his most pressing questions answered, he neglected his prayers for the night. Besides, his thoughts were fixed on Nessix, and about matters unrelated to combat, and Mathias wanted to avoid more of Etha's teasing. Inadequately wishing the pesky general from his mind, Mathias closed his eyes.

* * * * *

The pawn felt eyes track him as he stumbled in the dark. Unless minotaur and ogres constituted his audience, he was unafraid. Flemans wouldn't attack him out of simple recognition and demons wouldn't due to their fear of Shand. Mind preoccupied with whether or not his previous bout of verbal courage actually occurred, the pawn jumped when an alar dropped in front of him.

"It's not safe to talk here," the pawn growled. "If we're seen, I'd hafta kill you to save my cover."

"I've scouted and cleaned up any threats," the demon replied.

Man and demon stared each other down. "What d'you want?" the pawn asked at last, wondering how many sentries the beast had brought along.

"Words from your visit with Shand leaked out; things she couldn't have wanted us to hear."

"I deserve Elidae, if that's what you mean." He watched for a visual response. "But I'm not stupid enough to think your people aren't after your own share."

The demon crossed his arms and nodded. "We've noted much more about you than you'd care for us to know. Your political mind and lack of concern for your own would make you a fine governmental figure."

He chuckled. "You're assumin' Shand'll let any of us see the end of this war. The bitch is just as likely to kill us all and end it herself as to follow through with any promises she's thrown at us."

"Our solution is simple. A representative of the horde would govern beside you. If the flemans won't coexist, we can either exterminate or enslave them. Either would allow both of us what we want. Elidae would be yours to rule, ours to inhabit."

The pawn took his time thinking over the proposal. It was a novel idea, the demons respecting him, but they couldn't be trusted. It was just as probable they'd butcher him in his sleep as honor these terms. Every ounce of logic told him not to agree.

"You overheard me and Shand talkin'," he slurred. "How're you so certain we're not bein' listened to now?"

The demon spat and curled his lip. "I told you. We've secured this location." He inched closer despite the claim, twitchy with the thought of being spied on. "Even if we hadn't, Shand likes you." He glanced the fleman over and shook his head. "For whatever reason. You've at least got something to show for your obedience. All we get are orders and untimely endings."

"And me dealin' death to you on the field means nothin'?"

The demon shrugged. "You do what you have to. We're glad to give our lives in battle, and it certainly beats standing by while Shand cuts us down at her leisure."

Even through the tumbling in the pawn's head, it was a good point. "What makes you think I can help you?"

"Shand trusts you. We are her pets, but you are her child."

The pawn distinctly recalled Shand putting things differently, but his distorted comprehension hindered further debate. "If I went along with this, who'd I take orders from?" He'd already figured out how Shand worked, and didn't favor the notion of sorting out a rapport with the demons.

"You would follow the lead Shand set up for you until we were ready to revolt. At that time, you wouldn't be following orders as much as you'd be agreeing to them."

"And if I don't survive that long?"

"We haven't killed you yet."

Keeping his eyes open made the pawn tired. "I'll think about it," he muttered.

The demon nodded and followed with a stiff bow. "I think you'll find we need each other more than either of us wants to admit. Shand will never let either of us win."

"All she's after is that White Paladin," the pawn sneered. "Once he's taken care of, she'll be done with Elidae."

"Don't be so certain. She's a beast of power. If she can take control of the holy land, the entire Order is bound to retaliate. What better way of seeking her vengeance?" Besides that, the demons had spent ages trying to remedy the problem that was Mathias Sagewind and were no closer now than they were in the beginning.

"Be gone, demon," the pawn spat. His words grated against his pounding temples. "I told you I'd think about it, and don't have the desire or ability to figure anything out right now."

Darkness swept across the demon's face. "We will await your decision, then." Nothing else had to be said. The demon departed.

* * * * *

Mathias hadn't intended to sleep so late, but considered it a blessing. Rest refreshed his troubled mind and his thoughts moved about in order once again. Etha's insight comforted him from immediate military concerns. He dressed and dined, mingled among students and civilians, then climbed his way to the battlements in search of Nessix.

She sat on the edge of a secondary wall, stabilizing herself with her hands as she leaned forward to gaze at the field of decaying demon carcasses. Her hair traced down the length of her back in a single braid, as opposed to one of the intricate styles that better suited battle. Tiny wisps had pulled free and fluttered about in the breeze. Wearing a simple bodice, Nes's shoulders and arms were exposed to the sun. A belt fit with two daggers slung around her waist, the flow of ceremonial skirts hanging behind. If she knew Mathias stood there, she made no sign of it.

Mathias opened his mouth to address her but he didn't know what to say. He ached terribly inside, worse now that he saw her. Etha had been right. Nessix had lost everything that made her strong, the life that had dealt her an unfair hand had thrown in a joker. Those fears and pains vied to destroy her, but she remained as dutiful and diligent as ever. This position, with its crushing responsibilities, was the only thing Nessix had ever known.

What do I say to let her know her people are here for her? What do I say to let her know Etha's watching over her, even if she doesn't want to believe it? What do I say to let her know I'm here for her?

Mathias stared at Nessix a bit longer, her uncertainty reaching timid fingers out to him, begging him for guidance he didn't have. He murmured her name.

Nessix jerked at the sound of Mathias's voice. A deep breath raised her shoulders as she looked down again. "I didn't know you were there."

"I didn't mean to startle you," Mathias said. "It's just... forget it." Modesty withheld his deeper sentiments. "Nessix, I'm sorry."

"This fortress is nearly as much yours as it is mine. There's no reason to apologize for exploring it."

Mathias frowned at Nes's effort to dismiss the prevailing topic. "That's not what I meant. If I could change any of this for you, I'd do it without hesitation." He looked away from those bare shoulders before they brought on more complications. "I'm sorry for all of this."

"If any of it was in your control, then I'd be angry with you." Nessix curled her legs up to the wall's ledge and stood on the security of the battlements. "You've been doing all you can. A warrior doesn't get strong through coddling. All that's bothering me now is..." Nessix stopped and looked down, heaving a sigh. Her mouth fumbled in her attempt to murmur her greatest regret. "I'm the only one left. No ancestors, no siblings. When the demons take me, that's the end."

Mathias stepped forward, reaching a hand toward her shoulder. Grateful that Nessix still looked away, he awkwardly withdrew the gesture. "Your line will live on with you, Nes," he assured.

"You really think anyone's going to live through this?"

"I think a lot of your people will live through it. They've been tested from the start. The gods tore apart their homeland, men exiled them, and after they made it across the sea they were greeted by monsters. This is no different from what your ancestors went through. A few demons can't change who you are."

Nessix chuckled, turning to face Mathias with empty eyes. "The only hard thing my people survived was their journey to Elidae. The beasts here are nothing to boast about defeating, not anymore."

"You'll overcome the demons, just the same."

"If you're so sure we have what it takes, why did you bother to come?" The question was bitter, but not malicious.

Mathias smiled at her recollection. "Maybe I'm here for this moment, to remind you of your people and their strength. I don't know," he confessed. "I was called, so I came."

Nessix tore her eyes from his and looked at the stones of the wall. "This is my first actual war; I've never faced a battle I couldn't see the end of. I don't want this to happen to my people, we've come so far."

"You'll see this one through, I promise. You'll see your people free from war and terror and get them back to thriving. Cities will be rebuilt and your kingdom will rise to glory again."

Nessix turned back and smiled at Mathias, not noticing the color that trickled to his cheeks. "You're lucky to have your Etha to listen to you." One last envious moment passed before she returned her attention to the crows tearing demon bodies into their meals.

Fighting off the flutter in his heart, savoring the effect of Nes's smile, Mathias stammered his reply. "She would speak to you, too."

"Perhaps when she quits answering you, I'll give it a try," she said.

Mathias continued to watch her, his eyes tracing the laces against her back as he tried to come up with a reason to prolong their conversation. *She's just a girl*, he told himself. *No different from the peasants, save station and spirit.* Her spirit, he knew, was what called to him. She was noble and loyal. Devoted. If it was up to Nessix, she would give her life to free her kingdom from danger. Mathias would not allow her such a sacrifice.

Balling his hands into fists to keep from reaching out to touch her, Mathias sighed and left Nessix to her thoughts before his own devoured him.

TWENTY-ONE

Eager for a reprieve from obligation, Nessix indulged Brant's request of a leisurely gallop, visiting childhood haunts and reminiscing over old adventures. Both Logan and Armina savored this freedom and gamboled playfully to their riders' whims. When the horses tired of their shenanigans, neither of the cousins objected to a slower pace. With the war far from over, they treasured this day of peace.

Nes leaned back into the pillows of grass, listening to the pleasant bubbling of the Spring. The horses eagerly accepted the offer to satiate themselves in the lushness across the stream, and the sun beamed down on the remnants of the noble family.

Defying nature's orders, Nes continued to brood over matters out of her control. In her heart, she trusted Mathias, and there was no doubt in her mind that he was the only one able to keep her people thriving. Yes, he had unique powers, feats which had awed and delighted Nes when Inwan had shown her such wonders, but the inconsistency of Mathias's miracles frightened her. Mathias had kept hope's head above water, but the brewing storm was becoming too strong. If his abilities stabilized consistently, Nessix was certain they'd win this. She twisted her mouth at how easily she'd credited the paladin for what she'd once insisted were fraudulent tricks.

"What do you think's causing it?" Nessix turned her head to gaze at her cousin.

Brant peered back at her through the curtain of grass. "Causing what?"

Having not meant to speak her question, Nes stared back at the sky. She knew better than to mention Mathias to Brant. "Hmm?" she mused, hoping he'd accept her implied request to steer the conversation in another direction.

"You asked what I thought was causing it." Brant propped himself up on his elbows and watched her expression keenly. "What are you after, Nes?"

"Nothing." She glanced away from his prying gaze.

"Right," he grunted. "I know you better than that."

"If you know me so well, you'd already know what's on my mind, so why bother asking?"

"Sagewind."

Nessix bolted upright and looked over at her cousin, an awkward flush flawing her cheeks. "How'd you know?"

"Because," Brant sighed. "He's *all* that's been on your mind. What he thinks, what he does." Speaking that truth soured Brant's mouth.

"Well, what if that's not what I meant?"

"Was it?"

"That's not what I asked."

Brant sat up and plucked a stem of grass to tuck between his lips. "You asked my opinion, and this is it. Mathias is the cause of this war, and before you started swooning over him, that's what you thought, too. There were no real problems before he came, and I can't help but think they'd leave with him."

Nessix remembered those accusations well. While she longed to revert back to such simple reasoning, Mathias's dedication to her people—to *her*—motivated Nessix to keep him close. She couldn't confess her change of heart, not out loud or even to herself. If Brant picked up on her feelings, so be it. That didn't mean she needed to admit them.

"He's the only tactical mind we have left," Nes said, hiding behind a safe excuse. "At least he's making a positive contribution."

Brant sighed. "It'd be much easier for him to lead the demons away. We could handle everything that's left, even Veed."

"And we can handle the demons," Nessix said belligerently. "Our people do not run."

"I'm not saying we should." Nes's dismay over this topic twisted Brant's stomach, and his sense of peace faltered. "Come on, Nes. Let's keep riding and put our worries aside for the day."

"No!" she insisted. "Something isn't right."

"Of course it isn't—"

"I listened to Grandfather and did my reading. You can't tell me that Sagewind's a fleman, and everything else about him is supported in the histories."

"Except for the fact that he should be dead."

Nessix was running down the road to Mathias's defense now and couldn't stop herself. "If what I read was true, he doesn't die, something to do with his goddess."

"Would you listen to yourself!" Brant scolded. "Where's your faith in Inwan?"

A sharp gasp interrupted Nes's renegade thoughts. Her heart tugged at her mind painfully, reminding her of all she believed in and what kept her going. "Inwan will come back to us," she murmured, avoiding Brant's glare.

"And until then, we'll be fine on our own." Not so long ago, Nes had tried to convince him of the same. "We've made it this far, we can make it longer still."

How much longer, Inwan? Nessix didn't want to let go of hope, but began to feel helplessness take over. She longed for divine counsel once more, and Mathias had promised her that Etha held no grudges of her past or follies. Afraid of where her mind wandered, Nessix shook her head.

"You still haven't answered my question," she said.

Brant offered a grudging snort in reply.

"Please, Brant. The sooner we can establish what we have at our disposal, the sooner we can move to the offensive. If there's anything we can do to keep Sagewind functioning the way he's supposed to, we need to do it." She reached out and grasped his hand. "I need your advice."

Brant hated disappointing Nessix more than he hated Mathias, and seeing her so forlorn gutted him. "My advice? Quit worrying about Sagewind. Even if he has all the knowledge in the world, he's not better than you. This great Etha's given up on him, and maybe it's time we did, too."

The longer Brant spoke, the further Nes felt herself slipping. She hadn't banked on the idea of Brant supporting anything about solving Mathias's problems, but his callous responses cut her. Normally, he at least pretended to respect her opinions, whether he made an effort to mask his displeasure or not.

Brant had intended to put Nes's mind back on course, but when she offered nothing in rebuttal, he reconsidered her fears. His perception of Mathias aside, Nessix had clearly developed a fondness for him. Disappointed in himself for hurting her with his cruelty, Brant redirected the conversation.

"Let's head back," he suggested. "You were right. With or without Sagewind's help, we've got to tidy things up." Brant stood and offered a hand to her. "We've enjoyed being children long enough."

The regret in Brant's voice and sorrow in his eyes reinforced Nes's misgivings. *Give me anything, Inwan….* She forced a smile and accepted her cousin's offer. "I suppose you're right. The demons won't get rid of themselves."

* * * * *

Brant narrowly succeeded in cheering Nessix up on the ride back, allowing her to return to her quarters with a mind free to articulate decent tactics. She proceeded to make herself scarce for two days, only seen when visiting with Logan. Brant and Sulik took turns checking on her, making sure she ate and watching as her mood fluctuated between frustration to humming battle hymns. Her preoccupation freed Brant's mind to tend to his own concerns and he grudgingly addressed Nes's growing interest in Mathias. Brant was aware how his harshness on this topic troubled Nes, but that only motivated him more.

He sent out a note for the paladin, mentioning concerns for Nes's well-being. A short hour later, a polite knock announced Mathias's arrival. Personal preference urged Brant not to answer, but his heart insisted he solve this problem before it festered out of control.

The door opened slowly and Mathias studied Brant. He'd been aware of Nes's current state of distraction, but hadn't thought of it as a concern. A gentle whim suggested maybe these concerns lay more in the heart, something Mathias realized would infuriate Brant immensely, but he denied himself to believe it. Brant's hostile posture assured Mathias he wasn't after small talk.

"Commander," he greeted.

"Sagewind," Brant gestured for Mathias to enter. "I didn't think you'd come."

Mathias walked forward, surveying the lavish interior of Brant's chamber. The door closed behind him. "There are matters concerning Nessix, why wouldn't I?"

Chivalrous bastard. "She's been planning our next movement on a troubled mind, with you her greatest concern. Nes doesn't function well with distractions."

That didn't sound right. Mathias had felt quite good about his relationship with Nessix following their last encounter. "What problem does she have with me?"

"Your value to the army, primarily. Whether or not it's worth our effort and safety to keep you around." Brant looked Mathias over, lip curled. "I don't think you need me to tell you my opinion."

The corner of Mathias's mouth twitched, but he wouldn't clash wits with Brant right now. "She tried to get rid of me in the past and failed. I won't leave her to face this alone. You'll find—"

"You stay away from her."

The order was cold and unwelcome to debate. The last of Nes's surviving family, Brant was dangerously serious about protecting her. As the commander's eyes swelled with menacing storms, Mathias braced himself for this inevitable battle. Brant's fierce devotion to Nes touched Mathias, but it wasn't up to him to dictate her interactions with others.

"She and I are both adults and can handle any issues between us in a mature fashion. Her regard for me is understood."

"Quit filling her mind with your shit."

Mathias would allow Brant's personal grudge, but not blatant disrespect. "Like the filth that's kept us alive so far?"

"Like how history says you should be able to wave your sword at the sky and make the demons drop."

The accusation coaxed a chuckle from Mathias. "Most of history is an exaggeration of the truth," Mathias said, wondering what Brant had learned about him. "I've been doing everything I can."

"Tell that to our dead." Brant's voice trembled with a regret Mathias had never considered appropriate from him. "And to their families. To the knights who lost their mounts. Tell them, great *savior*, that you're not the hero you've made yourself out to be. My life is expendable, Sagewind, and my brush with death has been rightfully ignored. You wouldn't mourn my passing, but what about the innocents who died?"

"I mourn none who pass," Mathias answered firmly. "They have reached their paradise."

Brant frowned. "Then what about Nessix? You know better than I do how close she came to dying. What do you think would have happened if she had?"

Mathias thought over that day again, still caught up in the communal fear and his own doubt. "Her maiming hadn't been intended to be her end, it was a statement to me."

"Another fine reason for you to get out of her life."

Mild mannered, slow to anger, and a man of painfully few desires, the resentment which churned in Mathias's core startled him. "Commander, I believe I've heard enough from you."

Brant laughed mockingly. "Where's your bold tongue now?"

"It's been sheathed out of some form of respect!" Brant could not possibly want to see what happened to Mathias when pushed. "Do not try to anger me, Brant."

"Am I supposed to take that as a threat?" Brant's disdainful eyes narrowed at Mathias's growing assertiveness.

"You can take it however you'd like. I'd suggest a warning."

Boundaries laid out, Brant continued to pierce Mathias with

his burning gaze. If Mathias truly wanted Brant to let this drop, he'd step out of Nes's life, simple as that. The door flew open and Nessix burst into the room.

"Oh, good," she breathed, brilliant eyes contrasting to the established hostility. Grabbing Mathias's forearms, she pushed him to Brant's side. "Now I don't have to say it twice."

Brant frowned and shifted his weight from Mathias. "Sagewind was on his way out."

Disappointment etched a fine line between Nes's brows and Mathias answered her with a pleasant smile. "That's fine. I can stay for whatever she has to say."

Brant's scowl drowned in Nes's enthusiastic nod. "I think I've finally got our next movement planned out."

"And it's feasible?" Brant asked, willing to suspend his hatred for Mathias, if only to please Nes.

"It's fantastic!" The grin Nessix tossed them soothed Brant's mind and melted Mathias's heart. "The scouts reported demons still milling about in the east. I want Veed to lay low in his fortress and send Commander Falk with a small force in our direction."

"You think Veed will agree to hold his action?" Brant asked.

Nessix closed her eyes, letting the interruption slide. "He owes this to me, and if he doesn't have any better ideas, he'll have to. Now, once Renigan secures our fortress, we'll ride out to the east."

"We?" Mathias dreaded the sound of combining such strong temperaments in one force.

"Yes. I'll need every one of my officers to make this work. We'll split the force that's there, push a chunk of them further north to the mountains, maybe get them caught in the forests. The other shove will be south, where Veed will engage. We can cover almost every front this way."

Brant eyed the paladin astutely. "It's good enough for me," he said, silently gloating over Nes's satisfied grin.

"I'll lead part of the army to clean up the north the following day," Nessix continued, oblivious to Mathias's disapproving frown. "Not many people know those forests as well as I do." She turned to Brant. "You and Sulik relieve Renigan so he can go back and help Veed if he needs it, and Sagewind, you'll circle around the other side to give support to the rear."

Nes's proposal assured abundant destruction, and Mathias wasn't in a position to try coaxing sympathy from her. "It seems like you're stretching your resources thin."

"We'll be fine," Brant insisted. "I told you before, our people don't run like yours would. It's a brilliant plan, Nes. Don't let his doubt sway you." Mathias may have been glaring at this point, but Brant neither cared nor noticed. "I do wish you'd let me join you on your ambush."

Nessix had spent the past two days wrestling with these plans and shook her head. "I've run through every option and this is the best one. You and Sulik made a good team before. You'd be much more help to me this way."

"Well, if your mind's set, I wouldn't be able to change it, anyway." Brant's steady gaze challenged Mathias to speak up. "What about you, Sagewind?"

Nes missed Brant's perturbed glower, but Mathias didn't. Tucking their feud away for future consideration, Mathias contemplated whether or not Nessix ever got around to asking Veed where his aid had been in the previous fight. Veed had since provided his promised goods, but with much less fanfare than he had in the past. Mathias longed to know the vile man's intentions and doubted his reliability.

"Sulik's already said this sounds feasible," Nes prompted. "Veed'll be fine with it, and if he's not, Sulik offered to stay behind so we can lead the demons to him." Her eager eyes begged for Mathias's approval and her head unconsciously bobbed in excitement.

Mathias expected Nessix to disregard any protests right now, anyway. Her plan was riddled with holes waiting for the demons' exploitation, but the gleam in her eyes coerced Mathias stronger than common sense. "How could I say no?"

"Great!" Nessix didn't turn in time to catch Brant's scowl before it hid behind a smile. "Now, let's get a move on. I've got to get word out to Veed."

Brant continued to smile at Nessix as she scrunched her shoulders in delight and flitted from his room. The further she went, the more his expression faded to a frown. Mentally exhausted from the whirlwind of events, Brant sighed.

"You'd better not let her down," he told Mathias. A sinking feeling suggested Mathias aimed to avoid just that.

"I will do anything I can to fulfill her wishes," Mathias vowed, aware of Brant's scrutiny, "but I am, after all, human."

Patience worn to the limit, Brant settled on the assumption that Mathias would remember their discussion. "You are free to leave." His words were clearly not an invitation. "I'm through with you."

Considering it graceless to remind Brant that he'd been through long ago, Mathias nodded insincerely. "Of course, Commander. It was rude of me to overstay my welcome."

TWENTY-TWO

Mathias had hoped Veed's pride would bar him from accepting Nes's suggested movement but, as usual, Veed disappointed him. A response arrived not two hours after Nessix issued the request, and she wasted no time informing her captains of the following day's plans. Under the cover of darkness, Renigan led the appointed force to Nes's domain, the mix of soldiers coexisting better than expected.

Stopping to review her maps, Nes climbed aboard Logan and nodded to Veed's commander. After receiving a respectful reply, she rode to Mathias.

"We're going to need fierceness out there," she told him. "Every demon left standing is one of my men dead."

"I'll act as we agreed," Mathias promised. "Whether I like it or not."

"Prove your heart's with my people."

His spoken reply would be coarse, so Mathias settled for a silent nod to move Nessix along. Brant and Sulik rode by shortly after, the former not acknowledging him. Death must come to the fallen. Nessix ordered it. The safety of the people relied on it. Etha insisted upon it. But none of that eased Mathias's conscience, and he tried to block out the fact that the demons had once been mortals.

The sun's hazy glow cast out from the distance, and the freshness of dawn energized the army. No horns or drums or rallying cries called to the men, but Logan collected himself on his haunches and galloped toward the pocket of hidden demons. The commanders spurred their way to the outer lines of the force, and the army mobilized.

This isn't how I wanted it, Mathias prayed. *Let us be swift and merciful.*

* * * * *

Whispers of stadium games hovered between the demons, offering everyone their fill of excitement. Toying with the flemans entertained them, but Mathias was a far more delectable target. Etha had made it clear after the Divine Battle that she had no regard for the demons, and from then on, they vowed to do her no favors. The few who remained civil enough to befriend Mathias had been pushed away by their peers, too weak to hold a spot within the horde. In the ages the demons had dealt with the paladin, they only succeeded in killing him once, and were repaid with his resurrection. The demons would never know how passionately this modern Mathias pled for their salvation, and now they had a goddess of their own backing them.

The demons didn't waste time on formal orders. Today, the opposition was nothing more than means to exhume Mathias's anger. Eager to meet the fleman army, a handful of alar took wing.

Nessix expected a much larger unit, and her men hesitated in their confusion. With her officers dispersed, Nessix relied on her herald to sound the advance. Ceraphlaks's shadow flashed overhead and in the same breath, a mangled demon plummeted to the ground in front of her.

She silently cursed Mathias's carelessness. Brant had better be happy with the paladin's disregard, because he'd given his position away completely. Nessix grit her teeth and concentrated on her immediate concerns, praying Mathias took care of himself.

As the flemans approached, masses of demons leaked from

hiding. Still confident in her strength, Nessix adjusted course. Drawing her sword, she stabbed the sky and swept the blade downward, Logan's lengthened strides bearing her to the enemy. Jubilant songs of battle embraced her, bolstering her fortitude. Logan bounded two exuberant leaps to land in the middle of the front lines.

Instinct instructed Logan to keep Nes in the saddle, and he danced about actively to thwart any attempts she made to dismount. Nessix didn't quite understand his motives, but trusted his judgement enough to remain fighting from his back. Ceraphlaks's calm whinny announced his departure as he shot from the clutches of a trio of demons without Mathias. A roar flooded from demon throats as the fiends threw themselves at one target.

He couldn't be that stupid...

A fevered cry erupted from the bevy as Mathias hefted himself to full height. He tossed one of the creatures aside and turned to tear through another. Even his nearby allies paused and shifted away from the deranged heat in Mathias's eyes, his blood-spattered grin, the brutal curses hissed in a foreign tongue. A ghastly beast of a man possessed the gentle soul they trusted and loved. Gallant Sir Sagewind flicked a hand toward himself, beckoning the next demon to engage.

Logan bellowed as a blade sliced into his flank, jolting Nessix from her stupor. She swung her sword rhythmically from either side of Logan's neck, but they lost their forward momentum. Demons penetrated every level of Nes's army, and plenty more waited their turn to jump in. Out of all the men in her sight, only Mathias pushed deeper into enemy lines.

"We're following him, Logan!" she urged.

Logan grunted and planted his hooves stubbornly against the influence of Nes's voice and legs. No amount of obedience would force him to put Nessix in the middle of that.

"We need to see this through," she insisted fiercely.

The demons rushed forward and Logan trampled living beings of undetermined allegiance to avoid impact. Too numb to move, Nessix held her breath as a wall of demons fell over Mathias. The field drew a collective breath before a primal cry cut through the air. Shooting an aura of blue flames from his core, the White Paladin sent dozens of demons scattering. Renewed with Etha's blessing, he turned as briefly as possible and roared a firm order to his comrades.

"Abandon your orders! Retreat!"

Concern warped into contempt as Nessix's mind processed Mathias's words. Yes, things looked much worse than she'd anticipated, but he had no right! Terrifying power or not, Mathias was not the one in charge. If for no other reason than to assert herself, Nessix countered his demand.

"We will not run, men! Stand and fight!"

It seems she doesn't agree with the danger you're in, Etha chimed to Mathias.

Whether she agrees or not, I need them gone.

The closest I can get to her is Sulik, and he's far from her vicinity. You're going to have to do something to convince her yourself.

Just grant me the strength you can. I don't think they'll have much of a choice but to run in a moment.

Mathias repeated his orders, and while Nessix doggedly sought to hold her ground, Logan knew better. Outnumbered and outmatched by the enemy, he could not keep her there in good conscience. Wielding his superior strength over his petite rider, Logan turned and ran.

Nessix tried to rein him in, resorting to brutal yanks on his mouth. "Hold your ground!" she screamed, cursing Logan's rebellion. "We must fight!"

A moment's uncertainty passed. The majority of the army favored Mathias's sound order, but Nessix insisted they follow course. Devotions tearing through fierce hearts, the fleman warriors turned to Logan's lead. If they escaped the field before comprehension dawned on the demons, they stood a chance at outrunning them.

Frustrated screams from Nessix wound back to Mathias until Logan had whisked her out of harm's way. The horse ran too fast for Nessix to risk launching herself from his back and Mathias breathed a sigh of relief. With bystanders gone, he was ready to accept the demons' challenge. By the time Nes's objections disappeared from earshot, the masses surrounded Mathias in a living arena.

The paladin had dueled demons more times than he cared to recall. Over the years, they'd made a game of hunting him, and their efforts often culminated in this fashion. They were bound to hurt him plenty, but they wouldn't succeed at killing him. Etha forbid it and, unbeknownst to Mathias, so did Shand.

* * * * *

Logan compromised with Nessix and stopped at the top of a hill to let her watch Mathias's fate. The army pulled up behind her and the commanders joined her side. All eyes strained to see what would become of their savior. Even Brant held his breath as he watched on.

Mouth working in hushed, uncertain prayers, Sulik contended with his insufficiency. "Nessix," he choked, throat dry. "I'd like to escort the wounded home."

"Will you be able to heal them?" She stared ahead where the demons scurried around Mathias, throwing lively blows toward him.

"I'm ready to try."

Nes's jaw kneaded her anxiety. "If Sagewind taught you anything that'll help us, I think you're our best hope right now."

"Until Sir Sagewind frees himself," Sulik corrected.

Nessix pinched her lips between her teeth, clenching her opinion with them. Too many ears monitored her reflections, and while Mathias's outcome looked grim, no one would admit their predications. Sulik turned from Nes's silence and called for captains to gather their wounded. His actions distracted concerned eyes, but the stoic cousins maintained their focus on Mathias.

A full arena of bodies assembled around the lone man, evil intent snapping dastardly pledges at his placid demeanor. As the odds stacked increasingly against Mathias, Nessix bleakly wondered what would happen if he died. She once looked for excuses to try and get rid of him, but the thought of losing him now taxed her breathing and weakened her knees. Without Mathias, her men would continue to throw down their lives until only she survived, crawling to Veed if he was still around. Losing Mathias meant losing her people's only real power over the demons. It almost meant losing a friend. A smaller demon lurched at Mathias from the crowd. The paladin moved into action immediately, his response carefully calculated.

Mathias expended minimal effort to slay that first demon and a ripple of gasps alerted Nes's troops that the fight was underway. A second attack came from behind and Mathias allowed the weight of his assailant to topple them both to the ground. The army sucked in a communal breath as the paladin fell from sight, not releasing it until Mathias rose and heaved a limp body back into the force around him. Opponents took turns challenging him, most falling and a few skittering to retreat. Steadfast to his disposition, Mathias brought merciful ends to his assailants.

"Why don't they move in on him?" Brant murmured to Nessix, more concerned than he'd intended.

The same thought echoed in Nes's concerns. Her mind reeled back to the first book En made her read following Mathias's arrival, recalling details she'd only half paid attention to. Mathias had faced demons on his own before, ordering his army to retreat when the enemy proved too powerful. He fought them like this for nearly a day before exhaustion struck and the demons disposed of him. As Mathias picked off each new demon, this tale retold itself in her mind.

"They don't want him dead," Nessix said quietly, "at least not yet."

"But why waste the energy when they could just end it now?"

"A mockery? Toying with him? I don't know Brant, but the end of this can't be good."

Brant gaped at Nessix, seeing for the first time how deeply she cared for Mathias. While he had no intention of fostering such affection, the army truly did need the paladin and the resolve he cultivated. One more heartbeat of studying his cousin and Brant uncovered a grossly familiar quality in the set of her jaw. He reached a hand toward her.

"Nessix—"

Heels dug into Logan's side, eliciting an indignant grunt. He hopped half a stride forward before throwing his head back and dancing closer to Armina. Valuable or not, Mathias was not worth running back down there.

"We will not leave him to die," Nessix insisted, trying unsuccessfully to haul Logan around.

Logan's fit broadcast Nes's intentions to the troops. Confused faces searched her for guidance, hope tainted with terror. Regretting his decision to allow Nes to watch the fight, Logan pushed against her restraints and sprinted toward the back lines. The war would continue, whether or not Mathias survived, until one side suppressed the other. If Nessix couldn't handle that, Logan would remedy the situation through any means necessary.

Under normal circumstances, Nessix found excuses to overlook Logan's flits of disobedience, but not now. If he wanted to leave, she wouldn't stop him, but neither would she allow him to force it on her. Jerking one rein to her hip, Nessix pulled Logan's head around and vaulted to the ground. Ignoring her mount's frantic attempts to stop her, Nessix stormed toward the rise.

"I will not sign him over for dead," she told Brant's stony face.

"Nes…" he warned, his voice rising in apprehension. "This is a terrible idea."

"I don't care." Nessix grimaced as Mathias took his first hard hit. "He's never left any of us to die, and I will not abandon him. So be it, if none of you will come with me, I'll go by myself."

Brant closed his eyes, fully aware that Nessix meant for others to hear her declaration. "He ordered us away for a reason."

"Will you honestly just sit here and watch him be slaughtered?" As promised, Nessix darted ahead.

Brant hastily navigated Armina to block Nes's advance. "You cannot go down there alone."

"Then come with me."

Brant looked down to where Mathias retreated two steps from his current opponent, shaking the daze from his eyes. Sighing, Brant turned back to Nessix. Determination was engraved on her face, and he knew better than to try and chisel it out. *Great Inwan,*

why did you give her such fire?
"Give us your orders," Brant said.

* * * * *

The attacks wore on him, but Mathias had plenty left. A startled roar coursed through the back lines, croaks of agony telling him what his eyes couldn't stray to. Mathias stretched his arm out and adjusted his grip on his sword.

More cries followed and the ring of danger rippled apart as the fleman force beat down around him. Perverted by adrenaline, Mathias growled at Nes's recklessness. The break in concentration cost Mathias as an alar latched onto him from behind. Pinning Mathias's arms against his body, the demon propelled them both into the air, wings drawing them higher. Mathias dropped his center of gravity, trying to impede the demon's effort. Hissing at the inconvenience, the demon leaned forward and bit him behind his ear. A tormented cry tore from Mathias as teeth sank in and removed a mouthful of flesh. He didn't begin to struggle until the demon raked her teeth down her own arm.

Her wings folded around Mathias, holding him close as she pressed her open wound against his. Screams ripped from both throats as good and evil mingled, invading each other's systems. Etha's blessing purified the demon on contact, and her wings released their embrace. Lifeless arms fell away from Mathias and he writhed in his descent. Tears streaked his face as his hands pressed against his neck. Demon blood pulsed through his body, scraping the walls of his veins with its toxicity. Mathias opened his eyes to see the ground speeding toward him and braced himself for impact. Blessed armor absorbed the brunt of his landing, but Mathias struck the ground and gasped for air as he waited for the agony to stop.

Swords clanked against one another and booted feet kicked dirt in his eyes. He coughed between sustaining breaths and hefted himself to his stomach. Still gripping the side of his neck, Mathias wobbled to his knees. Instinctively, he whispered pleas for divine assistance, but Etha's name burned on his tongue. Chin trembling at this distorted emptiness, despair threw Mathias back on the ground.

A hoarse cry cleaved Mathias's anguish and a shadow passed above him. Heart racing, he peered up to see Nessix straddling him protectively. Teeth brandished in a ferocious snarl and eyes ablaze with possessive fury, she wielded his sword with both hands, throwing her entire body behind each swing and thrust. Five demons fell to her and the sacred blade before they thought better than to rush her. Nessix remained poised above Mathias until nothing else threatened to charge her, then lowered the sword's tip to the ground.

Mathias's discipline insisted he snap at her about the danger of ignoring his direct order, but the rest of him was too thankful to allow it.

"Are you al—"

"Fine," he coughed. "A hard fall, that's it."

Nessix breathed her relief and dropped his sword to offer a hand to help him rise. Mathias accepted the gesture politely, but stood with his own strength.

"Where's Sulik?" he stammered.

"Escorting the wounded back home. And before you say it, don't tell me you didn't need us." Nessix looked Mathias over, unsuccessfully attempting to pull his hand away from his neck. "Because you did."

He averted his eyes and shoved past her, glancing at his sword where it lay on the ground.

Nessix followed his eyes, biting the inside of her cheek as he strode away. She nabbed his faithful blade and tracked after him. "Where are you going?"

Mathias wheeled to face her, the brisk movement spinning his head violently. All he wanted was to lay back down. If death evaded him, he at least wanted to forget. Etha couldn't come near him in the presence of evil. The taint would cycle out with time, but until then, he'd been leveled to an ordinary human warrior. Losing his physical abilities meant very little to Mathias, but losing Etha? If Brant and Nessix wanted to see brutality, they only had to wait for

Mathias to regain himself. Nes's question forgotten in his jumbled thoughts, it took her gasp and rush forward to catch him for Mathias to realize how close he was to losing consciousness. Two soldiers stepped forward to offer further support.

"Get him back to the fortress," Nessix said. "It should be safe here now."

They nodded and hauled the paladin between them. Nessix watched them leave, not knowing if she should be relieved that Mathias had survived or frightened by this change in him.

* * * * *

Mathias sat under the moonlight, absorbing the stillness he'd long ago grown unaccustomed to. He gave up trying to reach Etha hours ago, aware that the blight he carried forced them apart, and asked for a simple poultice and bandage for his wounded neck. Once again, he hid the extent of his spiritual damage from the flemans in the hope of keeping what little positive momentum the army carried alive. The lights of Veed's fortress flickered in the darkness and Mathias contented himself in his solitude until cautious footsteps crunched in the grass behind him.

"Tonight isn't well." Nes's softened voice jarred him from his dour reflections. "You can feel it, too."

"What we accomplished today was by luck alone." Mathias didn't look at her.

Nessix nodded grimly and frowned at his gloomy demeanor. "But we did win," she tried. "I'd have led the rescue sooner if it hadn't taken so much rallying."

"If you had to push so hard, you shouldn't have bothered." A bitter laugh scorned her sympathy. "Etha was watching over me. It's the reason I'm still alive."

Nessix pinched her lips together and sat down beside Mathias, hugging her knees. "We did what had to be done."

Mathias focused on the distance, unwilling to reveal the doubt in his eyes. "Your strength is what won today. I had nothing to do with it."

She ignored his modesty. "For a while there, I was afraid we wouldn't make it. Part of me expects the same tomorrow."

"We won't lose tomorrow," Mathias assured. Of course, the demons were past the point of playing, but Nes's confidence mattered much more tonight. He missed her sorrowful smile.

"I hope you're right. If you want to get even with them—"

"That's not my way."

This cold side of Mathias rattled Nessix. She ached to know what bothered him so deeply, to get him to open up, but if he'd wanted to talk about it, he'd have done so by now. Nessix understood pride well enough to let him keep his. "Will you promise me one thing?"

A long blink later, Mathias finally shifted his position to look at her. "What's that?"

Nessix hesitated to gather her wits. "If I don't... I mean, if something happens and the troops need you... "

Mathias forced himself to relax for Nes's benefit, smiled, and laid a gentle hand on her shoulder. "I'd keep them safe for you, but am trusting your stubbornness won't let it be an issue."

Her smile tempted his mind away from darker thoughts. "Let's hope you're right." She fell to her back and stared up at the sky. "I wish I understood..."

"Understood what?" Mathias asked after several breath's silence.

"Why bad things happen." Nessix intentionally kept her answer vague, losing the courage that initiated this poignant conversation. She trusted Mathias not to judge her, but erected preemptive walls just in case. "You know what tomorrow is?"

Her tone struck Mathias with a startling truth. Nessix had walked behind shadows from her past since the day he met her, and she was finally ready to ask him to help hold a torch to them. "What?"

Her gaze drifted from him and a deep breath drew in her wits. "Eleven years since father gave his last orders." Pinching her eyes shut against the promise of tears and shake of her lower lip, Nessix struggled to maintain her dignity and stared up at the sky once more. Mathias watched her curiously, but she didn't dare confirm the nature of his interest. "How can you stand to live forever? To see everyone important to you have their lives snatched away? How do you deal with the doubt and the—" *The fear?* She wouldn't let that escape her. "How do you do it?"

Mathias had seen Nes question herself before but never so in need of support. "I can't answer that for sure. All I've ever done is continue with my duties."

"Just like that? Keep on working and everything's better?"

He chuckled. "I help people, it's what I do. If they need healing, I mend them. If they need a bit of happiness, I offer what I can. In caring for others, I care for myself. You can't concentrate on the evils of the world, or you'll lose yourself. That's why I always try to find the good."

Nessix processed his words and picked a blade of grass. "I... I prayed for the first time in nearly a decade last night." She twirled the grass between uncertain fingers in an excuse to not look at Mathias.

"I see." A content smile turned Mathias's lips. "What did you say?"

Nes's eyes grew blank and she pinched the grass still. "It's not important. He never answered."

"Still praying to Inwan?" No wonder she was disappointed. "Next time, try Etha. She might surprise you."

"Inwan's the only god I know," Nessix said. "Why would your Etha waste her time on me after all I've done?"

At least she admitted her blasphemy. "You've never given her a chance, but she knows you well." Mathias watched Nes hopefully. "She's been waiting to accept you when you're ready. It might be time to move on."

The words carried the intent to encourage her, but left Nessix much more alone. Out of everyone she knew, Mathias was the only one she assumed could relate to this fear. "If your Etha stepped out of your life, left you in silence after everything you'd been through, how long would you keep praying to her?"

Mathias clamped his jaw at the untimely irony of Nes's question. No matter how much he wanted to deny it, his answer was exactly the same as hers. As powerless as he felt right now, he'd hear from Etha once the demon blood cycled out of him. Nessix trudged through life with the same helplessness, nothing but her steady faith pulling her along.

"I don't know any other way," she concluded to his silence. "What else would you have me do?"

Now that she'd explained herself, Mathias hurt for Nessix. "I don't have an answer for you."

Nessix masked her disappointment with a short sigh and looked away from Mathias. She debated getting up to leave, but didn't want to muster the energy. Her doubt wound around thoughts of Mathias's instabilities, Inwan's absence, her father's death. Tomorrow, she'd ride into battle, taunted by these reminders of how little she knew herself. She'd failed in her attempts to hate Mathias, failed to keep her family together, failed to prove herself a competent general. Her stomach curled.

"You once said we'd win no matter what," Mathias said, thwarting her glum thoughts.

Nessix sat up, uncomfortable and anxious. "I've learned a lot since this war began, and I regret all of it."

"Then you want to just lay down and let them take us?"

Mathias's accusation hurt an already flawed mind, and Nessix faced him abruptly. "This isn't easy for me, Mathias!"

"So you *do* still have your spirit," he said. "You need to keep it for tomorrow, whether you find it from anger at me or Etha or anyone else. Your men need it. They deserve it."

She turned a shoulder from him. "None of this is fair."

"Do you know where the demons came from?"

Nessix started at the question, unable to connect it to their current discussion.

When she slowly looked back at Mathias and shook her head, he continued. "That's truly an unfair story, more than a tale of hard lives or unfulfilled promises. They were once men and elves and all manner of people like we are now." Nessix listened politely, but not without doubt.

"The first children gods, in all their pride and hatred for each other, waged a war across Abaeloth, tearing the lands apart. The people too near their wrath were perverted by the raw energies of their magic. Misshapen, broken, some hurt just from surviving. The fallen were outcasts, desperate to be whole beings again but shunned by their kin. Within a few years, they united to form their own society. They carried on peacefully before a few twisted mortals offered them assistance and corrupted them with words of evil. The first of the demons set out to obtain flight. Before anyone knew it, the fallen became true demons, monsters that had only been heard of in children's tales. The demons fell from their mortal grace, and from Etha's as well. Ages have fostered their hatred and now all anyone remembers is war."

After Mathias stopped, Nessix kept silent for a while longer. "And you're okay with this?"

"No," he answered honestly. "I hate it. The fallen have become far too vile and powerful to ignore, the few who know or remember kindness toward the mortal races have either been killed or exiled. The only joy they know anymore is how to spread their pain. We have no chance to reunite with them at this point, too much has been put between us. So, we fight. There's no other way. And I *hate* it."

"But this isn't what I want to do anymore!" Nessix pounded a fist against the ground. "I want to battle the minotaur and ogres, get caught up in petty arguments with Veed!" Common sense screamed at Nes to shut up, but the words gushed out of her control. "I want my life to make sense!"

Mathias smiled in gentle understanding. "When we seal the demons back in their realm, you can have your life back. Until then, you have a commitment to your people."

His spoken truth didn't make Nessix feel any better. "I wish I was commanding beside Father again. He always knew how to handle things."

"He'd do no better than you. There's no way to prepare for demons. You're as strong as him, no doubt, just younger."

Warmth tickled Nes's cheeks at the compliment, but it hid in the darkening night. Only one other concern troubled her, and Mathias was quite possibly the only person able to understand. Prepared for the worst, Nessix divulged her final secret.

"Do you know why I'm still hung up on Inwan?"

The fact that Nessix volunteered such precious information snagged Mathias's attention. "No, but I've been wanting to know."

Nessix heaved a sigh. "He loved my people." A nostalgic smile hinted at existence. "Especially those of us with noble blood. He'd always been a generous god." Fighting off her discomfort, Nessix raised a hand to her chest and her eyes drifted closed. "I never knew my mother, she died in childbirth, and Father was left to raise me alone. Inwan loved us so much that he answered Father's prayers by blessing me as an infant; 'No mortal power will make her fall.' I still carry the mark of his touch." Her eyes peeked open, the reminiscence replaced with anguish. "It's more of a curse now than a blessing."

Mathias nearly corrected her, to tell her it was never a bad thing to be touched by a god who loved her, but understood exactly what Nessix meant. This one confession explained not only her adoration for her god, but for her father. They'd meant the world to her, and both had left her. Etha had warned Mathias early on that Nessix survived a traumatic youth, and while her history held nothing to the demons', he no longer blamed her for her behavior. Nessix lived with a constant reminder of the greatest betrayal Mathias could imagine. He knew the nature of Inwan's departure—that the god had taken inappropriate liberties with the mortals under his peers' custody—and frowned at the thought of him choosing whores over Nes's devotion.

"So you miss him," Mathias concluded.

"Dearly."

Mathias stood and turned from Nessix to relieve his scowl. "That's why you're so resentful of the gods. Your own left you unjustly burdened. Next time I see him, I'll remind him of his priorities."

Nessix looked up at Mathias from where she sat, eyes finally at ease. "Are you turning in for the night?"

"I think I need to go for a walk." His tone was hardly inviting. "And you need your rest. Nes, if it was up to me, I would drag Inwan here personally and force him to ride out with you tomorrow." Nessix flushed awkwardly as Mathias continued. "Those touched by the gods are always in their minds. If Inwan's still within the reaches of Abaeloth, he'll see you tomorrow."

After so many years on her own, Nessix had ample reasons to doubt Mathias, but she liked the thought of his sentiments. She rocked herself to her feet and held Mathias's eyes. "You and I aren't that different from each other, Sagewind," she murmured.

"No, we're not."

The statement wore on Nes's courage, and she looked away. "I don't know why I told you any of this. I've never shared it with anyone, not even Brant."

Mathias relaxed into a nod. "You'll understand someday," he promised. "Now, go get some sleep. Your men will need you at your best."

Nessix nodded slowly, racking her brain for something to prolong their conversation. Disappointed with her results, she turned and trudged back toward the fortress, listening to Mathias's footsteps fade away behind her. She stopped, a final thought beating against her desire to put up a strong front.

"Forgive me," Nessix whispered against the speckled darkness. "We should have had this talk months ago." A smile crossed her face and a wave of ease washed over her. She felt good about tomorrow.

TWENTY-THREE

A wicked smile danced across Nes's face as Logan leapt into the tangle of demons. The mounted elite raced after them, her soldiers trailing close behind. Inspired by the previous night's talk, Nessix was certain the demons looked forward to a substantial defeat today. She released her hold on Logan's reins and drew her sword to sever an arm off the first demon that tried to pull her from the saddle. The bloodshed began.

More demons had surfaced since yesterday, but that only encouraged Nessix. The flemans progressed through the opposition, aiming to clear the way to whatever portal their foes used to access Elidae.

Deep in the enemy lines, razing demons before their faces were clear, Logan's charge met an abrupt end as a war hammer connected with his left knee. The joint shattered on impact, no longer able to support his weight. It struck faster than Nes's confident mind could comprehend, and the severity of the situation didn't hit until the rotation of Logan's fall landed Nessix on her shoulder blades. The instinct to survive propelled Nessix to the side while Logan contorted his body to avoid crushing her. Disoriented from the fall, Nessix watched the legs of her allies rush past her to engage the enemy. Logan's wild grunt announced his frenzied attempts to rise, but the pull of his hoof's weight against broken bones kept him down.

Danger rained all around her, but when Nessix saw Logan's obliterated leg, her lips went cold. The sound of combat muffled in the tumult of her blood and breathing. Surrendering to his physical limitation, Logan lay heaving on the ground and rubbed his face in the dirt. Nessix dropped her sword and scrambled to her knees. Her hands reached out to him, arms pulsing while she tried to figure out what she could possibly do for her beloved mount. Nessix understood this injury and knew the death sentence it carried, but she refused to believe Logan would succumb to it. Staring at his fractured knee with helpless glances to his anguished expression, Nessix shook off the daze of both physical and emotional impacts. She couldn't feel anything right now, anyway.

Launching to her feet, Nessix protected Logan fiercely. She held nothing back, slaughtering any demon that wandered close enough to her blade with the same corrupt intensity they employed. Her men struggled with the fight, but Nes's only concern wrapped around her dearest friend and lifelong companion as he suffered ingloriously on the ground. Fecklans were born for their generals, and Nessix being raised on the milk of Logan's dam had intensified their bond. She'd quit counting how many times he'd carried her battered self free from harm years ago, and in this moment, Nessix was beyond compelled to return the favor.

By the fled god's blessing or simply a stroke of luck, the army persisted without Nes's guidance. Not straying from Logan's proximity, her participation was limited, but when the demons sounded their retreat, Nessix wasn't ready to let them run.

"Stop them!" she shouted from her station. "Not one of these sons of bitches escapes!"

Hooves dashed past her and the rallying cries of those on foot left Nessix behind as they chased down what demons they could catch. Nessix panted from her efforts, the hilt of her sword slipping in her bloodied hand, and she sank to the ground. As the demons drifted away, the fleman clerics moved in to tend to those in need, and the rumble of wagons followed behind.

* * * * *

309

Nessix reserved her tears for very special occasions. When the demons killed En, she responded with a healthy dose of self-reflection and renewed determination. She ignored wounds taken in battle, save vindictive snarls and increasing vigor. So long as an injury didn't hinder her performance, she preferred to refuse Mathias's healing.

The only times Mathias had seen tears in her eyes came from a much simpler emotion. Witnessing the devastation in Sarlot. Coping through the terror of her curse. Nessix only cried when she felt utterly helpless, and though Mathias tormented himself with his personal strife, seeing Nessix cry left him empty inside.

She lurched down the hall toward his chamber, eyes vacantly focused on her set path. Tears coursed down her cheeks and rapid breaths passed through an open mouth. The report Mathias received had said the battle went well, but Nes's agitated state spoke of a much different outcome. Unwilling to let a chance to win Nessix over pass him by, Mathias rushed to her, gently calling her name.

His voice dug coherence from Nessix, and she blinked back her confusion. Her face collapsed on itself as a sob announced her quickened pace. She reached Mathias and frantically clutched his hands.

"You have to help," she begged between sobs, shoulders hunched forward in the closest thing to despondency Mathias ever hoped to see from her. "Sagewind, it's Logan…"

Mathias winced. No stranger to typical wartime battery, Logan must have sustained serious damage to garner this response in Nessix. "What happened?"

She shook her head, fingers scratching at his palm as she searched for the words to answer him. "You have to help him," she repeated. "Please."

Nes's anguish sapped the resolve from Mathias, and he ached from her hurt. Even worse, he agonized over the fact that the demon taint prevented him from channeling Etha's grace, and Nes's persistent despair affirmed he'd need those blessings now. Swallowing his regret, Mathias leaned his weight forward to prompt Nessix back into motion.

Etha, I know you can hear me. Whatever happened to Logan, I'm begging you to allow a way for his recovery. Nes isn't ready to lose him.

Nessix accepted Mathias's lead and resumed her hastened shamble down the hall, clutching his hand to keep him in tow. She made no effort to maintain her dignity, wiping her nose with the back of her free hand and sucking the taste of her tears from her lips. Nes pulled Mathias along, unable to respond to his repeated requests for more information. They wound down the stairs and rushed through both doorways of Logan's stall. A tent stood three paces from the exterior door, rapidly pitched and lit from within. Nes's frantic hands clawed across the fabric panels, and Mathias calmly reached out to pull open the flap. Nessix darted inside and Mathias drew a deep breath and followed.

Logan lay on his side in the middle of the shelter, massive frame drained of strength. His great sides heaved with painful groans. Nessix tumbled over herself to sit beside him, stroking his coarse mane. Sending a second plea in Etha's direction, Mathias shuffled over to them and knelt down.

"He didn't even have a chance," Nessix stammered, tear-battered eyes scouring Mathias's face. "They hit him as soon as we engaged, took his knee—" A bout of sobs crippled her ability to continue.

Mathias didn't need Nessix to explain anything else to see the damage dealt to Logan. Such injuries weren't terribly uncommon for warhorses, and Mathias had never seen one survive. In a frightfully delicate spot, Mathias closed his eyes to search out even the tiniest spark of divinity. He found nothing of use inside him.

"Did the rest of the battle play out as planned?" he asked, trying to buy time to figure out an alternative.

Nessix nodded, choking on the influx of mucous from her sniffling. "I stayed with Logan," she said. "Fought off what was around me, but the army made up for me."

Etha, please!

Nessix uncoiled her fingers from Logan's mane to grab Mathias's arm. "Fix him, please."

Mouth agape, Mathias looked into Nes's wild eyes. She trusted him. She needed him. And there was nothing he could do for her.

Etha' voice remained lost in the haze of Mathias's mind and his heart throbbed around the shard of Affliction that kept him sparked with life. The bottom of his stomach dropped out and he pointedly looked away from Nessix. "I can't."

Nessix quit breathing at receipt of Mathias's statement, staring at him with wide eyes until panic spurred her on. "No," she begged. "You have to!" She grabbed his hands and pulled them toward Logan's knee.

Mathias had no way to explain his reasons for failing her, not in a way she'd understand. He snatched his hands away and closed his eyes. "I can't," he repeated.

"He needs you!" Nessix insisted. "I need you!"

"I cannot do it. I'm sorry." Mathias stood before her devastation overcame him and turned to leave the tent, chased by her broken screams for his help.

Tears streamed down Nes's cheeks as hope abandoned her. "Fraud! Get back here!" She collapsed against Logan's side, fingers tangling in his mane. "I need you…" Nessix sobbed, laying there in as much of a shattered mess as her mount until her choking forced her upright. She pulled her face away and stared at the disfigured, swollen joint.

Nessix had thought the previous night's confession had meant something. Mathias had been Logan's best chance at surviving, but desperation suggested one last option. Nessix crawled over Logan's head, cradling it in her arms as she stuffed away her tears.

"I'm not giving up." She pressed a kiss beneath his forelock. "Hold on for me." Rising on uncertain legs, Nessix scrambled from the tent, past people she didn't notice, and down to the stables.

* * * * *

Nessix rode out wildly, spotted easily by Veed's watch towers. Intrigued by her urgency, he waited for her outside the gates.

"You're a mess, Nessix," Veed mused, grasping the heaving horse's reins. Nes never rode a horse other than Logan, and Veed's keen eyes sparked with suspicion. "Would you like to come inside and tell me what's wrong?"

Nessix rolled her shoulders, stretched her neck, and dismounted. Lips tight, she shoved past Veed to stalk into his home. Her stony demeanor and rigid gait encouraged Veed's smirk. Leaving the horse with a guard, he turned to follow.

"We engaged in the north and the demons—damn it, Veed! I don't have time for explanations."

"So, Logan's wounded?" Veed opened the door to his conference chamber.

"Yes," she piped, "and I need to know... your practice of the dark arts covers healing, right?" Nessix took her seat quickly and leaned her head against the back of her chair.

Veed sat across from her, amused by her attempts at nonchalance. "What about Mathias?"

"He said he can't. He wouldn't tell me why."

"You're surprised?" Veed asked, pouring some wine for himself and offering the same to Nessix. She shook her head. "His luck's run out, if you ask me."

"That doesn't matter to me," Nessix snapped. "I need to know if you can heal Logan or not."

A depraved grin crossed Veed's face and his eyes bore straight into Nes's soul. "I believe I can, but there will be a price."

"Name it, Veed, and I'll get it."

Veed sounded a gentle laugh. "Payment's not something you have to get, Nes, consider it more something you have to give."

What does...? Nessix gagged on a disgusted gasp and snuck a fleeting glance at Veed's perverse eyes. Clenching her jaw to keep back anything she might regret, Nessix fought to compose herself.

"*You* are payment," Veed said, standing to saunter over to her. He devoured her with his eyes, smirking at the shock and abhorrence that held Nessix immobile. "I'm not looking for commitment, love." He pulled the pins from her hair. Each one dropped from his grasp, tinkling to the floor in the thick silence. "Just enough that I can assure your father you were properly taken care of when next we meet."

Nessix didn't dare close her eyes as Veed's fingers picked her braids loose. She'd come here willing to pay any price, but in her desperation, she'd overlooked Veed's obsession with her. "There's nothing else you want?" She turned her head from his lustful gaze.

Veed pushed the back corner of her chair so she faced him again. "You said any price, and I have access to anything else I want. I'd never take you by force; this seems my best opportunity."

Her eyes hardened as she fortified her walls. "This is business, Veed. Nothing more."

"I'd expect nothing else from you." Veed leaned closer and grinned as the chair restricted Nessix from shying away. "You know you don't have to be afraid of me, and if Logan's really so bad off, it'd be a shame for us to waste any more time with silly formalities." He took a step back and offered an arm to her.

Nessix closed her eyes to muster her courage. She was painfully ignorant to the value of intimacy, and tried to convince herself that this would be no different than battle. Combat saw her body touched all the time and she considered it more a tool than anything else. Somehow, that rationalization only made her feel worse. Veed cleared his throat and Nessix opened her eyes again.

"Time's wasting, Nes."

She'd known for some time of Veed's less than appropriate attraction to her, but never dreamed it would culminate to this. She stared at the chalice on the table and snatched it up, hoping the concoction within would help her quit thinking. She wanted to forget about this demoralizing arrangement. She wanted to forget about Mathias. She wanted to forget about that damned goddess who never bothered to show herself to the person who needed guidance the most.

Rising on legs of steel will alone, Nessix hung her head and approached Veed. A shudder passed through her and she awkwardly rested her hand on his arm.

"That's my good girl," Veed murmured, throwing the door open.

Wrapping her mind in a sturdy blanket of resolve, Nessix held her shoulders as proud as she could while they passed smirking soldiers and knowing leers. She forbid herself to let Veed defeat her, as she knew he aimed to. The sun had already disappeared below the rise of the mountains as Veed paraded Nessix through the halls and up to his chamber.

* * * * *

Frustration boiled inside Mathias. He'd finally come to terms with Nes's personality and thought she'd learned to tolerate him, and he couldn't deny his fondness for her any longer. This one night, ravaged by the depravity of demons, threatened to ruin everything he'd worked so hard to grasp. Mathias knew the limitations he suffered from, and the temple was the only place he and Etha could coexist until his body purged this evil from his veins.

"Mother, help me!" His voice rebounded in anguished strains against marble walls.

His fear clenched Etha as thoroughly as the despair radiating from within Veed's fortress did. She stared into Mathias's soul, her ageless eyes losing their youth. *You must let him decide when to play hero.*

She turned her gaze from him. "The only thing I can tell you to do is have faith."

"You know I do!" Mathias reached out to Etha before clenching his hands into fists to draw them back. "There has to be something—"

"Mathias, there is nothing I can do. You know the laws of—"

"Fuck the laws!"

A heavy breath pulled Etha's shoulders taut and her mouth gaped with a silent, despondent gasp. Mathias hadn't raised his voice to her since their early days together. In all her power, the only thing Etha could not stomach was Mathias's pain. She'd seen him through tortures no man should ever bear. He'd thrown himself into agony in her name. But this pain, the pain that she could do nothing to help him ease, tore Etha apart. Mathias's chest heaved and a dismal pink stained his eyes. As valiant as Mathias had proven himself to be, this was the first time Etha had ever seen him truly helpless.

"Mathias…" she murmured. "You know I *can't*—" This time, her gasp culminated and her eyes shot open as though she'd been run through.

"Etha!" Mathias drew the longsword that filled in for his blessed blade's absence to avoid grasping his goddess with his cursed hands.

"No, my dear." Etha placed a hand on the blade to lower it, eyes haunted in a manner Mathias had never seen before.

He allowed Etha to redirect his weapon and his eyes misted over in the fear of losing more than just Nessix.

Etha stared pointedly through the walls of the chamber. A shudder worked through her frame and she pinched her eyes shut as she shook her head against the devastation. "You must do something for me," she begged, keeping her face turned from him.

"Anything," Mathias swore.

"You must forgive her."

Questions leapt through Mathias's mind at a feverish pace. "What do you mean?"

"I can't tell you any more, it's not my place, but you must forgive her. She's hurting, too."

Mathias shook his head, brows drawn close. "Nes?" he asked brokenly. "Etha, what's wrong?"

The goddess trembled, wringing her hands as she paced away from her guilt of being unable to answer him. "You can't worry about that now. Only remember that she's as desperate as you are." She regretted her choice of words when Mathias's lip twitched and primal anger lit his eyes.

"Etha," Mathias growled, a tone he seldom used with her. "I need to know what she's doing before I can forgive her." His mind already presented the most probable horror, but his heart shrieked for alternatives.

"She'll tell you," Etha said. "She has to. She's afraid, Mathias. You must forgive her!"

Etha's fear confirmed Mathias's worst suspicions. "Where is she?" he demanded.

"Please, my child, I can't tell you anything else! If you want to try and fix things, go back to Logan, doctor him the best you can. He's the one that needs you right now."

Neither Etha's strange behavior nor her disjointed answers

suited Mathias, but even with this terrible, unspoken confirmation, his options were limited. If watching over Logan was the only way he could benefit Nessix, he would do so. His eyes trailed away, staring intently at the feathering in the marble floor. Mathias had loved before, and felt his share of lust, but a new, perverse feeling transcended his guilt. He was jealous.

Afraid of this feeling, terrified of any misguided desires that rode in on it, Mathias knew only one option. "My—" As he looked up, Etha was gone. A firm curse accompanied the slam of his sword back into its scabbard. He set his jaw and stalked out of the temple to do as he'd been told. Logan would live through the night, and Mathias would tend to Veed later.

TWENTY-FOUR

His eyes fondled her as she laced her breeches and though she only showed her back to him, Nessix averted her eyes. She didn't know how long it would take to write this from her mind, but trusted Veed to do everything in his power to make sure she remembered. Nessix clamped her teeth and bent down to retrieve her blouse.

"Father would have killed you for this," she snapped with what venom she had left.

Veed, still lounging in the blankets and furs, chuckled softly.

Nessix yanked the shirt over her head and wheeled to face Veed. His eyes still held their repulsive greed and she regretted turning around. "What's so funny about that?" she demanded, compulsively withdrawing a step under Veed's steady gaze.

"I'd have killed him over much less," he said, stretching lazily. "Something as insignificant as a kingdom, perhaps."

Nes's breastplate fell from her grasp and clattered to the floor. She'd had nightmares about Veed faltering in his service following her father's death. Inwan left before she'd found the nerve to ask him about it and so she suppressed her fears, hiding the ridiculous notion even from Brant.

"You loved my father," Nessix insisted, making a second attempt to buckle her armor.

"I've loved many things," Veed said. "Battle, fine wine, Solvig." He stopped to let Nessix secure her armor. "You."

"Don't say that."

"And why not?"

"One time deal, remember?" Nes's heart raced at Veed's exaggerated confusion. "You weren't looking for a commitment. It was your own terms, Veed!" She clenched her teeth to fend off resurging tears.

"You know, this war's going to ensure you live on in the histories. I'd hate to think they'd label the great demon-slaying Nessix as a whore."

Nessix shuddered at Veed's words and pinched her eyes shut. Trembling hands snatched up a vambrace and fumbled through the familiar motion of strapping it to her forearm. She rooted her tongue firmly against the roof of her mouth.

"You *are* the last of the Teradhel line," Veed continued. "This nation will fall into disorder if you don't do something about it. Think, when the war's over, once we get rid of the demons and Mathias, you and I could reunite Elidae. I could save you and the nation with one simple arrangement."

Nessix had no more dignity left to lose. With a fierce shriek, she grabbed the nearest piece of armor and swung it toward Veed's head.

"Kill me." Veed's calm instruction halted her action at once. "I'll be sure to tell Logan why I never healed him when we meet in the afterlife."

Nes's arm plummeted with her heart. Whether or not she wanted Veed dead right now, she needed him. If Logan died, her foul actions would mean nothing. She hated the demons for interrupting her skewed life. She hated Mathias for making her believe in him. Perhaps she hated herself. She hated—no. Inwan had his reasons to leave, and no one could dispute the decisions of a god.

"We need to get back to him," Nessix murmured. "I kept my end of the bargain, please find the decency to do the same."

"Now, Nes, have I ever been one to go back on my word?"

"I've never known you to, but a reminder doesn't hurt."

Veed accepted her terms and pulled himself out of the bed. Nessix quickly looked away, coaxing a broadened smirk from him. Her innocence moved him as effectively now as it had earlier in the evening, and he did Nessix the favor of letting her ignore him until he'd sufficiently clothed himself.

"I assume you'll be riding with me?" Veed circled close behind her, kissing the back of her neck as he secured the clasp of her pendant.

Nessix didn't move. "Would you have it any other way?"

"It would serve us both much better if you'd drop that tone. My question was simple."

"If you would be so kind," Nessix seethed with undue politeness. "I don't know how much longer Logan has on his own. So please, if you can assist my way home, do so."

Veed rather liked the authority Nes's words attempted to gain her. "Certainly, love. I don't expect Solvig to be too far off."

Curling her lip, Nessix lowered her head in fabricated respect. "Then do take me to him."

* * * * *

Mathias ceased his pacing as footsteps grew closer. A familiar baritone murmured something not quite audible, answered by a choke of discontent. Mathias would recognize that growl anywhere.

Veed flung the tent flap aside, boldly escorting Nessix inside by a hand on her waist. Mathias bristled as Veed flashed him a provocative grin. The paladin glowered foul curses back at him, more repulsed by Veed now than ever before. Content with the information conveyed, the dark general briefly pressed Nes's body against his before she shrank away from him, then moved ahead to Logan. Nessix tried to follow but a firm hand on her shoulder stopped her.

"We have to talk," Mathias growled.

"Stay out of my affairs, fraud," Nessix spat. "You wouldn't help me, so I went to someone who could."

"I'd like to thank you for that, by the way. She had me singing the praises of a *true* goddess," Veed threw in, not even bothering to turn from Logan. He knew the reaction he'd receive.

Nessix shuddered at Veed's words, her skin crawling at his vile reminder. "I'm trusting you, Veed." Afraid of cracking in front of either of them, Nessix fled the tent.

Mathias longed to throttle the man in front of him with every last impure fiber of his being, but right now, Nessix mattered more. Eyes darkening with the hateful promise to deal with Veed later, Mathias followed Nessix. He caught her easily and she made no attempt to prevent him from turning her to face him. Her hair, previously trained over her shoulders, displaced to expose her neck and a pair of physical remnants of her misadventure. Mathias's eyes burned through those badges of shame, and she swept her hair back into place. A ragged breath and short nod later, Nessix changed course to the left to try to avoid this confrontation.

"What were you thinking?" Mathias demanded, stepping in front of her to block her retreat.

Nessix tried to step around him again. He clearly knew what happened, not that it was any of his business, and she owed him nothing. Before she attempted another evasion, Mathias pinned her shoulders against the wall. This time, Nessix didn't bother to fight him.

Mathias's heart fell to his soles and he nearly released her. "Nes, what—"

"Nessix." Her correction was terse and she met his gaze just long enough to convey her sincerity.

"Nessix." He swallowed. "What were you thinking?"

"I told you once and it doesn't need repeating. Let me go." She made a halfhearted move against his grasp.

One hand guided Nes's chin to face him, though she kept her eyes directed away. "You have to believe me," Mathias begged. "I *tried*." He knew Nessix needed more than that to heal her heart, but maybe admitting his failure would mean something to her.

"How can I believe you?" she asked, voice breaking. "Why did I ever?"

"I tried to heal him, but—"

"But you couldn't!" The dying embers of trust and hope

flickered from her hollow gaze. Nessix leaned her head against the wall and pinched her eyes shut in an attempt to conceal her dishonor.

Mathias smoothed the renegade tears that seeped past, and Nessix tried to recoil from his touch. He searched his distant soul, toiling over how stupidly he'd kept his feelings from her. Beyond losing Etha, his failures had driven away the woman he'd hoped to find a future with. Mathias snatched at the courage to come clean, unable to admit to Nessix his deepest flaws.

"Please," she bid, her voice soft and shaking. "If you won't do anything else for me, at least allow me the chance to bathe."

At a loss, Mathias lifted his hands from her and stepped aside. He watched brokenly as Nessix hung her head and disappeared into the fortress. So much hope had filled her when she'd gone to him after the previous day's struggle. Mathias knew Nessix had approached Veed with a request for help, not an offer, and that this method of payment had come from the wretched man's own mind. Sick with the thought of what memories now tarnished Nessix, Mathias returned to the tent to demand an explanation.

"You do know I didn't hurt her, right?" Veed didn't bother to look back as Mathias fumed behind him. "I'd *never* damage something I own." His lips wrapped around that final word brazenly.

Darkness welled about Mathias and he fought to choke it down. "Owning a woman is something for cowards. Nessix belongs to no one and she will never return to you."

Veed laughed impulsively. "You really think she'd protect your desires before her own reputation? You certainly are conceited." He reveled in the power he had over the situation. Mathias didn't dare lay a hand on him, and the rage radiating from the paladin twisted Veed's grin perversely. "For what it's worth to you, she made quite pleasant company, surprisingly submissive, actually."

Mathias's reply was lost in Veed's depravity. Letting the dark general get a rise out of him would only deteriorate the situation further and risk Logan's chance at recovery. Instead, Mathias stood rigid, festering in his rage.

Veed gave Mathias ample time to muster the wit to retaliate

then returned his hand to Logan's withers to resume manipulating his energy against the horse's. "It's alright, boy," he said. "I understand. I've chosen my goddess while you've wasted your time on yours. Maybe if you weren't so uptight, you'd have got to see a little something, yourself."

The tension of Mathias's clenched jaw tore at the back of his neck. Devotion to Etha came before everything else, but she had made him human. Veed's pointed leers about his desecration of Nes's innocence burned Mathias's heart more than he cared to admit, and the longer the loathsome man exulted in his sin, the further Mathias moved from mere jealousy. Veed continued to flaunt his indecency with the fact that part of him had intended to break Nessix all along. Bitter fury blazed inside the paladin, an ugly emotion he hadn't felt in quite some time.

"Relax, Sagewind," Veed sighed when Mathias's breathing grew heavier. "There's nothing you can do about it now. Nes made her decision. It was a fair trade, my service for hers—"

"Silence yourself, miscreant!" Mathias roared. The power he typically held dormant inside seeped from his heart and into his limbs, ready to carry out whatever action he deemed necessary.

Veed lifted his hands and sat up. "Don't think you're going to punish me. There's nothing forcing me to finish this job."

Nessix had sputtered with some degree of conviction that she trusted Veed, but Mathias didn't. Clerical tricks and a touch of magic could easily mend a flesh wound, but reconstructing a shattered joint took something more powerful. Not three days ago, Mathias possessed that ability, but now he only bested Veed in terms of morality. Veed had quite possibly lied to Nessix about his abilities simply to have his way with her. Mathias scowled at Veed's back, watching carefully as the other man rose and turned to face him.

"Are you wanting me to stop?" Veed asked.

The heat of madness seared along Mathias's nerves, and he doubted his ability to control his tongue well enough to not push Veed past his limit. With Nessix already emotionally vanquished, Mathias didn't dare give Veed an excuse to to leave. Veed and Mathias had never shared even a remote sense of camaraderie, and

Mathias wouldn't pretend otherwise. Veed had spoken his terms, and Nessix had paid the price.

"Never again will you defile," Mathias growled, the wrath of the heavens in his eyes.

A smirk tugged at the corner of Veed's mouth and, before he could rattle off his next taunt, Mathias left.

* * * * *

Unable to avoid people on the way to his makeshift school, Mathias's baleful scowl effectively held all greetings at bay. He violently resisted blaming Nessix for her contemptible decision; she'd used her only available option. Never one to dwell on the past, the question of why this happened reeled through Mathias's mind. Flicking the hilt of his dagger to send it spinning on the table in front of him, Mathias sat and moped.

"Sir Sagewind…?"

Sulik's intrusion startled Mathias and he slammed his palm over the flat of the blade to stop its motion. When the commander poked his head into the tent, his eyes were panicked and Mathias leapt to his feet.

"What's the matter?"

"It's—" Sulik stopped speaking to secure the tent flap closed. He moved closer to Mathias. "It's Nessix."

Mathias's heart plunged deeper still and he paced half a stride, throwing a fist at the ground. "What happened?"

"Well, sir," Sulik said, still trying to piece the situation together. "She locked herself in your chamber. Crashes and one of her tantrums alerted some soldiers to her distress and they sent for me and Brant." A timid chuckle accompanied the shake of Sulik's head. "Brant's been trying to coax her out, but she hasn't responded to him and I was afraid you might be in there and rendered silent." He fixed Mathias with an inquisitive stare. "Would you mind me asking if you know what this is about?"

Jumbled whispers drifted to Mathias's ears, a deliciously familiar voice hanging in them.

324

Etha, are you there?

Distorted words flit through the haze, still indistinguishable, but there all the same.

"I'll get to the bottom of it," Mathias promised Sulik, "and I'll alert you if there's need for further concern."

Sulik nodded, trusting poor Mathias's intuition. "Best of luck, sir."

Mathias silently pushed his way past Sulik. He didn't care what damage Nessix dealt his furnishings, but he hoped to soothe her out of hurting herself. Against his better judgment, his mind wandered to the things that were said and done, and he wondered if she'd been afraid. Mathias doubted Veed, in his infatuation with her, would have intentionally brought physical harm to Nessix, but his act of domination would affect her for the long haul.

Rushing back into the fortress, Mathias paused at the beginning of the hall that led to his quarters. Brant stood at the door, one forearm braced against it and his forehead pressed into his elbow. Mathias cycled through a deep breath. Whether or not Nessix wanted to see him, he needed to see her. The incoherent chatter persisted in his mind as he approached.

Mathias prepared for a forceful yell, but barely managed to speak at all. "Nes?"

Brant turned his head, eyebrow cocked. He'd been trying to get Nes's attention for nearly twenty minutes with no luck and Mathias expected *that* to work? The routine pattern of glass shattering against the stone floor ceased and neither man dared to breathe. The swish of a blade whipping from its sheath whispered from the other side of the door.

"I don't want to talk to you," came Nes's furious and muffled reply.

Mathias closed his eyes, trying to quell his emotions and summon patience.

Brant lifted his head from his arm. "I guess she's coming around."

"Oh, she's been around," Mathias muttered.

Brant made careful note of the untimely insult. "I haven't been able to get her to talk to me, and she's out for blood. If you want to stick your neck in there, be my guest." Brant left, trusting Nessix's behavior meant she planned to rip Mathias something long overdue.

Once Brant had disappeared, Mathias wasted his effort trying the door's handle. It held fast, and he used it as an excuse to release his stress in a more satisfying manner. "Nessix, get out here, now!"

No sounds of frustration or anger answered. As far as Mathias could tell, Nessix didn't even move. Glaring at the door, he shifted his weight to his back heel and drove his shoulder against it. It shuddered, but held against the force. "You wanted my attention, now you've got it!"

That jolt coerced Nessix from her inactivity and she resumed the destruction of his room's interior. A grunt preceded the collapse of what Mathias believed to be his bookshelf. "If you want in here, you'll have to break the door down."

"Fine." Mathias threw his shoulder against the door again, hinges voicing their protest this time. He stepped back to gain momentum for the next strike. "I still think it'd be easier if you'd just—"

The door cried open courtesy of a trembling hand. Nessix stood in the entryway, encompassing all signs of danger and insignificance. Her teeth clenched obstinately, enhancing the frame of her cheekbones. Bloodshot eyes wavered, lost on a pale face stained with the memory of tears. She needed her father now, needed someone who dared to hold her. As Nessix stared at Mathias, he hardly recognized her. He opened his mouth to scold her actions, but nothing came out. At last, Mathias understood. Memory would serve as punishment enough; the only thing Nessix had left of her spirit was a ghostly aura of pride. Drawing on that last pinch of herself, Nessix pulled her defeated gaze from Mathias and stumbled toward the window.

"Now what do you want?" she muttered.

All of Mathias's fury diffused in this moment. Nothing made sense, and he had only one demand. "Why?"

A tiny shift of Nes's shoulders spoke her opinion of the question. "Because you demanded entry. I don't want you here any more than you want me to be here."

"That wasn't what I meant and you know it."

Oh, Nessix knew, but that didn't merit her cooperation. "Logan's saved me more times than I'll ever admit. I couldn't find it in myself to sit back and watch him die." A shudder battered her delicate frame, and Mathias barely caught a glimpse of her profile as she shook her head. "This wasn't easy for me." More of an explanation tried to follow, but choked itself away. "It wasn't."

"There had to have been another way."

"I thought there was."

Mathias choked on Nes's abrasiveness, shifting away as he pinched the bridge of his nose. Once his guilt had settled, he turned back to her. "I never thought you were the type to do this."

The verbal slap stung Nessix hard and she crossed her arms tightly. "Like what?" she spat, turning her chin to catch Mathias's pitying glare from her peripheral vision. "Help a friend?" Unable to look at Mathias any longer, Nessix traded her attention for a smirk of fabricated confidence. "No, I suppose you wouldn't think so. I'm sorry to disappoint you, but if there would've been another way, I would have taken it."

Mathias no longer faulted Nessix for her actions. His failings had led to this. Nessix had finally accepted him as her hope, and he abandoned her, saddling her with this shame wrought of desperation. Jealousy prevented Mathias from offering her comfort, and he could say nothing to her tears. With Logan healed, Nessix should have found some peace, but her bitter sputtering exposed another concern.

Is she afraid she hurt me? It seemed a ridiculous thought, but what else could be the matter?

"I'm sorry," Mathias murmured at last.

Nessix swallowed and stared into the same night sky that had encouraged her to open up to Mathias in the first place, and the same darkness that had torn her apart. She was through hating Veed and had shut out Mathias's moping. The only logical thing left was to hate herself. Logan would run again, Veed had assured her of that, but she'd wear these shackles forever. Looking down at the glitter of broken glass at her feet, Nessix faced the reason behind her fit.

"There's no need to be," she said numbly. "I'm the one who needs to be sorry."

Mathias shifted behind her, prompting Nessix to elaborate.

"I'm sorry I didn't see this coming. That I let you lead me to believe in you so strongly."

The darkness that whispered loathsome memories to Nessix moments before drew her closer, and Mathias held his breath as she climbed on the windowsill. Nes brandished her temper as an immature response to regret, but Mathias wouldn't blame her for it. He should have told her of Etha's silence and what happened during that last attack. Sulik could have called on Etha if Mathias had conveyed how to—Nessix would have had to believe him then. None of those thoughts had crossed Mathias's mind when options still remained, and it was too late for them to matter now.

A noise that could have been a laugh left Nessix as she glanced over her shoulder. "Why did I ever believe you?"

"Once, it was all true."

Accepting Mathias's words would have been so much easier than this, but Nessix had run out of faith hours ago. "You are not a paladin. There are no gods, no goddesses. Admit it already and set my people free from your spell." A new wave of sorrow crept over Nessix, and her knees no longer declared their trustiness. She stepped down from the sill, turned, and slid to the ground. If Mathias saw her vulnerable, so be it. She had nothing left to defend, anyway. "Set *me* free…"

The agony in Mathias's heart jerked toward overwhelming with each stifled sob that racked Nes's body. Neither he nor Etha had put anyone under a spell, and he'd given such strong evidence of the heavens, but Nes had spoken some amount of truth. What kind of paladin was he if he couldn't serve? This time, Mathias's eyes grounded on her. No matter what he thought of her behavior, Mathias ached in light of Nes's self-loathing.

A moist cough intercepted Nes's tears as the strings of pride caught what she'd been doing. Nessix hadn't tried to hide her emotions from Mathias, but she hadn't been entirely aware they'd shown themselves. Curling a lip at her own sniveling, Nessix rubbed the tears from her face and dragged herself to her feet.

"We'd been getting along so nicely there for a while."

Mathias studied Nessix hard. Her tone had been too bland to decipher. "I will find the answer."

Tears sought to flow once more before Nessix shook her head to warn them away. She stopped beside Mathias on her way to the door. "I beg you. No more lies."

"I have never lied to you, Nessix."

She stared at him, tears pooling behind the walls she frantically tried to repair. "Are you through with me?"

Mathias would never be through with her. No matter how badly he wanted to fix this, Nessix made it clear that she had no other thoughts to share with him. Desperate laments tangled around broken advice and insignificant promises, rendering Mathias unable to deliver the most basic reply.

His silence was answer enough. Nessix lowered her head and walked away.

* * * * *

Nessix had turned down all company, sending even Brant away. She insisted on her privacy, ordering the guards far from Logan's tent. Her men accepted that she wanted to be left alone, but Mathias was not one of them. He'd dispatched scouts to ensure the fortress would sleep peacefully and received reports of more movement. Eager to rid Elidae of the demons now more than ever, Mathias set out to demand Nessix's approval to take action. He anticipated another tremendous fight, but if he phrased the report properly, he stood a chance of leaving unscathed. Carefully, Mathias pulled the tent flap open and crept inside.

The broken woman nestled in the arch between Logan's neck and back, and Mathias snuck quietly past the horse to check on Nes's condition. Her cheeks were still flushed with pale traces of dried tears and the gentle gape of her mouth suggested some amount of residual congestion. A glint of steel in her right hand caught Mathias's attention, and he crouched down to gently lift the blade from Nes's grasp. His heart fluttered as he noted blood on the blade, proving relatively fresh when he touched it. Mathias scanned Nessix for injuries and discovered her wrist wrapped securely in a strip of white cloth, just barely stained through with the same crimson as the dagger.

Logan snorted in his sleep, startling Mathias. Nessix groaned and shifted position. The robe she wore peeked open to near indecency, and before Mathias averted his eyes, he saw a second flash of blood across her chest. Centered above her breasts were two parallel lines devoid of pigment, no more than three inches long and the width of a man's fingers. Inwan had blessed her with his touch, alright, but the bleeding gash that intercepted those marks proved Nessix no longer appreciated his gift. Mathias gazed at her stricken face, his pain rivaling what he imagined she felt.

"Etha, help me," Mathias breathed, cradling Nes's wounded wrist in his hands.

He watched Nes's face intently for signs of her waking. Finding none, he unwrapped the rough bandage to appraise the damage. If Etha couldn't reach him, as her silence proposed, Mathias would force his own life energy into Nes and fix her that way.

Closing his eyes, Mathias rubbed Nes's hand between his, willing his strength and vitality into her. He'd denied and feared his affection for her for too long and would not let his heart be broken, not this time. Etha help him, he needed Nessix. Moments passed in an unblessed silence before Nes trembled and murmured incoherent objections. Mathias held his breath, waiting to see if Nessix stirred, and relaxed only after she remained still for several heartbeats.

Tentatively, Mathias reached out to brush the backs of his fingers across Nes's cheek, shaking in anger and disappointment at the reason behind her disheveled appearance. He recoiled his touch slowly, took a deep breath, and plucked at the neckline of her robe to reveal the more sacrilegious mutilation now stamped over by a bloody, lily-shaped laceration. A fled god's broken promise overwritten by Etha's eternal one.

Accepting the forced breath that hit him, Mathias quickly covered the wound with his hand. Even muted, Etha was clearly with him. "I don't know what you're trying to tell me," he whispered.

Slowly, almost unnoticed and easily confused for the heat of Nes's body, warmth pooled in the air beneath Mathias's hand. It intensified to a burning sensation against his palm until he feared it would scorch their flesh. He grimaced and reinforced his hand's position by gripping his wrist, and then, nothing. A moment of hesitation passed before Mathias scratched together the nerve to pull his hand away.

The wound had healed in a pale, unfitting gray. Nessix now wore the brand of two deities, whether or not she wanted to accept either of them. Mathias had healed her, but why after the doubt? Why with such pain? And why, in all of Abaeloth, had it resulted in a scar? His touch mended flesh much more damaged than this, leaving nothing but memories. Not knowing the answers, not caring at the moment, Mathias's hands eagerly wrapped around Nessix's wrist. The same burning coursed between them and yielded the same result. He suspected Nessix would be displeased to find her anguished handiwork tampered with, but she no longer had a choice. Facing even more questions, Mathias squeezed Nes's hand and slowly stood. Nessix needed to sleep away her internal battle.

"Wherever you are, Mother," Mathias murmured, "do what you will to me, but keep these two safe. Forgive my doubt in what you've given me." With more urgent matters to attend to, Mathias forced himself to leave.

TWENTY-FIVE

Each passing day provided Nessix more time to mull over what she'd done. She refrained from participating in the next few attacks, raising a silent concern among her army. Nessix exploited Logan's condition as her excuse, but worried more about how to mask the physical evidence left behind from her actions once properly prepared for battle. No one pressed the issue of her fouling mood, and she never offered an explanation. With the same good faith Nessix had trusted from Veed when this entire avalanche of pride began, she trusted him to keep his mouth shut. News of Logan's plight spread quickly and Nessix allowed those who wanted to assume Mathias had healed him that luxury. Trying to force her doubts in him on those around her had grown exhausting, and the fewer people who knew of Veed's involvement, the better.

While her conduct disgusted her, Nes accepted it and tried to forge ahead with grace. As Logan regained his strength, so did Nessix, and she pulled herself from the ashes of her shame. After discovering Etha's icon where she'd tried to erase the last dreadful remnant of Inwan's affection, Nessix didn't doubt Mathias had come by to mend her flesh, and she resented the holy imprint now branded on her. She hadn't wanted healing from that pain, at least not physically, and especially not from Mathias. It made everything so much harder that she had actually grown fond of him. Until Mathias, Nessix had never met someone else touched by the gods, and while she would never accept Etha's superiority over Inwan, at least she had someone to relate to. It seemed, however, that she'd been misled.

Brant watched Nessix's sanity degrade, worrying for her as much now as when the demons had nearly killed her. His delight of seeing her revitalized disregard for Mathias was dampened when the direction of her indifference reached out toward others. Brant hated pressing issues Nes obviously wanted to keep private, but he'd always been her confidant. Besides, he missed her voice.

He knew where to find her, and waited out by the conditioning track for her to wrap up Logan's breezes. They completed a stretch of cantering with a toss of Logan's head, skipping shortly in the last stride. Nessix dismounted and felt his knee over for heat. With a smile and a brief nod, she approved of his limb's soundness. She appeared in good spirits, and Brant considered this as good a time as any.

Greeted warmly by a spirited whinny from Logan, Brant smiled tightly as Nessix rushed back around the horse. It took her a moment to fully recognize her cousin's intent before she returned the gesture, though it lacked her former gusto.

"You two are looking great." Brant patted the horse's shoulder.

That inspired a more genuine response from Nessix and she reached up to unbuckle Logan's bridle. "It shouldn't be much longer until he's back on the field."

"And what about you, Nes?"

She shrugged. "Certainly, I haven't been working as well without him, but I'm not—"

"No." Brant stopped her weak explanation effortlessly. "I've seen you out there and know your heart's not in it. I need to know when we'll have Nes back."

She held his eyes calmly, instinctively clenching her jaw. Ashamed, Nessix refused to answer the question, letting Brant concoct his own assumptions. She moved around to Logan's side to loosen his girth and quickly found her forearm in Brant's grasp.

"Where did this come from?" he demanded, his free hand pulling Nes's sleeve up to better view the scar across her wrist.

Nessix tried once to draw her hand back. "Nowhere," she insisted, losing the small amount of glee she had scratched up. "I've always had it."

"You didn't have it as of four days ago."

A stubborn dispute almost came out, but sense caught her. "If it's only four days old, how is it already scarred?" It wasn't a lie if he couldn't give her a logical answer. Nessix watched Brant's mind turn its cogs and corrected his obvious theory to spare him from speaking it. "Do you really think I'd have let Sagewind touch me?"

"You let him heal Logan, didn't you?"

Nessix drew a sharp breath and blinked. Not even Brant had caught on? Over the past two days, Nessix had managed to avoid dwelling on her self-destruction and she'd been content with that. In the dark about her shame, Brant hadn't meant to hurt her, but the memories that leered at the reminder left Nessix eager to scratch Veed's touch from her skin all over again. Scowling, not regretting if Brant took it personally, Nessix snatched her arm away and yanked her sleeve back down. She pulled Logan's saddle from his back.

Brant believed he understood what Nes conveyed, and frowned at having unearthed her turmoil. He made his observation and would conduct his future relations accordingly. Nessix didn't have to speak of the matters involving her self-mutilation, but Brant had other means to uncover what he was after.

"Nes, what's wrong?"

She hefted the saddle against her hip. "Nothing. Don't worry about it."

A flicker of compassion danced through her words, and Brant caught a glimpse of warmth at last. "I have to worry," he told her. "Consider it my duty."

"Your duty is to oversee the cavalry and interpret my orders."

"That's my job," Brant corrected. "Something's wrong with you and it's making everyone uncomfortable. You rode into battle, Logan fell. It was expected for you to be off, but this has gone on too long."

Nessix couldn't fathom where this lack of respect came from. If anyone else dared to interrogate her in this manner, she'd have had no problem issuing a formal reprimand, but her soft spot for Brant kept her a breath toward civil. He pressed this issue out of concern, and she owed him some sort of answer. Fumbling over the truth, Nessix shrank from the confrontation and walked toward the stable to deposit Logan's saddle.

Brant glowered at her persistence and followed. A lifetime of putting up with Nes's temper had taught him how to bend her if necessary, and he was not above abusing that power now. "If you're so relieved by Logan's progress, what's been fueling your terrible mood?" He expected Nes's silence, and his reply followed fluidly. "Have I wronged you?"

"No."

"The only other person you've spent any amount of time with is Sagewind," Brant said. "Is *he* the problem?"

"Not that it should matter to you, but I've written him from my mind as thoroughly as possible." Now, if only Brant would shut up about him!

The commander refrained from asking Nessix to elaborate, but held his course. "Then what's he still doing controlling your men and doctoring your wounded?"

"Pissing me off," she spat, stalking ahead.

The thought had been tearing Nessix apart. Only a day after Veed saved Logan, Mathias resumed healing those off the field no differently from when he'd first arrived. The coincidence tormented Nessix and to add more pain to the punishment, she knew he'd healed her, as well. Scars didn't tattle the tales of those injured in combat, but Mathias had left her with a nagging reminder of her stupidity. Nessix didn't particularly mind carrying physical flaws, but these ones would glare at her for the rest of her life.

Brant stubbornly tracked after Nessix. Her answer elated him, and if the rigidity of her stride suggested anything at all, he'd soon have a reason to be even happier. "If he's your problem and what's been hurting morale—"

"*I* am what's been hurting morale."

Brant darted in front of her and grabbed her shoulders to

make her stop. "Get rid of him, Nes."

"It's not that easy."

"Of course it is." He'd dreamt up a plethora of methods for months now. "Ask Veed to withdraw from the pact and you follow him. It'll force Sagewind out of power."

Nes's lip curled and she jerked her shoulders free. "I will do *nothing* with Veed, and you know as well as I do that the troops would happily follow Sagewind over me."

"I would do anything for you, Nes, even deal with the bastard myself if you asked."

Whichever bastard Brant had referred to, the practical side of Nes doubted he'd be able to carry out the task. "What I want is for you to quit talking about it."

This had gone too far. Nessix didn't have to give him any details, but Brant desperately needed to soothe her, to divert her frustrations back to where they belonged. The sorrow in Nes's eyes struck Brant the hardest.

"Nes," he said, trying with eventual success to coax the saddle from her arms. "We are all we have left. I won't stand here and watch you fall apart."

"I know, but—"

Brant shook his head, intolerant to her excuses. "If I can stop any harm coming to you, any at all, I swear to you, I will."

Nessix never doubted it, but none of this was in Brant's control. "The only thing you can protect me from anymore is death."

"And does Sagewind endanger your life?" It was a chilly thought. Mathias had better hope she answered with a resounding no.

"It's the only thing he hasn't tried yet."

Brant didn't know what had transpired between Nes and Mathias, though his mind tugged frequently at the memory of their discussion by the Spring. Mathias's influence had a history of providing abundant ways to trouble Nessix, some more obvious to Brant than others. Even if Mathias didn't threaten Nes with death, there were equally horrible possibilities to account for. Obviously, the first warning failed to adhere, and this time, Brant swore to make it stick.

* * * * *

On quiet days, Mathias preferred to station himself on the battlements. Those on duty milled about their tasks and Brant's lip twitched at the thought of gaining their attention. Mathias, vigilant as ever, concentrated on the distance, at least appearing oblivious to Brant's presence. Scowling in every manner of detestation, Brant rushed forward and grasped Mathias's arm, spinning him around to shove him against the wall. A dagger quickly found its way to the paladin's throat.

"You've overstayed your welcome," Brant growled.

Mathias stared back at Brant with subdued eyes. "Perhaps you're right." A firm honesty backed his words.

Brant read the reply as contempt and voiced a vicious yell as he hurled Mathias to the ground. "Damn you!" He pitched the dagger down as well. "*Damn* you!"

Mathias had thought this feud written off long ago and hoped to avoid another dispute. He was past being courteous. "I can assure you, that won't happen."

Brant scoffed and briefly turned away to refrain from kicking Mathias. The small crowd around them averted their eyes and pressed away from the encounter, but Brant remained aware of his audience. "What purpose do you serve here?" he demanded. "Bastard!"

A cocky smile etched across Mathias's face as he propped himself up on an elbow. "My parents bore me within wedlock."

Mathias's scorn drove Brant past the desire to defend Nes. He crouched down to grab Mathias by the collar and jerked him to a half-seated position, eyes savage and dark. "She was a child before you came."

"She still is." Mathias kept his further opinions of Nessix to himself. He still loved her, but even he was entitled to bitterness. "Using impulsive measures to get what she wants, regardless of what it costs anyone else in the end."

The implications escaped Brant; evidently they were on different pages. Brant snarled and shoved Mathias back down, drawing his sword. "You don't get it, do you? She hasn't been so far from herself since the day we found Laes." He was unwilling to elaborate any further. "You will not be forgiven for that. Mock me all you want, but leave Nes alone."

Mathias laughed shortly. "I have. For several days now, if you haven't noticed. I've done nothing to quell her spirit. Such a task would be far too great for a man like me to undertake. Nessix chose to fall. You couldn't possibly understand."

"Enlighten me."

It would have been sadistically delightful to divulge such horrid news, to watch Brant's face and heart fall, but Mathias didn't have it in him to disgrace Nessix in that manner. "Go ask her to tell you what happened and what choices were made."

Brant sneered. "You had her eating from your palm, digesting the shit you fed her. No one—not me, not Laes, not even Inwan— has held that sort of influence over her."

"Your devotion to her blinds you to the difference between her initiative and mine." Mathias shook his head. "You are a fool. I suggest you walk away, Commander."

"I do not serve you."

Already at the end of his rope, Mathias glanced away and hissed out a sharp breath. "Do not push me, Brant."

"You think your threats make you more of a man?" Brant laughed. He'd pieced enough together to know Mathias wasn't responsible for Logan's recovery, and since no one else made any claims, that left one person. "That the fact that a practitioner of the dark arts saved Logan's life makes you better than me? Where were you, Sagewind?"

"I was here," Mathias spat.

"Exactly. Perverting her men and her townsfolk, using her supplies. Filling fragile minds with the garbage you, yourself, have been unable to uphold." The more Brant spoke, the bleaker Mathias's outlook became. "How can you call yourself a man of the gods when you're barely a man at all?"

Mathias had weighed those exact accusations over the past

several days. "It's not for you to judge me."

"Nessix is the last of Elidae's nobility and it is my duty to protect her. With you serving as a threat to her station and well-being, I am making it my place to judge you."

"The nobility of that line…" Mathias's thoughts indulged themselves in silence, more from respect for Laes and En than anybody currently alive.

"What about it?"

Mathias answered in stride, no longer caring where Brant aimed to goad him. "That line failed long ago. You hold on to a dream that was, in a world that woke up without you." He regretted the next, but couldn't hoard this truth any longer. "Nessix is not the best person to lead your people, not with her impulses, but she holds their loyalty. I haven't found the man who should take her place, but I know he's out there. Blood's all you care about, though, and you'll continue down this path, clutching to this impotent line."

Morbidly pleased by Mathias's insult, Brant savored the valid excuse to press the tip of his sword against the paladin's throat. "A smart man would choose his battles with more care."

Mathias swatted the blade away, unimpressed, and stood at last. "A battle that must happen, must. Often, the inexperienced force their hand prematurely and that's when people die."

Brant narrowed his eyes and leaned closer. "We would rather be dead to the demons than slaves under you."

Finding the haughty commander had earned a lesson in dominance, Mathias seized Brant's wrist, crushing down with his restored strength and twisting the joint against natural movement. After a yelp, Brant dropped his sword, the blade clattering to the ground.

"Slaves are made through force," Mathias said. "This is the first time I've used such means against you, and I pray it's my last." As proof, he loosened his grip and Brant quickly retracted his arm.

"I told you before," the commander said through gritted teeth, "threats do not affect a warrior race."

"That wasn't a threat. It's a fact. If I wanted your people to be slaves, I would have brought armies and used strength of arms you could not hope to match. Instead, I came alone with my faith to stop a threat that could tear across all of Abaeloth." Mathias scowled at Brant's arrogance. "I came to you and found disgraceful children fighting for scraps left of a once-proud people, lost without their god. I showed you the strength to live, a strength that flourishes in your people for all the wrong reasons, yet you cling to memories as if they'll answer your prayers."

Mathias could spout flowery words all day long and Brant wouldn't believe one of them. "Leave Nessix out of your plans."

"Nessix is not in my plans." It stung Mathias to admit as much. "Safeguarding your people is the only agenda I have, and that's something that requires the only competent leader you have left. Hope guides your people and they look to Nessix for that. She needs to be stronger, she needs to be smarter." He smirked at Brant's increasing agitation. "She needs to not fail those loyal to her."

"She has never failed us!" Brant screamed, unable to overlook the dissection of his cousin any longer. "Not the way you have. What *you* have been too blind to see is that she took the waste left from tragedy and forged it into a powerful force with nothing but faith backing her. She raised us into something to be proud of, something you've taken advantage of."

"She makes choices and all of you follow, whether it's the wisest move or not. She gave me the position I have, coming from her own free will. If you are so determined to defend her actions, you need to remember that. Stop blaming me for everything that's gone wrong. I'm just a convenience for you because you are a hurt little boy."

"I am not hurt. I am livid." Admitting the next to Mathias left a sour taste in Brant's mouth, but he needed to make his point. "Nessix needed provisions. She needed the brute strength of Veed's army. She did everything she had to in order to keep her people safe, and you do not give her half as much credit as she's due."

"And you have let your petty hatred for Sir Sagewind carry on for long enough!"

Both men spun to find Sulik standing in the doorway to the battlements.

"You are abusing your station, Brant," Sulik scolded, prepared to rely on seniority if need be.

"Maybe," Brant seethed. "But with all due respect, Vakharan, maybe you are neglecting yours?"

"I have done nothing against Nes's wishes. She may not declare love for Sir Sagewind, but she has never ordered otherwise."

"Seems to me she did. The only reason you even got to know the son of a bitch is because she sent you to spy on him."

Mathias caught the fleeting, daunted glance Sulik shot in his direction. He'd expected Nes to have tried something like that, but hadn't pinned Sulik as one to stay quiet about it all this time. Mathias longed to intervene the commanders' quarrel, but it seemed a prior tension existed between them.

"I did exactly what Nessix asked of me," Sulik insisted.

Brant shook his head defiantly. "You left her side for his—"

"I never—"

"And here you are!" Brant shouted. "Abandoning Nessix, spitting on the last ounce of trust Laes put in you! All for what? Some piddling thanks and unfulfilled promises?" Disgust coursed through Brant as thick as blood. "We were supposed to have been through with this war long ago."

"I have neither abandoned nor betrayed anyone," Sulik said, reining in his temper accordingly. "If it weren't for Sir Sagewind, the war *would* be over, because we'd all be dead. Nessix doesn't know how to win this one. Not this time."

"Is that something *he's* been telling you?"

"I didn't need to be told, because everyone but the two of you knew from the start."

Concern over Mathias was shoved aside, and respect alone held Brant back from throwing himself at Sulik. His teeth creaked as he clenched them. All this time, had this eager following of Mathias come from a lack of faith in Nessix? Brant shunned the notion. Nessix belonged to her people. They loved her, regardless of outside factors, but a squall of apprehension clustered in Brant's gut. The family resemblance became blatantly obvious as his shattered pride tried to piece itself together to serve as something worthy of commanding with. He never had the chance to get angry.

"Sulik, don't be misled to assume victory from my presence alone." Mathias had no true fondness for Brant, but destroying one of Nes's family was enough for him.

"But, sir—"

"Seems your change of trust yielded nothing at all," Brant scoffed, ignoring the favor Mathias gave him not two seconds prior.

"No," the paladin corrected. "The trust was once legitimate."

"And it still is!" Sulik cried in disbelief. Walls were crumbling down, and the commander had the feeling it was up to him to catch the stones.

Mathias, with the sliver of pride he carried around, hated to devalue himself so, but posed his question out of concern for the future. "What is my advantage over the rest of you?"

"You've healed our army." Sulik would gladly spit out praises for the rest of the afternoon if it made Mathias quit belittling the power he provided.

"No, he's talking about experience." Brant rolled his eyes, bored with the explanation that had carried Mathias this far. "You're the only one who knows how to fight the demons, because you've fought them before."

Mathias nodded. "And with my experience is theirs as well. They know who I am and what I'm capable of."

Brant raised an eyebrow and whistled impassively. "Surprise."

The retort, while something Sulik would have loved to return pleasantries on, flew straight past him. On the brink of Mathias confessing truths he didn't want to hear, Sulik held his breath.

"No matter if you want to believe my past or not, they know I can be defeated, but they also know it takes a great deal more weakening than they are physically capable of."

"If they're incapable of hurting you, why are we still at war?" Brant asked.

"They can't hurt me on a physical level, but they are intimately in tune with the spiritual world." Mathias sighed, fearing the worst response, but stuck to the course he'd started. Giving Brant valid ammunition beat letting him draw his own conclusions. "They

342

wield a horrible power that at least you, Brant, are incapable of understanding."

Brant's guffaw passed Sulik by, overshadowed by a frightful tugging at his heart. "Sir, what have they done to you?"

"I'm immune to poisons and direct spiritual intervention, but they've cursed me twice now. Someone's been serving as an agent for this, which is the only reason they've been successful."

Sulik's pointed gaze drifted to Brant. "What does that mean?"

Mathias missed the suspicions behind Sulik's eyes, but Brant saw them plainly. "It means those times he refused to heal our troops, his precious goddess was failing him," he said, not at all appreciating Sulik's implications. "Perhaps if you weren't inclined to believe me and Nes before, you can see the lies he's weaving now." Brant turned to Mathias. "Nice of you to come clean."

Mathias's lips pursed in a tight grimace to Brant's response. He didn't care what Brant made of him, but was compelled to console Sulik. The more pleasant of the two commanders stared at him in dejected shock. Guilt wriggled through Mathias's veins. He should have told Sulik about his problems from the start.

The paladin turned to Brant. "You have your leave, Commander."

Brant assumed as much. "Hurt her one more time, and I will see you dead," he swore. "I may not be able to do it myself, but I'd easily be able to find help, should anything we've discussed leak out." Civilly for a change, Brant accepted Mathias's stern nod. "I would trade my life to see yours end, if that meant Nessix wouldn't hurt anymore."

Mind thoroughly spoken, Brant turned to tell Nessix everything.

TWENTY-SIX

Another week passed with Nessix going out of her way to avoid Mathias, and the grudge slowly wore on her. After Brant hurried to disclose the confession from the battlements, she longed to forgive Mathias, but self-preservation forbid it. Nothing would erase what happened, and as long as those memories persisted, part of Nessix could never trust him again. The sole pleasure she found came in the form of her daily runs with Logan, gratified by his growing strength.

Mathias scheduled his classes around those rides, as watching Nessix and Logan dash out from the fortress gates was the most invigorating feeling he knew how to find anymore. He thanked Etha daily for the pair's recovery.

Though never one to turn down the concerns of her men, Nessix had coldly brushed off Mathias's single attempt to speak with her. She no longer sought his advice when the scouts announced an approaching threat, and though the first battle she led completely unassisted resulted in an abundance of wounded, Nessix gained experience readily. As if simply to prove Mathias wrong, left to her own devices, Nessix developed into a powerful enough leader to make him feel ineffective. There were plenty of men educated in clerical knowledge now and Mathias couldn't take Nessix striding by, deliberately blind to his presence.

Despite Etha's gentle urging to back off his obsession, Mathias worked ceaselessly to win back Nes's confidence. He looked past the physical needs of rest and nourishment to personally lead raiding parties. He set out on his own to flush out potential ambushes. Between the splinter of Affliction that kept his heart pumping and Etha's blessing that supplied him with might, Mathias stopped at nothing to prove himself to Nessix.

The quality of his lessons deteriorated as Mathias's preoccupied mind droned through the simplest of teachings. Nessix found more value in valor than scholarly pursuits, and he'd trained Sulik well enough to fill in the obvious educational gaps. For Mathias, this approach flowed smoothly, but his lack of attentiveness disappointed more than just Sulik and his students.

Etha didn't know what Mathias prattled on about and reflected her regrets for interrupting class accordingly. *You need to get past blaming yourself and start recovering.*

Mathias shook his head and swallowed a bitter laugh. *Because that's such a simple plan.*

She hadn't anticipated such a dour retort. *It beats what you're doing now. Don't make honest men out of Brant and Veed. If you keep this up, you'll lose the faith of the people and open the door for the demons.*

"But I don't know what to do!" Mathias said, unaware he'd spoken his words until the startled handful of men and women present in the tent looked up in confusion. Mathias grit his teeth and discounted Sulik's pitying look. He turned from his audience. They could figure out their own ways to pass the time. *I've already destroyed too much. Nessix has seen enough of the demons now, maybe it's time for me to duck out and let her handle things the way she wants to.*

Shame on you, thinking of leaving! Etha wanted nothing more than to pop in front of him and slap his nonsensical face. *And this destruction you speak of has been anything but at ease in your mind. You cannot mean what you've been brooding over.*

Etha's words buried Mathias deeper in his gloom. *What else can I do?*

Go talk to her, Etha said. *Tell her what you told the commanders.*

Oh, Brant's already shared, be sure of that.

And you can be sure he told her exactly what he wanted her to hear.

Mathias frowned for not realizing that sooner. Feeling even shoddier than before, at least now he had a thin line of hope. *Can you tell me if she's forgiven me?*

I can't. And he knew better than to think otherwise.

Is it even worth my effort to try?

Mathias made slow progress this time, but progress nonetheless, and Etha commended him for that. *I wouldn't have suggested it if I thought it was a waste of time. She needs the truth before she can understand, and she needs to understand before she can forgive. Don't let her entire vision of you be distorted by Brant's misgivings.*

No matter how freely Etha made her stance, Nes's vision of Mathias was already distorted, and he doubted any amount of groveling would change that. *Is it too late to wish I never came?*

Yes, Etha snapped. *And thinking as much makes you a coward. Face this, Mathias, and get back to being yourself.*

He flinched at her stern demand. Even through Etha's silence, Mathias had maintained his faith in her, yet he'd spent the past several days routinely questioning her intentions. Petty fears pounded at his resolve. If Nessix chose to never speak to him again, Mathias would respect that, but he so desperately needed to convince her that he'd never meant to let her down. An effort at explaining himself offered the potential to heal much of what went wrong, but digging out the pluck to come clean daunted him.

I'll do what I can.

Etha believed those words as much as Mathias had, himself. *The only thing you can do to disappoint me is lie,* she said softly, hoping to trigger him into his hunt for reconciliation. When Mathias refused to release any more thoughts to her, Etha left him to sort through logistics on his own.

* * * * *

The day's ride rejuvenated Nessix, reminding her what it meant to live. She and Logan set out simply to enjoy their leisurely lope through the fields, but their ride yielded much greater results than providing Nessix a mental escape. Logan heard it first—a distant clacking. *Pop! Crack!* He yielded to face the sound and raised his head, ears pricked forward. Nessix followed his gaze. A great tree shuddered its way off balance and crashed to the ground, clawing at the limbs of its neighbors along the way. Nessix held her breath as Logan's nostrils flared in uncertainty until the clacking resumed. Her eyes traced the leveled clearing to where it led to a path up the mountain, ending in a darkened depression.

For several heartbeats, Nessix squinted at the cavern. Common sense told her exactly what it was, but the simplicity of finding the portal the demons used to ravage her country surprised her. Another tree creaked in its last attempt to cling to stability and as it tipped to the horizon, Nessix gathered Logan up and turned him back toward home.

The adjustment to tackling these problems on her own was one of Nes's least graceful transitions, but she found pleasure in the growth of her self-sufficiency. Each beat of Logan's strides bolstered her confidence. Pleasant enough, Nessix halted Logan upon their arrival and found Brant instructing drills at the stable. She dismounted, leaving Logan to his own devices, and wandered up to her cousin.

She watched silently as Brant put the men through their paces, unsure if he was aware of her presence. Several movements later, he nodded, clasped his hands behind his back, and turned to her.

"Glad to see you out and about." Brant's carefree smile brightened his eyes.

Nes reciprocated as genuinely as possible and shrugged. "I saw you out. Guess I'm tired of being alone."

"Well, that's what I'm here for," Brant said, though he knew other matters occupied her mind.

"You're here for much more than that," she teased.

"Maybe so." A long silence passed between them, neither comfortable with their usual small talk. Nessix still hid much inside herself, and Brant dreaded the thought of delving it out. "How's Logan doing?" he asked instead.

"He's great. I'm sure you've noticed our rides getting longer." Nes's best intentions still produced a lackluster response and she wrinkled her nose as Mathias floated through her mind again. She stubbornly shoved her thoughts back to Logan and his improvement. "I'm about as happy as I can be," she decided at last.

Brant barked a laugh. "You used to be much happier. Quit trying to lie to me. It won't work."

Nessix heaved a sigh and glanced at the ground. "That was before a lot of things happened. I've grown a lot, Brant."

"I know," he groused. Vague rumors had bubbled up over the past few days, catching Brant's attention in all the wrong ways. He didn't want to confirm their validity, but knew no other alternative. "Forgive me for prying, but you've been pretty unapproachable lately and Sagewind said something about—"

Nessix caught Brant's discomfort immediately, and his words warned her of the nature of his pending question. "Sagewind says a lot of things," she interrupted firmly.

Brant sighed, saved from the gracelessness of his inquiry. "I hope none of it's been directed toward you in a while."

"No," Nessix said, resulting in Brant's satisfied smile. "The closest I've come to speaking with him is through Sulik, and even that's more than I'd like." While Nes spoke an honest enough truth, her mouth twitched toward a frown. "I heard he's acting strange again."

Hoping to prevent Nes from seeking answers firsthand, Brant indulged her curiosity. "He's still patching up everything that comes to him, but from what I've seen, he's not the same cheerful bastard."

Brant shrugged off the statement, but it hung heavy in Nes's mind. Of course, she blamed herself for the paladin's change of behavior. If Mathias's vehement response to Veed's gloating that night pointed toward anything, it was that he cared about her. Had that battle lined up a few hours later, there would have been no need for such loathsome actions, Mathias would have still been her secret mentor, and these foul memories would not lurk inside her. Nes shook her head to steer her mind back on course.

"We've been doing fairly well on our own," Nessix said, more to soothe herself than inform Brant. "I don't think we'd be too bad off if Sagewind felt he had to leave." The question still remained as to whether or not she wanted him to.

"I doubt he would," Brant said. "You know as well as I do that he feels like he belongs here, like he has some spiritual debt he owes our people or something."

Nessix crossed her arms, eyes darting away above flushed cheeks. "Something like that."

Brant's heart sank as Nessix flailed for control. He should have known better than to open this door. "Do we have any new plans coming up?" he asked.

She brightened at his effort. "As a matter of fact," she boasted regally, "I was getting ready to process some reports of my own when I saw you." A brilliant grin gleamed past her previous torment. "I spotted some surefire signs of movement not too far off, but can't tell how many demons to expect. Let's just plan on our victory when they finally show themselves."

"Why?"

"Because my people do not lose!" she cried victoriously, mistaking Brant's question for playful rallying.

"No, Nes. Why are we waiting for them to attack?"

"So we can drive them back," she said slowly. "What's the alternative?"

"Before these brutes came here, you flushed your quarry from hiding and forced them where you wanted them. Up until last year, the word defense wasn't even in your vocabulary." Brant missed those days fiercely. "You let us be warriors."

Nessix choked on Brant's words, features falling with each accusation. "A lot's changed—"

"Quit with that excuse!" Brant scolded. "A lot may have changed, but you said so yourself that you have, too. We've all grown stronger, and if you want to show our people that you're the same passionate leader, you need to make the statements instead of finishing them."

Brant's honesty didn't make Nes feel any better. "You've never corrected my actions before."

"Have you heard the rumors Veed's army's been whispering about you?" A shudder told Brant that Nes didn't want to know, so he added, "Or even our own?"

That startled Nessix, as Mathias was the only person with the knowledge to spread any valid gossip. "No, what?"

"They see you as Sagewind's puppet. They miss the old you, Nes, the one who didn't hesitate to risk it all for glory." Brant looked her over, wondering what she doubted in herself. "You're more than capable of taking the demons, you've seen it, yourself."

Nessix appreciated the vote of confidence, but her mind pulled up memories from the last time she thought she had the strength to take on the demons on her own. Unwilling to owe anything else to Mathias, Nessix didn't want to hazard the gamble of coming home wounded again. "There's always the chance something stronger than me is out there," she said.

"That's part of war. Laes taught you that, and I'm ashamed of you if you've forgotten. There may be something stronger out there, but there are more that are weaker. You have an entire army behind you to deal with those you can't take on your own."

"Do you really think I can lead my own attack?"

"Yes."

"Even if they're coming from the mountains, themselves?"

"That's even better. They wouldn't be able to surround us."

Nessix closed her eyes to process her cousin's faith. She knew she had this in her, not because Brant told her so, but because history had proven it. Yes, the demons were stronger than the foes of old, but the flemans were stronger now, too. There had to be a way to successfully attack the enemy, and Nessix knew that only one person could tell her how to do it. She hated that option and knew better than to ask Brant his opinion on it.

"Laying low isn't your style," Brant continued. "If there's any doubt in your mind about the outcome of this war, wouldn't you rather go out with your pride intact?"

Nes's eyes opened and met Brant's decisively. The risks danced through her mind before pro met con and they clashed. If she kept waiting for the demons to surface and move in on her, she'd never get the upper hand. While everyone seemed confident, Nessix knew better than to believe it. She also had to consider the filth Veed would spread about her, and the disgrace to follow. Past experience screamed of the stupidity of leading her own assault, but it had to be done. Brant was right. Nessix didn't see herself surviving this war, anyway, so why go down quietly?

"You've always been here for me," she said.

"Always."

"And I would trust you with everything I am and that I own. Should anything happen to me, you are the closest thing to nobility Elidae would have left."

Brant lowered his head in modesty and fear of the words he anticipated. He hadn't intended to plant such thoughts in her. "I don't like where this is going."

Nessix smiled sorrowfully and spared Brant the rest of her thoughts. "If it's an attack you want, it's an attack you'll get."

He nodded silently and watched Nessix set off to form her strategies. Her mixture of grief and fear and excitement jumbled themselves into a knot Brant couldn't even begin to pick at. Praying he hadn't initiated the biggest mistake in Elidae's history, Brant sighed and turned back to the men on the field.

* * * * *

"I haven't even *smelled* an effort on your part, so how can you honestly tell me you've tried?"

Mathias refused to look at Etha, hoping she'd let him escape this confrontation. "I had to finish class, and Nessix was still out. You can't blame me for matters out of my control."

"I would hardly call what you hosted today class," Etha snorted. She considered ruining Mathias's efforts of avoiding the topic, but activity outside the room interested her more. "And you could have been more productive in searching her out."

"I told you I'd try," Mathias repeated. "I never said when."

Etha's brow arched in maternal demand. "Walk out this door."

"Excuse me?"

"Walk out this door. Do not make me force you to."

Etha's open threat hastened him into action to keep from disappointing her further. Mathias plowed through the door and intercepted Nes's determined route down the hall. He gathered himself in an awkward flurry of crossed arms and shuffling feet. Internally muttering about Etha's lousy sense of humor, Mathias marched past the encounter, hoping his purposeful stride suggested to Nes's fiery temper that he intended to leave her alone.

"Sagewind."

Her subdued voice noosed him immediately and halted his departure. Mathias held his breath, heart pounding. He refrained from turning, not knowing what his dumbfounded expression might convey. Nessix had come to his room with the intention of finding him. She'd *wanted* to subject herself to him. After his shock tapered, Mathias realized this meant something must be wrong.

"I know we haven't been on decent terms," Nessix said to his silence, "but I have a request."

Composing himself at last, Mathias breathed, "I am at your service, General."

"Then quit cowering and get over here."

Whether Nes's motive was jest or malice, Mathias followed the order. If he could please her now, there might be the chance for him to continue doing so. He gathered the courage to face her and looked her over. She seemed well enough and less angry than he'd anticipated. Encouraged by the absence of spite in her eyes, Mathias donned a pleasant smile to try and coax the same from Nessix. That attempt failed.

"Go on," he said.

Nessix nodded slowly, suddenly unsure why she'd been so compelled to speak to him in the first place. She owed this to her people, and that alone pushed her along. Wrapped in pensive silence, Nessix led the way downstairs to the war chamber and motioned Mathias inside. She shut the door, sealing them off from the rest of the fortress. Together.

She stood with her back to him. "No thanks to you, Logan and I were on our ride today when I saw what had to have been demons clearing a road through the woods."

Mathias sighed inwardly. "Alright. How do you want to handle it?"

"They were coming from a cavern in the mountains." Nessix moved to her chair and sat, focusing on her hands as they fidgeted atop the table. "That's where I always thought they spawned from." She snuck a glance at Mathias and his nod of confirmation allowed her to continue. "We're going to take the initiative this time. Ask your goddess what they're doing and tell me if it can be done."

Mathias hoped Etha was inclined to be more sensible by now. *I guess I was a fool to think she wouldn't figure this out eventually. Did you hear her, Etha?*

The goddess giggled back in his mind. *I most certainly did. And I'm guessing by that tone you're not going to help me. Apologize to her first. For what? Apologize!*

Mathias contemplated Etha's motives. With Nessix finally approaching him after their weeks of conflict, the thought of revisiting the recent past turned his stomach. His wants notwithstanding, he needed Etha's insight and to get it, he had to play by her rules. Mathias looked down, shoulders drooping.

"Before anything else, General, there's something I must tell you."

The penance in his voice caught Nessix off-guard and for a moment, she lost her breath. Remembering how much she meant to hate Mathias, she scoffed. "If it doesn't have to do with—"

"Nessix, there is nothing I wouldn't do for you."

His declaration stopped her hastened attempt at pushing him away. Eyes wide and misted with bewilderment, Nessix stared up at his resolve and held her breath, willing him to keep talking.

"I would give my immortality to ensure nothing ever brought you harm. You've criticized me in the past for going easy on the demons, but that won't happen again. In the brawl you rescued me from, they bled their evil into me. They stopped the flow of my divine strength and I was too proud, too *cowardly*, to tell you. I will never be able to make it up to you, I know that, but I will never stop trying."

Color crept to Nes's cheeks and a delighted spark turned cartwheels in her head. Her lungs pressed out her reserve of breath, serving poorly as her only response to Mathias's confession.

Mathias sighed, liberated to get that off his chest, even if it meant nothing to Nessix. *Was that good enough?*

Such pretty words! Etha sang. *Tell her it can be done.*

A smile eased his lips. *Thank you, my lady.* Mathias searched Nes's confused eyes for her tactical side. "Your attack can be done, but I beg you proceed with caution. The demons' caverns are a treacherous place for mortals, and it wouldn't be out of the question for them to spring on us from the back lines."

Nessix waited until her heart quit choking her, and even then, her first attempt at speech came as a garbled mess of syllables. A brief growl sounded her frustration and Nessix closed her eyes, turning her face from Mathias. "Do you know how to navigate those tunnels?"

"These ones in particular? No. But I've been in more than my share of them, I'm comfortable with their patterns, and would be able to clear an emergency path if it came to it."

When Nessix's eyes opened, they were deep and clear and the most radiant things Mathias had ever seen. She glanced at him until she caught his gaze and hastily looked away.

Nessix cleared her throat and pushed herself from the table. "Then we need to plan our assault." Turning her back to Mathias, she paced along the table's length. "You've won the hearts of my men and for that, I can wish no ill will toward you. Please use what you know of the field to schedule our strike."

"Now?"

"Yes, now." Mathias's willingness to accept her pitch pleased Nessix immensely, though the residual wisps of bitterness refused to let her admit it. "I'm going to gather the captains. I trust the strategy won't take you long."

Mathias hadn't wanted to choreograph this battle and had no idea how long doing so would take, but he wouldn't argue. Etha willing, he would come up with something sound. "Then don't let me waste any more of your time."

Nodding again, Nessix turned and left Mathias to his assignment.

TWENTY-SEVEN

Nessix left behind just enough men for basic defense of the fortress and townsfolk, and hid Mathias's involvement from Brant to the best of her ability. In light of Mathias's soul baring confession, only her cousin's watchful glare kept Nessix from regressing to old habits. She chose to ride on the opposite side of the field from Mathias to save face, but he remained hopeful. If Nessix hadn't been ready to begin healing, her pride would have barred her from requesting his assistance altogether. Letting Nessix have her way now would ultimately serve Mathias better.

Armed with an overdue ferocity, the flemans struck. Before this rush, part of Mathias expected another pitfall, but for the first time in recent recollection, the demons genuinely seemed unprepared for the attack. As Nessix insisted and Etha confirmed, nearly one thousand fiends had gathered in the mountainous portal between realms. Even if the flemans only succeeded in destroying this one unit, it would serve as a firm statement that Nes's people had not given up.

The army plugged the demons' access to Elidae, offering retreat as the beasts' only viable option. Brant remained at his cousin's side, leaving Mathias and Sulik floating somewhere behind. Nes's confidence soared with each foe that crumbled to her blade. She quickly reverted to the charismatic warrior she'd once been,

355

fighting alongside her lifelong companion. The cousins fed off each other's enthusiasm, falling into an undeclared competition of slaughter as they tore down whatever threw itself in their direction. More demons surfaced to reinforce their comrades, but only enhanced the number of bodies gathering on the ground. Slowly, the fleman army pushed deeper into the demons' domain; they couldn't pull back without losing the upper hand.

Mathias did his best to respect Nes's desire to fight well ahead of him, tracking her progress by the volume at which battle hymns rebounded from stone walls. She pressed ahead beautifully, and just as Mathias thought it might serve him better to withdraw and watch the back lines, Etha chimed in with news he didn't want to hear.

They're sending up the big boys.

Mathias frowned. *Inoga?*

Yes, and a whole mess of them.

He swore beneath his breath. Giant swells of beasts, the most diminutive inoga Mathias had seen was nearly four times his size. Even in peak condition, part of him was intimidated by these monsters. He gripped his sword tighter and shouldered his way through the troops that plugged the hall.

You need to get these people out of here, Etha urged, her voice trilling.

I know.

Inoga throw even you around like a rag doll.

I know!

A pair of heralds waited near enough to Nessix and Brant to deliver orders, and Mathias reached the young men before either officer noticed him. "Sound a retreat," he instructed. "Whatever will make the troops move the fastest."

Not questioning Mathias's discretion, the heralds announced his order.

What's your plan? Etha asked.

Mathias steeled himself as Nes's furious glare turned to him. *Well, that depends,* he said grimly. *What I said earlier—did it mean anything to Nes?*

You get to figure that out for yourself. Etha's voice shook with urgency. *They're closing in, Mathias. What are you going to do?*

He smirked. *I'm going to break her heart again. Just a little bit.*

The heralds continued the song of retreat, followed closely by Mathias's shouted order.

"Everyone, get back to the forest!"

Nessix shoved her way over to Mathias, Brant pressing behind her. "What do you think you're doing?" she demanded. "We've come so far, we can't—"

"Do you hear that?" Mathias waved his sword toward the growing commotion deeper in the cavern. He met Brant with somber eyes, trusting the commander to see Nes to safety. "That's reinforcements. A *lot* of them. They'd been clearing that path through the forest to move heavy weaponry. I won't let any of them pass, but I need all of you out of here to do it."

"What do you mean, you—"

Brant gripped Nes's forearm. "Nes, let's go."

Mathias pressed his lips in a tight smile and delivered a curt nod to Brant.

"No! We can't just—"

"Nessix!" Brant hissed. "We have to go!"

"I came here to keep you alive and fend off the demons," Mathias said. "Let me do my job."

The rumble amplified into distinct footsteps and creaks of massive, load-bearing wheels. Nessix opened her mouth to object, but her efforts tapered off in a breathy squeak. Stubbornness wanted to argue with Mathias. Frustration wanted to argue with Mathias. Her desire to prove to Brant that she still hated Mathias wanted to argue with Mathias. Her trust in him, in his duty to her, told her something else entirely.

Nessix turned and ran, Brant staying at her heels to shove her along in case she stopped. Mathias watched them near the cavern's exit and hefted a sigh.

This is going to hurt, Etha murmured.

Only now did Mathias frown. *I've been through worse. Right?*

Etha's silence did nothing to comfort him. The demons rounded the corner and hastened upon finding him standing alone. Mathias's racing heart sparked Affliction to life, and he set about

357

his prayer.

The emblem on Mathias's breastplate erupted into a golden light, a metallic squall singing of the power generated by his divine fortifications. He squinted against the luminosity, unable to see the demons in front of him clearly. Their hisses and curses suggested the radiance affected them as well, and Mathias looked over his shoulder to ensure the cousins had cleared out.

"*Mathias!*"

The paladin's breath caught in his throat as he saw Brant grab Nessix by the arm as she attempted to dart back in. Brant flung her to the ground behind him and when Nessix scrambled up, he tackled her to hold her back. The sheer devastation in Nes's voice when she'd shrieked Mathias's name, the broken panic in her eyes, comforted him in light of his pending action. Mathias smiled at her then turned back to the demons and closed his eyes.

Mathias Sagewind, radiating his goddess's justice, held his arms open before the demons, sword glowing.

Etha, I'm ready.

* * * * *

A blaze of light blinded Nessix, and even though Brant had his back to the tunnel, he pinched his eyes shut and pressed his face into her shoulder against the brilliant flash. The concussive force that followed hurtled them further down the mountainside. Brant clutched Nes's head to his chest, shielding her from the tumble and the rocks that crashed around them. When they quit sliding, he looked up to see a cloud of debris rushing toward them.

That fucking idiot!

Nessix pushed herself to her knees beside Brant, rubbing the daze and dirt from her eyes. The dust choked her as she tried to hold her breath and squint up the mountain. She had no way of knowing what Mathias had done, only thankful he'd cleared everyone out first. Her trust in Mathias's good sense and resiliency thrashed against a darker murmur in the back of her mind, and as the debris settled, reality struck Nessix in the chest.

"No."

For the first time, Brant couldn't object to her grief.

The cave's entrance was gone, swallowed up by jagged boulders and fallen trees. A massive indention folded in on the rocky face. Nessix shook her head in staunch disbelief, desperately scanning the side of the mountain in case their slide had skewed her sense of direction. Her breath pummeled its way from her lungs as her mind sorted through hope and reality. Smaller rocks bounced down the path of destruction, chased by a greater slide once gravity pulled the larger stones over the collapsed cavern.

Unsteady legs lifted Nessix from the ground as the troops climbed back up the foothills, murmuring their confusion. Nessix didn't hear them. She didn't hear Logan plod up behind her. The only sounds she registered were the shrill ringing in her ears and the thud of her heart. Coherent thoughts evaded her as she stared dumbly in the direction where she last saw Mathias. Brant's call to action registered as little more than an annoying hum behind the tumult of questions spinning through her head.

"There's nothing else we can do here," Brant insisted.

Nessix didn't move when Brant grabbed her arm. Mathias had ordered them away with the intentions of sacrificing himself. No matter how powerful he was, no man could survive a mountain collapsing on him. Nessix didn't respond to Brant's shove, either.

"Get it together, Nes. The troops need you."

Brant turned to descend the mountain, head bowed with stoic sobriety, and reached his arm across Nes's torso to grasp her opposite shoulder. Too numb to resist, Nessix staggered two steps backward as Brant pushed ahead before turning to pick her way down the rocky face. She didn't protest to him giving her a leg up on Logan, and instinct alone allowed her to safely navigate the great horse back home. A stuffy silence hung about the army on the march that should have resonated with so much triumph. Hushed whispers attempted to sort out what happened, but nobody dared to breathe the answer.

Once they reached the fortress, Nessix dismissed herself from the chaos of her reassembling army. She left Sulik's distraught authority to handle the uncertainty with the faith he'd gleaned from

Mathias. Tucking herself into the stairwell, Nessix ordered her legs to hasten to the privacy of her room. Footsteps hustled after her, and she frowned.

"I need time to think, Brant."

Her words didn't thwart him. "With where your mind's going, thinking's the last thing you should be doing."

Nessix closed her eyes to pinch off her tears. "Unless you can explain to me what's going on, I don't want your help right now."

"Nes…" Brant jogged to catch up to her. Gentle hands on her shoulders coaxed her beaten form to a halt. "Even I'm willing to admit how terrible this is—"

"The last thing he said was that he was doing that for me," Nessix insisted, shoving Brant's hands away. "He died because of me."

"The last thing he said was that he was going to do his job," Brant corrected. "The demons lost their portal. Nes, no matter how bad you feel right now, he stopped the demons. The end is so close now."

Nessix stepped back until she reached the wall and leaned her head against its support. Pressing her hands against the coolness of the stones, she tried to believe Brant. Mathias's sacrifice put the war's end right in her grasp. He'd successfully removed the demons' access to her home, but that reassurance alone didn't clear her conscience or ease her heart. She didn't dare tell Brant how badly she wanted to dig Mathias's body from the rubble so she could see him one more time. Nessix pinched her eyes shut as she reflected on how this had been her idea to begin with.

"The movement was a success," she admitted at last.

Her remorse rubbed off on Brant and he shifted his weight uncomfortably. "I think it'd do us well to concentrate on that and nothing else tonight."

Nessix opened blank eyes. "You're probably right." She pushed herself away from the wall. "Go drum up as much spirit as you can. See if you can lighten this gloom a bit. I'll be down as soon as… as soon as I get cleaned up." Her eyes darted in every direction but Brant's, her tone drab.

Brant frowned. "Try not to keep us waiting too long," he said.

"You need a distraction more than anyone else. I'll be up to check on you if you're not down soon."

It would have been easy to fall back on station and correct him, but Brant's concern for her silenced the dreadful whispers gumming up her mind. "I won't be long," Nessix promised.

Empty and numb, Nessix resumed her trek down the hall, leaving her cousin behind. She knew part of Brant had hoped for something like this to happen all along, and she imagined Mathias taking both himself and the demons out in one shot elated him. She tried to reflect on the times when she'd hoped for the same, but those feelings were so shrouded in the past, buried among a much more delicate sensation, that Nessix couldn't find them anymore.

Her eyes stayed trained on the ground, counting the steps to her chamber. She stopped in front of the door, hunched over with regret. None of this felt right. This had never been Mathias's war, not his responsibility. With a rattled breath, Nessix flexed her fingers and retrieved the key from her belt. Hands clumsy with grief, she bumped the handle as she reached for it, and the door creaked open. She sniffed back her anguish, suspicion effectively roused. A demon would have already jumped on her, which limited her dismal options to Veed. Tonight, Nessix was ready to deal with him properly. She drew her dagger and pushed her way inside.

Looking out the window, as he so often did, Mathias spun to face her. The cuts and bruises on his face enhanced the startled expression he feigned, contrasting with the courtly attire he wore. Nessix stared at him and her dagger clattered to the floor. Common sense objected to the truth of what Nessix saw, but once her mind justified this circumstance with everything else Mathias had pulled off, she snapped her teeth shut around her shock.

"You son of a whore!" she spat, rushing up to him.

Mathias laughed and raised his arms in defense as Nessix swatted him on the chest. "Come on, Nes, take it easy! Can't you see I'm hurt?"

His calm voice still held its good nature, and Nessix ventured to scathe his warm eyes for confirmation. Lost in the deluge of the day's emotions, Nessix sputtered her relieved frustrations and pushed Mathias a step back. She never imagined it'd be so good to see him.

"What in Inwan's name happened?" she demanded.

"I collapsed the tunnel. You're welcome."

"That's not what I meant and you know it. How are you..." Too modest to show Mathias the depth of her concern, Nessix jutted her chin and looked away. "How are you alive?"

He furrowed his brows, lifting one corner of his mouth. "Are you upset about it?"

She crossed her arms. "Maybe."

Mathias grinned. "I told you before. I'm a lot tougher than I look."

Show off...

As irritated as Nes wanted to be with Mathias, all she could do was breathe gratitude that all of his big talk had been grounded in honesty. A smirk wearied her filthy face and she dropped her guard. "Is it over?"

His smile faltered just enough to reflect her dashed hopes. "Not quite, but we're a lot closer than we were a year ago."

When are you going to tell her about the other access point? Etha asked.

Mathias studied the way Nessix gnawed at the inside of her cheek. *I'll tell her when she needs to know. Tonight's not that time.*

Etha tried to delve deeper into Mathias's thoughts, but he actively blocked her intrusion. *Mathias, why don't I like how that sounds?*

"So, what do we do now?" Nes asked, providing Mathias with a valid excuse to brush off Etha's fretting.

His smile returned. "You ought to enjoy the moment. The demons we have left to clean up won't organize overnight—"

Mathias... Etha warned.

He continued in stride. "And you and the army have earned a bit of a break, I'd say."

This is a terrible idea.

Nessix's shoulders relaxed and she smiled. "I sent Brant to try to stoke morale in light of your... conduct." She rolled her eyes at Mathias's grin and set to unbuckling her armor. "And you look like you were expecting to attend some sort of celebration."

Mathias nodded enthusiastically. "I'd like to think the party will liven up once we've made an entrance." He held up a finger. "Which reminds me."

Nes's brows furrowed as Mathias darted behind the partition that screened her bed and reappeared shortly with a wrapped parcel. He took the loosened vambrace from her hands and replaced it with his gift. Still confused, Nessix looked up at him.

"For you," Mathias said.

Nessix stared at him a moment longer, unsure what to make of the peculiar gesture, before walking over to place it on her desk. "I have no idea what motivated you to get me anything." Even as she spoke, her cheeks warmed and a tickle in her chest swooned over his flattery.

Mathias watched her attentively. "I need motivation to do things for you?" He laughed. "You certainly are a hard one to please."

She grinned and untied the string that held the parcel closed, peeling back the paper with eager fingers. Beneath the crisp covering lay an intricately gilded bodice in silver and blue, folded over top affixed tails. The fabric was rich and elegant, its cut promising to reveal a figure Nessix always kept hidden. Her hands recoiled to her lips and Mathias's smile melted into his eyes.

Moments into staring at the garment's exquisite perfection, Nessix snuck a glance back at him, blushing at his gaze. "Mathias, I can't wear this," she murmured.

His heart ached at her obvious conflict, and he so badly wanted to see her smile. "Well, not with your armor on," he agreed. "At least see how it looks. If it's too overwhelming, you can change into your normal attire. No hard feelings." He'd find a way to let her be a lady, if only for one night.

Frightened of the reaction she predicted from the army, of Mathias's vivacity, and of her own cavorting heart, Nessix looked between the paladin and his gift. Slowly, she reached out and touched the bodice, tracing the silver embroidery. Her fingers curled back as the excited girl inside her jumped up and down.

"You don't think I'll look silly?" she asked meekly.

Mathias thought she'd look ravishing, but felt her modesty

wasn't quite ready for that confession. "Do you really think I'd do anything to embarrass you in public?" he asked instead. He winked at the incredulous look she gave him. "And do something simple with your hair. I'll wait for you outside."

Before Nes had the chance to argue, Mathias stepped out of the room. Biting her lip, Nessix pulled the garment from its wrapping and pressed it against her chest. She walked over to her mirror, marveling at how the color complimented her eyes. This was a special occasion and she deserved to have a little fun, didn't she? She twisted her hips a few times, sending the tails swirling against her legs. A special occasion, indeed! Nessix looked into her glittering eyes in the mirror and grinned.

TWENTY-EIGHT

Even though she inwardly approved of her unconventional attire, it took Mathias's quiet confidence to reassure Nessix to step out in public dressed halfway near ladylike. She couldn't remember the last time she'd been so nervous, but followed his lead toward the drab music and smell of cooking meat. The usual bouts of cheering and rowdy conversations were devoured by a melancholy air until the first pairs of eyes spotted them.

Nessix stood out in her unusual formalwear, and Mathias's regal presentation gained instant attention. With no further effort, the generals restored the atmosphere from its dismal hue. Mathias eased Nessix into the crowd, pleased to note the overall acceptance of her appearance. He stayed with her until her shoulders relaxed and her eyes quit darting about in anticipation of ridicule. Coaxing a drink into Nes's hand as she recounted the success of their last fight, Mathias quietly slipped away to find Sulik.

The commander had taken charge of the infirmary and held down his role solidly in Mathias's absence. Satisfied with Sulik's growth on the spiritual front, Mathias was reluctant to interrupt his progress until the awe-struck whispers of recovering soldiers spoiled his efforts. Sulik did a double take and suppressed his urge to rush over to greet Mathias.

"I'd heard a rumor you were still kicking about," Sulik said, finishing his work with the current patient. "I've gotten in the habit of not doubting your actions, but you had me worried for a bit."

Mathias chuckled. "Etha wouldn't let me die that easily."

Humored wrinkles pinched the corners of Sulik's eyes. "That's what you tell me."

Mathias observed the room quietly, pleased to see all of the grave injuries tended to and healing. Sulik had certainly come a long way.

"I'd like to have a word with you, once you can spare a moment." Mathias clasped his hands behind his back and waited.

Sulik nodded and hastened his efforts of tidying up his supplies. Once through, he walked up to Mathias and clapped him on the shoulder.

"This is best discussed in private," Mathias said, leading the way out of the infirmary. "You seem to have been preoccupied. How much do you know of our current position?"

"Besides the fact that logic insists you should be dead?" Sulik laughed. "I heard there are some stragglers left and that we've been granted a break while they regroup."

Mathias creased his lips and nodded tightly. His hand snapped forward to open the war chamber's door.

This somber reaction was not the one Sulik had anticipated, but he politely waited for Mathias to conceal them from prying public ears before continuing. "Sir Sagewind, what don't I know?"

Mathias sank in a chair and leaned his head back.

Sulik, Etha said. *You're going to tell Sulik and not Nessix.*

Mathias worked his jaw slowly. "What would you say if I told you there was a second tunnel?"

Sulik had spent months building his relationship with Mathias. He trusted his mentor explicitly, but this was not something he'd expected to hear. "Is there?"

Mathias met his friend's gaze, catching the first disapproval he'd seen in quite some time. He swallowed his deceit. "Yes."

Sulik blew a sigh through puckered lips and looked away. "With all due respect, sir, what business did you have telling Nessix to take a break from arms if you knew that?"

I rather like this boy.

I never asked you. Mathias averted his gaze and sighed. "She's spent, Sulik. The troops might be fine, but Nes needs a reprieve if we hope to keep her sharp enough to survive."

Sulik processed the different scenarios before them. Mathias was right. Nessix didn't have much of herself left to give, and he knew she'd run herself into the ground to uphold her duty. These past several weeks, she'd been unstable at best and today's emotional overload couldn't have been gentle on her.

"How do you think she'd handle it if I sent out my own attack?" Mathias asked.

Sulik winced at the notion. "If you allowed her the time off first, she'd probably let it go if you convinced her it was her idea. Any time sooner…" He shook his head. "It wouldn't make her happy."

Mathias rubbed his chin and leaned his weight back against his chair. The demons were going to be livid and violent, and there wasn't time to let Nessix recover. "Think I could pull it off without her knowing?"

Mathias!

Sulik grimaced, but lowered his head dutifully. "If Brant didn't get word, either, but we'd have to sneak off while they slept and hope they stayed that way." His brows furrowed and he shook his head at the logistics. "This movement could take days, sir. Even if we managed to mobilize the army quietly enough, there's no way they wouldn't wake up before we returned."

"You let me worry about that."

Right when Etha thought Mathias had learned something about a woman's heart. *You can't seriously be thinking of doing this behind her back!*

"This might be our only chance to secure our position," Mathias declared to both of his critics. *I know how these tunnels work. If I make the maps—*

That still doesn't fix your problem with making peace with Nessix.

Mathias was eager to move on from Etha's scolding. "Would you be willing to distribute orders to those you consider trustworthy?"

Sulik puffed out a dry laugh, not even sure Mathias met his

own criteria right now. "I'll do my best, but—"

"That's all I need to know." Mathias hated interrupting Sulik, but wanted a dispute from him even less than he wanted to deceive Nessix. *What do I need to do to ensure Nes turns in early enough for us to gather tonight?*

Etha rewarded Mathias's rashness with a moment of silence. She didn't like this plan one bit. *Promise me when this is over, you'll tell her you did it all intentionally.*

Mathias grumbled and curled his lip, but agreed to her terms. "It shouldn't take me long to sketch out my plans," he told Sulik. "Go and relax for a bit. I'll send for you when I'm through."

Sulik cleared his throat and rose, uncertain about Mathias's judgment for the first time in a long while. "Yes, sir." His chest tightened at the idea of betraying Nes's trust. Unable to stand thinking about the alternatives any longer, Sulik left.

You haven't recovered enough to pull that stunt again, and it'll be some time before you're able to.

Mathias watched the door fall shut behind Sulik and sighed. This was about as far from ideal circumstances Mathias wanted to get, but he couldn't fathom any other way. *I know, but the demons are likely drawing into position already and we have to hold them off at the source until I'm strong enough to finish the job.*

You're missing my point.

No, I'm not. Mathias leaned forward and propped his elbows on the table, dropping his forehead against his thumbs. *I'm doing what I can to keep Nessix safe.*

Mathias was quite possibly the only man capable of making Etha regret the law of free will. She couldn't deny his desire to physically protect Nessix from the demons' next lashing, but she balked at the betrayal he was set to commit.

You'd better not make me regret this, Etha warned.

A smile crossed Mathias's face at the closest thing to Etha's blessing he expected to get, and a rush of enthusiasm swept over him. *I always aim to please.*

* * * * *

"What do you *mean* they just obliterated the portal?" Shand hissed.

The demon cowered from her, having seen his share of terror for one day. "We couldn't push them back, my lady," he blubbered. "Nessix led her army into the threshold and Mathias ran in and collapsed it."

"Did it at least kill him?" Shand asked, feeble hope begging for an affirmative.

The demon sputtered over an answer he didn't have.

A shriek of madness spewed from Shand's unearthly lungs as she snatched the demon by his throat and lifted him from the ground. "We do not get defeated!" she declared indignantly. "*I* do not get defeated!"

The alar standing patiently by her throne remained silent, watching with impassive orange eyes as Shand dismantled the unfortunate nominee who delivered the report.

Kicking the remnants of her wasted servant aside, Shand's fierce gaze locked on this winged demon. "Nobody leaves tonight. I have to orchestrate something more powerful than a simple rush."

The negative energy emanating from Shand as she whisked away to her pawn's quarters raised the hairs on his arms seconds before she fully appeared. The blood of her informant still painted her hands, and she didn't think twice about it. Perhaps the pawn would take note and comply without debate for a change.

Having been lost in reflections over the war's change of events, the pawn raised his eyes from the map he'd been studying, prepared to bark reprimands at whoever dared disturb him. Instead, he turned to face the enraged eyes of his goddess.

"My lady." His voice ticked with unease, eyes darting to his chamber door. "What are you doing here?"

"It is not your place to question me," Shand snapped. "General Nessix no longer has a place in this war." She pulled the corner of the map depicting fleman movement to get a better look at it.

"My lady?" he asked quietly.

"It's a shame," Shand sighed, finally channeling calm from her inner depths. "If you'd taken control over her from the start, like I told you to, we wouldn't be discussing this right now. As it is, she's become too strong and knows entirely too much."

"What are you suggesting?"

"Dispose of her," Shand answered coldly. "I don't care how it's done; I need her and her influence off the mortal plane."

The pawn loathed to think of the girl's death, even more so to be the one responsible. "Perhaps if we push once more—"

"With what?" Shand demanded. "She's destroyed enough of the demons and you know you'll be next if she discovers our alliance. You'd better heed my words. I can take everything and so much more from you."

"I know." He heaved a sigh and rubbed his tongue on the roof of his mouth. The thought of losing the noble line sickened him, even with his daydreams of personally surpassing that family's clout. "Must *I* see to her undoing? I'd hate to dirty my hands with her blood."

Shand's smile broadened in understanding. "Of course not. You have disposal of the third squadron. The alar there have matters to settle with the little wench, anyway."

He tapped his teeth together and nodded once more. "Do I give them free rein?"

"Do as you see fit. I don't want to trouble my mind over her any longer."

The pawn bowed his head. "It will be done," he swore. "She will be gone before tomorrow's sun sets."

* * * * *

Expelling a jaded sigh, Mathias leaned his sword against his bed post and moved to his desk to look over his battle plans once more. If Sulik succeeded in the task given to him, this next push ought to be the war's definitive end. Mathias's eyes bore through the maps, praying he missed nothing and invoking protection for the ranks. The one variable he couldn't plan for was the persistent hunch of a traitor living among the flemans.

Veed remained the most likely culprit, his conduct doing nothing to convince Mathias otherwise. The dark general knew too much about the war and had proven himself unusually capable compared to his peers. His warped sense of nobility was Veed's one chance at saving grace. A faint scratch at the door pulled Mathias from the path his mind rolled down and compelled him to cover his plans.

The door peeked open upon his invitation for entry, and Nessix slipped inside. She'd donned a cloak against the unusual summer chill and her hair tumbled loosely over her shoulders, crimped with the memory of braids. Mathias's face eased in contentment. Nessix looked much more comfortable without her hair pinned up so tight. Her longing for this proposed break from combat was apparent by this fact alone, and a tiny storm of regret rumbled in Mathias's core. Desperate to distract himself from blurting his guilt, Mathias drifted closer to her. It wasn't until Nessix threw her shoulders back and gasped that he realized he'd reached out to touch her hair.

Mathias cleared his throat and retracted his hand. "Is something on your mind?"

Nes's eyes fleetingly passed his as a timid smile raised her cheeks. "I'm not very good with humility, but you've become quite the asset to my people." Her eyes wandered to the desk where Mathias's plans lay hastily hidden. "And I have to thank you, Mathias, for not letting my temper deter you from our cause."

He casually stepped across her gaze to better shield his deceit. "I've had faith in this cause far too long to let one woman throw me off course." Mathias gave her a smile that softened her expression.

Nessix fidgeted with a toggle on her cloak. "Attendance at the festivities tapered off soon after you left and I—we'd hoped you'd come back to join us." She sighed. "But, I'm through for the night. Call me vain, but I've earned my rest."

Etha bless you, Sulik! "You have," Mathias agreed, crossing his modest chamber as he finished removing his weapons and loosened the cuffs of his sleeves. "Go to bed, sleep in tomorrow. You deserve it."

A distant bliss swelled in Nes's eyes. "I suppose I could manage that." Even with her exhaustion and agreement, Nessix stood still.

"Is there something else?"

"Yes." The answer slipped from Nessix completely, and she curled her knuckles against her lips and spun from him. "I mean, no. That was all."

Mathias craned his neck to try peering around to catch her eyes. "Are you sure?"

Nes's cheeks flushed and she shuffled another quarter turn away from Mathias, sealing his curiosity.

"I've never seen you so flustered," he said, rocking back on his heels. "What could've possibly grabbed your tongue?"

"I was just—" Nessix caught herself again and turned to face him briefly, gaze pointed at the floor. "Forget it. I really should be going."

One step carried Nessix toward the door and then Mathias's hand caught her arm.

"You were just...?" he prompted, freeing her from his hold when she awkwardly recoiled.

Nessix huffed her frustration, battling down the hiccups in her heart. "I was just reflecting on your popularity among the silly village girls." There. She said it. But the longer that sentence hung in the air, the more insecure Nessix felt about it. She shifted her weight and sighed. "They're pretty, proper ladies and there seems to be an ongoing challenge between them over who can snag the most looks from you. Nonsense like that."

Mathias chuckled and closed the stride she'd taken from him. "Then they must be incredibly jealous of you, General."

Heat pinched at her cheeks again, and she turned around once more. "That's absurd. They're much more— They know my position, and I'm sure they're comfortable in their lofty feminine ways."

"Yes," Mathias granted. "But maybe that's not what I'm looking for."

Nessix focused her gaze on the floor as Mathias walked up behind her. His left hand brushed over her hip, fingers crinkling the fabric of her cloak. With his right hand, he gathered the length of her hair and swept it over her shoulder to expose her neck. His breath warmed Nes's cheek and his stubble grazed behind her ear as his lips parted and wrapped around the crook of her jaw, tugging gently at the tender skin near her throat. A ragged breath shook Nes's frame and her hand clutched at his as he slid it over her stomach.

"If I've misunderstood your intentions, you need to tell me now," Mathias murmured.

Nessix blamed her euphoric dizziness on her clothing's restrictive fit. Heart skipping, Nessix abandoned her attempts at dutifully denying what she felt was right. After all the mistakes she'd made and hardships she'd endured, it was time for her to do something for herself. Nessix turned around against Mathias, letting his hand peel the cloak from her shoulders, and caught his lips with hers.

Mathias knew Nessix had been causally drinking prior to this encounter, and the honorable side of him whispered the suggestion of being a bit more responsible. She leaned into their kiss, curling her fingers in his hair, and effectively silenced that prude's voice. As they pushed the limits of decency, the greatest resistance Mathias met came from the laces of Nes's bodice. Ensuring she slept soundly proved much more gratifying than Mathias had ever imagined.

* * * * *

Fighting the urge to sleep while Nessix nestled up against him was one of Mathias's most trying battles to date. The gentleness of her hand on his chest and the blissful dependency that left her draped in his arms stirred a youthful side he hadn't acknowledged in years. Admiring the curves of Nes's body, Mathias longed to stay in this moment, knowing how angry she'd be when she woke. He kissed the top of her head and smiled.

Indigo pre-dawn light leaked into his chamber from beneath drawn curtains, and quiet footsteps rushed down the hall. Mathias played with the idea of rousing Nes to see if she'd be inclined to revisit the past night's activities, but the deceit of his prior arrangements stood firmly against such fancies. Mathias stretched the side of his body Nes wasn't attached to and sighed. He had to ensure the safety of Elidae before exploring any personal desires.

Mathias yawned and suppressed his urge to play with Nes's hair. *Please tell me Brant got drunk enough last night to pass out.*

He's out cold.

Etha's tight voice discouraged Mathias from even thanking her for the insight. He brushed two fingers against Nes's forehead. *Let her sleep until she's consciously woken.*

Etha scoffed. *That could be days.*

She deserves good rest and sweet dreams. If not for my benefit, at least give her the chance to sleep off her horrors.

Mathias never received a spoken answer, but considered Etha's lack of argument as receipt of her assistance. He traced his fingers down the bridge of Nes's nose and swept his thumb beneath her lower lip. When she failed to stir, he slid out from under her, tilted her chin and kissed her. Indulging his inner grumbling, Mathias slipped out of bed.

Etha stewed in silence, waiting for guilt or lust to talk Mathias out of this movement. He dressed and equipped himself, interrupted only by tender glances at the woman he was about to deceive. Too afraid she'd hit him if she showed up physically, Etha settled for a healthy dose of scolding.

You should have told her.

Mathias heaved a sigh, wondering how many more times Etha planned to chastise him over this. *If I'd told her, she'd have tried to come along. We both know the sort of trouble she'd get into. This is for her own good.*

I still don't like it.

Mathias knew he wouldn't win this debate and opted to not even try. Etha was displeased with him, he understood that, but she wouldn't abandon him. Not when he needed her this badly. Picking up his sword belt, Mathias looked down at Nessix once more, eased by her peaceful expression. He pressed his lips against her shoulder, and slipped quietly from his room.

TWENTY-NINE

"Nessix, where *are* you?"

Sleep fled Nessix at the urgency in Brant's voice, though the memories of the past night still tickled her mind. Her feet hunted through the sheets for Mathias's warmth. Eyes pinching tighter in her displeasure, Nes rolled to her back to find herself alone in the bed. She sat up in a flash to glance through the chamber, finding Mathias's sword and armor equally absent.

"Nessix!"

Shoving the covers off herself, Nessix jumped from the bed, drowsy mind not yet wrapping around reality. She snatched her cloak from the floor and secured it around her bare shoulders, rushing from Mathias's room and directly into Brant's agitated path.

"Thank Inwan I—" Brant froze, his mouth hanging open as he looked from the door his cousin had emerged from to her scantily clad body. *That son of a bitch...* "You have some explaining to do."

Nessix lost her attempt to curb her flush and kept her gaze pointed at the wall. "I'll explain what needs explaining," she snapped. "Now, what's wrong?"

"This!" Brant shoved past her and into Mathias's room, throwing the heavy curtains back to reveal a sun well into the afternoon. "You've been asleep all day." His words steamed with condemnation.

Nessix raised her free hand to block the invasive light and sighed, hoping to redirect Brant's ire. "We're supposed to rest, remember?"

"Oh, I remember," Brant hissed. "And that's why Sulik, two thirds of our force and your *dear* Sir Sagewind are nowhere to be found?"

Out of all of the things Mathias had implied to Nessix last night, combative movements had not been among them. "What do you mean?"

"Exactly what I said. Your White Paladin and Commander Vakharan are gone. We barely have men left to hold the fortress. I almost expected you to turn up missing, too."

"Have you sent scouts out to—"

"None are left, Nessix! He betrayed us!" Brant's eyes darkened. "And I am so sorry you didn't see it coming."

Nes's gut flooded with a devastating chill of shame and disbelief. Mere hours ago, Mathias had murmured such delicious words of what she meant to him and had backed up those sentiments quite believably. She'd trusted him to replace her skewed view of intimacy with something delightful, and this is what he'd planned all along? Shaking as fury joined the tangle of her heartache, Nessix clutched at her cloak as she tried to figure out what to do next. She could not allow last night to soften the blows to come.

"Nes, you better come see this."

She looked up to where Brant stood over the desk and slowly joined him. What waited for her numbed her mind even further. There sat a detailed map of Mathias's proposed movements, along with a rough estimate of the numbers he needed.

"Brant, go get yourself ready. I want you to start armoring Logan as soon as you're fit for combat. And prepare Armina."

"We're following them?"

Nessix whirled on him, knuckles paling as she gripped her cloak. "What else can we do?"

"Want me to rally who's left?"

"No. This is between me and Sagewind. We still need him for this war; you're coming along to make sure I don't kill him."

Nes's solemnity curbed Brant's smirk. "I'll meet you in the courtyard?"

"Yes," she snipped.

Brant left the room promptly, and Nessix glared out the window, wondering why she even bothered to care.

* * * * *

The map Mathias had left behind disclosed his location and Nessix drove her chase of him hard, Brant and Armina trailing behind. A filthy pleasure filled Nessix as the army spotted them and scattered frantically. She slowed Logan to a walk once she was certain her troops had gone crying to Mathias.

Armina, sides heaving, dropped her head to pluck at a few blades of grass as Brant loosened his grip on the reins. "What are you going to say to him?"

Nessix's tongue pressed against the roof of her mouth, but failed to force it open. If not for her need to regain control of her men, if not for her duty to her nation and its safety, she very likely would have succumbed to the pathetic desire to wither away in tears and her shattered heart. Nessix despised herself for falling for Mathias, feeling so stupid for letting his sweet words, noble façade, and enchanting eyes snare common sense from her.

When a handful of jittery troops pointed in her direction, Nessix saw Mathias walk ahead of them and cross his arms. He stood there calmly, turning his head briefly to dismiss the soldiers around him. As they scuttled off, Nessix sent Logan forward in a trot, focusing only on her intended mark.

You have to go easy on him.

Nessix choked on those words, hearing them so clearly she snagged Logan in the mouth and staggered him back to a walk. "What?"

Brant pulled Armina up as he passed and turned in the saddle. "I didn't say anything."

Please, you must trust him!

Nessix shook her head to scatter these tainted thoughts.

"What's wrong?" Brant asked, afraid Nes's recent acts tempted her to change her mind.

"I'm... angry. That's all."

Brant eyed her skeptically. "There's something else bothering you. You'd better not be planning on backing down."

Shooting Brant an angry glare, it took Nessix a moment to find the concern in his declaration. "Oh, you don't have to worry about that."

The sun continued to draw the day toward evening, mocking the recently woken general. No smoke rose from the campsite, though that didn't surprise her. Mathias obviously wanted to keep his plan a secret. They rode toward him and he watched Nessix with illegible eyes. She gave him the length of time she was within earshot to beg her for forgiveness, and when she met silence through her entire advance, she flung her foot from the stirrup and aimed for his face.

Mathias caught her leg before she connected and held it immobile. "Go home, Nessix."

"Not without my men."

When she tried to squirm her leg free, Mathias gave it a stout yank and deposited her to the ground. More furious than hurt, Nessix leapt to her feet and waved her arms at Armina to keep Brant from interfering. The few eavesdropping soldiers shared subdued whispers and shifted farther away.

"Your plans were to rest," Mathias said. "My plans were a little different. I'm in competent control of the troops. There's no room for you here."

"You left the fortress completely exposed."

"And *you* left it without any sort of commanding officer. Go back and make sure nothing happens."

"Don't you dare give me orders!" Nessix spat. "I did you a favor letting you get this far, and this is how you repay me?" More important debates weighed heavy in her heart, but an internalized growl and twitch of her head chased them beneath her objective.

"I do dare give you orders. Get used to it."

"It wouldn't make any difference if I went back. If the fortress is attacked as it is now, we'll all be dead. Or is that what you were aiming for?"

Mathias paced away from Nessix and flicked his gaze to the sky. Etha had warned him about this, but his desire to keep Nessix safe had trumped even divine influence. "You can't keep following your foolish impulses—"

"Brant!" Nessix snapped. "Go cool out the horses."

Her cousin nodded in compliance. His prying mind itched to know how Nes planned to ream Mathias, but he respected her enough to give her privacy in this critical moment.

Nessix waited for Brant to clear the vicinity before taking a step closer to Mathias and gripping his arm. "Foolish impulses? Like talking to you last night?"

"Right now, you're acting like a child, and there's no room for children on this battlefield."

She slapped him. "How *dare* you say that to me!" Shoving Mathias away, Nessix drew her sword and held it ready. "I grew up on this battlefield. You, the son of a common human, have no right to tell me where I belong!"

"And that explains why I'm the one who still has my temper?" Mathias plucked her weapon away.

Nessix snarled at him but made no move to reclaim her sword. Everything but her pride agreed readily with Mathias. Fear of failure completely exhausted her and she no longer had the strength to hide it. Torn down by the repeated trials of this war— her fragility, her inadequacy, her weakness—part of Nessix wanted to give in and let Mathias have his way. The thought of surrender disgusted her, but she'd grown tired of not living up to her heritage.

"I knew exactly what I was doing when I came after you," Nessix insisted.

"Apparently, you didn't," Mathias said. "This is one of the worst decisions you've made to date, and it's going to get hard to top them if you keep it up."

"I took care of the matters concerning me, didn't I? I'm looking out for myself for once," she said bitterly. "You should be proud of that."

"With your reasoning, I've never had the incentive to." Mathias avoided her eyes to escape the feral beauty of her rage.

"Damn you!" Nessix growled at the smirk that tugged at the paladin's wretched lips. "Forget it. I'm going for a walk. *Not* back home, but if I don't release some steam, I *will* kill you."

Mathias watched Nessix bluster off, his smile withering away in the depths of dejected eyes. Regret for not telling her of today's movement and working with her upfront would do nothing for the situation now. He felt her slipping away from him and that emptiness frightened him. Releasing his breath, Mathias tested the weight of the sword he'd taken from her and let the immediate rush from their debate settle at the bottom of his shaken heart.

* * * * *

"What does he know," Nes muttered, smothering her urge to scream. With no destination in mind, she trudged through the brush, waiting for the warmth of forgiveness to find her. A tremble of anger rippled through her body. "I don't care *how* old the bastard is or what he can do. I'm capable of handling myself." She kicked a rock, the dull thud of it hitting a tree flaring her agitation.

A raspy whisper breezed through the timber, stalling her thoughts. Nessix shuffled to a stop where the trees met a dirt road and listened for what else the waves of the evening air carried, not quite convinced she'd heard anything in the first place. She held her breath and just as she contented to shrug it off, the sound babbled again, tugging at her curiosity. Looking both ways down the road, Nessix ventured a timid step into the open. She straightened to reestablish her jarred confidence and turned a slow circle to survey the location.

"Show yourself!" The thickness of the surrounding woods devoured her demand.

Incoherent murmurs rose from behind her and she wheeled around, backing into the middle of the road. Nessix cocked her head, straining to catch more of the garbled message as she peered into the forest.

"You've really got some nerve, following me like this!" she called.

"Come back to camp." The message formed clearly in her left ear.

Nes's heels scuffed in the dirt as she braced her stance. Those words hadn't come from a voice she knew. "Would you knock it off?" No attempt at outward confidence could slow her heart rate or keep the tremor from her voice.

The demand echoed all around her, eventually becoming multiple voices cackling through the air, assaulting her from every direction. Nessix instinctively flinched and raised her arms toward her head as the sound's origin continued to elude her.

"Lead us to camp, lady," it ordered wickedly from behind.

Nessix whipped around, face to face with a demon's toothy smile. He grasped her forearms and attempted to throw her to the ground, but Nes's petite size allowed her to wriggle her way out of his manipulation. She grabbed for her missing sword, but settled for the dagger at her hip. No worries; she'd handled more dire situations before.

"Lead us to camp," the demon repeated, chortling as he appraised his feisty opponent.

Nessix's eyes narrowed. "Over my dead body," she seethed, bracing herself for his follow up.

A fiendish smile stamped the demon's face. "We'd be delighted." In that instant the trees, the road, and the air flooded with demons.

The only thing instinct allowed Nessix to do was scream.

* * * * *

Brant's squared shoulders and tight frown warned the soldiers against approaching him as he waited for Nes's permission to return to her side. Her inevitable loss of temper and subsequent departure gave him ample room to move in on Mathias and deal with him properly. Brant stormed up to the sullen paladin.

"What do you think you're doing?" General or not, Brant

would not show Mathias a breath of obedience.

Already in a foul mood, Mathias attempted to push past the other man to resume his duty, but was pulled to a stop by a firm hand. He turned to glare at Brant. "If your cousin is too thick-headed to go back, you'd better go hold things down until I'm through." He jerked his arm free from Brant's grasp.

Brant clenched his teeth, hesitant to crack in front of the troops. "I asked you, Sagewind, what the fuck you're doing!" he demanded once more, hostilely blocking Mathias's path.

You'd be wise to get to Logan right now.

Mind caught in a whirlpool, Mathias didn't know what to make of Etha's unusual suggestion. He glanced at Logan, meeting a pointed glare and flared nostrils. The horse stomped a hoof and tossed his mane fitfully. Mathias pinched his brows a notch closer and shook his head to tend to his immediate concern.

"I told you, Brant. I'm the commanding officer here. If you want to serve right now, go track Nes down or go home. I have no use for either of you."

Brant encroached well into the bounds of Mathias's comfort zone. "That would be because you've already taken what you wanted from her?"

Mathias! Etha's voice trembled.

"This is not the time to be testing me," Mathias growled back at Brant.

"I'm making it that time. I warned you to stay away from her."

Mathias's joints quivered and his breath came in sweltering bellows. They didn't have the time to hash this out right now, and Brant couldn't possibly want him to act on the rage boiling inside him. Respiration rate increasing, Mathias worked his jaw, trying to come up with a way to save them both from public shame.

Get to Logan! Now!

Frustrated with Nessix, fuming at Brant, and thoroughly confused by Etha, Mathias caved to the disorder in his mind and acted on his goddess's demand. Shoving Brant two steps back, Mathias strode rigidly to the perturbed horse, not knowing what the fuss was all about.

"I'm talking to you, you yellow-bellied prick!" Brant spat,

puffing himself up to give chase.

Brant's heated insults didn't concern Mathias half as much as Etha's urgency did, and even that was trumped when Logan nearly plowed him down. Mathias still didn't know what was going on, but Etha's insistence and the great horse's mobilization complimented each other a little too well. Grabbing a hold of Logan's barding as he dashed by, Mathias scrambled to keep from falling beneath trampling hooves. He pulled himself against Logan's shoulder and used the push of the horse's speed to spring into the saddle.

A distant scream pierced the air and comprehension hit at once. Nessix had found a fight. Shaking his head, Mathias almost dismissed the predicament until he realized he still held her sword. A morbid cacophony of laughter resounded through the forest, followed by a second, more panicked shriek. Nessix would never scream over an idle threat, and an ice-cold hand reached inside Mathias's chest and smothered his heart.

* * * * *

Forty-five demons assaulted Nessix from the trees. They'd stripped off the majority of her armor, leaving her limbs exposed and vulnerable to their attacks. Unarmed, Nessix wielded her left vambrace in her defense. She hissed as a demon's knife sliced through the leather of her breeches and the skin of her thigh, spinning around to try and pummel the offender with pieces of her armor. The demon dodged out of the way and Nes's momentum sent her tumbling to the ground.

Nessix was so tired of this war. Blood seeped into her right eye from a gash taken from her brow, tinting half of her world in the hue of death. Fear gave way to exhaustion and she panted as her weary limbs shook just to raise her onto her hands and knees. She spat out a mouthful of blood and internally screamed at herself to get up.

The demons regarded her down their noses, arms crossed, eyes mocking her with their superiority. Muffled musings left snide lips and while Nessix soaked in the casual way they'd quit coming after her, she knew. Helplessness seeped into her gaze, overlapping the shameful terror she'd previously limited herself to.

Her assailants parted to allow a lanky alar to pass them. He targeted Nessix with glittering orange eyes and a conceited smirk.

"Make her squirm, Kol!" one of the demons called. A few others cackled their commendations.

Kol cocked his head, unkempt black bangs sweeping across one eye as his lips twitched their way into a smile. Nes's muscles protested, and she jerked her right knee underneath herself to try and stand. Her trembling thigh prevented her from rising and her mouth parted in a silent gasp. Kol slowed as he reached her, squatting down to meet her devastated gaze.

"This is the best part, you know." He ran his tongue over his teeth. "Watching the hope and fire simmer away. Tell me, Nessix. Are you afraid?"

She persisted in silence, latching to her pride, if nothing else.

Kol rocked back. "You know, I'll bet your dear paladin is quite close now."

That reminder—that single, bitter whisper of hope—sparked one last ounce of determination. Drawing on the feeble remnants of her energy, Nessix lurched forward and tore Kol's dagger from his belt. He met the action with a broad grin, springing to his feet as Nessix sliced erratically at his face. These weren't the calculated strikes of a seasoned general; they were the final thrashings of a dead woman.

"She still kicking?"

"You weren't kidding, Kol! You picked a good one!"

"You sure you can tame her?"

Kol's eyes narrowed and he turned to slam a wing against the side of Nes's head. The impact flung a cascade of multicolored starbursts across her field of vision, and she staggered and dropped the knife. A kick to her calf sent Nessix to her knees as a second demon stepped on her ankles and pinned her arms behind her. Kol's cocky lips continued to twitch as he closed the distance between them. He grabbed a fistful of Nes's hair and tilted her face up to meet malicious, rusty eyes.

"Oh, I'll tame her," he swore.

Tears battering the backs of her eyelids, Nessix twisted her arms until it felt they'd roll from their sockets. She shrieked as she threw her all against her restraints. Kol stood calmly, a patient look of expectation on his face while Nessix tried to thrash her way to freedom. Her protests tapered off to a whimper as she faced the fact that she didn't have the strength to win. Not this time. Her tears rolled silently free.

Kol wrenched Nes's head as he bent down to pick up his dagger. He ran the flat of the blade across her cheek. "What's going through your mind, little one?"

Nes's resigned eyes met his gaze. With nothing left to lose, she spat on Kol's face. The demons surrounding them snickered at her audacity as Kol closed his eyes and snarled. A slow breath calmed him, and when he opened his eyes, their glower was three shades darker. He slid the knife under Nes's chin and pressed the tip into her flesh. Bending forward, Kol licked the most recent layer of blood from above Nes's eye, receiving her revolted choke in reply. Laughter wafted from behind them and Nes's arms were jerked again.

Staring back at the demon, seeing for the first time the intelligence there, Nessix relaxed enough to speak. "Why are you doing this?"

The laughter hushed.

"This is the way Etha made us," Kol answered. "We fight to protect ourselves and to punish those who hurt us, just like you do." He looked over his shoulder. "Brothers, take wing. Our visitor's nearly here."

In a whirlwind of wings, every remaining demon darted into the sky, save Kol and an oraku standing three paces behind him. Kol still restrained Nessix by the hair, but no other bounds held her. Slowly, he moved the knife to lie alongside her throat, the pounding of her heart lifting the blade with each beat.

"I am doing this as cleanly as possible," Kol promised, adding a touch of force behind his hand. "No disrespect is meant."

Pinching her eyes shut, wishing Mathias had been just a little bit faster, Nessix accepted her fate. "To be singled out and taken with a fight, where's the disrespect in that?"

"Your honor should be a lesson to us all."

Nessix drew an uncertain breath as the demon twisted the blade. Her stomach heaved.

* * * * *

Each of Logan's strides jolted painfully on something deep inside Mathias that he always refused to acknowledge or name. This sensation exceeded the concern he felt for his troops in battle. He thought he'd killed and buried it long ago. *But some things never die.* Mathias clenched his teeth in determination.

Instinct insisted Mathias spur Logan on faster, though he knew the horse had reached his limit. The air hung heavy with the stench of demons, their laughter sifting to his ears over the pounding of hooves and hearts.

"She's strong!" Mathias shouted to Logan. "She can handle a few of them until we get there."

True, a handful of demons posed little danger to Nessix these days, but as Logan leapt into the road and slid to a stop, Mathias realized why his fear had overwhelmed him. Dozens of demons circled and spiraled into the air, obscuring any sign of Nessix. Roaring out her name, Mathias launched himself from Logan's back and tackled the nearest opponent from the sky, slicing through its throat with Nes's sword.

Logan did his best to fight the winged brutes as they swooped in mocking attacks. Mathias pushed himself to his feet and cut down the most foolish assailants as he plowed through the madness. The horde of demons gradually thinned and revealed a roadway speckled with blood. Nes's dagger, the only weapon she'd had, lay alone on the ground.

The anxious horse did Mathias no good, save for fending off the last of the demons. Weary but frantic, Logan trumpeted his distress and trotted down the road in search of his rider. Mathias watched him for a moment before turning in the opposite direction to cover more ground.

Frustrated at his futile attempts, Mathias concentrated on following the faint flicker of Nes's soul. Hopeful eyes darkened as they raised to the last two demons. The lanky alar stood from where he'd knelt on the ground and backed away slowly. He looked up at Mathias with a grin and quiet confidence as his unusually brutish oraku companion took his place on the side of the road. The truth dawned on Mathias the moment he recognized Nes's still body.

"What are you doing?" Mathias demanded as the oraku loomed closer to Nessix.

"They call me the Spirit Binder," the oraku replied. "What do you *think* I'm doing?"

Mathias had never heard such a title before, but didn't like the sound of it. Leaping forward with a primal yell, Mathias dropped Nes's sword to draw his own. The creature cupped his hand over Nessix's mouth. A milky fog condensed and painful convulsions contorted her body, accompanied by a tortured moan.

Despair.

The rush of blood in Mathias's ears muddled his senses. He slashed out with his sword, bent simply on destroying this demon. Entertained at the human's efforts, Kol intercepted Mathias's thrusts to buy his comrade time before they both spread their wings and lifted into the air. Squinting against the dirt kicked up by the haste of their departure, Mathias swung again, catching part of the thin webbing of the alar's wing. The beast lowed an uncomfortable croak but flew higher, leaving only a spatter of blood behind.

Chest heaving and mind lurching, Mathias dropped his sword and clutched at his hair. Logan's overwrought cries and thundering hooves grounded Mathias just enough to rush to Nessix. A faint trail of blood guided him to where a patch of brush gave way to her body.

Laying there in the crimson weeds was all that remained of General Nessix Teradhel, the fierce warrior maiden reduced to nothing more than a shattered and hollow hull. Empty eyes still peered open and paling lips parted in a final, silent gasp. A trickle of blood ran from the corner of her mouth, tracing her jaw to her neck. Holding his breath, Mathias stared at her, praying for her to move, or criticize his concern, or jump up and hit him. He didn't care what she did, so long as she did *something*! Dizziness forced Mathias to his knees as he reached forward to close Nes's eyes.

His mind numbed as the seconds elapsed, and Mathias weighed the consequences of trying to heal her. A body needed its soul to receive such blessings. His eyes crossed over Nessix, visions of the Spirit Binder snatching her essence lashing his mind, and Mathias realized that nothing else could be healed. He had failed his mission. Nessix was gone, and he hadn't been there to save her.

The Afflicted Saga

Deception

Tale of the Fallen: Book II

DEMONS ARE NO LONGER LEGENDS…

Kol pressed his cheek against the cool stone of the tabletop, watching as Nessix's soul swirled about in its despair. She'd quit trying to fight her way out of confinement for the time being, and the muddy green of her misery soothed the alar's demented mind. Footsteps clomped down the hall and Kol lifted his head to rest his chin on the table's surface. Moments passed and an imposing air rushed ahead of those steps, jerking Kol upright. Suppressing a scowl, he cleared his throat and stood, laying a protective hand on the lid of Nessix's glass cell.

Not all inoga were equipped with wings, but Grell was. A beast even for a demon, Grell hunched his shoulders forward and twisted his body sideways to clear the doorway, though Kol knew his lord could just as easily crash his way through the walls. A quick assessment of Grell's scowl, enhanced by a scar stretching from eye to lip, confirmed a preexisting irritation. Kol swallowed hard and waited for whatever the inoga's temper sought.

Grell spared Kol little more than a glance, choosing instead to snatch the jar from under his subordinate's hand. He tilted it roughly, raising it up to eye level, and a bolt of red agitation crackled through the confines. Kol would have corrected anyone else, even some other inoga, but not Grell. He pinched his lips tight.

"This is your Nessix?" Grell's voice boomed loud enough for dust to sift from the crevices of the walls. He continued to focus his scrutiny on Nes's soul.

"I harvested her myself, my lord."

Grell curled his lip at the clip of Kol's reply and tipped the jar the other way, enticing a greater flood of red from Nessix. "What did you tell Shand?"

"Exactly what we'd discussed."

"And she believed you?"

"She was too delirious not to." Kol wound his fingers into fists of restraint as the red haze warped into an insecure yellow. Nessix was meant to be his masterpiece, and it took the entirety of his will and common sense to hold himself back from snatching the jar away. The days when he'd have survived such a bold action rested well in the past.

"Good." Grell plunked the jar back on the table. "Keep things that way and notify me when you move forward with her. I trust it won't take you long."

The only thing that truly frightened Kol was Grell investing faith in him. Even demons feared the right kind of pain. "We will work as promptly as conditions allow."

Grell still wore the same unimpressed frown he arrived with, but nodded in refined satisfaction. Acutely aware of how little Kol wanted to disappoint him, Grell left to entertain himself in the holding cells. Once his massive frame vacated the room and his shadow disappeared down the hall, Kol sank to his seat.

Pulling Nessix back in front of him, he lowered his chin on the tabletop once more. She swirled about in a fiery confusion, reds of anger, yellows of fear, reeling through a plague of worry. Kol wrapped his hands around the jar, darkening its interior until Nessix's foggy mass stabilized and settled to the floor of her prison.

"That's a good girl," Kol murmured. Pressing Grell's insistence on hastening to the second phase of Nes's transformation aside, he sighed and let himself get lost in his delight of Nes's increasing gloom.

Keep up to date at www.katikaschneider.com

ABOUT THE AUTHOR

A lover of literary adventure and notorious breaker of writing rules, Katika Schneider's been an obsessive writer for most of her life. She started out writing for herself before surrendering to her characters' demands, and began pursuing publication in 2014. She's a firm believer that everyone has a story to tell.

Holding her degree in Animal Science, Kat planned on attending veterinary school until incisions started making her faint. She lives with her husband and their abundant family of critters.

Made in the USA
Monee, IL
22 January 2020

20724347R00231